# IN THE SHADOW
# OF THE MOUNTAIN

U.K best wishes.

## Also by Fergus Smith

*Sunlight in the Valley*, published by Headsail Books 2014

# IN THE SHADOW
# OF THE MOUNTAIN

## Fergus Smith

Published by Headsail Books

© Fergus Smith 2013

Published by Headsail Books, 55 Westgate, LEEDS, LS20 8HH
www.headsailbooks.com

First published in the United Kingdom in 2013 by Headsail
Books.

ISBN 978-0-9926872-0-5

Cover design: Claire Simpson claire@clairesimpsondesigns.co.uk

Cover photo: copyright © 2013 Victoria Nabours photography

Cover portrait: Faye Kenny-Broom fkbphotography@gmail.com

Page design by Clare Brayshaw

This book has been produced by York Publishing Services Ltd,
64 Hallfield Road, Layerthorpe, York YO31 7ZQ
www.yps-publishing.co.uk

*For Tom*
*Who always inspires*

# Praise for 'In the Shadow of the Mountain'

*The true scale of the impact politics has on modern military operations, from an individual mission to the grand strategy, is one of the taboos of recent history. This book breaks that taboo with brutal clarity and should be as thought-provoking as it is enthralling. In many ways, this is a story which has needed telling since Kosovo.*

James Clark, former Defence Editor,
The Sunday Times

*Students of leadership will find much here to confound and contradict more conventional texts on leadership. Using the Northern Ireland conflict as a backdrop, Major Smith draws the reader into the experiences of a flawed but ambitious young officer. This fascinating book unpacks the day-to-day practice of front line professional soldiers in the British military as it follows one particular new officer through the conflict as he learns to lead. Major Smith uses a semi-fictional narrative approach to demonstrate that leadership is a complex and uncertain business.*

*Anyone with ambitions to lead should read this book. When the pressure is on, we learn, rank means little and the 'right to lead' is hard won and easily lost: 'command', it transpires, is an anxious and ever insecure place. Humility, sacrifice and integrity are every bit as essential as toughness, confidence and competence.*

Professor Chris Ivory
Deputy Director, Institute of International
Management Practice
Anglia Ruskin University

# Glossary

Bergen: a military rucksack

Boot-necks: Royal Marines

Callsigns: radio code names for a unit of people, for example 'Zulu-two-zero'

Casevac: Casualty Evacuation

Chinese writing: faecal stains down the back of a toilet bowl

Chin-strapped: a little tired, to the extent where the jaw hangs down on the strap of the helmet

Crabs: the Royal Air Force

Crow: a new member of the platoon

Comfy-bum: soft toilet paper

Dickers: young children employed to watch military patrols and report their progress

Dixies: washing up detail after a meal

Endex: The end of an exercise, or, colloquially, death

Exfil: Exfiltration, leaving a theatre of operations

FRV: Final Rendezvous; the last checkpoint in a series

Hexamine: solid fuel blocks for cooking on portable, folding stoves

Jaffa: a castrated man, hence seedless

LOD: Line of Departure; the line that marks the start of a battle once crossed. Now called the Start Line

NATO: The North Atlantic Treaty Organisation

Noduf: Real, as opposed to exercise

Ooloo: Originally a Malay word meaning jungle, now used to mean 'countryside'

PJHQ: Permanent Joint Headquarters, the Army's command bunker in Northwood, London

PIN: The Province Incident Net, a radio network enabling the security services to communicate with each other

Rat Pit: a pub in the 'Shot, now closed

RHQ: Regimental Headquarters, an administrative body that provides back office support to operational battalions

RTE: Irish national television

Scran: food

Screws: Corporals

Shebeen: drinking den

Shrapnel: spare change. Also broken bits of metal designed to injure and kill as part of a fragmentation munition

'Shot: Aldershot, a military town in Hampshire

Sneaky-beaky: under cover soldiers spying on IRA activity

Tab and tabbing: A march or the act of marching, carrying full scale weight of rifle and bergen

Taig: a derogatory Protestant term for a Roman Catholic

Tiocfaidh ár la: Irish phrase meaning 'our time will come'

Wokka-wokka: a helicopter, usually a Chinook

*I must follow the people. Am I not their leader?*

Benjamin Disraeli

# PROLOGUE

*Belfast, Northern Ireland; March 1995*

*Keep true, son*, his Da used to say. *If you keep true, you'll always be safe, always be respected.*

Sitting behind the wheel of the car, gnawing at the black hairs on his forefinger, Liam Gerard watched the policemen climbing out the back of the armoured Land Rover to swagger about by the entrance to the chippy, their hands hooked into the arm holes of the body armour.

"There they are now," said Jamesy. "Let's get it done."

Liam shook his head: "There's only four of them, but. There should be more, this time of day."

One of the coppers remained inside the vehicle, obscured by the protective mesh on the windscreen. The three others barged past the students to place their orders at the counter. Enraged, the students jostled and flicked signs at them behind their backs.

"Don't you be shirking on me now, Liam," said Jamesy, pulling his seatbelt down across his shoulder.

Liam scowled at him: "What the hell are you on? Since when have I been chicken?"

Jamesy held his gaze: "Keep it cool, boy. I'm just codding you."

Liam shook his head again, tutting, then returned his eyes to the policemen. He had liked living in this area as a student, sharing a house down by the little theatre. He'd eaten in that chippy several times. It was famous for the curried sauce and the massive portions, a blessing after a feed of beer down at Lavery's. At the minimarket on the next corner he had bought his fags – the woman behind the counter as bent as a hairpin – and down the hill, in the park, he would walk to get air when the exams were on. The trees were in bud now, new leaves bringing a liveliness to the street. It felt familiar. They had been happy years, the first couple anyway. But then the SAS had shot Mairead out in Gibraltar and that was when things changed.

"This is stupid, Jamesy," Liam said, watching the coppers scoff their chips on the bonnet of the Land Rover. "How is shooting some old guy in the leg gonna help? We need to top him. You know this. You do, Jamesy, you know this."

Jamesy said nothing, watching. "We've been over this," he said. "We've been told not to kill him. If he's killed, they'll give our boys a kicking down the Kesh. There'll be block searches. Just follow orders: *stand behind the men behind the wire.*"

Liam shook his head slowly. Jamesy Horgan was an eejit; as slab faced as the Divis and brainy as a lift shaft. No wonder the troops never left. "I know the fucking songs," he said and then, "Look, there you go. There's the other one." A second Land Rover came up the hill towards them, pulling in behind the first and parking on the diagonal lines by the road crossing. Five men got out and once again the students jeered in protest as they were elbowed aside. There was no point delaying. It was going to be as safe now as ever.

Liam turned the key and indicated, checking carefully in the mirror before pulling out and following the road down the hill, through the lights and right past the university. Turning off the Malone Road he took one of the litter-strewn streets of student rentals, following a route he remembered from years before. The houses round here were all the same: four-room brick terraces with a small yard and an entry at the back. He wondered why Pearson, a retired prison officer, would choose such a place to live out his days. He'd be sitting on a nice little nest egg, the house prices in Belfast doing what they were. Surely he'd be better off moving out to Cultra or Comber or the like?

I bet he moves now, Liam thought.

At the bottom of the hill he turned down a short link road parallel to the river that made the one-way system navigable. They swapped seats, Jamesy taking the driver's position and Liam reaching inside the glove box for the pistol, the arm band and the collection box. The hat with the Salvation Army badge was on the back seat. He checked his watch then nodded: "Let's go." It was five in the afternoon and the streets were empty. Rounding the corner he could tell immediately which one was Pearson's because it had a Sierra parked outside, the only car on the road. The driver's mirror dangled by a cable. Jamesy pulled up ahead of it. Liam got out, time slowing around him. He placed the hat on his head and adjusted the peak. He pulled on the arm band.

*Be true, be true*, he thought to himself.

Pearson's door was red. The knocker was gold and he rapped three times. He folded up the collar of his coat, hiding his face as much as he could. The living room window was to the right of the front door. It had lace curtains. A man pulled them aside; he had a long face and glasses and a mug of tea in his hand, the draw-string label hanging over the side. It was him, certainly, though the hair was now grey. Liam held up the collection box close to the glass, showing the logo. The man looked at it carefully through the glass, head tilting slightly back. With a final lift and fall of his eyes, he let the curtains drop. Liam waited, listening. Inside the house, doors banged. Bolts were drawn. The door opened half way and the old man smiled, extending a clawed hand with small change in the fingers. "Don't get many of you coming round here," he said. "Nice to see a young lad like yourself..." Liam held out the box for him to slip the coins into the slot then lifted the gun and fired once, straight into his thigh. The shot was sharp. The man buckled sideways against the wall, grimacing, glasses askew. Liam looked down but didn't fire again. He'd got the bone and missed the artery. He stepped up and pushed the man backwards: "That's for the boys in the Kesh, you Brit fucker," he said, then pulled the door closed. He shoved the gun into his pocket and got back into the car without looking round. He was ten feet tall. He was champion of a nation; as bold as a bull and straight as an arrow. "Drive," he said, the blood thumping behind his ears like a galloping horse.

# **PART ONE**

# Canning Town, London; April 1995

Paul woke to the sound of a taxi horn down the street. It was early evening. He had slept for over an hour and now felt guilty for the self-indulgence. Propping himself up on one elbow, he pushed the diaphanous curtain aside. A party of girls were laughing as they climbed into the cab. Planes were stacking up against mauve-coloured clouds for their descent into City Airport and judging by the chatter, Clare was in the kitchen with Yvonne. He let the curtain fall as wakefulness mugged him. Clare's bedroom was cramped and prim, a wardrobe slotting snugly into a recess by the door, the walls dotted with pin holes and tack marks. Underneath the mirror, four pastel coloured novels lay ready for donating to charity. His patrol-sack was propped in the corner with his clothes draped across it. On the bedside cabinet was a photo of him, taken some years previously, when his hair hung down to his shoulders. Paul sucked his teeth. He detested the dowel-jointed, flat-packed cheapness of it all. He now held the Queen's Commission and deserved so much more.

The door pushed open and Clare shuffled in carrying mugs of tea, the belt of her bathrobe swinging behind her like a tail. "You're awake! You were out for the count, sleepyhead," she said and slipped into bed beside him, kissing his chest and nestling her head into the well of his shoulder. Unable to say anything beyond a mumble of thanks for the tea, Paul ran his fingers through her hair. Before sex he had been aroused by her moistness. During it he enjoyed the vigorous oscillation of her breasts and the high-pitched panting. Afterwards, he found her proximity distasteful and it took half an hour for him to feel like engaging. She sensed the change and drummed his chest with her fingers: "Did you ring your parents, Pauly? You should, you know. It's an important day for your Dad, what with the conference and everything."

"I'll ring tomorrow," Paul mumbled. "There's no point today. If he got the vote he'll have gone out with his mates. If he lost he'll be a bugger to talk to. I'll ring him tomorrow, from Brize Norton."

"But it's important, this vote. The future of the party's at stake. If they don't change Clause Four, Tony Blair will have to go. You must..."

"I'll ring," Paul insisted, "Tomorrow. It's not as if I've been idle, you know."

Clare softened. "Yes, tell me," she said. "How was it? Did you meet your soldiers? Were they nice?"

Paul winced. Soldiers were not *nice*; they were *soldiers*. "It was good, really good," he said at last. "Me and Rolly – Rolly and I, even – we reported to Aldershot in the morning. The Adjutant, that's the Commanding Officer's right-hand-man, a Captain, he told us we were both posted to B Company. Rolly will command Four Platoon and I get Five."

"So you and Rolly are staying together, in the same..."

"In the same Company, yes. Like I said before, lieutenants like Rolly and me command platoons; majors command companies."

"So a major is higher than you?"

"More senior, yes."

"And did you meet your Major as well as the, er, Adjudicant?"

"Adjutant. I did, but it were only very brief. The Company's just back from Northern Ireland. They've been away six months. The last person they were interested in was me, really. It were their families they were after." Paul fell silent, recalling the feeling of trespassing on the intimacies of others.

"And did you meet your Sergeant as well? Is that right?"

"Yes it is, well done. Rolly met his; a man called Taggart, a Glaswegian."

Clare snorted. "Has there been a murder?"

Paul had to laugh. She could still make him do so, even now. "Well, yes there has actually."

"How do you mean? What's happened?"

"I won't get a sergeant when I get to battalion. Mine's in prison, in Northern Ireland. He's accused of murder."

"He's what?" Clare propped herself up to look at him, the joviality gone. "What do you mean? What's so funny?"

"It's nothing like that," Paul said. "Don't you remember the joyrider shooting a month ago? Teenagers driving through an army checkpoint? It was on the news."

Clare's face clouded: "I don't really..."

"Doesn't the name *Sergeant Bryan Moor* mean anything? He's all over the tabloids." She shook her head. "Well Sergeant Moor will be my sergeant, if he gets off, that is." Paul was excited. He had not yet taken up his command and yet was already throwing headline names into conversation. Clare did not understand how thrilling it all was. She settled her head against his chest and threw a heavy arm over his stomach. He could feel her blinking. "Well at least you and Rolly are staying together," she said. "I'm glad you are anyway. And I'm glad you're not going off to Ireland, at least not yet." Paul studied the shapes cast by the street lights across the ceiling. Going on operations was what he wanted more than anything. She must realise that.

A car sped down the street, scraping its exhaust on the speed bump. The girl in the house opposite slammed her front door. Her footsteps receded out of earshot. The day had been dazzling, too dazzling for him to explain. The Adjutant was only in his late twenties but his hairline had already retreated behind the crown of his head. When Rolly had knocked on his door he had affected an air of aggressive austerity, examining the two young officers from tip to toe: "You were right to come. Time spent in reconnaissance is seldom wasted. Follow the Duty Sergeant and he'll show you round."

The Sergeant, an amiable Welshman, talked constantly about the coming rugby World Cup. He escorted them round the training wing, the guardroom and the squat, utilitarian barrack blocks where the soldiers lived. Since the battalion were on their way back from Northern Ireland, the buildings were almost deserted. At midday he deposited Rolly and Paul by the door to the Officers' Mess at the top of the hill: "Right Sirs, I'm off for a spot of scran. You've got lunch booked in here at Twelve-thirty. Just a plate of sarnies I expect. I'll meet you here at Thirteen-fifty and take you down the gym so you can see B Company coming in. After that you can thin out, unless the Adjutant has something for you." Tucking his pace-stick under one arm he saluted, turned quickly on his heel, and strode away before either Rolly or Paul had fumbled a reply.

The Mess was silent and unwelcoming. Rolly called out from the hallway and a chef, not in uniform, appeared with a tray of sandwiches heavily wrapped in cling-film. They followed him up the stairs to a dining room, where a long oak table had been recently and poorly dusted. Paul was obsequiously polite, asking if they should take the dirty plates through to the kitchen after they had eaten. The cook shook his head and told him to just leave them on the side. Rolly and Paul ate in silence, looking out through vast windows across the buzzing entirety of Aldershot's military town.

After lunch, they explored. The bedrooms on the upper floor were locked. The box-room contained all the accoutrements of young, sporty men: wetsuits, cross-country skis, climbing ropes. The showers were communal with stained tiles. They climbed down a spiral stairway to the middle floor. The anteroom was furnished with robust chairs and veneered coffee tables. The air smelled unused and stale. Beyond the anteroom was a small bar in which pewter mugs hung from hooks below the glass shelf. A pad of bar chits lay next to an upturned ice bucket. Plaques emblazoned with military insignia decorated the dado rail. In the corner, an industrial vacuum cleaner hibernated with its cable coiled around the body. The whole building had an air not of desertion but of rapid and deliberate evacuation, like a school building over the summer. Before long, life and laughter would reflate the empty spaces.

Rolly shouted from the anteroom: "Hey Paul, check this out!" An AK rifle with a folding stock was mounted on a wooden plinth inside a glass cabinet. Rolly opened the case and lifted it out. He felt for the magazine catch. He looked down the length of the barrel, weighing the weapon in his hands, and assessed its balance. The bolt ran smoothly forward and back. He cocked it and fired off the action, taking an aimed shot at a mark on the carpet. He offered it over but Paul shook his head, shrugging to appear indifferent. Rolly placed it back in the case and closed the door.

Looking for something to do, Paul inspected the pictures on the wall. By the door to the bar a huge oil painting was illuminated with overhanging lights. "Christ," he said under his breath, "Would you look at that!" The painting was of a soldier charging an Argentine bunker, firing from hip level, bayonet fitted. In the bunker, one Argentinian lay dead and a second was collapsing having just been shot. The third, eyes wide, was aiming his rifle and about to fire. "Inspiring, isn't it?" Paul whispered, almost to himself. He recognised the event at once: the charge by a Sergeant that had turned the tide of battle. After this, the mountain had been taken within a few hours and Port Stanley within a few days. It had been the bloodiest battle of the Falklands war. The Sergeant, a man called McKay, had been posthumously awarded the Victoria Cross and Paul could still remember watching the news as a teenager:

a piper playing the lament; a helmet upturned on a rifle to mark the place where he fell. It was the moment he had started to dream of military glory.

"That's what we're here for, matey," said Rolly from behind him. Paul was unsure if he meant charging the enemy, or the responsibility for inspiring others to do so. "Same thing," Rolly replied.

The Duty Sergeant called for them exactly on time and again saluted as they appeared at the door. The gym was bustling with giddy women wearing regimental sweatshirts, leggings, and white high heels. They sloshed pink wine into polystyrene cups. Their faces glowed with the anticipation of sex, the frustrations of delay and the need to share in something special. The chef, now in uniform, was laying out oval trays of chicken wings on a table covered by a bed sheet. The climbing bars had been hung with bunting and a poster taped along the end wall was daubed *Welcome Home B Coy* in maroon paint. Paul had the vague recollection of being at one of his father's fundraising parties – too young to have an opinion but too old to be cute. Rolly leaned against the wall with his arms folded and knee bent. A Sergeant approached him, exchanged a few words, saluted and disappeared. Preferring to be useful, Paul served cups of juice to the children. They ran up, snatched one and scampered away. Thus employed, he was spied by a scrofulous, sharp-elbowed woman in a leather blouson jacket who seemed dominant among those near her. "What are you doing here – why are you back ahead of the rest of them?" she demanded in a nasal, Belfast accent. "I'm not yet posted," Paul explained, almost bowing as he did so. The woman studied him with tight lips. She held an unlit cigarette in puffy fingers laden with jewellery. Paul expected her to say something else but she turned away and muttered to those nearby: "Bloody officers never did anything for my Bryan after the shooting, so they didn't." Paul took this as a cue to back away.

As he did so the double doors opened at the far end of the gym. Everyone turned. The Belfast lady immediately clapped her hands, calling out to any who would listen: "Come on now; you know what to do ladies," and the gathering reluctantly formed itself into an arc with the mothers calling for their children. From outside came the hiss of air brakes, the issue of final instructions and a guttural cheer. Then a figure strode into the hall, a Private. He was thick set and grinning, his beret pulled down low across one eye. Unfazed by the semicircle of women, he found the face he wanted and strode towards her. The Belfast woman clapped her hands again and started singing, *For they are jolly good fellows*... and was joined for a line or two by those nearest to her. Further away, discipline broke down as one woman surged forward to greet her man, followed by another with tears streaming down her face. Soldiers entered, found their wives and swept them off their feet: long-imagined lips, so much said without words. Couples embraced, heedless of those around them. Children tugged at trousers to be scooped up, kissed and held high. Tiny fingers pulled the berets off their fathers' heads and placed them on their own. They hung low, hiding everything but wide, peggy smiles.

One woman, mousy haired, bobbed quietly near the back with a child standing obediently either side of her, each holding a plastic England flag. Their mouths hung open. Their eyes yearned. Standing on tiptoes, the woman peeked through the melee. A tall man appeared, a Major, carrying a heavy bergen over one shoulder. He let it fall with a thump. The woman melted into him, absorbed by his body and the wrap of his arms. One child, the boy, tripped over in his rush for attention. He started crying.

It was a moment of intense privacy. Having not served with these men, known nothing of the pain of separation, Paul was an intruder. Rolly had already gone and so he ducked out the side door and breathed deeply. By the buses, the Belfast woman was smoking and talking in angry tones with the Duty Sergeant. Driving up to London he could still feel how the men had been clotted together like blood. Their bond had been tangible. It would be an honour to be part of such a family.

As he lay in bed, Clare drew circles on his chest with her finger. "I think you're so brave," she said. "I can't tell you how much I admire what you've done, Pauly."

"You know what, Clare?" Paul said, his eyes shining. "I realised today that this is undoubtedly the regiment for me. I just know I can lead those men."

# B Company Block; May 1995

We are Five Platoon. Our last officer didn't last ten days. We was in Dungannon at the start of a six-monther when he turned up; straight out of Sandhurst, a fresh little Second-lieutenant with one star on his shoulder and a head full of bullshit.

He was standing in the cookhouse with his tray in his hands, looking round for other officers. He didn't know that on operations, in Ireland, we all eat together. He clocks a Captain and sits next to him. *Didn't know we'd be eating with the plebs,* he says and then we knew we've a dickhead.

First thing Sergeant Moor does is tell him to carry the fire hydrant in case of petrol bombs. For three whole days he's sweating his knackers off with this big red aiming mark sticking out the top of his patrol-sack and all of us trying to keep a straight face when he turns round. Even the officers are in on it. They've clocked he's a dick as well.

Then we're out on patrol and he throws up and he gets on the ration wagon and goes back into camp without clearing it. When the OC calls for him over the net we can hear him shouting *Two-zero-alpha... Fetch two-zero-alpha.* Sergeant Moor says he's fucked off, he's not at this location, and when we get back we find the Colonel's put him on the next flight. *Not the right calibre of officer to command my soldiers*, he says.

We're pissed off. We deserve better.

And then, when it's raining so hard you can't see, and we're out looking for Liam Gerard, the fucking Engineer,

11

this joyrider drives right at us, almost kills one of the blokes, and Beefy Moor and Mercy get arrested for shooting the cunt. I mean what can you do?

At the end of the tour we're snapping. When we're back in the 'Shot we find our dickhead officer hanging round RHQ. He's living in the garrison mess cos none of the battalions will have him. But he's got this fuck-off Jap eleven-hundred, a monster thing it is, parked round the back. Except we know it's there. And one night we creep up like we're in *Mission Impossible* and steal the bastard thing. The police find it in the canal a few days later and the wanker has to explain why it weren't insured.

We're howling when we hear that. Serves the cunt right. That's what happens to officers if they don't earn our respect.

And now we've another one just turned up.

# Montgomery Lines, Aldershot; June 1995

After crossing the footbridge over the dual-carriageway, Rolly and Paul ran round the rugby fields and under the Wellington Memorial. Out on the garrison training area, the Sunday sun caused mirages along the sandy basin of the tank circuit. The air hung thick, needing rain, and the swallows swept low in expectation.

To the two men this heathland was a vast stadium in which to display. Beyond the tank circuit they revelled in long, determined strides down the fire gaps between the conifer plantations. They powered up the flinty slopes of Seven Sisters to the ridgeline, sweat dripping from their faces and darkening their tee-shirts. From here they followed the high ground overlooking disused target ranges and trench systems to Flagstaff Hill and its panorama of the Hampshire countryside. Only on the final straight, homebound along the canal some eight miles later, did they slow to a steady jog with their shirts pulled off and chests glowing. It had been three months since they had first reported to the battalion. Both now commanded platoons and were hopeful of operational service, the more dangerous and exotic the better.

"Did you see Percy Andrews on the news?" snapped Paul, puffing sweat from his lip.

"That fat bloke from Sandhurst? Joined the Cheshire Regiment?"

"Him. He's going out to Bosnia. He was interviewed on telly last night." The two men fell silent, sharing the same jealousy. "The fucking Cheshires!" muttered Paul, shaking his head. "Why not us?"

"Don't know, matey. They're armoured infantry, not light-role; I guess that's why."

Paul grunted: "Maybe."

"But they'd better be up to it," said Rolly. "Did you see the UN did nothing while the Serbs slaughtered all those people? There's been over six thousand shot!"

"In Srebrenica?"

"Sure."

"I heard it was over eight thousand."

"Christ!" said Rolly, "I just wouldn't let it happen. No matter what the orders were, I'd put a stop to it. I mean this is Europe not some tin-pot African state."

"You reckon? If you're UN you have to follow their rules of engagement."

"Sure, matey. But give me a platoon of our blokes any day. Warfare's a matter of will not skill, remember? Nobody's standing up to these Serb fuckers." Rolly clenched his fists. "The only way to keep the peace in places like that is to batter them all into submission. Peace enforcement. Peace through superior firepower."

Paul chuckled: "You mean like Tito?"

Rolly snorted, nodding, and the two men trotted in silence for the last mile, trying to imagine what it would really be like to command in war. They thought of the assault and fight-through, the noise and blast of battle, the casualties and the singing shrapnel. They thought of glory and fame. They thought of self-sacrifice and what it would take to inspire others to follow their example.

They halted where the canal passed through a tunnel underneath the dual-carriageway next to camp. They warmed down. As they pulled their shirts back on, a black labrador appeared from under the bridge and trotted along the footpath to cock a spindly leg against a tuft of nettles. The owner followed behind; a short, round-bodied woman in a waxed jacket. Fawn jodhpurs clung to vast thighs.

Along the footpath she pulled a ball from her pocket and threw it in the canal for the dog to splash in and retrieve.

Rolly sniggered: "I thought Clare was looking bonnie last weekend, matey."

"Fuck off Rolly!" laughed Paul. "I like a bit of meat on them, sure, but not that fucking much."

Chuckling, the two men elbowed each other through the tunnel and trotted the final hundred metres back into camp.

# Aldgate, London; July 1995

Kirsty was early, unusually so, but apart from her timeliness little seemed to have changed. Her skin was perfect and carefully powdered. The spiral perm elongated her face and drew attention to the glossed pout. Her wedge-heel, hessian-effect sandals were stylish without being tarty. Her coat was from the new range at Top Shop and her bag had that lovely print of Audrey Hepburn wearing pearls and waving a cigarette holder. By comparison, Clare's shoes had been chosen to minimise the pain of standing all day. Her trench coat, the pockets full of tissues, did well to hide the crime scene of her hips. The plastic bag at her feet contained low-fat cream cheese and a packet of crackers.

"It's so good to see you!" Kirsty exclaimed as she approached the table, arms wide. "It's been ages and ages. It must be like six months or something. You look super..." The pair kissed, studied each other, and realised they were still friends.

"Actually it's been over a year, Kirst," Clare said as she shuffled along the velvet bench. "No! Fancy!" said Kirsty, brushing her skirt underneath her legs. They had chosen the pub because it was easy to find: an oak-lined, triangular affair nestled alongside a tangle of traffic lights; a venue favoured by city men and secretaries. Kirsty's arrival caused heads to turn, a fact that she put to good effect while Clare went to the bar.

"I got your usual; a spritzer."

"Wow, thanks, Clare. So tell me what you've been up

to! There must be so much and I'm so sorry, I only have an hour before my train."

Kirsty's finger was ringless but a thin rope chain bore a locket in the shape of a broken heart. "No, you tell," she said. "I said mine on the phone. How was France?"

Kirsty sucked in deeply. "Aw, it was lovely," she said. "Have you ever been?" Clare shook her head. "Well me neither. We didn't go in for that sort of thing. Dad said he learned to ski when he was young but I don't remember. It must have been Susie made him go." Her face brightened as she put a hand on Clare's arm: "But right at the start, right, I was so nervous and there was me all dolled up and standing on skis like I was afraid to move and every time I tried to go forward I fell over and when you go skiing it's really cold, especially high up on one of them lift thingies. And then I hurt myself and was all for coming home and forgetting about the whole thing, but Dad said I should stay another day. And that's when I met Gustav."

"Oh yes? A Latin lover?"

"No, not Latin. Hungarian. He was a skiing coach and he taught me how to ski and by the end of the holiday I was really good; I mean I was doing blue routes, top to bottom without stopping, all the way down, weeee, just like that..."

Clare laughed.

"So then I stayed on after Dad and Susie went home because Gustav got me a job as a chalet girl. That's not just a cleaner; it's like a personal coach and holiday rep and everything all rolled into one. Just as well I listened to old Mrs Morgan, I can tell you. French was the only thing I was any good at. So then I got taken on by this company, really big it is, based in Portsmouth. I came home for a week in March to see my Mum but then went back to do the same thing till the spring. Now they've given me a place in the call centre in Dulwich, booking holidays for the customers. It's good it is. I love it, talking to people about their jollies..."

17

Clare squeezed Kirsty's hand: "And Gustav?"

"Oh well, nothing really. When I went back I found out he'd shacked up with some teenager. He's eight years older than me so I thought that's going to be the way of things is it? So we left it there. I still shagged him mind, after his little tart went back to Germany. Thighs like iron he had, and such a lovely bum. I wanted to pinch it all the time." Kirsty trailed off, smiling to herself.

"And now?" asked Clare.

"Not much. Just a few irons in the fire, you know me. I started seeing a boy from home, Gary, as we said on the phone. He drives a cab for his Dad. He's quiet. He wasn't at school with us; he was at St Luke's and maybe a year behind or something. But I like him and he gave me this, look..." Bending forward, she allowed the necklace to fall. Clare took it gingerly, swallowing a whiff of spray-on deodorant: "It's lovely..."

Kirsty straightened: "So listen to me, gassing away. It's been so long and you're like my best friend and everything. Tell me about you. Tell me you're still with that boy. He left the supermarket didn't he? Did he join the army like he said? Is he like really high up or something?"

Clare nodded: "Yes he joined up and yes he's an officer. He left Aldi, the supermarket, two years ago and then went to Sandhurst. He's now in Aldershot now. You should see him in his uniform. He's gorgeous."

"I can imagine. You've been with him for ages now. Is it three, four years?"

"Three years, eleven months and eight days. Since Africa."

"Listen to you! You're like Sinead O'Connor you are! And wasn't he really into politics and that?"

"Yes he is, his family is anyway."

Kirsty smirked: "Imagine! A young Tory! Does he wear tweed trousers?" Chuckling at her own joke, she pulled a menthol cigarette from a packet in her handbag.

"No, it's not like that at all. His family are Labour, New Labour; into Tony Blair."

"Who?"

"Tony Blair. He's the leader of the Labour Party, the one that took over from Neil Kinnock."

"Was he that Welsh bloke with red hair? Fell over in the sea?"

"Yes, that's him. Paul's Dad's on the Executive Committee. He's a branch delegate from Bradford... But you did meet him that time at the Windmill didn't you?"

"Oh yeah! I thought he was lovely; such long legs and very handsome. How on earth did our Clare pull that one, I said? She did well there."

There was the truth of it and Clare ignored the barb. As a schoolgirl she would stand stork-like at the end of the nightclub bar while Kirsty kissed older men to get drinks for them both. Africa had unshackled her from the confines of Hatfield and in Paul she had found someone who listened to the world. He was like St Christopher, carrying the needy across the river. They'd even managed to stay together when he went back to university despite the distance, the cost of weekly calls, and the nagging awareness of her intellectual inferiority. The graduate programme with Aldi had brought him to London, but he had hated it.

She had always been sceptical about soldiers. They were either tattooed thugs on the night club doors or curmudgeonly old grumps in the care home. Then Paul said it was really about helping people less fortunate than yourself. It was about protecting the weak. At the Sandhurst Ball the officer cadets were charming, genuinely so, not at all like the boys from home. They were posh, proper posh. They spoke nicely. They stood when she entered a room. They pulled out her chair. She had not sat next to Paul at dinner but opposite him and the cadets on either side had spoken to her by turns as if they practiced doing so. After the main course they moved round so she got someone new to talk to and the second pair was even posher than the first.

Paul then started working full time while she finished her training. He was away often and did not always return to London, even at weekends. She never knew where he would be one week to the next.

"Crikey," Kirsty said, unable to hide the gloat. "So you don't get to see him every week, even?"

Clare blushed. "No," she said quietly.

Though she would not admit it, the recent phase of life had not been easy. After Sandhurst, Paul had done a selection exam for the regiment he wanted to join; lots of running in the mountains with a rucksack. It had made him leaner and fitter, his body hardening every time she saw him. There was no fat on him, not a bit. He was far stronger than anyone she knew, broad in the shoulders with powerful, clutching fingers. His physicality was unashamed and raw. But he had withdrawn also. He had become curt and absorbed in the news – what was happening in Bosnia or the gas attack in Japan. They had never argued, not once in nearly four years, but recently he had made a comment that at first she had thought was a joke. When she saw it wasn't, that he genuinely wanted her to lose weight, she asked him what he disliked about her body. He had clammed up, unable to say anything. But it had been just the once. All in all, Paul was a lovely, lovely man.

"He is special isn't he?" said Kirsty. "I thought I'd lost you there. Away with the fairies, you were. It was like me going *Hello Clare Briggs... come in please... earth calling...*"

Clare squeezed her hand.

"So has he... ?" Kirsty whispered, "Is it time I bought myself a hat?"

# Montgomery Lines, Aldershot; August 1995

When the alarm went off at Zero-five-thirty, Paul asked himself if there was any other way to do this, but his conscience pricked him out of bed. *There is no such thing as a bad regiment; only bad officers.* Making the training both demanding and realistic required imagination and solid preparation and Paul was determined to prove himself. He pulled on his running kit and by the time he had covered the four miles to the far end of the training area, life was shining inside him. The day had limitless possibilities. If his men saw how hard he was working they would surely warm to him more.

A mile beyond Flagstaff Hill, looking over the brow of the ridge, he found a location perfect for his needs. The ground sloped away to form a natural arena. There was a parking area to the north-west and what could be an admin area to the rear by some trees. He wanted to teach his men how to direct mortar fire with a radio. He would seat them at the top of the bank with a map. In the bowl would be a target made from a high-visibility marker panel. The corporals would be scattered around the bowl and indicate the fall of notional rounds by shining their torches upwards. If the rounds landed off the target the soldier would correct the fire using the radio and the corporals would indicate the more accurate fall of shot as a result. It was not the map reading that mattered, but the radio procedure, the wording. Paul nodded to himself. He thought the plan simple and effective. He had ordered the radios, maps, packed lunches and transport and checked mentally through the day's timetable. Happy that everything was in order, he jogged home along the back roads with the soft, morning sunlight filtering through the elder trees. Back at the Mess, he felt radiant. After showering and changing into his field gear he ate an enormous breakfast, collected his packed lunch, and drove back out to where he had just been. It was then things started to go wrong.

A unit of engineers had occupied his chosen area and were rapidly turning it into a defensive position. A combat tractor dragged at the heather, the sand dribbling through the teeth of the digging blade, while an officer marked out the corners of a four-man trench. A squad of men bounced rolls of barbed wire along a line of iron posts and the entire arena reverberated with the juddering and clanging of military plant.

There was no point wasting time. He would have to find a new location and do so quickly since his platoon would be arriving in fifteen minutes. Rummaging in his patrol-sack Paul looked for his map case. It was missing. He searched again but it was definitely not there. Nor was it in his car. He slapped his head, remembering where he had left it: on the bench by the door in the Mess. "Fuck!" He pressed the heels of his palms to his eyes, embarrassed at his own stupidity. "Bollocks, bollocks, bollocks." The beautiful crispness to the dawn was surrendering to the dull monotony of morning. Traffic noise hummed from beyond the car park.

The lack of a map was not insurmountable, he decided. The corporals had been told to bring out a stack of them and he could use one of those. Paul jogged along the ridge to find a new location for the exercise and in doing so quickly became sweaty and red faced. Thankfully, he found a similar if slightly smaller bowl a kilometre to the south-west. It was not as good as the first, but it would do. The soldiers could sit in the heather just below a lone ash tree, as if in cover. The digger could barely be heard. Looking round, he mentally revised the briefing script: *You are alone behind enemy lines after your patrol was ambushed. Making your way back to friendly forces you find a company of enemy infantry in the open blocking your route home. You have a radio rescued from your section commander who was killed during the ambush. You decide to call down mortar fire to cover your escape.*

He checked his watch. Despite the setbacks, he was pleased with himself. *Improvise, adapt and overcome.* The day could still be a success. It was Zero-eight-forty and along the ridge, above the original position, the platoon were congregating as instructed. Corporal Smith, known as Delta, was studying a map. They had not seen him and could not hear his shouts so he strode over, conscious of the time ticking by. When he arrived the soldiers were smoking and gassing with each other. Corporal Smith called the platoon to attention and saluted: "This is the grid you gave Sir, yeah? This is where we're meant to be?"

"It is, Corporal Smith. But the engineers have taken the area I wanted, so we have to move. We've to go along the ridge a click. Get the blokes ready and we'll go."

"You didn't book the area Sir, no?" Smith's moustache was twitching.

Paul coloured. "I didn't, no. I didn't know we had to, for a platoon exercise." This was the root of it all. "But there's another area along here. Follow me." He strode off, leaving the platoon to rush along after him, giggling like children. Knowing they were mocking him, his ears glowed. It was after nine before he finally had them in orderly lines by the ash tree.

"Right, well, let's start, shall we?" Paul said, rubbing his hands and looking first at Corporal Smith. "Who's got the kit I ordered?"

Smith placed his patrol-sack on the ground by his feet but then shook his head: "The signals platoon said they can't give out seven radios, Sir. The scaling is four. They said if you want more you have to get permission from Major Casenove."

"They what?"

"That's what they're like Sir, in the sigs; a right bunch of jobsworths. And the Sergeant, Rosy Russell, he said you never filled the form in right."

Paul stared at the ground feeling the men's eyes upon him. With only half the radios it could still work, but he would have to make it more stage managed. "Maps?" he asked, looking at Corporal Hudson, whose vaguely Asian appearance had earned him the nickname Chink. The NCO nodded, pulling a roll from the side of his patrol-sack: "Same detail, Sir: three of them, brand spankers from the training wing. I know you asked for one per man, but they won't issue that many as there's a limit to what they get. But most of the lads have their own, from various exercises going back. They're one to fifty, not one to twenty-five. If you can navigate on a one to fifty, the larger scale's easier."

Paul wanted to express his displeasure but knew better than to sound off in front of the men – all three of the corporals had served in the Falklands and in truth he was slightly in awe of them. "Well what *have* we got?" he demanded huffily. "Did we at least manage to collect the packed lunches?"

"What packed lunches?" frowned Delta.

"The packed lunches for today," Paul said. "I booked them myself. I told Private Banks to get the blokes to collect them after..."

Delta turned swiftly towards the squad of men, voice rising: "Banks – did you pass the message about the packed lunches?"

Banks, looking small and narrow shouldered, nodded along the front rank of men to indicate two Lance-corporals. "No, I told Matt and Brad and they..." The two men immediately shook their heads. A small soldier in the rear rank, his arm in a cast, shouted out that he had collected a box for himself and one spare; they were on the table by the door after breakfast and marked for the platoon. The man next to him, an imposing South African, hissed for him to shut up and he immediately did so. Delta poked Banks in the ribs. "Well? Did you pass the message or not?" The Lance-corporals looked down the line, shaking their heads. Banks, caught between being outranked and being outpunched, simply shrugged.

Paul shuddered. No maps, no area, no lunch. The day was slipping through his fingers. His attention was then taken by Corporal Weston, the largest of the NCOs, who was sitting apart from the squad, studying his map and the bowl below them. "You want us to do what Sir? To go where?" Paul knelt quickly, not wanting the soldiers to see he did not understand. They would think it his failure to explain rather than Weston's inability to listen that was in question. Having repeated the instructions, he asked quietly if Weston understood. The man looked at the map and then at the bowl: "Yeah, if that's what you want us to do Sir, fine, but..." His voice trailed off, leaving doubts hanging in the air.

Briefing his NCOs the night before, Paul had painted a wonderful picture of what the exercise would achieve. The reality was proving somewhat prosaic; a comedy of errors even. It was nearly Ten-hundred and the sunniness of the morning had been replaced by an icy wind that penetrated his smock. Sweat was chilling on his chest. With the men starting to chatter to each other he dug the warm kit out of his patrol-sack – a fluffy green fleece he had bought at an army surplus store, a bit of kit he prized highly. It was lighter, warmer and more windproof than the issued, elbow-patched woollen jumper. If only he had bought the bigger size, he thought, as he tugged the zip round his chest. He took a moment to think. Since they had no lunch he would have to get a move on and do something. Without transport until Sixteen-hundred they would have to march back into camp and that would take at least an hour. This was a classic military problem. He had a specific task and insufficient resources. It was his job to make it work. The platoon's eyes were on him.

"Stop! Just stop and listen in," he said loudly, zipping up his smock over the fleece. "We're going to do this exercise for an hour. Then we'll march back into camp for lunch. This is what needs to happen now..."

He issued instructions chopping at the air with his forearm. The Corporals slid away to their tasks. Paul taught the soldiers as best he could but found them so slow and uncomfortable with the voice procedure that only two of them managed to complete a turn. At Twelve-hundred it started to rain and he shouted for the Corporals, who had spent most of the time in the bowl smoking and looking up for instructions, to come back up to the ridge. "Chink, bring that marker panel back as well. We're going in."

They marched back in silence. Paul was surprised that the soldiers were so unfamiliar with the material. He was angry with the Corporals, thinking them unhelpful; frustrated by the bureaucracy of the system; and most of all he was livid with himself for letting it all happen that way. He should have thought it through in more detail. Because he had to march back with the men, he would now have to ask Rolly to give him a lift back out to collect his car. How would he debrief this fiasco with the Corporals? The men seemed morose and rebellious. As they marched to the cookhouse to collect their forgotten lunches, they made catcalls to their friends in the scoff queues until Delta told them to stop. Inside the accommodation block they disappeared to their rooms. The corridors echoed with mocking laughter and the sickly stench of cheap lemonade. What a clusterfuck.

Paul directed the Corporals to join him in his office: "Gents, I don't like looking stupid and that's what happened this morning..."

Delta immediately raised his hand, his moustache emphasising a scowl that soured his face. "Sir is this going to be like a bollocking or something? Cos if it is you better get your facts right."

Paul was so dumbstruck by the challenge that his hands started to shake.

Delta continued: "You never told us anything about this exercise, never gave us any instructions or anything we could prepare. I'm the Acting Platoon Sergeant in this platoon. If you're gonna treat us like this then you and me's gonna have to have words." Chink Hudson was straight faced, nodding. Corporal Weston chewed gum, his pale eyes fixed on Paul's. Delta was insistent: "It's not your job to book the admin Sir. It's mine. If I'd done it we'd have everything we needed. You just do the planning."

Paul felt his cheeks redden. He had to reduce his boil to a simmer and from that to a whimper: "Look, I wanted this to be good, right..."

The three Corporals all started speaking at once. "Well delegate then! We know how to do this! When we were down south, in the Falklands, Delta was calling down fire all the time..."

The comment killed what was left of Paul's ardour. There was nothing he could teach those who had done it for real; those who had been, as they often said, *down south*. He had no way of ending this conversation without looking a fool. He blinked as the room fell into an angry and unsatisfied silence. The fabric of his authority felt tissue-thin, his dignity vaporous.

Delta caught the others' eyes and with a flick of his head, sent them out. Paul did not object, his chin falling to his chest. With them gone, the Corporal's manner eased into something almost paternal. "You tried hard, Sir. You tried really hard, and to be fair it was a good idea, that exercise." An unspoken word hung heavily between them before he said it. "But for fuck's sake trust us to do our jobs."

## Toomebridge, Northern Ireland; August 1995

It was raining. A convoy of industrial tippers chugged past, spluttering dark smoke and spraying the kerbside with run-off slush. It being Saturday, men were playing football on a pitch beyond the houses and the periodic shrill of a whistle punctuated their clamour for the ball. The sound brought back a mixture of memories for Liam: the shame of his clumsiness and the strapping exhilaration of the changing room.

He'd been a week hiding in the back room of this wee bar, waiting for Michael, one of the Big Men, to come see him. Right after the shooting, Jamesy'd driven across the border to a safe house in Sligo. They'd said he was to stay out of sight and he'd done so, despite being bored out of his wits. There was only so much RTE a man could stand. He'd watched the news every hour and flushed with fear and pride when they said his name and given a description. They were calling him The Engineer, a sobriquet he liked. It conveyed the arts of destruction and construction in the same word; the removal of colonialism and the building of a free, united Ireland. But his mood had been mixed. The elation of the job had been scorched by the army killing a wee boy out with his mates. They'd thought it was him in the car, Liam thought, fascinated by the consequences of what he'd done.

*Be true, be true*, he kept telling himself. *That way you'll be safe.*

Then at last Jamesy'd brought him a book, apologising that he'd only just remembered as he left his Ma's with the food box. He'd grabbed what was nearest on the shelf and hoped it would do, hadn't even looked to see what it was. The complete works of Oscar Wilde was not quite as delicious as Liam had hoped, but at least it was Irish and of a time before partition. He'd devoured it page by page until, thank God, the pressure from the police eased off. Command said it was safe for him to come home if he stayed low. He'd not wasted any time in getting the late night bus and Jamesy had met him and taken him to see his Da, slipping him in through the back doors of the care home after hours. God, his Da had looked old, his skin as bruised as an apple from the bottom shelf. In the morning, when he came out with tears in his eyes, Jamesy'd brought him here and left him.

Liam stepped back from the window, pulling the curtains together. The two men who had come to talk with him kept glancing over from the other side of the room. They whispered to each other. He became afraid he'd said too much, been too bold. They had listened to him while he told them what he thought, their faces as implacable as a pair of dustbins. They'd nodded and looked at each other and then told Jamesy to go wait in the car outside. Jamesy had patted Liam on the knee, told him to pin his ears back. Michael, the Big Man, told Jamesy to hurry the fuck up and get out and he'd disappeared in a flash. Now Michael was nodding and making a move to sit down, so Liam did the same.

"You done a good job on Pearson," Michael said at last. "He's to have the leg off, but he's alive – just what we needed." Liam swallowed. He felt nothing for the man. "So the boys inside are singing your praises," Michael said. "The guards got nasty and it makes our lads happy, seeing them panic like that."

The tall one sitting next to Michael was called JP. He was unshaven and scratched his chin, nodding. He winked, which made Liam a little less afraid of him. Liam opened his mouth to speak but Michael held up a hand to keep him quiet, his shoulders slanting thick and broad from the base of his neck. "But you've to be certain in your mind that there's to be no killing till we say. There's a ceasefire. There's talks going on, and the negotiators are tight up against it. They're round the table with these fuckers every day. Every day they're looking them in the eyes, working out what we can get and what we can't. The stakes are high. This is like 1920, but more important. It's history we're making."

He paused.

"So what we don't need is some young buck thinking he's the new Patrick Pearse. We've to be sure you'll do what's needed, when it's needed; not before and not after. Are you clear on that or do I need to spell it out for you?"

Liam's mouth was dry. He nodded.

"You sure now? There's to be no more talk of fighting unless I say."

Liam nodded again, his voice sounding strangled. "No. I mean yes, I've got it." The men stared at him, assessing. He was shackled under their gaze, shoeless.

"Good," Michael said. "So we'll not talk of it again. We've something special we need a man for, something big. We think you might be the one. It'd mean living in London, away from your Daddy. You'd have an alias but that'll be no surprise, since they know your name and you can't go out. We'd get you a job, something to give you cover. You'd be spying. You'd be planning... in case we have to end the ceasefire."

Liam's mouth fell open. He couldn't believe what he was hearing. And London as well; away from here, out of the claustrophobic morality of the place.

"So you're up for it?" Michael asked.

"Yes, I'm up for it," Liam said without thinking further.

Michael looked at him hard again. "Was it electrical engineering you did at Queen's?" he asked.

Liam shook his head. "No, civil," he said.

Michael nodded. "That'll do. That'll do rightly," he said.

# Montgomery Lines, Aldershot; August 1995

"How's your training, matey?" Rolly asked as they climbed the stairs to Major Casenove's office for the weekly conference. Paul answered in non-committal terms. It was going fine; a bit of learning perhaps, on his part, but overall it was going well. He had got to know the corporals and identified the immature soldiers from the promotion-ready. In fact some of them had been almost infantile, come to think of it, goosing around like children. "What about you?"

"Oh, I've been out on the ranges all week, shooting. Sergeant Taggart managed to scrounge some ammunition and we did a cracking first aid exercise on the way back; something he knocked up himself." Paul was jealous. Rolly spoke of his Sergeant as if they were already firm friends and never seemed to agonise about his platoon's internal dynamics. "Sounds great. Give me the exercise instruction and I'll see if I can work it in."

In the long mirror by the door to the Company office, Paul and Rolly adjusted their berets. Suitably fierce looking, Rolly knocked. "Come," called Major Casenove and the two marched in, saluted and sat down, laying out their notebooks ready for instruction. While they did so, the Major leaned back in his chair with his fingers interlaced behind his head. There was an air of supreme calm about him. He had the phlegmatic self-assurance of someone destined to command at progressively higher levels of the army's pyramid, as both his father and grandfather had done before him. His ambition in this regard had been made clear to the two young officers. If he was to be successful he would need subordinates of quality, men he could trust, to follow him up the ladder. The edge this created between them was subtle but undeniable. It never paid to come second in Major Casenove's eyes.

"Gentlemen, there are two things we need to discuss today. Firstly, I want to give you the latest outlook for the chances of an operational deployment." Both Rolly and Paul looked up. "In short, since we have only recently come back from Tyrone, the Chain of Command is saying that there is little chance we will deploy again in the immediate future. The Operational Tour Plot doesn't have us down for another two years, until May Ninety-seven. It is quite possible you will both serve out your time as platoon commanders without gaining operational experience. Not ideal, but that's the price we pay for peace.

"As for Bosnia, you will have seen that it's all over the television and no doubt deduced that it is the focus of the government's foreign policy. But sadly we don't see a place for light-role infantry such as ourselves. If there is a ground war after the bombing campaign, it will be the armoured brigades that are best suited to the terrain."

Paul tried hard to look impassive but the disappointment sang keenly within him. "Is that definite Sir?"

"Nothing's definite in this game, Paul. That's why we have high readiness built in to our DNA. The men, I'm sure, will be keen to do anything new. But you need to put it across to the blokes that we are a strategic asset. Any student of military history will tell you that Churchill always kept his best troops in reserve and that's where we will remain for the time being. It's not much of a sweetener, but there you go. Our time will come, as they say across the water."

Paul and Rolly glanced at each other. They would have to wait and see.

"But let's not dally on all that," the Major said, tapping the end of a pencil on the desk. "That's for info, not action. The main reason I brought you here is to give you a heads-up about the Longdon Assault Competition. It's an inter-platoon march and shoot conducted at the end of every training year. It was developed, obviously, in the aftermath of the Falklands war, in honour of the battalion's attack on Mount Longdon. It is designed to test the full range of military skills we require in this regiment. The next one will be held on Salisbury Plain – the Operations Officer is already down there booking training estates. It will take place in December. Although that will seem a long way away, think hard about your time estimate. After summer leave, time will be precious. You must anticipate what's coming and start to plan your work-up training.

"And gentlemen, let me be clear about this. I expect this Company to win and I expect you two to beat every other platoon in the battalion. This is not a threat, it's a promise: there is no second place in war. If we think we are the best, we have to constantly prove it. The armoured brigades might well be babysitting the UN in Sarajevo or coddling the RUC in Belfast. But in this regiment we train for real wars and real fighting. We train hard so we fight easy."

The Major's inflection became more insistent, making Paul's heart pump harder. He wanted to prove that he was the best platoon commander and in the absence of going to war, this would have to be the next best thing.

After he had outlined the logistics of the event, the Major quizzed the young officers about their training plans. His questions were direct and uncomfortable, giving Paul the impression that he knew more than he let on. Eventually, he dismissed Rolly but asked Paul to remain. A chill of self-doubt rippled up and down his spine.

"Paul there's nothing wrong, so relax. I want to talk about your NCOs." The Major placed his fingertips along the edge of the desk as if playing a piano. Paul shifted his weight, unsure of what was coming. "Paul this is not about you, it is about your Sergeant, Bryan Moor." Paul nodded. Getting to know the Corporals he had asked about the joyrider shooting but his men rarely opened up. Delta had said he was not in the platoon at the time. Chink Hudson had said he was elsewhere on the road when the shooting happened. Weston just shook his head and continued to stare at Paul with pale, penetrating eyes.

"I don't really know what happened, Sir," Paul said.

"No? All right. I'd better fill you in," the Major frowned. "Last March we were looking for a versatile little bastard called Liam Gerard. The sneaky-beaky teams had been trailing him for a week, following a tip off, but they lost him. Then he popped up in the Holy Lands – that's one of the gentler suburbs in south Belfast. He shot a sixty-five year old retired prison officer in the leg and robbed him. The man had to have his leg removed and has since died. Gerard was, at that moment, the most wanted man in Ulster. Intelligence suggested he would escape south-west, to Monaghan. This meant he had to drive round Lough Neagh to get on one of the back roads across the border. We were tasked with setting VCPs – vehicle checkpoints – to prevent him. Your platoon, led by Sergeant Moor at the time, had VCPs just south of Aughnacloy. Unfortunately, a young joyrider called Andrew McGiven made the fatal and unconnected mistake of using that road to take a stolen car full of his mates to one of the shebeens across the border. They drove into Moor's VCP and given the choice between stopping and going for it, they made the wrong decision. A Corporal called Mercer... ?" The Major raised his eyes and Paul nodded. "Yes, Sir, I've heard the blokes talking of 'Mercy.' He's got a room on my floor; it's got his kit locked away in it still."

"That's the man. A damn good man as well; very reliable. On this occasion Mercer had a split-second to decide if the car contained Gerard or just some pissed-up teenager. It was driving directly at his men so he opened fire, sending it off the road. The driver was killed. Because of the peculiarities of the law in Northern Ireland, he had to be charged with murder.

"Now, the Adjutant tells me that we've just been informed by Brigade that Mercer's trial will be separated from Moor's. The issues are more complex. Although Moor was in overall command, he did not open fire. The forensic report said that Mercer's shot killed the driver. So his trial will start next week and Moor's will be set later in the year. You may notice that this affects the morale within the platoon. I am giving you this information so you can manage your men better."

The comment seemed barbed.

"I mean," the Major qualified, "That you must stop them doing anything stupid. Both Mercer and Moor were very popular. Moor is something of a legend in the battalion. I'm sure you've heard stories about him." Paul nodded. Yes, he had heard the men talking about Bryan Moor all right. "So the long and the short of it is that we will find out very soon if you are going to get your Platoon Sergeant back, or if we will have to promote someone else in his place."

Paul frowned. "It doesn't sound like there's a lot I can do to alter the outcome of the case."

"You can't Paul. But you can affect how the news influences your men. Nothing lifts morale like a victory, even a small one. The best thing you can do is win the Longdon Assault Competition."

# Chelsea, London; August 1995

As she walked down the King's Road past the iron gates of the army barracks, Clare briefly felt the warmth of the sun on her cheek. A little further on she returned to the shade of shop buildings, and a little further on again she crossed the road behind a pair of taxis to have a peep in the window of a boutique on the other side. It was the second weekend in the month. Paul was on leave, but having lost three consecutive games of Connect Four, he had begrudgingly agreed to repaint the bedroom in her flat. This provided her with the opportunity she needed. Money had been tight when Paul's birthday had come around earlier in the year but, with the passing of her intermediate exams, her salary had risen slightly. Now she wanted to get him something nice.

Paul's clothes were enduringly unfashionable and whenever they went shopping he spent most of the time in military surplus stores buying heavy-duty, forest-coloured gadgets or yet another pair of boots. He dressed, she decided, as though he expected to be stranded on a desert island for years at a time; his outfit always thorn-proofed and double-stitched. He would need to be coaxed carefully into something hip, something that only the King's Road would provide.

The sloany trend, she observed, was for branded, pastel-coloured polo shirts, Chelsea boots and Australian jeans. Paul would hate it. By comparison, Rolly took his grooming seriously, favouring a classically English look of tailored jackets, natural fibres, and quality labels. It suited him and Clare wished Paul would oblige. Not far from Sloane Square she found a place selling the sort of expensive, high quality shirts that Rolly might wear and into which Paul might be persuaded. There was a sale rack, but the items were either too small or would never do. She could picture him pulling a face. But against the back wall a rack of underlit glass shelves bore a small pile of dark grey, V-necked jumpers. The wool was from New Zealand, the girl explained. The knit work was wonderfully fine and a metal button sewn onto the right arm acted both as a fitting for an epaulet and the manufacturer's label. She held one out at arm's length. Would he like it? Would he wear it? It was more money than she had intended but it was on offer, stock not sold from the previous winter. That would appeal to his pragmatism, no doubt. She would certainly like to see it on.

"Hi Clare! What's up?" It was Rolly, wearing a citrusy aftershave she had noticed before.

"Oh, Rolly! How lovely to see you! Listen," she said, "Just stand there with this, will you? It's a present for Paul. Do you think he would like it?"

Rolly held the jumper up against his chest and felt the wool. "Merino? Very nice, very nice indeed. That's very generous, Clare. Are you sure he's worth it?" A smile dimpled his cheeks. His eyes were kind. It was flattering to have him with her while the shop assistants gawped. He pulled the jumper on, exposing much of his chest and stomach as he did so. His hairiness was an attribute she always found attractive, perhaps because Paul did not possess it. Patting Rolly's chest, she decided to make the purchase and at the tills he stood beside her, winking at the teenager who folded the jumper into a cardboard box. Clare could not help but enjoy the display. His girlfriend was beautifully slender but a little insipid. It would not surprise her if Rolly undertook some extra-curricular studies.

"Were you in there, Rolly?" she smiled, once they were out on the street and could feel the sunshine on their faces. Rolly grinned, reflecting her face in his sunglasses. "Not my type Clare: bone from the neck up. Anyway, I'm meeting Evelyn by the tube in ten minutes. We're going into town for an exhibition at the National. Would you like to come?" Clare smiled in thanks but no, she had work to finish and had promised to cook Paul a curry for dinner. Rolly insisted: "Have you time for a drink instead, there's a coffee shop on the Square. Can you stay another half hour?" Pushing his glasses up onto his head, he looked her straight in the eyes: "Please, Clare; let me give you one."

It had been a deliberate choice of words. He was grinning. Paul had once been like that: boyish, flippant and fun.

"Yes, Rolly. I'd love you to," she said. "Covered in chocolate, please."

## Montgomery Lines, Aldershot;
## September 1995

The Longdon Assault Competition was set for early December, the Major said. That sounded a long way off, but once Paul took into consideration the exercises in Otterburn and Wales, the cadre period, an exchange exercise with the French Foreign Legion, the officers' planning exercise and all the annual training tests, the time between the end of summer leave and the planned departure for Salisbury Plain dwindled away into nothing. With all the commitments plotted in the diary, Paul was only left with a couple of weeks to prepare his platoon.

He had also learned in his first few months that managing the frenetic activity of barracks life was too much for him on his own. Though it made him feel important to be the sole decision maker, he was sufficiently self-aware to notice that he quickly became a bottleneck and the pace of activity slowed. Soldiers spent more time on their beds waiting for training to start than actually being out on the ranges. As the NCOs had told him, delegation was key.

This in itself was not difficult. He found it easy to carve up the training into subject areas and give each to the most qualified Corporal: Delta Smith took the fieldcraft lessons since he used to be in the reconnaissance platoon. Corporal Weston, a sniper, ran the shooting. Private Horne, the platoon medic, did the first aid and Chink Hudson, with a personal best at the London marathon of less than two hours fifty minutes, planned the fitness. But the difficulty for Paul was how far he *should* delegate. If he gave too much away he felt exposed, as if he was not leading from the front. If he interfered with the Corporals' lessons they quickly told him to back off. But if he did not interfere they tended to drift off the subject matter that Paul had expected them to cover and this made him embarrassed for having been unclear during his briefings to them. Additionally, Paul had come to realise that he knew considerably less about soldiering than they did. Hudson was far faster than him in a straight race. Weston could put ten rounds through the same hole at two hundred metres. Delta, it was said, had narrowly missed out on a gallantry medal down south. Major Casenove reassured him that being in the top three in the platoon was good enough, providing he was in the top three for everything. But this did not make it easier. He had expected to be better than his men but, on finding that they out-skilled him, had to learn to ask rather than tell. Leading the platoon became an awkward surrendering of responsibility pitched in such a way that he still felt in command.

But there were times when Paul had to be seen to take the lead and the battle march was one of these. It was something he enjoyed, trotting alongside a formed body of men, their feet pounding in unison. Every now and then Paddy Connolly or Geordie Dickinson, the platoon comedians, would crack a joke and the men would gurgle with deep laughter. As they ran, they asked if there was any more news about Corporal Mercer and Bryan Moor, but Paul shook his head. He said he'd let them know as soon as he heard anything.

Along the ridge of Seven Sisters after the morning's rain, they splashed happily through the shallow puddles. Over the brow of Flagstaff Hill, the track turned from flint to sand and here Paul increased the pace, leaning forward. The platoon picked up the cue, leaning into the march with him; rifles swinging across the front of their bodies, lips pursed and sweat pouring. The last four miles took them off the open serenity of the training area and along one of the tight, meandering roads that webbed across the Hampshire countryside.

Overhung with branches and sided by drainage ditches long lost to brigades of nettles, the road encouraged drivers to enjoy the exhilaration of fast, canted turns. As Paul marched the platoon along a narrow track to meet the road, he could clearly hear the sound of a motorbike approaching from the left and a van approaching from the right. The bike roared with the decline in its favour while the van crunched its gears as it climbed. Each would have little idea of the imminent appearance of the other and instinctively Paul slowed. Just ahead they could see a twenty metre stretch of tarmac framed by trees.

The van appeared first, leaning over into the middle of the road, the wheels lifting as it took the bend. The bike, appearing from the opposite direction almost in the knee-down position, found the van tilted into his lane. Breaks squealed. Wheels skidded. The rider swerved by instinct. The platoon held their breath, certain that death had placed his hand before them, but once they got to the road they saw there was no smash and no helmet bouncing down the tarmac. "Christ that was close," said Paul. "Only a gnat's pube in that one," Corporal Weston added, shaking his head. "Thought that was endex for both of 'em."

The van driver fought to bring the skidding van under control. The bike slowed to a crawl. The van driver, hearing nothing of a crash, sped off. The biker's head started lolling and his movements became sluggish. The engine roared and the bike swerved from one side of the road to the other. He could not get his feet back on the footrests. "He's gone," said Weston. The bike suddenly accelerated, struck the kerb, smashed into a traffic sign and threw the rider into the road, where he collapsed like an empty wetsuit. The bike span into the ditch.

"Follow me!" ordered Paul, his mind suddenly sharp with responsibility. The men were at his shoulder. "When we get there: Delta you and your section take the far side, block the road and cordon it. Chink you take this side, where I say so. Westy, you take the casualty and sweep the road of debris. Get the bike out of the ditch if you can."

Paul looked at each of his corporals. None of them challenged.

A short distance from the motionless body, Paul snapped, "Here, Chink," and Corporal Hudson pulled out of the formation, five soldiers peeling out with him. At the casualty he told Delta to run on and get beyond the next corner so no-one would plough into them on the road. Scouse Horne needed no instruction and was already pulling off his rucksack next to the rider. Paddy Connelly went with him and Westy told the remainder to grapple the bike out of the ditch.

"Sketchmap, yeah, Boss?" Westy said, "for the insurance and the police, yeah?" Paul nodded: "Good idea; do it. Let me sign it off."

He pulled off his bergen and took up a position where he could observe all three of his sections at work. The bike was too heavy and too far wedged into the ditch to be moved so he called the men off, telling them to cut branches and sweep the road. This they loved, jumping enthusiastically into the copse to snatch at the saplings.

In five minutes there was a five-car tailback on both sides of the incident, Corporal Weston had drawn a sketch map and the road had been swept of the shattered glass and fairings.

The rider was still lying prone in the middle of the road, one arm beneath him and the other stretched out at an awkward angle. His leathers were torn down the back, exposing the armour. The helmet was cracked where he had hit the road sign. Scouse had the visor up. One of his legs twitched and then lifted to Scouse's instruction. The other could not move. Scouse was soothing: "That's OK mate; that's OK. Can you move your right fingers for me, yeah? Just your right fingers? Just a little?" Paul did not quite understand how he had collapsed. "Me neither, Boss," said Paddy Connelly. This was the second time one of them had called him 'Boss' rather than the more formal 'Sir' and to Paul it meant that he was on the verge of acceptance. "But the guy's fecked now," Paddy said. "I don't think his neck's gone but he's in and out of consciousness. We need an ambulance quick."

Paul was a little stunned that he had not thought of it. Having just come out for a march he had not brought any radios. "Right; hold on…" He shouted for Delta and Chink to come in to his position and briefed them to find a driver with a mobile phone in their respective queues: "One casualty, very serious injury, conscious but incoherent, three miles west of Aldershot on the Crookham road, police and ambulance needed immediately, traffic halted and building up fast." The corporals disappeared to their respective positions and soldiers immediately started along the cars, knocking on the windows. Very soon Chink raised his hand: "Lads have found one, Boss. Message sent."

It was only a matter of time now. All they had to do was control the traffic, keep the casualty alive and wait for medical attention to arrive. Paul stood back and surveyed the incident. It was working. He was in control. He was in command. But after thirty minutes the police had not arrived and the halted lines of traffic were doubling in size every ten minutes. The drivers who could not see the incident became impatient. Horns blew. Delta shouted that one driver was in a hurry: he was a plumber on an emergency callout, a gas leak. Chink shouted that a woman in his queue was asking how long they would be; she had her mother in the car and needed a loo.

The pressure mounted in Paul's mind. It swept over him. He looked at Scouse but the soldier shook his head: "Can't move him, Boss. Neck might be broken, not sure. Never move a head-case, yeah?"

Delta appeared at his shoulder: "Sir, the traffic's getting angry. We're not coppers. We don't have a right to stop them. We should let them go, but under control."

"Scouse says we shouldn't move him."

"We'll have to, Boss. Just put him on a stretcher; four man lift. If he's alive now, he'll survive a quick shift to that parking area. We did it down south, with much worse injuries."

There was indeed a very suitable concrete lay-by just metres away. "And I guess the queues are blocking the ambulance..." Paul whispered to himself as he swayed between options. Delta nodded. Scouse, on his knees next to the casualty, looked up at him. At that moment, a car from Delta's side of the accident pulled out of the line and drove towards them, forcing Private Pietersen to jump out of its way. Paul and Delta both stepped into the road with their hands up but it drove straight at them and got round the casualty by mounting the kerb and scraping the exhaust. As he sped away, the driver looked angrily in the rear view mirror, sticking up a finger.

Paul was astounded, unable to fathom such behaviour.

"Fucking cunt," said Delta. "Come on, Boss. Let's get the road clear."

The world was looking at him for an answer. "All right, do it," Paul said.

Scouse immediately protested but Corporal Weston silenced him: "Scouse, shut it. The Platoon Commander's made a decision. Get fucking on with it."

Within half a minute someone had improvised a stretcher from a plastic sheet and Scouse fed it underneath the casualty's limbs, one by one. Since he could not fight the decision, he was ensuring the rider would be moved with absolute care.

Paul felt control returning. He watched as Weston and Delta both got involved with the haul, a careful but speedy drag across the tarmac: "Two-three move... two-three move..." It was a timeless sight, soldiers moving a body by stretcher.

Kneeling down, Scouse peeped through the open visor. "You all right there mate? Still with me, yeah?" The man's

45

eyes were open and he responded slowly but clearly. Paul reorganised his men to get the traffic flowing, keeping one man watching out for the ambulance while the others made statements in their notebooks. The paramedics took another ten minutes to arrive, sloughing to a halt just short of the casualty.

"Who's in charge," Paul demanded as the driver dismounted. "What's happened here then, mate?" the man replied, a frown colouring his face. The second medic, a fairly attractive, middle-aged woman dismounted from the back of the ambulance dragging a large plastic box. She began looking to the rider, assisted by Paddy and Scouse. Paul was outlining the events when the woman shouted: "Jerry, he's been moved. They've moved him."

The man scowled at Paul. "Why did you do that?" he demanded.

"Because he was blocking the road and delaying your arrival. If we didn't clear the road you might never have got here." There was an inflection in his words that Paul had not intended, a criticism that was not lost on the paramedic. He was about to rise to it when his colleague called over: "Jerry, he's lost consciousness. Need you now!"

Ten minutes later Paul felt his limbs starting to stiffen. They had never warmed down. The soldiers would be feeling the same. With the traffic now flowing he told the corporals to collect and check the men's statements. Scouse and Paddy continued to help the paramedics; the latter holding a saline drip and the former studying everything they did.

After the police arrived and Paul had briefed a laconic sergeant about what had happened, he asked if they might now get away. The policeman replied that of course he could, surprised they had remained for so long.

Rather than the march finishing on a high, it now felt as limp as a rainy afternoon. Paul presented the handful of scrawled statements to the police sergeant and called Paddy and Scouse to fall in for the remaining three miles home. As he did so, the male paramedic stood. Paul stretched out his hand, expecting him to shake it but was surprised by the invective he got instead: "Listen dumb-arse. Next time you fancy playing God, just leave the fucking casualty where it is. Let the professionals do it. You could have killed him."

# Canning Town, London; September 1995

Clare sat up in bed, pulling the duvet up to her neck: "You look super, Pauly, you really do! I knew you would as soon as I saw it." Paul laughed and started to dance, thrusting his hips to the French song coming from Yvonne's room. Wearing only the pullover Clare had just given him, his cock slapped gaily against his thigh. Clare giggled, hair falling over her eyes. Seeing her like that always made him happy; a fleeting vision of the girl he had known before life became serious: "It's super, Clare. I wasn't sure at first, but now... is it wool?"

"Yes, merino; from New Zealand. It's the best you can get, Rolly says."

Reverentially, Paul pulled the jumper off and folded it along the creases, replacing it in the box. "Was it very expensive?" he asked.

"Don't you like it? I can take it back..."

"No don't do that. It's lovely, Clare. I just wasn't expecting it. Is it our anniversary? What's the occasion? Have I forgotten something?"

"It's a present, Pauly, that's all. Just something to say I love you."

"No strings attached?" He smiled. It was a standing joke between them from his university days. Clare giggled: "Well, maybe..." and Paul slid back into bed and pulled himself up to her, his cock hardening against her thigh. She smelled of skin cream and her lips lingered on his, drawing him in. When his tongue touched hers, she exhaled, closing her eyes. He took his time, wanting her to feel his appreciation. Probing with his lips he traced her cheek, her neck, the lobes of her ears and the softness in the well of her shoulder. "I need you," he whispered and her nipples hardened in his mouth as she moved to welcome him. When they made love, she called out, repeating his name. When she came, tears moistened her cheeks. When it was his turn, she cried out again. Sated, they lay together for another hour, drifting in and out of sleep. At seven she shook him: "Pauly – we've got to be there in an hour. Come on, get up." Paul looked over his shoulder at the clock, swore and threw his legs out of bed. He took first shower while she made tea then she showered and he pulled on a tee-shirt and the merino jumper. In the mirror he did not quite recognise himself. "You really do look smart," Clare said, emerging from the bathroom with a towel over her hair. Paul nodded at his reflection then kissed her cheek saying he would order a cab and get the champagne out of the freezer box.

They were only half an hour late when they arrived outside the small bar in Putney. A bouncer directed them up the stairs and into the chatty clamour of the private room, where they immediately saw Evelyn draped in bunches of flowers and looking like a film star. Paul kissed her cheek and seeing she turned, kissed the other as well. "You northerners," she smiled, "We do both in London!" Paul grinned back and held up the champagne: "This is for you, Evey. Very many happy returns. I'll put it with the others, shall I?"

Leaving the ladies to chat he stalked off to find Rolly at the bar, asking if any help was required. Rolly said no, it was all done: the nibbles and dips were out; a short, red haired teenager was serving a glass of bubbly by the door and the DJ was setting up for later.

"I appreciate the invite," Paul said, pulling off his coat.

"No worries, matey. I told Evey I needed some moral support if she was going to invite all her civvy mates." Then noticing Paul's jumper, he added: "Hey, look at you! Don't you look cool!"

Paul frowned: "You like it? Clare gave it to me. I think it makes me look like a security guard at a train depot."

Rolly shook his head. "No matey. It's great. I ran into her when she was buying it. And it goes well with that tee-shirt. You look very swish." Dragged over by Clare, Evelyn came up to admire him and was equally complimentary. Paul blushed. Self-conscious, he thanked Clare publically and raised a toast to Evelyn before getting in a round. The room was filling and Evelyn glided away to welcome a couple bearing another large bunch of flowers. Cooing, Clare was sucked towards a couple seated against the wall with a baby in a carrycot at their feet.

Paul and Rolly stood with their arms folded and backs to the bar, watching the guests arrive. "What did the Adj want you for on Friday, matey?" Rolly asked.

Paul swore angrily, shaking his head: "It was about that biker. He's afraid someone might tell the press I blocked the road off for an hour. I mean, I saved the bastard's life and then, when the ambo turns up fucking forty minutes late, I get gripped for having moved the twat. I tell you, civvies are fucking arseholes. I bet if any one of these cunts witnessed a crash, they'd either walk off and leave him or just sit there and gawp. I got the blokes to make statements in case they found the van driver, and gave them to the police. Now they're saying it was me caused his broken fucking neck. I tell you, Rolly, they can go and fuck themselves next time. No way am I putting my cock on the block if that's what happens." Paul shook his head angrily. "I've to go see Major Cas on Monday morning. I'll find out then what's going to happen."

Rolly started a deep and resonant guffaw: "Touched a nerve there, matey eh? Come on! Don't let it get to you. The Adj has a tiny prick anyway. It was weeks ago. Let it lie. They'll not do anything." Rolly winked at him and nodded towards the gathering crowd: "Just look... this place is bursting with gorgeous totty. Relax, matey. Have some fun."

The conspiratorial nudges took Paul over his sudden flash of rage. This was neither the time nor the place to worry about the Adjutant and a steady flow of beer would blunt any fears he harboured. And for sure the room was crammed with the most beautiful women Paul had ever seen. As the alcohol took hold of him he became rather jealous. Evelyn's male workmates were mostly thin-necked and thin-legged with coiffed hair and gay-looking, open-neck shirts. Their voices were plummy. More than half of them wore glasses and yet all of them had slender, graceful, wide-mouthed honeys hanging from their shoulders. He, by comparison, was a prime physical being yet his girlfriend was a dumpy little thing with broad hips and pendulous breasts. The world wasn't fair.

"Fucking stupid civvies," Paul mumbled as he ordered their fifth round. Then for the sake of good manners and considering himself part of the hosting detail, he tried to engage an insular group of people that included Evelyn's brother and his painfully beautiful girlfriend. The brother introduced himself as "Marcus. Marketing. Not for myself you understand, but one day. What's your business Paul?" Paul replied, rather modestly he thought, that he was a platoon commander in an infantry regiment. "But what does that mean?" Marcus asked. Paul tried to explain but found Marcus kept asking really dumb questions: "So when you say you train your men, does that mean you're in HR?" Paul's increasingly inebriated responses did nothing to enlighten him and when both parties had tired of trying to unpick the other's language, each retired to their respective corner.

Clare cautioned him to slow down on the drinking but he responded by grabbing her hand and dragging her to the empty dance floor. Ignoring everyone else in the room, he sang as he danced: *My girl's mad at me*, the other guests looking at him for a while with uncertain smiles on their faces. But after another song and his carefree dancing, others joined in. The DJ then stuck happily to pop tunes from their school years and Paul, Clare, Evelyn, and Rolly ensured that the collective mood spiralled into noisy revelry. They were, in their minds, the life and soul of the party. Four hours and several pints later Paul instigated a dance somewhere between the *Gay Gordons* and the *51st Division* (Aberdonian version) when the DJ played *Five Hundred Miles*. Sweaty, Paul pulled off his jumper and collapsed into a circular sofa in the corner to be woken by Clare when the lights were on, the hoover was out and the taxi had finally arrived.

"See you in the morning Rolly... happy birthday Evening," Paul shouted as Clare pushed, tugged and fumbled him down the stairs and out into cold fresh air.

# Strood, Kent; September 1995

"Where you from then, Curly? Scotland? Just down from the hills? You're new here aren't you?"

Liam's heart thumped. The boy was slight shouldered and short, coming up only to his chest, but he had beautiful, almond coloured skin and almond shaped eyes. He smelled of citrus trees and his teeth were shiny and white beneath wholesome, thick lips. Liam's mouth was dry. He hoped the boy could not tell how nervous he was. "I'm from Ireland," he said. "County Antrim. And yes, I'm new here."

The boy studied him, one eyebrow raised. It was early but there were already couples starting to form among the mass of dancing men.

"You sound Scottish," the boy insisted and Liam shrugged. "People always say that if you're from Ballymena," he said. "But I am Irish. I'm sure of it, now."

The boy smirked, taking a swig from his beer bottle. As he did so, someone jostled him from behind, jolting him forward. He turned, dabbing at his mouth with slender, perfectly manicured fingers. "That really hurt," he said.

Liam looked at his wounded face. His heart raced. It was now or never. "You need someone to kiss it better?"

The boy looked up, surprised at first, but then started laughing in colourful, high-pitched peels. He slapped his thigh. "You're new to this aren't you?" he said.

Liam blushed and looked away. Tears sprang to his eyes. He stopped laughing. Liam prepared to leave, reaching up to the fruit machine for his coat and scarf.

"Easy, easy there, Curly. Don't be so precious," he said, four fingertips lightly pressing against Liam's chest. "I didn't mean it. It's cool. Relax. You're in good company here. There's no need to go if you don't want to."

The boy's lips were pursed. There was a smear of blood on one front tooth. Liam felt afraid and angry at the same time. The devil was prodding the thick sausage in his underwear and it made his breath jagged and uneven. The boy placed a hand against his cheek and moved closer. Liam thought he would explode. The boy's eyes glowed in the neon lights. His face was smooth, his fingers unbelievably warm.

"It's Fergal," Liam stammered.

The boy reached up on tiptoes and sucked at his lips, tickling inside his mouth with his tongue. There were fingers on his chin, on his ears, on the tuberous swelling in his trousers.

"Hello Fergie," the boy said. "I'm Mo. Welcome to London, Irish boy."

# Aldershot; September 1995

We are Five Platoon.

It's the end of the month. We're Aldershot Orphans, stuck here on a Friday cos we can't afford to get home. Nobody's got any money to go on this piss and no one on guard wants to sell their duty. We walk down to the cinema to watch *Seven*, the new one with Brad Pitt and the guy who played Kaiser Soshay in *Usual Suspects*. Daz and Brains and Banksy think it's great but the rest of us think it's shit and pass the time throwing bits of popcorn at the bald civvy sitting a few rows in front. He turns round all frowning-like, sees us all together, cap-badges on our sweatshirts, and decides to say fuck all.

Then, on our way back up the hill, we're gassing and having a laugh when a car pulls up just short of the roundabout. TP sees it first. It's got one of those Ulster number plates that civvies pay money for. It's stopped on a double yellow. The driver watches the guards at the back gate as he talks on a phone.

Instantly we're tight. TP clicks his fingers to Paddy and Dicko and they're over the other side of the road. If the cunt's got a gun, they're to go for the driver's door. Daz and Taff stay low and step out into the road. Banksy slows down to halt the traffic if it comes.

The blood starts pumping. We're unarmed, off duty, but alive as fuck. Back in the seventies the IRA blew up the Officers' Mess in revenge for Bloody Sunday. No way that'll happen to us, not now. We're alert. We're keen. We're fucking sober. If they're dumb enough to come and have a pop at us on our turf, so be it. TP and Tiny close quickly on the car, watching the driver through the rear window and in the offside mirror, trying to get a description. Dicko repeats the VRN to himself so he can report it: *yellow Citroen Xantia, registration DAZ 445; yellow Citroen Xantia, registration DAZ 445.* TP and Tiny start jogging, shoulders set. The driver looks up and sees them coming. His head turns. We are all around him.

There's an IRA saying that they only have to be lucky once. We, on the other hand, have to be lucky every time. It could be any day and any car. It could be a parcel through the post. It could be a drive-by and could be a bomb. They even landed a mark-ten mortar on Downing Street a few years ago.

But they ain't doing us, not here, not now.

Before we get close, the car speeds off, spewing smoke. It could have been just a civvy, just lost his way, but we ain't taking chances. He'd have shat himself if we got to him. TP reports it to the Guard Commander and then, back in the block, we set up the telly and spend the rest of the night watching porn. We know that out there, somewhere, Liam Fucking Gerard is walking free while Mercy and Beefy Moor are up in court.

# Montgomery Lines, Aldershot;
# September 1995

On Monday morning the office felt cold and cramped. Paul sat with his feet on the desk, chewing a pen and waiting for the Company Clerk, Corporal McGregor, to summon him. It was to be an interview, as Delta put it, 'without coffee'. He felt lonely, listening to the murmuring in the dormitories through the walls. Were the platoon enjoying his discomfort? His imagination flew in terrifying circles and he wondered if he could be sacked for the incident, if he could face the ignominy. Turning events over in his mind, he kept telling himself that he had been the commander on the ground. He had made decisions based upon the best information available. Had he not, the ambulance might never have got through. But he found it difficult not to imagine the worst. "Fucking hell." He threw the pen at the wall. It marked the paint, tumbled, and rolled across his desk to clatter on the floor. If this was what life was like, a prison of self-admonishment, then he might not be cut out for it after all. He pulled his feet off the desk and looked out of the window. He could just imagine Scouse telling everyone that he had advised against it, but the inexperienced young officer just wouldn't listen.

And it wasn't just the incident weighing on his mind. Clare had thrown a track when he admitted to leaving the jumper in the pub. He had rung up but nothing had been handed in and Rolly had even gone round on Sunday night. There was nothing more that could be done now.

The jumper was gone and there was little point making a song and dance about it. But Clare made a song and dance about everything these days. It was nothing against her, it was just that he had other things on his mind much of the time. The more he got into his job the more he found there was to do. She did not understand he could not turn it off every evening like she did. A bloody jumper was a bloody jumper, nothing more.

A light tap at the door made Paul tuck his shirt into his trousers and straighten his beret before calling "Come." It was not Corporal McGregor but Delta, half entering the door as though sensitive to his mood: "I'm making a brew Boss. We're out of sugar but I can send Dickinson down to the NAAFI if you want some. And we're talking about the next period of training, out here. We could use a little direction if you wouldn't mind."

It was such a gentle nudge that Paul felt guilty for brooding. The NCOs' room was a dormitory with the beds removed. An old telly with a coat-hanger aerial was perched on a chair in the corner, a stack of porn films nearby. The locker doors were decorated with rock posters, centre-folds and photos of the platoon on various tours of Ireland. Corporal Weston was smoking rollies and Paul scrounged one for companionship. The three Corporals were sitting in a circle and had been joined by Lance-corporal Steele, a Welshman Paul couldn't help liking for this humour. They looked up at him, expecting him to speak.

"Right. What's on your mind chaps?"

It was Weston, stubbing out his fag, who spoke: "It's like this, Boss: we're not doing enough map reading for the Longdon Assault. The last one was a bastard. Must have done twenty miles at night, in fog. Teams that made the FRV only did cos they were shit hot with the nav. It was forestry block after forestry block. Easy to lose track unless you're ninja at bearing and pacing. We need a cadre on this for the blokes." Weston shrugged. "That's what I think, anyway."

"Westy's right, Boss," Chink nodded.

It made sense. Who should do it though? Him, on top of the fitness training? It was an easy matter to combine the two; just jack up a lot of orienteering and night navigation exercises, maybe some micronav. He was about to speak when there was a tap on the door and Corporal McGregor slithered in, smirking: "Major Casenove will see you now, Mr Illingworth, if you don't mind."

Paul had been waiting for this and was immediately on his feet but Delta turned sharply to McGregor: "Don't you salute an officer on entering the room?" McGregor quickly drew his heels together and straightened before saluting with an odious indifference. Paul said thank you and asked him to lead on. He might as well get it over with. As he left the room Delta called out, "Good luck Boss, don't take any shit." It was a warming, supportive gesture.

Paul followed McGregor to the Company offices. On the drill square, the Provost Sergeant was beasting a very large soldier who had been late for guard duty. As he shouted drill instructions in double time, the soldier, dripping with sweat and carrying an antitank shell on one shoulder, responded as quickly as he could. Seeing Paul, the Provost Sergeant saluted without breaking rhythm and ordered the soldier to about-turn and march in double time to the far end of the square. Paul smiled. *If you can't take a joke, you shouldn't have joined.* In the Major's office, he stood erect and firm, bracing his legs and feeling for his neck in the back of his collar. *You can't crack me, I'm a rubber duck.* Major Casenove smiled, shaking his head. He cracked his knuckles then leaned forward on his desk: "Paul relax, stand at ease. You are not in trouble. In fact, sit down. Let's have a little chinwag."

With the change in mood, Paul felt himself in confident hands but remained attentive just in case he had misread the situation. His cheek twitched under the Major's unwavering gaze and conscious of looking foolish, he engineered a sort of cough-sneeze to allow him to get out

59

a handkerchief, rub his face and restore a more confident expression.

"Let's start with the casualty," the Major said. "I have read your report and understand your thinking. I fully support the decision you made although I don't think I would have done the same. If there's a risk of neck injury, leave the casualty where he is. The traffic could find other ways to go where they were going – understand?" This summary, in a couple of simple sentences, belittled all Paul's fears and yet reinforced the learning he had made. An enormous weight was lifted from him. He nodded, a smile bursting across his face: "Yes Sir."

"The casualty, a Mister John Bird, was not injured further by being moved. After the surgeons had dealt with his broken pelvis, fractured skull and concussion... he was found to be quite well. I spoke to his family and they were anything but critical of you. In fact his mother said you were nothing less than a gift from God, to have been there at the time. In her eyes you saved his life..."

Paul smiled. The Major was toying with him a little. It was the Adjutant who had first summoned him to explain himself after the paramedics had made a formal complaint. The Adjutant had been so vocal in his criticism that Paul had felt alone and unwelcome: the officer who cracked under pressure. Now he saw he had been partly right. There was sense and scale to the world again and a flush of anger surged through him.

Major Casenove nodded: "Don't let the Adjutant get to you. He is a very busy man, as I hope you will one day realise."

This, the first inkling of his future potential, curbed Paul's rage. "It is Scouse Horne who should get the credit Sir, not me," he said.

The Major nodded again and made a note on a pad, but his face suddenly clouded. Paul knew at once what was wrong and was about to speak when the Major waved him to silence: "But let's talk about the wider issue, Paul.

I think you need to be clearer with your men about who is in command of them." Uncompromising eyes fixed him to his chair. "It is not Scouse Horne, it is Private Horne; or if you prefer, Horne five-nine-eight. Soldiers should not be addressed in familiar terms, no matter how well you admire them. And although you do not have the benefit of a sergeant to guide you, you must quickly build a picture of when you are being given good advice and when not. You will have realised how strong willed corporals are, especially your three. They were all down south and have all been to Catterick to train recruits. All of them could make excellent platoon sergeants if slots were available."

Paul nodded. He would have loved to have Delta as a sergeant.

"But you should also understand that their range of vision, their intellectual reach, is going to be less than yours. If you give them enough rope they will drop you in it. One reason Mercer and Moor are on trial is because they falsified the evidence. After the car went through the hedge, Mercer broke a junior soldier's arm to make it appear as though he had been hit."

Paul went cold. That's why Carroll, the platoon booby, had been in a cast.

"So it's like this, Paul," the Major summarised: "Don't be aloof of course. You must know your men better than their mothers do. But don't undermine your position by being over familiar. It will only breed contempt."

# Canning Town, London; September 1995

Clare knew that the Mess payphone was in a small cubicle by the letter rack as you went in the front door. She also knew that the officers never answered it as doing so meant having to go and find the person requested, an action that usually resulted in them losing their seat in the TV room. But Clare also knew that the Duty Officer's phone, the one with a completely different code and number, usually lay on the floor of the top corridor where the bedrooms were. When she had gone down to keep Paul company during the weekends he was on duty, he had plugged it into the long extension cable so that it reached his room. He had told her to ring it only in an emergency as it was an army phone, not for general use. But this *was* an emergency. It was Wednesday and they always spoke to each other on Wednesdays. She had been angry on Sunday and their parting had been resentful. Now she felt guilty and wanted him to know she had forgiven him.

How often couples called one another was something they agreed in the early days. Kirsty rang Dave (the boyfriend after Gary the Cabby) every lunchtime and then saw him most evenings round at his. Yvonne rang her boyfriend every Thursday even though he lived in Toulouse. The sound of her breathy whispering would always be one of Clare's abiding memories of the flat. For her and Paul, the midweek chat was sufficient for each to know the other was thinking of them. They had been going out longer than most couples and therefore did not need daily reassurance.

But this week Paul had not rung. Clare dialled the duty phone thinking she would ask someone to tell Paul she would ring the payphone in two minutes. Her call was answered after three rings: "Duty Officer, Lieutenant Rawlins speaking."

Clare blinked. "Rolly?"

"Duty Officer."

"Rolly is that you? It's Clare, Paul's..."

"Clare! Hi! Sorry I didn't recognise your voice. I'm so sorry. Are you after Paul? He's downstairs in the bar. You just wait there, I'll get him..."

He had gone before she could say to put the phone down. The line clicked for a minute or two and she could hear the sound of feet plodding by, laughter, and someone playing *Going Underground*. Rolly's voice came back on.

"Hi Clare. He's just coming. He was in the bar. He got another rollicking today from the Adjutant and then Major Cas.

"Oh, is everything... ?"

"Yeah it's fine. We all get told off now and then. It's part of life."

Rolly's voice was warm in her ears and he asked how she was, what she had been up to that week. She answered in platitudes, making his tone change: "Clare, are you two all right? You seem to be bickering a lot. I thought we had walked into a war zone when we saw you both..."

The truth stung. Clare did not know what to say. The need to talk to Paul had swollen within her all day, swollen until she had made a list of things on her mind. "Clare, are you there?"

"Yes, I'm here," she said, suddenly conscious of twisting the cable round her fingers. "I was just thinking, that's all. I'm sorry about Sunday. I hope it didn't spoil Evelyn's weekend. It was just the jumper thing. I was angry, that's all." She looked at her nails then placed her hand firmly on her knee.

Rolly's breathing was slow and deep: "Clare listen. It's nothing to do with me but if you need someone to talk to, I'll be here, OK?"

"Thank you Rolly," she said. "I guess I was just angry about the jumper, that's all." Her hand lifted again to twist the cable. This call was costing her tons of money. Paul's voice was audible in the distance. He sounded drunk. He started laughing, like boys did when they were trying to be quiet.

Rolly spoke again: "Well listen Clare, I hope you're OK. Look, Paul's here. I'll hand you over, OK?"

There was just time to thank him before Paul came on. It was as though she could smell the beer and fags from London: "Clare? Clare? Look I'm really sorry. I was going to ring you earlier but I got caught. I'm sorry. I'm really sorry OK?"

Clare tittered to herself. When he was like this he became as soppy as a labrador. "I just wanted you to know I love you, that's all," she said.

"And I you too Clare," he replied. "But I'm going to have to ring you back tomorrow. I'm pissed as fuck. I'm drunk. I'm off my trolley. I'll ring you later OK?"

The line went dead before she could say anything. The smile slipped off her face as she replaced the receiver on its cradle. She sat in silence until nearly midnight when Yvonne came back from the hospital. He wouldn't ring, she knew. The discussion would have to wait till the weekend. It just wasn't healthy to be on the pill so long.

# Montgomery Lines, Aldershot;
# October 1995

One week later Paul was again summoned to see the Major. Not expecting the call, he was worried he had done something wrong but could not imagine what it might have been this time.

The Major was abrupt: "It will be on the news at lunchtime, Paul. Corporal Mercer has been found guilty of the murder of Drew McGiven. He's got eight years. You had best tell your men quickly, so they hear it from the Chain of Command, not rumour control. And then I want you to box all his kit in the bunk room on your floor. Get a key from the Quartermaster and detail an NCO to witness it all. Separate the military kit, which is to be returned to the QM, from his personal kit, which we will post back to his family – but do a sense check and take out anything untoward. Understand?" The Major was on his feet, a piece of paper in one hand and a pen in the other. The telephone was ringing and the Sergeant-major tapping at the door. Paul nodded.

After collecting the key from the QM Paul went straight to the NCO's room and told Delta to get the blokes in, no matter what they were doing. They knew from his face it was serious and asked him straight away if it was about Mercy. With the platoon assembled in various forms of dress, less Cunningham who was on guard duty, Delta called for them to brace up. The youngest ones were on chairs at the front while the NCOs stood at the back.

Putting on a grave face, he was sure he had their attention: "Gentlemen. I have some bad news and there is no other way to express it so I'll just tell you. Corporal Mercer was found guilty of murder at Belfast Crown Court this morning. He..."

"The fucking cunts!" There was a sudden and dramatic change. Pietersen, the South African, sitting in the centre of the room, shook his head in disbelief: "What the fuck do these bossie fuckwits think they're doing, heh?" Mouths fell open in shock, turning quickly to snarls of anger: "You're fucking pissed!" They looked quickly round at each other, then to Paul, and then round again. It was the moment at which a crowd becomes a riot. The clamour rose. Lance-corporal Quinn, one of the men Paul had identified as a future star, swore bitterly to himself as he crushed a can of pop in his hands and threw it against the wall. Scouse Horne punched the nearest locker door, then did so again and again, each time harder. Weston, leaning against a wall, buried his face in his hands, his head shaking. When he looked up his eyes were hurt. "Why Sir? Why'd he go down? The cunt was driving right at us..."

"Yeah, and we thought it was Liam Gerard..."

"Do these fuckwits know anything..."

"Fucking civvy paddy cunts..."

The gap between the understood and the expressible was growing. Paul felt a surge of power, riding the anger in the room. It would have been easy to raise his voice and whip them up but it would have created a dragon he might never contain. He lowered his voice to a whisper, slipping unconsciously into his northern register: "Gentlemen. This is shit. It sucks. But losing the rag now ain't gonna do owt about it." It worked. The platoon fell silent, their anger unassuaged but at least controlled. "We've two hours before lunch. We'll do this afternoon whatever we were doing this morning but right now we're gonna burn off some aggression. Get changed, we're going out."

The platoon rose from their chairs without question, a single body of seething rage. Paul realised he was the conscience of the room; the only one guiding their behaviour. It made him afraid and excited at the same time. It was the most powerful feeling he had ever known, this tight body of men so absolutely under his control. Once changed, he knew they would need beasting hard. When they were this angry only two things worked: a wank or a run.

Paul took them down the canal path past the golf course and out onto the area across the soggy expanse of the tank circuit. They powered through the claggy sand, pumping their legs. At Seven Sisters they felt the first draw of fatigue, so they sprinted even harder up the flint-strewn tracks to the brow of the ridge then back down again and along to do the next one. The anger made them determined. Determination made them angry.

At Flagstaff Hill they stopped, gasping, their foreheads sweating, hands on hips, sucking hard at the air, sucking it in deep. Paul looked to each in turn. Weston nodded, almost imperceptibly. The expressions had changed. They were still angry, frustrated perhaps, but no longer destructive. Paul stood apart. Delta whispered: "Good call, Boss."

Paul smiled and realised the Corporal was smiling back. He looked at his watch then placed his fingers over his heart, feeling for the beat, slowing it down. He told Delta to form the men into three ranks. They would jog back past the rugby fields and do so as a unit, tight and disciplined. They ran together, feet striking the ground in unison, shoulders rolling in unison, chests breathing as one. Short of the main gate Paul slowed them to a quick march and told them to raise their heads, to walk proudly through camp. Everyone would know by now, rumour control being what it was.

"Walk tall, Five Platoon. Be as Mercy would have us be," he said, careful to show respect without overdoing the rhetoric. He wasn't Neil Kinnock or Michael fucking Portillo.

Outside the accommodation block he saw his job was done; mutiny had been averted. "Right, chaps. Lunch now then first aid with Scouse at Fourteen-hundred. Scouse, I can't attend training because I've got to box Mercy's kit and Chink I need your help with that. Any questions?" The platoon stayed silent. "Fall out."

Paul turned and nipped back to the Company office to tell Major Casenove why he had changed the training programme. The Major was impressed and having cleared his in-tray, joined him for the walk up the hill to the Mess for lunch. After Paul had showered and changed, they ate together, giving Paul a chance to ask again about the joyrider incident: "So does this mean Sergeant Moor will go down as well?"

"No, not necessarily, though it might look like it to him. Moor did not open fire. He was in command of the patrol and was arrested for being the responsible officer rather than the culprit."

"So Gerard got away? Made it to the Republic?"

"Yes. But we know he's around. I've a mate, he was my best man actually, working at HQNI. We know Gerard's father died recently and Gerard was spotted. It'll not be long till we catch him. Have you boxed Mercer's kit yet?"

"Not yet, I'm going to do it after lunch with Chink – I mean with Corporal Hudson." Paul checked himself and the Major looked up briefly from his plate but nothing more was said.

Back in the accommodation block he saw the soldiers off to their afternoon training then collared Hudson to help him. He had asked Chink, rather than Delta, to avoid a charge of favouritism. Being in command was like being a parent; his attentions had to be equal and unconditional. Chink had two copies of a form in his hands, something he had already collected from the Sergeant-major. Paul thanked him for his initiative, not knowing the form was required.

Having been locked for several months, Mercer's bunk was musty and damp. The window was jammed and the wall stained in the corner. In any other environment, the building would not have been fit for human habitation.

Paul started separating out the contents of the wardrobe. In the locker were jeans and some spare items of uniform. All the important stuff had been taken to Ireland with him and then surrendered to the police when he was arrested. Chink seemed unsettled. "Are you OK doing this?"

"Yes Boss. It's one of those things isn't it, boxing up a man's kit? It's just got to be done, so we may as well get on with it." He seemed superstitious so Paul took the task of pulling each item out, calling its name and placing it in one of the two boxes while Chink listed the item on the form.

Mercer had a Spanish grammar and dictionary tucked away at the back of his locker. "His wife, Boss, Rayna. She's Spanish. Met her on holiday when we went there, all of us, back when we were single."

"What was he like, Mercer I mean?"

"Good soldier," said Chink, without thinking. "A very good soldier. And he was good with the lasses as well; hung like a baboon he is." Chink smiled, rocking as he did so, making the curtain waft the light. "He was a character as well, Mercy. You don't get many like him nowadays. On the tour before this last one we were going to ambush the provos taking drugs across the border. Mercy liked to have all his kit just perfect before he went out on patrol. He was kind of picky that way. The ambush was at night so he was carrying illumination flares, schermoulies. But he'd taken the end caps off so they'd be ready in a hurry. So when we were getting on the chopper he had his bergen on one shoulder and we're all on board and strapped in and the Loadie pulls his bergen up and nods to Mercy to get on. The rotors were going round and he wanted to be safe and up at four hundred feet..."

"So you'd been collected from a pick up point out in the ooloo, not in the barracks?"

"Yeah, we were near Fivemiletown; I can't remember where. But there was Mercy looking up at us and I'll never forget it..." Chink started chuckling, holding his chest as he did so, "But there's Mercy looking up at us inside the chopper with his eyes all round and then he ran off into the bushes clutching at himself and pulling at the zip of his smock like there's a swarm of bees inside his shirt. And there's the lads laughing; we're laughing at him wondering what the heck he's doing. And the Loadie's going spare, asking what he's up to and pointing to his watch and shouting to the pilot on the intercom and then we realise what's happened. The schermoulies had gone off in his smock. He had them in the internal pocket. They were going round and round his body, firing off, sparks coming out his neck, his kegs, his sleeves. He was like Tower Bridge at New Year. And he was ripping at it, to get his smock off. So Bryan Moor leaps out and grabs him and pulls the smock off over his head. One of the flares hits Mercy in the face as it goes off in the trees. Poor bastard was screaming on the ground. He got second degree burns all round his back and sides and chest and we had to take him to hospital before we could do anything else..." Chink stopped chuckling, his mood fading.

Paul was unsure whether to smile or not. He was touched by Mercer's selflessness. It must have taken loads of courage to run away from the chopper so as not to hurt anyone else.

"He and Moor were close then, buddies?" The question sounded clumsy in his mouth but Chink didn't seem to notice.

"Yeah, sure. Mercy was a recruit coming through depot when we came back from down south. Beefy Moor was a screw, a Corporal back then. Until we went to Germany, anyway. Mercy was one of his recruits. And it was tough, depot, back then. All the instructors had been down south. We'd all done it for real. We weren't gonna put up with poor recruits getting to battalion. We knew what we wanted and maybe only a handful had it. Mercy was one of ten out of sixty who passed the course. He had to be harder than us, you know – better than us, the ones that were down south."

Paul was all ears. He liked Chink. He was softer edged than Weston or Delta and gentler with the junior soldiers. They blossomed because of this. His leadership style was more inclusive than directive and his observations of life were insightful. The best soldiers come through training after wars, not during them.

"And anyway, after the ambush – we never hit them, the provos, by the way – we got back to camp to find that Mercy had been casevac'd back to Blighty. We didn't see him for months." Chink suddenly started laughing out loud, his voice rising. "But then it was crazy! When we get back to Aldershot his little dance had become a legend. All the lads were doing it down town in the Rat Pit singing along to *Rocket Man,* you know, the Elton John song? *Rocket Man burning up his fuse up here alone...*"

"And Moor?" asked Paul, quietly, "what's he like?"

Chink fell silent, the hilarity evaporating as quickly as it had come. Perhaps he realised now why Paul had asked for his help. The shadows of Moor's presence seemed to reach across them both.

"I don't know if you'll ever get to find out Boss, not after the way they treated Mercy."

"I'm not so sure," Paul replied with an assumed authority. "It's a different case, being tried separately."

Chink nodded, acknowledging the bigger picture. "Beefy Moor is a soldier Sir; the most professional man you'll ever meet. He's like Robocop and Terminator all rolled into one."

"He was down south with you... ?"

Something flickered across Chink's face. He looked for a moment as if he would keep silent but then he opened: "It was like this. Beefy was down south, sure; he's got the medal. And he was besty mates with Curly McKay. On the march down, when we were tabbing with the boot-necks and they took a right for Mount Harriet and we went left flanking towards Longdon, Beefy was like a man mountain. Strong as an ox he was. Nobby Jones went down with hypothermia and so we put him in a dossbag with Beefy but then he couldn't walk the next day cos of frostbite, so Beefy carried all his ammo as well as his own. He must have been humping a hundred and fifty pounds for much of the march."

"And then what – was he involved in the attack where McKay got hit? The one in that painting? Were you?"

Chink frowned, reflecting. The muscles in his face twitched: "I was just a tom, Boss, in another Company. I was nowhere near all the action. All I ever did was make brews for the senior lads in my platoon and ferry them forward under fire. Combat brew boy, me." It was typical self-denial. There was a modesty about Chink Paul admired.

"Beefy was never on Longdon, see?"

"Why? What happened?"

"He got shot in the groin, the night before the assault. One of the lads in the platoon, a new boy that had just been posted, was cleaning his rifle and forgot to take off the magazine. He had a negligent; fired off a round by accident. He shot Beefy straight through the nads. They had to carry him back to the dressing station holding his cock in his hands. It was the first bullet wound we had."

Paul was amazed. "The poor bastard. So he never got to..."

"No. He never got up the mountain. And the guy who shot him knew that he'd have to prove himself as soon as we crossed the LOD. He went off like Audie Murphy and got slotted within ten minutes... can't remember his name."

Paul shook his head. What a piece of luck! Moor was the best soldier in the battalion and missed the one chance he would get to really go to war. "The poor bastard."

"Yeah, it's crap isn't it? But he lived and there were twenty-three lads that didn't. So he's got that to be thankful for. And when he came back from hospital with his prosthetics fitted, he was himself again, only more so. That's when he started weight training. He's a body builder, Boss. You've never met him so you won't know. But he's a big lad. And not many would cross him, not if they like their face."

Paul smiled. He was an officer. Officers didn't enter into scraps with soldiers. But he couldn't help respecting them. This was a professional fighting unit. War was work, and the sheer brutality of it required people to be brutal by nature. From what he had heard, there was something primeval about Moor. He thanked Chink for the insights and said it was time to complete the formalities. Chink started filling in his name and number at the bottom of the form and asked for Paul's number as witness. He had gone quiet, as if feeling he had given too much away. "You shouldn't go talking about this, Boss. Beefy, if he ever gets back, is a bit touchy about what people know about him. He won't like it if..."

"No, of course," Paul assured him. He needed something to change the subject so pulled the last two photos off the wall. One was of a suntanned, auburn beauty sitting at a beach restaurant, a glass of wine in her hand. The second was of a black-haired woman, naked and enormously chesty, squatting provocatively on the bonnet of a military Land Rover, parting her labia with her fingers.

"That honey is Rayna, his wife. But that one's Lara Croft, the girl he was banging when she was in Spain."

"Not one to send off then?"

Chink chuckled: "No, Boss. Best not." Paul tore it up and threw it in the bin. All he needed to happen now was to tape the boxes up and get the blokes to hump them over to the QMs for storage. Chink would then take the yellow copy of the form to the Sergeant-major. At the top of the box of personal kit was a green fleece, exactly like

Paul's own. Chink was taping up the box of military kit and while he did so Paul tugged out the collar to read the label. It was an extra-large; just the size Paul needed.

In all his reading about army life Paul had clocked how soldiers in Burma would swap one item of kit with that of a fallen comrade. It was a practice that served to remember the fallen and simultaneously recycle kit in a pragmatic way. Paul's fleece was too small for him. Mercy would no longer need his, and there was a battalion exercise in Wales in a couple of weeks where such an item would prove indispensable.

Chink finished taping up the military kit box and was about to start on the second. "Hold on, I'll be back in a mo." Paul ran to his office then returned with his own fleece hanging limp in his hand. Chink had already taped up the top of the box despite what Paul had said. He stopped him doing more. Deliberately, slowly, he picked at the corners of the parcel tape and pulled it back, opened the flaps and swapped the fleeces. The family would never know the difference.

"Any problems?" he said. Chink shook his head, shrugging, "No Sir, nothing at all."

He retaped the box again and Paul nipped back to his office with the new fleece. It had been a good day. He had got to know Chink better, helped the platoon through a time of pain, was getting told stories reserved for those in the know and to top it all, had found a fleece that fitted him.

# Shipley, West Yorkshire; October 1995

The four-day exercise in Wales was sufficiently arduous for the Commanding Officer to grant the battalion a long weekend. Paul had promised his mother he would drive up and would, since they insisted, bring Clare as well. After hanging one on in the Mess on Friday night in celebration of a brother officer's engagement, he drove up to London to find Clare ready by the front door. Standing with her knees together and a shapeless weekend bag in her hands, she looked like a spaniel being taught to stay. Once she was greeted, kissed and loaded inside the car, Paul took an intuitive rather than logical route through London, punching his way through the stalled traffic to gain even the smallest advantage. Turning up the radio, he talked little until they had passed Watford Gap, and it was not until they had crossed the M62 that he accepted the speed of the traffic, slipping through Leeds and then Bradford in ways that only a local would know. At a bend in the road near Shipley train station, three mud caked ponies stood in a tiny field and Paul felt himself to be on home turf.

His father had pulled the Rover out, allowing him to use the carport. As he reversed in, his mother appeared by the driver's door with tears in her eyes. Though not the longest time he had been away, it had certainly been one of the most eventful. His father beamed and shook him by the hand, then circumnavigated the car to kiss Clare on one cheek. Sitting in the kitchen round the small table, they drank tea. His mother served parkin with a thin slice of Wensleydale, which Paul gobbled before the cheese crumbled away between his fingers. The conversation didn't stop for the next hour. There was so much Paul wanted to convey: how good he was at his job; how he had taken the vicious humour of soldiers in his stride; how he had become hardened to the risks of death, injury, killing; how at one he was with the regiment and its uncompromising ethos. He told them how Paddy Connelly, one of his men, had tapped on the door to his office one afternoon, nervously asking if he could have a word. After a few minutes the soldier had blurted out that he could not satisfy his girlfriend; that she was too much for him. He was ashamed, he had said. He didn't feel like a man. His mother asked what he had suggested and Paul replied that he recommended spending more effort on foreplay. She sat upright, straight faced, nodding slightly. "Well you've obviously made an impression," she said, rising to lift the pot and cups.

"You never told me that, Pauly," said Clare in the ensuing silence and Paul shrugged: "It's not something to boast about."

After placing the cups in the sink, Paul's mother swivelled, shaking water from her hands: "Well listen. It's nearly six and Dad will want a beer before tea, won't you love? There'll be enough hot water if no one's too greedy – or there's always the shower. Clare, what would you like to do?"

"That's kind, Tina, thank you. I'll just have a quick wash."

"Very good love," George said and directed her up to the spare room in the attic. Paul would sleep in his old room.

With Clare despatched, Paul humped his bag up the narrow, twisting stairs to lie on his old bed, listening to the sound of the shower.

What sort of impression had he really made on his men? It was a complete lie to say he had them fully in the palm of his hand. In fact there was an enormous chasm between what he had just told his mother and the reality of the barrack block. The soldiers' cruelty was astounding. They held nothing sacred and if they found weakness, they worried it like a terrier, ripping at it until someone snapped. Then they laughed. After Connelly had been to see him he had finished writing up the shooting record cards and taken a final walk along the dark corridors of the block. In their room, Connelly and Dickinson were cackling with laughter, the Irishman clearly impersonating him and Dickinson giggling with glee: "Foreplay! As if he'd fucking know, like." His face had coloured at the time and coloured again on remembrance. But he could not let them think they had one over on him. He had burst into the room to stand in the doorway, one hand on the handle, a look of stern sincerity on his face. The room had gone silent as he looked from Dickinson to Connelly and back again. The soldiers' expressions mutated from innocence to arrogance to embarrassment. Paul slowly allowed a smile to tickle the corner of his lips. He had winked as he left, slamming the door. Yes, you got me; but I got you too. In the dark of the corridor, a fresh wave of clapping erupted from within the room.

He had won some of them over, certainly. Delta seemed loyal enough, as did Chink Hudson. Dickinson and Paddy would perhaps tell others how he had reacted and that would prove he could take a joke. Carroll, the youngest, would not say boo to a goose and was awed by his rank. Terry Pietersen, TP, the big South African, was also one of his fans. He was more mature than the others and very much a field soldier. What won him over was Paul making effective tactical decisions. Matt Steele was also warming to him. Paul had invested a lot of time in understanding him; the youngest son of a West Wales farmer, there was nowhere he could go apart from the army.

But there were many others. Corporal Weston, dour to the last, was always mumbling behind his back. Scouse Horne, the medic, and his buddy, Scotty Oldham, the Gecko, had never really trusted him since the biker incident. Brad Hyde, one of Matt Steel's mates, was much harder to converse with. Darren Rose was surly, as he was with everybody. It had taken Paul three months to learn he was a Quaker and that his reticence was down to personal struggles with the morality of violence. And Imran Kahn – Paki Khan as he was known – was from Bradford of all places. Paul should have been able to establish a connection with him based on that alone, but the soldier remained aloof, his dark eyes inscrutable.

Paul could never admit any of this to his parents. In their eyes he was a hero and in the warmth of their love he must not disappoint. Later, in the parlour, his father served half-cans of bitter for the men and a small gin for the ladies, the glasses carried through on an electro-plated nickel-silver tray. At dinner, as was the Illingworth custom, the conversation tackled the geopolitical issues of the day, the arguments bouncing from one side of the table to the other like a beach ball.

"Do you think we should be doing anything about the Serbs, Paul?" his mother asked. "Your father thinks we should."

Paul had to smile. His father's position had changed since he had got swept up in the New Labour movement. He was reenergised. It was not like the doomed years under Kinnock or Foot, it was different this time. George Illingworth advocating military action was indicative of that. "I think it's entirely consistent with democratic socialism for the strong to protect the weak," Paul pronounced, wiping his lip on the back of his hand before being reminded he had a napkin. "But you can't win a war through airpower alone. This was proven in Vietnam, in Suez, in... and in other wars as well. If we are going to win we have to send ground troops and send ones that can operate outside of the UN rules of engagement."

The wine was dulling his mind but it didn't matter. He was in his own home and surrounded by those who loved him. His school trophies adorned the dresser. His mother had attempted to cook something foreign but omitted to wash the rice. After pudding, the last of the frozen rhubarb, his father served a cheap port in the tumblers they used for orange juice in the mornings. At a nod from George, Tina asked Clare if she would help her do the dishes and the women rose, taking plates through to the kitchen. The men remained at the table to talk in vaguely interconnected ideas for another thirty minutes, George studying his son across the bowl of his pipe. When they went through to the lounge, the ladies were watching television. His mother turned it off and a brief moment of quiet descended. Clare asked George if he had met Tony Blair, how the party was.

"Kind of you to ask, love. It's going well, you might say, going very well in fact."

"Is there an election coming, a local one?"

"No, not for two year or so; but what matters now is that we reform the party, get ready for government. It's been near seventeen year of Tory rule and they're spent. No ideas, no investment, no benefit to communities. We're going to get them this time."

"You reckon?" Paul was teasing him. Most of his friends were conservatives and, because of the Falklands, lionised Margaret Thatcher as a latter day Boadicea.

His father answered sternly: "Oh yes, I reckon. It's Blair, you see: an ideas man, a leader. The party are behind him. In April we even changed the constitution. We got rid of the old Clause Four. Blair knows we cannot stay in the shadow of the old guard. We need the middle ground, see, the people who vote Tory because of money. It's not about nationalisation, you see. It's about making people think they have choices..."

Tina placed a hand on George's knee but Clare urged him on: "No, it's fine Tina, I want to hear this. I'm a teacher. We're desperate for a better education policy. The whole system's rigged. Go on, George, tell us what's going to be different."

The interruption had disrupted his flow. He sought for what he had wanted to say but failed and shook his head in apology: "Sorry love, it's gone. But never worry. You'll see. New Labour for a New Britain. It's coming, and it'll be good."

There was another pause as George looked around. "What about you, Clare love? How's your family getting on?" Tina asked. Squashed into the very end of the sofa, Clare replied that her parents were fine and yes, her father was still running his practice. If there was anything to say about people from Hatfield, they did like a good set of gnashers. But after this brief explanation she quietened, turning her glass. George suggested that it was time for bed. Clare rose, kissing them all good night, and Tina followed once she had heard the toilet flush. Paul and his father were alone once again.

"Do you want something else to drink? Something for bed?" his father asked. Paul shook his head. He was hankering for sleep. The bash the night before had ended only when Colonel Ivory had gone sometime around three. The drive up had been more tiring than he would like to admit. Yet something told him he was being set up for a special chat so he made a cup of tea and slumped down in the comfy chair by the gas fire.

"I wanted to ask you," his father began, making sure the door was closed, "about Clare. What your plans are?"

"About Clare? Why?"

His father looked at him carefully. "If she's not the one for you, son, let her go... if you've grown apart. It's normal. It happens. But do it sooner rather than later. It's not good to hurt people. But better hurt than to deceive."

Paul flushed scarlet. His thoughts knotted inside him. His father was right but also wrong. He liked Clare, respected her. But she had an arse the size of Egypt and her breasts swam before her like balloons. She required careful supervision in case she touched the silver or used the wrong fork. Evelyn, by comparison, could converse about anything from Caravaggio to Madonna and was often placed next to the Colonel.

"Promise me you'll think about what I've said."

Paul nodded, unnerved by the accuracy of this judgment.

"Listen, Paul. A good marriage is about leadership. I know you know all about that; that you've been taught how to lead and been to Sandhurst and so on. But hear me out. In a good marriage, someone has to lead and someone has to follow. It's no good two of you having careers. Someone needs to be at home for the kiddies when they come along. With us, with Tina and me, it was her career at first. She brought in the money teaching while I was with the union. You won't remember this, you were too small. But I followed, see – and let me tell you it weren't common then, a man looking after the kiddies all day. People laughed, they did. People said things behind us backs."

Paul nodded. He was listening.

"But then my career picked up in eighty-one and your mum and me agreed to swap. Her work took a back seat as I got promoted. You see what I mean? Someone has to follow and someone has to lead. The question you need to ask yourself – and this is what I wanted to ask you – is can you see this happening with you and Clare? Will she follow you, or will you follow her?"

The silence hung in the air like a cloud of swept dust. Paul turned to watch the flames on the fire, saying nothing.

His father's voice changed: "Well, I've said what I wanted and thank you for listening. It's because we've only got your best interests at heart, your mother and me. But say, what have you got Clare for her birthday? It is tomorrow, isn't it?"

Paul grimaced. "Nothing, yet," he said. "But I thought I'd nip into town in the morning, before anyone's up. I'll find something there."

"In Shipley? Well I'll wait and see what you come back with! Your mother got her some perfume, that one she likes; Japanese sounding."

"Issey Miyaki?"

"That's the one."

That was one option gone; but there were others. "Dad if I'm up early I'd best get to bed. Thank you for your... advice." George smiled and took the last glasses through to the kitchen, patting Paul on the shoulder as he went up to bed.

In the morning, painfully early, Paul woke to his little plastic soldier alarm. To beat the inevitable hangover he walked quickly up the hill, along to the market, and got a bacon butty from the cafe. The town square was unchanged since his last visit but it now appeared a bleak and ugly place to him. Old women hobbled along the walkways dragging wheeled tartan bags. Every other shop was a charity concern: for the aged, for dogs, for the mental, for kids. There was a bookie and a pawn shop that showed promise but proved to be full of old tat. There was Woollies of course, but all it had was party hats and sweets. He considered a *Take That* tape but was not sure if she already had the album. Should he get her a portable CD player? The idea was great but they were nearly thirty quid each and that seemed too much. The bus shelter was awash with litter. An elderly lady smiled at him, her face familiar. In the covered market he got some Poor Bens for his dad and flowers for his mother. It was nearly eleven; they would all be up and wondering where he was. Ratners was on the corner, so a pair of dangly earrings had to do. Thank god for Sunday opening. He would say they were only half of the present and then take her out to a show in London, something they could do together. Clare accepted the gift with grace when they were sitting in the parlour, snatching an hour together before a heavy roast lunch and afterwards, in the afternoon, they made their excuses saying they wanted to miss the traffic. Shaking his hand in farewell, his father fixed him with his eye. His mother kissed him warmly and said to drive carefully. Once underway, Clare stared silently out of the window, fascinated by the immediacy of the cooling towers that loomed over the motorway outside Sheffield.

It was over. They were on their way home. Driving, Paul thought again about his men.

Just before the exercise in Wales, Cheese Wensley had been to see him, knocking on the office door like a penitent. He had stammered something about his pay not being correct; could he go and see the paymaster? Paul had said yes, he must. Cheese had taken Paul's direction as an excuse to miss half a day at the ranges and Corporal Weston, Cheese's section commander, had been furious. Paul had heard a scuffle in the NCO's room and gone to investigate, finding Weston holding Cheese against the wall by the throat: "Go behind my back again and you'll get a fucking slap." Suddenly conscious of Paul's presence, Weston had released Cheese, telling him to fuck off and get the chinese writing off the back of the bogs. The soldier had vanished, leaving Paul uncertain what to do.

What *was* the line between bullying and a Corporal's right to maintain the standards in his section? Was Cheese coming to see him a subtle cry for help? Was Weston bullying others as well? They were all, certainly, very good soldiers. Lance-corporal Hyde, though not officer friendly, was one of the rising stars. Scouse was recognised as one of the most talented medics in the battalion. Even on leave he would go round to his local paramedic station asking for work. There had been no issues with Paddy or Scotty the Gecko either. Should he ask them, on the QT, if everything was all right?

Perhaps he should talk to Delta about it. He was the senior Corporal and might at least have a word with Weston; tell him to ease off on his blokes.

Or was he ducking the issue? Was it acceptable, the use of such violence? Or shouldn't a corporal, a Section Commander, be allowed to choose his own leadership style? War was a brutal and unforgiving thing. It would do Cheese no favours if he was allowed to be soft.

On the graduate entry scheme he did before Sandhurst, they would have said it was an issue of diversity. This was a classic example of the dynamic between a 'team worker' and a 'shaper' personality.

But something still rankled. Paul had been brought up to stand up to bullies, always. When the first Pakistani family had moved into his street, right next door, all sorts of unspeakable detritus was dumped on their drive. His father had not put up with it and seeing some teenagers hanging about on bikes, ran out to chase them away. The Lasharis were to be made as welcome as any, he insisted. It was not what decent people did, allowing that to happen. His interventions earned him respect but also enemies. Paul and his sister had been in the dining room when a brick shattered the large window and billowed out the curtain. His father had shoved them all under the table and ran into the street shaking his fist. Two youths had run off but were never caught.

Paul had been so proud of him that day, so proud it made his eyes mist over just thinking about it. The abuse had petered out. Mrs Lashari had brought round a tray of sweet pastries the following morning and their daughters, heads covered, had helped sweep up the glass.

The answer struck him as obvious, really. Delta's section was undermanned; an unfitting position for the most senior of the three corporals. He would move Cheese from Two Section to Three Section and brief Delta to keep an eye on him. His chairman-like, paternalistic leadership style would probably get more out of the soldier anyway. Paul felt pleased with himself. He had cracked the problem. A smile spread across his face as he drove and the song on the radio had a lyric he liked, something about belonging *in the service of the Queen*. A glance across at Clare made his chest contract: "What's wrong?"

Her face was sour, the lips trembling. Resting her head against the window, her shoulders were turned away. Paul went cold. She had been stewing on something and now that he had noticed, her eyes flashed: "You don't respect me, Paul. You just don't care for me at all."

Paul felt trapped by the steering wheel. He could not avoid this one. "For god's sake Clare, I thought you were hurt, in pain or something. What's wrong? I don't know what I've done." Letting go of the gear stick he reached out for her hand but she pushed him away then folded her arms. "Not one word. You said not one word to me all evening. Your Dad said more to me than you..."

"Clare, now come on. That's just... we drove all the way up here, remember? Weren't we talking at all?"

Clare gave him a look of utter contempt. Paul wondered if he should pull over. There was a service station coming up in a few miles. It would mean delay but at least he could get out from behind the wheel. Indicating, he pulled into the inside lane. Clare exhaled heavily, still avoiding him. "It's all right. I don't want to stop. I know you always want to get on. It's just that I've been trying for three weeks to have a conversation with you and you're never there. You're never in. I just want you to show me some respect. I didn't have to come with you, you know. I have work to do as well, papers to mark..."

"Yes I know that. But what have I done?"

"You don't know?"

"No. Look. This is unfair. I didn't know you were angry with me; you seemed quite happy when you went to bed. We talked about johnnies on the way up here. And this morning you were OK when I got back from town. Why didn't you say something to me then?"

She said nothing. The silence built up between them until he felt ashamed, his chest hollowing. "Listen, I know I could have... well... I want you to know how much I appreciate you coming, really. It's a long way and I know they're a little set in their ways. I thought Dad was going to do a royal toast for a second..."

"It's not them!" Clare snapped. "It's not them at all, Paul. I think your parents are great. I really love them.

Your dad is an inspiration and your mum – well she's your mum isn't she? That thing with the tray and the port – that was all for you. They're so proud of you and everything you're doing. I mean that. They tell me so.

"It's *you*. You don't look after me. You don't talk to me or involve me at all. I'm like an appendage to you, like one of your bits of kit. I don't matter. You never ask about me. You never ask about my work, my friends, the kids in my class..."

Clare was raging, weeks of frustration steaming out. Paul contracted inside himself, biting his lip. Her words held truth but also partial truths and the differences made him coil with anger. They passed the slip road to the service station. It would be another ninety minutes till they got home.

"Do you love me?" she said, her head leaning against the window. "Have you ever loved me, Paul?"

This was not the time, nor the place. "Clare, you're very special to me. You always have been. Of course I love you. We've been together for years, haven't we?"

"But do you really love me?" She looked across at him, confronting the truth, "Or do you love your soldiers more?"

Of course he loved her. But he couldn't say it with the conviction it deserved. He was angry. This was not how such things should be discussed. He did love his soldiers but that was different. It was his job, his duty, even. The two should not be compared. "Yes I love you," he snapped and Clare sniffed, pacified at last, or at least in part. Paul drove on in silence, the anger writhing inside him. It was not like her to cry, not like her at all, but when he looked over her face was glistening.

Was this some ritual they had to go through? Would she now tell Kirsty, that stupid friend of hers, that they'd had a domestic? Would Kirsty then say something banal about how good sex was after a fight? How fucking droll. Paul drove on, only breaking the silence when they were nearly at her flat.

But sex was not good that night. It was fraught and painful and one sided and quick and Paul was asleep within seconds, leaving Clare to stare at the shapes on the ceiling while the dribble ran out between her thighs.

# Montgomery Lines, Aldershot; November 1995

It was still inspiring, the painting of Sergeant McKay, even though Paul saw it every day. The other officers had gone out to a pub in Farnham but, since he was on duty, Paul remained behind in the silent Mess. Having an hour before the Defaulters' Parade, he got himself a coffee and sat in a chair below the picture to study it.

His first impression was always how terrifically scary the battle must have been. The mountain was steep and sliced lengthways by ridges of jutting rock. These were interlaced with boulders that would have provided limitless possibilities for building bunkers. The idea of fighting up a slope that steep filled him with horror. He recalled the recent exercise in Wales and how breathless he had been, forcing his body upwards. *Train hard, fight easy*, Major Casenove said, but that had not helped him. Fighting uphill, at night, over such terrain, must have been utter hell. The ground was strewn with stones which would have been agony to dive on and must have thrown up ricochets like a village fireworks display. There was no cover to screen an attacking force and very limited space for support fire. He had been in trenches during training exercise and knew exactly how easy it was to identify attacking infantry, even at night. Their bodies popped up, moved and then ducked out of sight and each charge provided ample time to train sights and fire. Attacking a well prepared enemy on a hill like this must have been an act of such unparalleled self-discipline that Paul could not quite contain his admiration. How on earth could a professional army actually lose control of it, he wondered? It was a natural fortification. To have been driven off was an act of absurd incompetence. Sitting in the Mess and staring up at the painting he was acutely conscious of the veterans of the battle all around the battalion. He felt humbled.

As he continued to study the painting, Paul's eye was drawn to more detail within the moody brushstrokes. There were four characters in the foreground of the picture: three Argentines and Sergeant McKay. McKay was firing with his bayonet fixed and the Argentine he has just shot could not have been more than two feet from the tip of the blade. The one he had already killed was almost under his feet. The live one, presumably the one that killed him, was tucked behind a rock. He was holding his rifle as if it was unfamiliar in his hands; the butt against his upper arm, not the shoulder. It made him look like a conscript. His face was a story in itself. There was a Latin arrogance in the set of his jaw and fear in his eyes – the wild panic of a man who must kill in order to survive. Had he lived through that night, Paul wondered? Was he somewhere, perhaps in a small flat in Buenos Aires, bouncing grandchildren on his knee, cognisant of the fact he had created a hero by killing him?

Paul's father had spoken in laudatory terms of Tony Blair. He had been on the news a lot since he had taken over the party because he was younger than any party leader for over a century; in fact he was barely older than Colonel Ivory. "Paul, Blair is someone that unites the party and inspires others to follow."

Looking at the painting Paul had another thought: there was no officer in the attack. The Platoon Commander had already been killed or injured. McKay had stepped up to take command. In the background there was another figure, a soldier sprinting out of the shadows, following where McKay led, inspired by his example. Even without an officer, the platoon were continuing their attack.

Paul shivered. It was time for the Defaulters' Parade. He got up, placed his coffee cup on the side table and slapped his beret against his leg to shake off the dust. Looking at his reflection in the mirror by the front door, he shaped it on to his head as if positioning a crown. This was a uniform he had coveted since his early teenage years. How could he ever prove himself worthy?

# Canning Town, London; November 1995

"But I just don't know what to do, Pauly!" Clare exclaimed. She was sitting on the counter, legs kicking, her face knotted. "It's really horrible when people talk about you behind your back like that, especially if it's all lies."

Paul was on his back with his head underneath the sink. What he had thought would be a simple job was proving quite complicated and he was surrounded by ever increasing piles of blackened towels and pans of odorous water. Grunting, he realised that he could not do justice to both the conversation and the leaking sink. Shoving himself outwards, he sat upright: "But why did she say that? Did she say it to you or to someone else?"

Clare blinked, her lips curling round each other as she thought. Paul pulled himself up to standing then poured washing up liquid on his blackened hands: "Look. You have three choices, yeah? You were on time, you always are. You've never been late. That's the fact in question. Some old biddy has accused you of being in the wrong place at the wrong time..."

"Not just some old biddy: Sister Jeanette. She's the Deputy..."

"Whatever. The person responsible for staff discipline has accused you of an error of professionalism. You have not been formerly disciplined but there are rumours circulating about you... ?" He raised an eyebrow to check he was right and she nodded, blushing slightly. She rubbed the tip of her nose. "Well let's acknowledge the terrain as it is," he said, "and I know how hard it is to deal with background muttering. Believe me, I know. But nothing's been said about you officially. You just have this fear, this sense that the head, Sister Maresa, is being turned against you. That right?"

Clare's face was round and open. She looked girlish. She nodded.

"OK, so what courses of action are there? You can do nothing and see what happens..."

"No, I can't do that Paul. I can't. She's out to get me..."

"Listen a second Clare would you? It's only one option, all right? Think it all through. You have three options, yes? You can do nothing. You could confront your accuser or you could go straight to the main man..."

"Main woman."

"Main woman, indeed. But having seen her I'm not so sure myself..." Clare was suddenly tickled by his tone and snorted with laughter, her head craning back to expose her throat. Paul wiped his hands on a tea towel, smiling. When she looked at him the sparkle had returned to her eyes. He checked his hand was reasonably clean before placing it on her shoulder to kiss her cheek: "You'll be all right, love. Honest. This is a bit of office politics, that's all. Look at it this way. You have three courses of action open to you. Do nothing; confront the accuser and go behind her to the boss. Left flanking, right flanking and two up, bags of smoke, straight down the middle. The question is – what's good and bad about these options? If you did nothing, what would happen? Think about the good things before you get drawn into the bad."

Paul turned away to press the button on the kettle, then took two cups down from the cupboard, half listening. He knew what was wrong with the u-bend now. It wasn't the plastic nut; it was the downpipe that was cracked. He'd have to nip back to the shop and get a length of it.

"... and the children mustn't know that we argue in the staff room. So that's why I don't like that idea, Paul. It's my integrity under question. I've never been late, or even missed a day's work, never..."

"OK. So let's drop that option... but we can do so now we've looked at it properly. What would be good and bad about confronting Sister Jenny?"

"Jeanette. She's French."

"Sister *Jinettuh*."

Clare's expression dropped but then, slowly, with the grace of the moon rising, a grin spread back across her face. "You know what? I think you're right. I wouldn't want to confront her. That would put her back up. But I could ask her for advice. I could ask her if she's seen anything I've done that was wrong. I could..."

Paul tried to interject but her excitement silenced him: "You know what as well? I've got her observing my class on Tuesday morning. I could do it then." She clapped her hands, pushing herself off the counter, knocking a teaspoon to the floor. She threw her arms around his neck and reached up with her lips to kiss him: "Oh Pauly, thank you! Thank you! That was really helpful."

Paul, keeping his dirty wrists off her shirt, held her as tightly and happily as he dared.

# Dartford, East London; November 1995

Liam Gerard sat at a table against the wall in the all-day cafe, spinning a teaspoon round on his thumb. It kept falling off and clattering on the formica and a man in blue overalls turned round to stare at him. "Sorry," he said, and put the spoon down on the far side of his mug, parallel with the edge of the table. He checked his watch. It was nearly two, and if Michael didn't show in the near future there was a risk he might run into Mo, who was coming at half past. A horrible tremor of fear rippled through him at the thought of being found out.

The bell above the door tinkled as a woman backed in, pulling a child buggy up the shallow concrete step. She was rosy cheeked, her hair windblown, and bags of shopping dangled from her wrists. She looked round, making eye contact with Liam, and nodded at the empty chair opposite him. He shrugged, shaking his head apologetically: "I'm waiting on someone," he mouthed and the man in the overalls looked round at him again.

*Come on Michael*, Liam thought. *It's been months since you call me and then you want to meet me here …*

The woman looked round the room again and smiled to an old couple who were getting up to make room for her. "There you go, dear," the old woman said, "You can sit here. We were going anyway." The young mother thanked her, jostling her way past tightly packed tables to push the buggy out of the aisle.

They weren't that bad a people, the English, if he was honest, Liam thought. They were an ordinary, rather unprepossessing race once he had peeled back the image he had built up of them throughout his childhood. They weren't the caricatures he had expected. In reality he had found them socially accommodating and professionally focused. They worked hard. They were liberal in their views and rather modest about themselves and their country. They were neither brash nor aggressive (except with France, when the ports were blocked by militant trawlermen), and it was impossible not to respect what they were doing in Bosnia. And now that Mo had taken him under his wing, Liam had discovered subcultures that simply did not exist in Northern Ireland: the spicy headiness of Brixton; the magic of theatreland, and then, of course, the flashing lights and thumping music of the club scene. He'd got a haircut at Mo's request. He'd lost weight round his middle and Mo had taken him shopping, choosing things he would never have dared wear back home: clothes that were dapper, clothes that were dear, clothes that were dandy.

Liam checked his watch once again. It was past two. On his wrist was his father's gold chain with a St Christopher's medal dangling from it. He liked its coolness, though touching it caused a shameful sadness to spread through him. This time, thankfully, the feeling was not as sharp as before. After Father Paul had eventually got hold of him after giving his Da the last rights, Liam had gone to find Helmut, his boss, and ask apologetically if he could have time off. He had been surprised by the kindly response. He had been on a flight from Heathrow by four that same day but it had still not been quick enough. His father had passed away holding a picture of him in one hand and a rosary in the other, the night nurse said. At the funeral the other drivers made an escort of black cabs round the hearse all the way from the chapel of rest to St Patrick's and he'd stood on the bridge watching them pass below him, knowing the police cars and army patrols were not there to manage the traffic but to arrest him.

The memory of it made his eyes water and he wiped them with the back of his hand, before checking his watch again. It had been the tall one, JP, who smuggled him south of the border that time.

The red-headed waitress appeared at his shoulder: "You want something else or can I get you the bill my darling?"

Liam stammered: "No, it's fine," but then he saw JP at the doorway, as lean and chiselled as a cowboy. Liam changed his mind: "Actually, I'll have two coffees please."

JP saw him, glanced up at the tinkling bell, took in the room, strode over and sat down opposite. Liam was surprised to see him. "I've ordered you a coffee," he said, and JP called after the girl: "Two sugars." The girl turned to point that sugar was on the table then swept away to speak to the young mother. JP leaned forward on his elbows, his thick fingers interlaced and head tilted sideways: "Michael's been taken," he whispered. "They got him at the border and planted a whole lot of guns and drugs on him."

Liam's mouth fell open: "No way!"

"The Council's decided to waken the sleeping men. There's work to be done now, Liam. We need you to waken yourself."

Liam nodded imperceptibly. Looking over JP's shoulder, through the front window, he saw Mo in front of the bank, walking up the hill, checking his watch. JP must never see him. It was exactly like being woken, Liam thought. He had become cosy and comfortable and warm in bed. He'd put Ireland aside. He'd found love and liked having his arms around him. The woken world felt cold and uninviting. He wanted to stay as he was, to be left alone.

JP watched him, his face unreadable: "Do you think you can just leave it?"

Liam blushed, mouth open. "I never said that."

"You didn't have to. Have you been careful?"

"Of course."

"You've not gone for Kilburn, the old places?"

"No, I've a flat here, in Dartford."

"A job?"

"Surely. I'm working on the underground, part of the planning team."

"A woman?"

Liam shrugged and pulled a face. "A few irons in the fire, you know." JP kept watching him, his face unreadable. "And you've been keeping out of trouble?"

Liam nodded. "Not even a parking ticket," he said.

"Good man." JP held him in his gaze for some moments as if thinking how to put something. Liam sat back in his chair and glanced out of the window again, hoping Mo was not there. He started nibbling at the hair on the back of his forefinger, not quite knowing where to look.

JP turned round to glance out of the window in the door. Liam shook his head: "It's nothing," he said. "Just looking at the weather."

JP said nothing, watching him. He started turning the spoon on the table in circles. The waitress returned with two white, large-handled mugs. JP grinned up at her and winked and she span on her heels to go back to the counter. "Red heads," he said. "Always a thing for me, red heads."

There was silence again between them. Liam chuckled to fill the space: "You know what they say here? Ginger locks, smelly box."

JP didn't laugh. Liam blushed. JP reached into the pocket of his jacket for a pouch of tobacco and a packet of papers. A square of the flap had been torn off and Liam wondered if discipline was slipping. Thank God his father was no longer around.

After rolling a thin cigarette, JP put it in his mouth and sucked the length of it twice, then placed it on the table and reached into another pocket for a rattle of matches.

"You'll have to go outside," Liam said, and JP checked round for signs then shook his head. "Fuckers," he said.

The men sat looking at each other for a few more moments and then Liam had to ask: "What's it to be?" he said.

"You'll be told in good time," JP said, then looked over his shoulder at the door and stretched his legs out under the table, making Liam move his to the side.

The clock on the wall said it was nearly half past and Liam drummed his fingers lightly on the table top. Mo was always on time. It didn't bear thinking about, letting them see each other.

"You in a hurry?" JP asked.

"Not at all," Liam said, leaning back to stretch his arms overhead and yawn in an exaggerated manner.

"You meeting someone?"

Liam looked past him onto the street. Mo appeared at the door, peeking through the glass with one hand shielding the sunlight. He smiled and waved, rippling his fingers, then pushed the door open. The bell tinkled. Liam held his breath. Mo stepped sideways round the central bank of tables, excusing himself. He appeared at JP's shoulder and looked down at him. He placed a paper bag from the chemists on the table. Liam could tell it contained condoms and baby oil.

"Hi there," Mo said, smiling at JP. "I'm Mo. Are you one of Fergie's workmates?" His voice was refined and musical. Liam cringed. "Shuffle up," Mo said, "I'll slip in there beside you."

JP didn't move but leaned back in his chair to run a hand through his thick, black hair. Mo, rebutted, flushed and then backed away to find the toilet. JP watched him go then leaned forward, placing his face close to Liam's: "You know what'll happen if you're caught back home, don't you, *Fergie?*" he said.

Liam shook his head, his heart racing.

JP held his gaze. His eyes were cold. "You know what'll happen to you if we think you've lost your nerve?"

Liam shook his head again, his throat constricting.

"You know what'll happen if we think you've turned?"

Liam shook his head again. "No," he said, beads of sweat forming at the roots of his hair.

JP pulled a piece of paper from his jacket pocket and slid it forward over the formica. It was the torn corner of a newspaper on which he'd written a phone number: "Every Sunday. Ring your Aunty," he said. "Then maybe I'll not say anything." Liam was struck dumb. The horror of the moment could not get any worse. He swallowed and blinked.

JP pushed his chair back, stood, and walked out the door. It was only then that Liam remembered to breathe. When Mo returned, Liam was shaking. He sat down where JP had been. "Who was that?" he said. "He was very rude. Fergie, are you all right?"

## Montgomery Lines, Aldershot;
## November 1995

Paul was in the office updating the training records when there was a flamboyant rapping on the door: "Did you want a word, Boss?" Paul nodded, inviting Delta to sit, then composed his words carefully: "It's about Paki Khan," he said.

"What about him?" asked Delta. "He's a good soldier, Paki is. And he's a senior Private. Next time we have a slot for a lance-jack he should be in for the running. He's easy good enough."

"Yes I know all that," said Paul, "But that's not it. It's the name – Paki. It's not right to call people that; not here, not now. It doesn't matter what background he has. If he's passed training he should be good enough. Can't we call him something else?"

Delta shrugged: "Like what?"

"I don't know; it's not for me to..."

"But most of the blokes have nicknames. There's Taff Steele and Geordie Dickinson... Scouse Horne..."

"Yeah, I know. But Rose is called Daz, not Jock. It's not every time is it? And what's wrong with Imran anyway? It is his name."

Delta was amused: another officer with silly ideas. "Yeah but it don't mean the blokes are racialist. They're not."

"Racist. The word is racist."

"Don't matter, Sir. I never had them electrocution lessons like what you officers done. Blokes still ain't racist.

Nobody says Paki's a bad soldier. In fact nobody'd want to go three rounds with him. It don't matter what he's called."

Paul nodded and looked out of the window. This was considered advice from his acting Platoon Sergeant. "So am I going to look stupid if I say I don't want Paki Khan called Paki anymore."

"Officers always look stupid, Sir. It goes with the job." His eyes were kind, but he meant it.

"I don't care, Delta. It's not what I look like that matters. It's what's right. And it's wrong to let people call Paki *Paki* just because he is one. It's not the same as calling Geordie *Geordie* and you damn well know it. So I won't speak to the platoon, fine. But you can. Please tell the screws and the lance-jacks to spread the word: the boss doesn't want to hear Khan being called *Paki*. They can blame me all they want. But I want it done."

The words came out stronger than Paul intended, tumbling over themselves, and he wondered if Delta would tell him to stick it. *Never give an order you know will be refused.* He didn't. He nodded, shrugging. "All right, Boss. If that's what you want. I'll put the word about. Now was there anything else?"

A curl to his lip that made Paul think that might be enough pet projects for one day. "You could always tell me how you got your name?"

"My name? Gary? Me dad called me it, Boss. It was his father's name..."

"That's not what I meant..." The man would take nothing seriously. "I meant *Delta*. Were you in the signals or something? Were you... I don't know..."

Delta shook his head. "No, Boss. It were nothing like that. It was at depot, during training. It's me name, Smith, see? There were four of us. The Platoon Sergeant, Big Zhukov – now the RSM – he stood all four of us in a line and told us we were to be called Alpha, Bravo, Charlie and Delta. And that was that. If anyone called me Gary or Smithy or Smudger I got smashed across the face with a black plastic mug. It were like that in them days, when only a handful got through."

"So what happened to the others, to Alpha and co?"

"Never made it. Fell out; got injured; jacked; got on the wagon, whatever. But they never made it to pass out. I never knew what happened to them afterwards but don't care. I was like: *Can I be Gary again please?* but Big Zhuk said *No, fuck off Delta* and the name stuck. It's been Delta ever since."

Paul laughed and rose when Delta said he had to go. They felt close. Paul thought he could do without a sergeant if he had a senior Corporal like him. He would show Casenove that he could lead the platoon despite what resources he was given. It was not a matter of sergeants but a question of skill and determination. The Longdon Assault Competition was nearly upon them and they would be moving down to Salisbury Plain in a few days. And if he was doing the right things and the Corporals were doing as he said, they were bound to do well.

"How's Cheese getting on in your section?" Paul asked at the doorway to the office.

"He's good. Westy gave me the gypsies, said he was a cock but I've found him OK. He gets on with the job whatever."

"So it was right to move him?"

Paul thought he was being clever. If he had been right about this one, he would be right about Khan. Team dynamics must be at their peak ready for the competition.

"I'll make it work, Sir. I always do."

# Canning Town, London; December 1995

It was a lovely weekend, Clare thought. She had cooked fish on Friday and on Saturday they caught the latest Bond film at Leicester Square, the early evening show. On the way back from the station they got a carry-out curry and watched some comedy on telly before collapsing into bed. The routine was familiar and comfortably happy and on Sunday morning Paul got the morning tea and was eager to make love before leaving. He was to be in Aldershot by ten, he said. There was a big exercise in Salisbury Plain, a competition. They were going down early to be ready for Monday morning. Clare tapped on the window when he slammed the front door, but he must not have heard. She watched him stride off down the street, head bobbing from side to side, his rucksack over one shoulder.

The rest of Sunday was quiet and restful. She went to the launderette to do the sheets and finished the marking while she waited. She wrote learning plans for the week and even completed her development log, a chore she found painful. She thought about Terell, the troubled child in her class, and went to early evening Mass because Father McColl was presiding.

Then Kirsty rang. She had been shopping. Would Clare meet her at the Grapes? Clare didn't normally like going out on Sundays, it being a day of rest after all, but since it wasn't often she saw Kirsty and the light chatter always made her happy, she obliged.

The pub had a very different clientele at the weekends. The suits and secretaries were replaced by East End locals, men with creased faces and comedy accents. Clare didn't care for it but Kirsty said she liked a bit of rough. After an hour of gossiping she leaned forward to whisper: "Don't look now, OK, but there's two blokes at the bar and they're checking us out." She straightening her back and conscientiously placed her hands on her knees. Clare did not look round but popped to the loo, making a quick and negative assessment of the two suitors as she did so. She was disappointed to find, when she returned to the table, that Kirsty had installed them both where she had been sitting.

The chatty one, Micky, was sandy haired. He had coarse hands, weather beaten skin, and wore a white football shirt. He was polite but informal in his manner, indicating to Clare to sit between him and his friend. The second man was too drunk to say much at all. He nodded at anything Micky said then grinned, revealing rotten, brown teeth. They'd been watching the game, Micky said. Never thought a pair of beauties would just walk into the Grapes on a Sunday like that. Clare pulled over a stool from a nearby table and sat with her back to the door. For the next hour, she watched Micky focus his wit on a flirtatious Kirsty but by ten she had grown tired of it. Nudging Kirsty with her toe, she shook her watch. Micky saw the action and quickly offered to get another round. Kirsty accepted but Clare refused. Finding himself alone with the two women, the drunken man stumbled off to the toilet.

Kirsty whispered urgently: "Clare – you're not going are you?"

"Well I can't leave you on your own and I'm not interested."

"What? They're lovely. Micky's a right hoot..."

"No he's not. He's horrible. And I'm not interested. We're going, Kirsty, come on."

"What? He's just getting me a drink. I can't just walk out. And listen to you all loved up. Oh come on! For old time's sake."

"No. Not this time and certainly not with them. Come on! I've work in the morning and so've you. What about your boyfriend?"

"Never worry there, Clare. All sorted. I've already rung and told him I'm staying at yours."

"You did what?"

"I'm staying at yours."

Clare was dumbfounded. "OK, but..."

Micky returned from the bar with two fizzy lagers and a spritzer held in a triangle between nail-less, sausage-like fingers. A thick gold wedding ring adorned one hand. The glasses were frosted with cold. "There you go darling. You sure you don't want one? It's no bother, honest."

"No, thank you," said Clare. "In fact I was just going... Kirsty look; I'm not staying up. If you're staying with me then drink up and come too. But I'm off. I'm really tired and it's an early start."

"Me too darling," chirped Micky. "Up at five, I am. Got to drive all the way to Nottingham, wherever that is. Then back via Oxford. But don't worry about your mucker. I'll take her to the station myself, I will. She'll come to no harm."

Clare did not even glance at him. She folded her arms, looking at Kirsty, who winked: "I'll be all right, Clare. I think I can handle Mr Micky here."

"Are you sure?"

"Yes I'm sure," she replied, leaning over the table to give Clare a hasty, awkward hug. "I'll ring you next week," she said.

# Salisbury Plain Training Area; December 1995

The training camp in Salisbury Plain had changed little since it was built, sometime during the Second World War. Wooden huts with white window frames and blood-red, vertically panelled walls were marshalled around a central concrete standing. Here the Company's four-ton wagons were being unloaded. Soldiers strode purposefully under the direction of sergeants: bergens to the accommodations huts; tentage, fuel and ration packs to the stores, rifles to the armoury and ammunition to the magazine. The men were expectant and excited. In the lines they always complained about this competition – *it was a soldier's right to chunter* – but once deployed, once caught up in the swell of activity, their competitive instinct was aroused. This was the crucible in which they were assessed. Each knew, beyond any doubt, that their Section, their Platoon, their Company, their Battalion was better than the next; and the urge to prove it was irrepressible. There was no second place in war.

Paul sat on the slatted picnic table outside the hut designated as the Officers' and Sergeants' Mess, studying maps of the exercise area. The Warning Order had been passed down the Chain of Command and he was busy marking the drop-off points, rendezvous locations and notional enemy positions. Laying the maps out flat, he took a green illuminating pen and highlighted all the easting numbers and did the same with the northings in orange. He stuck the adjoining maps together with tape, concentrating hard to keep the joins flat and even. Finally, to make the whole thing easier to handle, he cut the joined map down to the area he would need, discarding the legend and the trimmings. On exercises like this, weight saved meant time saved. He folded the map carefully, positioning it in the map case with the bit he would need first showing through the window, then stuffed it away in the top pocket of his bergen. This he lifted by the shoulder straps, checking the balance and weight. Having carried it for nearly four hundred miles in the previous nine months he was confident that nothing rubbed, dangled or rattled, and that he knew exactly where everything was stowed.

Rolly came out to join him, lighting a cigarette. Naked to the waist, he wore flip-flops and a pair of tight tracksuit bottoms cut off in a jagged line above the knee. He saw the discarded edges of the map and frowned: "Are you sure that's wise? What happens if they throw in an 'expect the unexpected' thing, make us go outside the map-fold?"

Paul shook his head: "I'll be fucked then. But my screws have maps; we'll manage."

"Are you prepared? Did you get all your training done?"

"You bet. You?"

"Yeah, sure did. It's going to be a good race. It's between you and me, I reckon."

The two men looked across the grass to the hard standing and the busy hive of soldiery striding to the shower block, towels wrapped loosely around their waists, wash bags swinging.

"The blokes are up for it," said Paul.

"It's a good exercise by all accounts; tests everyone."

"But what happens if we lose?" wondered Paul. "What happens to the platoon commander who comes bottom?"

Rolly sat down on the concrete step. The ridges of his stomach muscles stood out in perfect definition. His toes were hairy, unpleasantly so. "I don't think that matters, matey. What counts is who comes top. You know what

Cas keeps saying: there's no second place in war. I reckon whoever wins this will get the pick of the best jobs at the next round of promotions."

"You what?"

"Think about it. We've been here for nine months, yes? We'll command platoons for another year, eighteen months, maybe. After that there are captain's jobs to be had and I want one."

Paul shrugged. "Never thought about it. I just want to command soldiers."

"Well you should think about it. Command is not the only way up the tree, and if you want to do well in the army you've got to stand out."

"Why? What are you after?"

"Me? I want to be the youngest major in the army, matey. I want to be at the top of my game and that means getting yourself noticed."

This was the first time Rolly had been so overtly career focused. Paul was disturbed by the revelation, but the conversation was interrupted by the arrival of a minibus on the far side of the camp, the back windows of which were piled high with luggage. "What's this?" pondered Rolly. The minibus halted while the driver asked for directions. A soldier pointed him towards Rolly and Paul. "Ah! This must be Captains C Johnson and S Child, Royal Army Medical Corps," he said. "Their names are chalked on the door to the other room."

"Army doctors?" said Paul. "They'll sit in a tent all day, while we're out beasting ourselves, then go home and pretend they did some work."

Having driven round, the minibus hissed to a halt near their hut. The door folded open. Two young women in barrack uniform descended the steps and walked round the back of the bus to hoist down their bergens and medical bags. Both were in their late twenties. Paul and Rolly were instantly on their feet, offering to help; Rolly latching quickly onto the taller, blonde one, leaving Paul with the shorter one with dark, bobbed hair. She was cute, her boots uncommonly small, almost childlike. Her legs were short but her hips spread to fill the olive trousers in just the right way. She smiled up at Paul, extending a hand to shake: "Hello. I'm Captain Sarah Child. I'm looking for Major Casenove. We're here to provide medical cover for the exercise tomorrow."

"Step this way ladies," Rolly answered, "we'll take you to your rooms then help you find the Major."

\* \* \*

We are Five Platoon.

There's nothing to do after scoff. There never is. The blokes are gassing, telling ditties; waiting round for the next timing. Our stories are cruel but funny. It's these tales, told over and over, that bind us all together.

The screws have their feet on the table and hands in their pockets. The junior blokes are on the bunks, swinging their legs over the side. The room is full of smoke and Luke Banks keeps coughing and opening the window, but it's cold so Taff Steele tells him to shut it and keep it shut. Twat Carroll is making a brew for the screws cos he's the platoon crow. Tony Quinn, Brad Hyde and Taff Steele all have their backs against the radiator. Anyone gets on the wagon tomorrow and it's them they'll answer to. Scouse, Gecko and Paddy have been cackling away like children cos Scouse is good at voices and does this wicked impression of the Boss. Daz is silent. Dicko is on the bunk below him with one hand in a glove, reaching up to tickle the moody Scottish cunt with a length of nettle he brought in from outside. Tiny Haynes and TP are playing cards. Cheese is asleep, a porn mag under his cheek. Brains Beckett is having a shower cos he was on dixies and had to wash the pots after scoff. Foxy Cunningham and Paki Khan are repacking their bergens, putting the finishing touches to how they're gonna to hump the load. Both of them have an antitank missile weighing thirty pounds and they're trying to work out whether to have it cross ways, underneath the flap, or vertical, tied to the side. Either way it's fucking heavy. Foxy's tittering away to himself cos Paki just snapped and threatened to deck the next bloke who calls him Chaka.

We'll tell stories, sitting round like this, for eternity. It don't matter that the showers are cold, the scoff greasy, the beds too small and that when you get up for a slash in the middle of the night, you wake the guy below you. It don't matter that the rain's bouncing off the wriggly tin roof. We are Five Platoon. The beret, the cap-badge, is all the armour we need.

There's banging on the door. Billy McGregor, the Company Clerk, pushes in and knocks over the fire hydrant put there to keep the door closed. The wind scatters fag ash across the table. "Close the fucking door," Westy snaps and McGregor quickly does so, looking round for someone to latch on to. Delta's not here and he's afraid of Weston.

"What is it, Mac?" says Chink. "You got some gen for tomorrow?"

"Orders will be at Zero-four-hundred," says McGregor. "Your Platoon Commander and Sergeant to attend, maps and notebooks ready. Rumour is that orders will be given by radio so have your signaller ready as well."

We listen in, silent. Banks puts his book aside to check the frequencies are set and the spare batteries charged up. It's good having someone clever as rad op.

"You been round the other platoons?" says Weston, chewing gum. McGregor shakes his head. Weston smirks, lowering his chin into his chest and tugging at his collar. "Don't fucking tell them," and the blokes laugh.

McGregor shifts his weight, trying to laugh with us. There's something he wants to say: "You better get Delta to tell your Platoon Commander as well," he says. "I just been up the Mess and Mr Illingworth is taking some last minute first aid lessons off the dark haired doctor."

"He'd better be ready in the morning," mutters Westy. "He can do what he wants to her for all I care; he just better be ready for the exercise."

Chink glances over at him and looks like he wants to say something. There's something on his mind, something's bugging him. But now's not the time. He'll wait to see how Mr Illingworth performs in the morning.

* * *

Rolly and the blonde had already slipped away to bed, tiptoeing passed the Major's room. Sarah leaned forward, invitingly close. Her lips were glossy where she had licked them, as juicy as a plum. At one in the morning he suggested they go through to her room and she nodded. Her skin was smooth and warm and smelled of wood smoke.

He had not been drinking. Three hours kip would easily be enough.

* * *

It was raining. The biting wind made Paul turn his face and squint as he marched. He was soaked. Rainwater ran down his legs and pooled in his boots. Thinking of Sarah was the only thing that reduced the drudgery. Slender and lithesome, she had melted below him, glorious in his hands. The memory made his cock thicken and he enjoyed the feeling of it, tight against his trousers. He leaned forward, one arm holding the rifle at waist height, the other swinging hard across his body. The pace was good. Their time was good. Eight miles down, twelve to go.

He had expected to chivvy his soldiers but found they were throwing themselves into the race. Khan's dark eyes were piercing and determined. Corporal Weston kept shouting: "Come on Five Platoon; let's win this cunt." Brad Hyde and Tony Quinn were taking their turn with the antitank missiles, leaning into the march, their legs swinging underneath the bulk of the load. Carroll was exhausted. He was being pulled along by the webbing straps by Cheese and Paddy, his head lolling backwards.

By mid-afternoon, Paul was utterly chin-strapped. He had never known fatigue like this; a heaviness that pulled him downwards, sucking at his eyelids. Head lolling, he tripped over a stone and almost fell. He struck on, increasing the speed to drive through it. The men leaned in, keeping pace. At the next halt, he stepped off the track and knelt, facing left. Banks slipped in behind him, facing right: "You're showing off, Sir," he whispered. Paul grinned and took a splash of water from the bottle in his webbing. The blokes would expect a bit of flair in their officers.

He studied the map, pulling up a grass stalk to trace the route and pick out the next major turns. He was looking for a ring contour, a small hillock in the next eight hundred metres and after that, a major road. They were making good time.

He called another halt an hour later, forming a hasty harbour in the corner of a pine copse. The sections settled into a triangular formation and he took a place in the centre with Banks next to him. He rested his bergen against a tree trunk. They had some five kilometres to go before reaching the assembly area. A blister had formed on his right heel. He knew he ought to sort it before it got worse but he was flagging. He would do it at the assembly area, after some rest. He ate some chocolate and felt for the rush of sugar but none came. He ate some more. He should keep the rest for the night phase, he thought. He should see to the men but took a minute to rest, the straps of the bergen holding him in place, his head falling back. His discipline was slipping but it was difficult to care. He closed his eyes for a second and felt their weight: how easy it would be to drift off. Banks nudged his elbow. Paul grunted, slipped the bergen straps off his shoulders, and dragged himself to his feet. He walked round, asking if everyone was all right, holding the rifle consciously in both hands. He had to be seen to be alert. He called the Corporals in: "Check feet,

112

get some water down and take ten minutes; there should be only an hour's march to scoff in the assembly area. Each section put one man on sentry."

The Corporals didn't seem half as tired as he was. They slipped back noiselessly to brief their sections. Paul lay back against his bergen. Banks fiddled with the controls on the radio set, listening for instructions. The smokers scratched at wet lighters to get a flame. They shared drags and exhaled low across the damp brown needles. The next thing Paul knew was Delta kicking the soles of his boots: "Boss, that's fifteen. Let's get moving." Paul shook himself. That little kip had been enough to restore balance; he was up for it again.

Paul rose quickly and drove himself out of the copse and into the rain, taking a kneeling position a hundred yards along the track. He checked his map while the Platoon got themselves out of the wood and into line behind him. When Banks tapped his arm – "Last man, Boss," – he pushed up and on, returning to the rhythm of the march. The final mile was a slog along a track that curled uphill, open to the full blast of the wind. The rain had turned the sand to a claggy mush that stained their trousers orange. The men marched in file, evenly paced and determined. It was beautiful. He wanted to approach the assembly area as a coherent and disciplined platoon. He hissed back along the line for everyone to raise their heads, to look up, to be proud of themselves. The entrance was marked with mine tape. Mr Zhukov, the towering RSM, stood waiting for them, his beret darkened by the rain. "Who are you?" he shouted and Paul stuttered in response: "Five Platoon, B Company." The RSM splashed forward to grab Paul by the elbow: "Over there; get going, Sir."

Paul hurried away, throwing a conspiratorial look at Banks, who shook his head. It was not just the soldiers who were in awe of the RSM.

The assembly area at last. Rest. Scoff. Shelter from the wind.

Time slowed. The men pulled doss bags from their bergens and crept into them to keep warm. Rain spattered against the Gore-Tex shells. *A good soldier eats and sleeps when he can.* They ate the dinner meal from the ration packs, cooking on hexamine stoves. There was not enough time to sleep but too much to sit around.

Paul treated his blisters, taping them with zinc oxide, and checked that Carroll had done the same. He received orders for the night phase of the exercise, processed the information and issued it to the Platoon with all the panache he could muster: "Listen lads. We're not doing this for us. We're not doing this for Major Casenove or for B Company. We're doing this for Mercy and Bryan Moor. That's what this is all about. We're going to win for them."

Looking at their faces Paul instantly recognised he had overplayed his hand. He had wanted to say something to inspire them but the rhetoric had fallen flat. As they walked away Tiny Haynes asked Delta what he had been on about and Delta shook his head, shrugging. But there was no point worrying about it. He had tried something. If it didn't work, try something else. With the sections settled into their areas, the men smoked in silence, allowing the time to drift away. He walked round, chatting to each in turn. No one mentioned his speech. With the last of the light fading, he camouflaged his face, neck, and hands, smoked a cigarette, and changed into his last pair of dry socks. Delta told him he'd had a whisper from one of his mates in the Signals that Five Platoon were doing well and the news excited everyone. Now all they had to do was get through the march and finish the shoot. After endex they could all go home and get pissed down the Rat Pit.

An hour before midnight they were allowed to depart. It took an hour to shake the cold out of their limbs. At four in the morning Paul was hit again by a wave of fatigue. Sleep became as cosy as warm chocolate and inviting as a feather pillow. In the branches of overhanging trees he imagined he saw the shapes of animals and distorted, ugly faces. Dark recesses loomed out at him. Distance grew and shrank. The rain pattered to a stop but coalesced into a mist which thickened and congealed into a heavy, deafening fog.

By a small bridge, he pulled the Platoon off the road to shelter in the lee of a hedgerow. He checked his map. They were on the right track and two clicks further on was a disused farm where they would swing left and follow the two-fifty contour to a metalled road which would take them back round in a lengthy dogleg. Delta appeared at his shoulder, map in his hand: "What's up? I think we're OK, but I've not seen any others." Paul didn't look up, using one hand to cover the glow of his torch and the other to trace the map with a spruce needle: "We're definitely at this intersection here." Delta nodded in agreement. Paul could feel the warmth off his body, welcomed it. He pondered. If they took a left turn and followed the river uphill they would cut off a good five kilometres, saving about an hour.

"I don't know, Boss. If we cross-grain, the walking's shit. It's bogs and baby's heads up there. Nightmare after rain."

Paul looked round but could not see more than a few metres. It would be cheating, of course. The orders had been specific about the route. But he could bluff it. The two other corporals slipped up to his position when he called them. He asked them their opinion. "Risky, Boss," said Chink and Westy shook his head slowly. "I've been over this ground before, Sir, on the sniper's course. It's boggy as fuck."

The discussion was disturbed by a distant pattering, a shuffling noise. Delta shushed the Platoon and those that were smoking quickly dabbed their fags into the mud. There was silence, then the shuffling got nearer. They recognised the sound when the following Platoon was nearly upon them, striding passed, slipping through the night. Paul's heart raced. They had been only metres away, the front man unmistakeable: it was Rolly.

"That does it," said Paul. "We're not getting beat by fucking Four Platoon. Prepare to move. We're going cross country."

The Platoon pushed themselves up, now heavy with exhaustion and stiff with cold. Their trousers and boots were soaking. They stamped their feet to get the blood flowing. Beckett, taking his turn with one of the missiles, had to be pulled onto his feet by Haynes and TP. Paul led off, following Four Platoon, listening to their footsteps ahead of him. In a dip about five hundred metres further on a shallow valley swept up left through a copse and onto the high ground. If he could find a path across to the track on the other side, he would have overtaken probably three platoons.

But the hill proved hard walking and the pace slowed. After only a hundred metres Paul looked round to make a judgment as to whether to turn back but decided against it. Once out of the copse there was a tilled field where the soil was uneven and mushy. Mud collected on the tread of their boots. The pace slowed further as one after another the men slipped and fell. At first they swore and pushed themselves quickly upright but after the third time they started giggling at each tumble. After another few yards someone would fall again. At the edge of the field Paul was thankful that beyond a dry stone wall the ground was unploughed. He heaved himself over but it took another fifteen minutes for the rest of the Platoon to do the same. Crossing tussock grass proved even slower. Paul leaped from one clump to the next then checked his compass. Visibility was less than twenty feet. Smatterings of rain came then stopped then came again. Once out of the lee of the wall, the wind blasted his face and made his ears freeze. There was another eleven hundred metres of this to go.

Then someone fell. At first there was the usual giggle but an audible snap and sharp cry made everyone silent. It was real. They dropped their bergens and knelt in all round defence.

It was Beckett. He lay writhing, clutching his knee like a footballer, his bergen pinioning him in the bog. Paul quickly waved to Banks and grabbed the radio handset from him. This would require a helicopter for evacuation: "Hello zero, this is Zulu-two-zero-alpha, over." The radio was silent. Paul tried again: "Hello zero, radio check, over." The radio hissed with static. Paul chucked the handset to Banks: "Sort that out. Get Zero as soon as you can; check the frequencies."

The men nearest Beckett pulled him out of the straps of his bergen. Released from it, he screamed in agony: "My fucking leg; my fucking leg..."

Paul stepped in to issue instructions but Delta already had it covered: "Westy, take your blokes and set up a perimeter but leave Scouse here with me. Chink, get your blokes to the side, we might need them. Sir – have you got through to Zero yet?"

"No, Banks is still trying..."

"Well keep at it, Sir, will you. I'll see to the casualty – he's one of mine after all."

Paul stepped aside while there was a flurry of activity. Corporal Weston's men dispersed into the gloom. Chink's section formed a line, the men watching as Scouse tried to unlace Beckett's boots. Paul felt uneasy, as if standing on the edge of a party he had not been invited to. Delta was giving curt instructions which were followed quickly and efficiently by the blokes. Paul wondered if he should grasp command: "Delta, I..."

Delta ignored him, telling his men to hold Beckett down while Scouse cut through his laces. Paul felt purposeless and unwelcome then Delta turned back to him: "Sir, have you got comms back to Zero yet?" Paul was taken aback by the aggressive demand, expecting more reverence towards his rank. He shook his head and Delta turned immediately to Banks: "Banksy – get Zero on the net now – we have a serious noduf casualty and we're off route. Go where you need to go to get comms. If we're in a blank spot, move

117

somewhere you can get through. Mr Illingworth Sir – you go with him please."

It was not a request. Paul and Banks left their bergens but took their rifles and the radio back down to the edge of the muddy field, following the remains of a dry stone wall. They had been on the high ground for an hour. Paul was conscious that the men had watched Delta wrestle command from him. He felt embarrassed and angry and huffily trudged ahead of Banks in order to feel in control. After a hundred metres he realised that he would need the grid reference for the casualty but had left his map behind. Ignoring Bank's tutting, he ran back to get it following Beckett's screams.

Delta demanded to know if he had got through and Paul stammered that he needed his map. Scouse had the boot removed and was cutting the trousers up to the knee. TP and Tiny were holding torches to light up the scene, Delta having decided that the need for light was greater than the need for secrecy. The leg was colouring, a dark bruise spreading along the line of the ankle. Scouse pressed it gently and Beckett howled, the sound of bone grinding on bone audible to all.

Alone in the dark, Paul was surrounded by activity he could not control. "Sir, you still here?" snapped Delta curtly.

"Corporal Smith, look here, I command this Platoon, not you...."

"No Sir, you don't. Right now I command this Platoon. You were up all night shagging nurses and now you've led us into a bog and got a man down. He's a broken leg and will die of hyperthermia unless we get him treated. If you wanna command you'd better fucking wake up."

Paul felt his pulse racing. This was the moment he would have to impose himself or else lose the Platoon for ever. He stepped forward into the arc of torch lights: "Chink, please take your section to find Banks over the brow of the hill. Get comms and stay together..."

"I thought you were doing that?" snapped Delta. "Why are you sending Chink out? He don't even know where Banks is. You could lose the whole fucking Platoon in this fog. No – here's a better idea. Chink stays here and you go out and get comms then come back and tell me there's a chopper on its way."

The soldiers looked from Delta to Paul and back again. Paul coloured with anger. The moment swayed from one to the other. Paul wavered. He could feel himself falling through the tissue-thin authority of his rank. Out here, with these men, the star on his shoulder meant nothing. This was a world of men who fought for a living. Normal rules did not apply.

"No," snapped Paul. "You fucking listen, Corporal Smith. I command this Platoon and yes, Beckett has fallen over but I will still command this incident. Now you go over the brow of that hill, take a fucking map and find Banks. Get a chopper in here of if you cannot get through, come back here in less than five minutes."

Paul turned his back on Delta. "Chink, your blokes get out your ponchos and get a stretcher improvised. We're gonna move him back down to the road if we need to. If we don't, use the ponchos to provide us all with cover. Now get to it, all of you."

There was silence. The men looked at each other. Paul's eyes blazed, his shoulders set square, his feet apart. Delta blinked. The men moved.

# Canning Town, London; New Year 1995

Clare was dancing on eggshells but Paul could not be arsed doing anything about it. While she skittered about in the kitchen, he scowled at the television with his feet on the leather trunk and his arms folded across his chest. NATO had started bombing the Serbian capital and now the ground troops had seen action as well. A guy he knew from Sandhurst was to be awarded the Military Cross in the New Year's Honours List. Apparently he had been involved in a four-hour fire fight, personally getting his troops out when they were pinned down by snipers near Gorazde. He'd got trigger time! Paul shook his head angrily. Percy fucking Andrews: a fat, mediocre little man in a pissy little county regiment, getting a fucking gong! If only New Year would come and go.

But what would January bring? Paul dare not think.

Christmas had been dire. He had not known how to tell his father what a precarious position his career was in. Then he'd come to London but found little solace in being there: Clare had insisted they use condoms, which he hated.

He needed time to think.

Major Casenove had shaken him to the core; the way he had quietly and slowly demanded to hear what Paul had done and why. At each response his questions had become more piercing. He had thumped the desk. "It is my opinion that you lost control of your men; that you are not sufficiently strong willed when things go wrong." Paul had started to speak but a glance had cut him short.

"You have a weak leadership style. You want to be liked. You did some graduate leadership course before Sandhurst – where was it, Tesco? Marks & Spencer? – and you think you can apply all that shit here, in the field?" Paul had coloured. He could only nod. "Well it may surprise you to know that I too know about Myers Briggs and Meredith Belbin and all that gumf. You are not the only person who thinks they know what leadership is. Get it into your head that this is an operational battalion. We fight wars, the sort others avoid. We select the best; men with fitness, discipline and integrity. The civvies can call it what they like. In this regiment, officers need the character to inspire, Paul. And that is where you fail. When you command in war, it is not about popularity, it is about respect. You have three months to prove yourself. If I do not see an improvement, I will remove you from command. Do you fucking understand?"

The vein on the side of the Major's temple pulsed. Paul had shook so much he could barely salute. Later, alone in his room, he had cried.

But it had not been Major Casenove's bollocking that upset him most. It had been the way the blokes had turned their backs on him. He had given an order that put a man down and the weight of it was crushing him. There was nowhere he could go, nowhere he could hide. Every man in the battalion would think him the sort of officer that would put them in danger just to look good himself. If that was not a sure-fire way of getting a round in between the shoulder blades, he didn't know what was.

He had once been so certain, so positive. He'd started to win them over and adopted what he thought was a jovial, teacherly sort of style. It hadn't worked and now he had no idea what would. After the dispersal parade, when the soldiers had left the room, the screws filed out leaving him looking at the floor. At least Delta had been strong enough to wish him a happy Christmas, but it had sounded flat.

Paul could only hope that a week's leave would give them time to forgive him. He had done his best. He had wanted to win and not for his own sake, but for theirs. Could they not see that?

Poor Brains! His screams, as they lifted him into the chopper, had haunted Paul's sleep ever since.

But what else could he do? Must he storm in and impose himself? How could he do that now? What was so bad about first names anyway? They used them in the Israeli army, and the Australian. In the nine months he had been in command there had been some notable successes. He was not a fool. It wasn't weak. Had he not brought the Platoon to heel when Mercy was jailed? Had he not dominated the Platoon when they played up?

Was he expected to resign over this?

Watching the news, Paul fidgeted with the cover of the sofa, tugging threads from a worn patch. Clare came through carrying a bowl of Bombay mix and a bottle of wine and slumped on the sofa next to him. He placed a hand on her leg, gently squeezing her thigh. She was the only real friend he had. She nestled beside him, lifting his arm round her shoulders.

On the television, a journalist in a blue flak jacket and helmet was speaking from Bosnia to the anchor-man in London.

Clare stiffened: "Are you going, Pauly? Is this what it's all about?"

"All what's about?"

"You being so moody. You being so... so..."

Paul grimaced. The last thing he needed was to have another talk about their relationship. He pulled his arm back off her shoulders: "For fuck's sake, Clare..."

Clare shifted, pushing away from him: "Paul, we need to talk. I can't wait for you to be nice to me every weekend. You do this every time; arrive in a grump and sit around for hours. Yvonne even spoke to me last night, asking if we were all right. And we never go to bed until you're completely plastered."

"We're fine," Paul said. "We're good, honest. It's work, that's all. It's hard. Very hard."

He ran his fingers through his hair. He was almost telling the truth and it worked. Clare relaxed and settled next to him again, pulling his hand back around her. She was doing her best, he knew, to keep them together.

"I don't want you to go," she said, watching the television.

He wondered if she meant it, if she was genuinely afraid for his life. She shouldn't be. He wasn't. "It's my job, Clare. It's what I joined for."

"I know Paul, I know. But I don't like the thought of it. If you go, I want to come with you." The idea initiated a spark in her mind and she giggled to herself: "How about that? If you go, I'll come along and stay in a hotel. Those reporters must have a place."

Paul had to laugh. The idea was lovely in a childish way. He placed the back of his fingers against her cheek and felt the plump, pink, heat. She stroked his wrist with her thumb. She was no oil painting but she loved him, loved him deeply. She snuggled into his shoulder to play with the buttons of his shirt. He wondered, briefly, if they could have a quickie here on the sofa, if there was time.

"I want to go wherever you go, Paul" she whispered.

Paul nodded. Her hair tickled the underside of his chin. He took another slurp of beer.

# PART TWO

## HMP Maze, Northern Ireland; January 1996

The men were in H Block 6. The gym was the only place they could talk because of the hidden microphones. Michael sat on the stool underneath the shoulder press, one hand holding the bull-bars. Shamey went out to check the guards had gone then came back in. He nodded to the two youngsters to make some noise and they started lifting and clanging weights on the concrete floor. Shamey stood close to Michael, bending down so they only had to whisper: "It's clear."

Michael leaned forward, shifting so his belly hung over his jeans: "It's been decided by the Council," he said. "You've to get word out to JP that the Engineer has done a good job. We're taking his advice. It's to be London, then Manchester. It's to be done the way Liam says."

Shamey said nothing, thinking, then: "You sure?"

Michael nodded.

Shamey said nothing, looking at Michael's face for clues. "You haven't heard then, what they're saying?"

"What who's saying?"

"What we're getting back from JP."

Michael shrugged a little: "No, what?"

Shamey searched his face again. "You really haven't heard, have you."

Michael shook his head.

"Your man's a bufty. He's a shirtlifter. He's shacked himself up with some young city trader, an Arab."

Michael frowned.

"Straight up. No word of a lie."

Michael thought, then lifted his eyes to meet Shamey's: "It changes nothing. He's still the best we got there. Tell JP to keep a close eye on him and make sure he's still with us."

The two men studied each other, then both nodded at the same time. It wasn't the best, but it would do.

"I'll get onto it," Shamey said, then pushed himself off the bull-bars and walked round Michael to get to the door, nodding to the young lads doing the weights as he did so.

Michael stared at the floor, thinking. Just as Shamey was about to disappear, he turned to call after him: "Shamey!"

"Aye."

"Just give Jamesy Horgan a shout now as well, would you? Tell him to get down here and see me. I've some domestic work I need him to do."

Shamey stood by the door looking Michael's broad back.

"Dead on," he said, then ducked out into the corridor.

After five minutes, enough time for Shamey to have gone to the phones, Michael stood up, adjusted his jeans, and left. The clanging of weights hurt his ears. It would be dinner in an hour.

# Montgomery Lines, Aldershot;
# January 1996

The Duty Sergeant called the guard to attention, ordering them into open order so that Paul, the Duty Officer, could inspect them. The guard was comprised of men from another Company and he did not know any of them well. Each of them stood aggressively to attention as he examined their turnout. Starting with the beret, he checked for dust and alignment of the cap-badge over the left eye; that the face was cleanly shaven; that the smock was ironed and that sharp creases ran down each arm; that the rifle muzzle and magazine housing were oiled; that the belt was centred and the trouser creases ran crisply down the leg to where they broke in front of the man's shin. Finally, he saw that the boots were suitably polished.

The soldiers didn't make eye contact unless he spoke to them. They stared through him, daring him to correct them. Their moral superiority was easy to identify: every man had at least one medal dangling from his chest. The guard commander, a Corporal, had three: a Northern Ireland medal with a purple and green ribbon; a Falklands medal with a silver rosette and the Military Medal indicating that he had not only served down south, but had been fantastically courageous when he did so. Paul's eye graced across his chest and the Corporal, seeing him do so, puffed himself out. The medals armoured him.

Paul's chest was bare. He was unproven. He had never known effective enemy fire; the numbing, freezing effects of fear. He felt neutered. Mounting the guard was a charade he had to endure while the flaws in the underlying logic were obvious: he was inspecting the soldiers by virtue of his class and education rather than military prowess, a pretence neither he nor they quite managed to swallow.

The inspection complete, he thanked the Duty Sergeant and took his position in front of the parade. The Sergeant ordered the guard to return to close order before the final instruction: "To your duties, fall out." The men saluted, then turned smartly to the right and marched away.

Paul walked slowly up the hill to the Mess, his hands grasping each other behind his back. In the TV room, the officers were absorbed in the news. The Dayton accord was due to be signed, bringing another period of bloody Balkan violence to an end. The screen showed a retrospective of images from the previous eight months: a Serbian general handing out sweets to the children he would later massacre, Dutch soldiers in blue berets climbing into a jeep, and a mine exploding under the track of a British armoured personnel carrier.

One of the captains, the newly married Jarred Fleming, sat back in his chair and lit a cigarette. Seeing the look on Paul's face, a sly smile crept across his lips: "Never mind Paul. There's always Northern Ireland – unless the peace process works, that is." The other officers laughed and Paul stuck up two fingers in response but the Quartermaster patted him on the back. He was commissioned from the ranks and greatly admired by the younger men. "Don't listen to them Paul. There's always going to be wars. Trust me. No-one saw the Falklands coming, nor Ireland, nor Suez. You bide your time." Paul nodded in thanks and was about to leave when Fleming clapped for silence, pointing at the TV screen: "Look! It's Sergeant Moor! He's been released!"

A reporter was stood in front of some iron railings, voicing over images of the battalion's previous tour of County Tyrone: a lonely country lane with police tape draped between blackthorn hedges; an upturned Vauxhall Astra; Corporal Mercer being guided into Belfast Crown Court underneath a blanket; women kneeling, banging dustbin lids on the roadside and masked teenagers throwing petrol bombs at police Land Rovers. A bearded man with oblong, gold-rimmed glasses said that the court's decision would put severe pressure on the peace process. He would have to consult with the army council, he said, causing snorts of derision from the officers. Then the screen showed the face of a teenager, red haired and sallow skinned. The camera closed in on his eyes as the reporter drew her speech to a close.

"You see, Paul," said the Quartermaster. "Northern Ireland's always going to be there."

# Montgomery Lines, Aldershot;
# January 1996

Haynes was ironing a shirt and using a towel to prevent the table from burning. Gecko was looking in the mirror, thrusting out his chin to address his spots. Scouse had been summoned by the Sergeant-major and Paul was angry that he had not been told. Some of the men were dressed for a run as Paul had instructed and some were dressed for barrack duties. "What's going on? Where's Delta?" he demanded.

"Sergeant Moor's back Sir," explained Dickinson.

"So?" Paul looked round the room expecting the men to get ready for a run, but they didn't move. It was obvious they were waiting for him to agree the training programme with the newly returned Sergeant. There was little benefit in expressing his displeasure to them.

Following the unlit corridor round the building, Paul came to the NCOs' room and barged his way in. The NCOs were sitting on reversed plastic chairs, their attention entirely focused on a bald, simian figure sitting underneath the window. Dressed in tight jeans, desert boots, and a green bomber jacket, he emanated the powerful odour of stale beer. Ignoring Paul's entrance, he continued talking: "So I gets back at Thirteen-hundred, says bye-bye to the RUC escort and I've a pint in my hand by Thirteen-ten. The RSM, god bless 'im, has all the blokes he can muster come in to welcome me back, Scale A parade, and there's plenty others who've come down cos they heard it on the news. There's maybe a hundred blokes in the Mess all buying me a pint; and who am I to say no?"

Laughter rippled round the room, the lance-jacks slapping their thighs.

"And so we gets to Twenty-hundred and some of the girls thin out and – you'll like this – up comes that mincing chef who thought he could take me when we were out in Dungannon. I thought he'd got posted but he's still here. Up he comes and says *Welcome home Bryan; glad you got out Bryan; shall we let bygones be bygones Bryan?* the fucking poof. So I asks him if he still thinks he's hard or was it just the beer talking and you could see he was shitting himself. He starts stammering and he knows I'm gonna have him as soon as the RSM's gone. So when I'm away for a piss I comes back and there's Cookie getting his coat and saying he's away, he's got breakfast to do early in the morning and he doesn't want any trouble blah blah blah.

"So I tells Musher Deans to get a rope from his car and in two minutes we've got him strung up from that spar across the ceiling – Delta, you've been inside the Mess, you know the one I mean – and then someone's gone and kicked out the stool from under his feet and he's clinging on to the noose and kicking and looking at me like I'm gonna be the one to let him down. Eyes were like Scammell wheels they were. It was only when we thought he'd passed out that Musher let go."

The NCOs were laughing and Paul could not help chuckling along as well. He leaned against a locker door while Moor finished his tale. Perhaps this circumstance was exceptional.

"Will he go to the RSM?" asked Matt Steele, his voice higher than normal.

"He'd best not, not if knows what's good for him. He's got a bruise round his neck like he's been out in Hampstead Heath on a Friday night. But he can hide it. He knows better than to try it on with me now, anyway." A silence fell in the room as Moor looked towards the floor, his features twitching. Paul pushed himself upright and stepped forwards to introduce himself. Moor looked up at him as Delta started an introduction: "Beefy, this is Mr Illingworth, our new Platoon Commander..."

"Sergeant Moor. Very pleased to meet you. I'm glad your ordeal is over. I think we should have a chat in the office..."

"You're spot on there Sir, I think we should as well," said Moor jumping up on his feet. He was much shorter than Paul but his build made that seem irrelevant. His lips were fleshy and the skin round his eyes dark from dehydration. His head was scarred where he had shaved his hair. "I was waiting for you to come down; my kit's in the office and I can't get changed without the key."

"Oh, I'm really sorry," stammered Paul. "I thought you had one. But your kit's fine. I put your box in the locker and kept an eye on it."

"That's very good of you, Sir. Shall we?" Moor indicated with his arm and Paul turned to lead the way feeling a little like their roles should be reversed. He unlocked the office and went in. "We have Company Commander's briefing at ten. I was going to take the blokes for a run but it's too late now; we'll do it afterwards. Then I'm giving the Geneva Convention lecture this afternoon because we're doing training tests this week. There's a range day tomorrow and platoon training on Thursday – I was hoping to do ambush drills. Then on Friday we'll do the ten-miler and get away for the weekend. I'm sure you'll manage to work yourself back in. How do you want to reintroduce yourself to the Platoon? Would you like me to say something this afternoon?"

"You'll say nothing Sir, if you don't mind. I'll speak to the blokes myself, when I'm ready. I don't need anybody talking for me."

Moor opened his locker and looked inside as if checking to see all his kit was there. Then he placed his hands in the pockets of his bomber jacket and stood squarely in the centre of the room, facing Paul, feet apart.

Paul sat on the desk: "I thought..."

"That's good Sir. It's good you thought. But now I'm here we're gonna think together. I'm back now and I want the Platoon back the way I had it before. There's something you better get into your head from the start. I've had officers before, lots of 'em. I've had good ones and I've had bad ones but I never compromise. I never let my standards drop. If you can hack it, you'll do OK. But if you fuck me about, if you let standards fall – then you and me's gonna have words."

Paul held the ash-grey eyes. He'd been in post for nearly a year and thought himself beyond such a pissing competition. "That's good," he said. "But let's get something straight from me as well. I'm in charge of this Platoon. I'm the one with a Commission and..."

"I don't give a fuck what bit of paper you got Sir. And I don't give a fuck who's signed it, if it's the Queen or Ming the Merciless. I don't gives a shit. If you can lead these men, we'll see in the field. We'll see when it matters. But don't go waving commissions in my face. It don't make a difference when the shit starts flying. What matters is you can cut the mustard. You understand?" He squared his shoulders, standing like a concrete bollard, his voice rasping and certain. Paul held his gaze. He was not going to back down. "I understand very well. And I don't expect to have to have conversations of this nature with you..."

"We'll have whatever conversations..."

"Do not interrupt me again, Sergeant Moor!" Paul snapped. Men were in the corridor, listening. The conversation was unbecoming. "I will not put up with it. So if you don't mind, we are required at the Company office in fifteen minutes and I think you ought to be changed. I will leave you to do so and will see you there. Now excuse me, please." He stood. Moor's eyes narrowed and the head tilted back. The two men stared at one another and then Moor stepped aside, his eyes unwavering.

Paul thought he had won and to ensure the men knew this, he strolled slowly through the rooms making a show of talking to them. They looked at him askance, smirking. They all knew a battle was inevitable; it was the way of things.

In the Company office Paul sat next to Taggart, making sure Moor saw him chatting comfortably with another sergeant. When Major Casenove entered the room, everyone sat up while he wove between the chairs to get behind his desk. His brief, extracted directly from Commanding Officer's prayers that morning, contained details about the next round of promotions, the tenuous situation in Belfast, matters of training policy and finally the boring logistical issues. He applauded Rolly and Sergeant Taggart because the Colonel had again mentioned their performance during the Longdon Assault Competition, a period in the meeting when Paul avoided Moor's eyes, and the Major rounded off by stressing that the alert state in the lines had been increased. An IRA attack was not expected but was certainly possible. "And here's the reason," the Major smiled, making a drum roll on the desk with his fingers. "Welcome back Sergeant Moor. It's been a long time."

"Thirteen months is a long time in a grey box, Sir," said Moor, peeling back fleshy lips to expose his teeth. "It's good to be back with the Company again."

It was obvious Moor and the Major knew each other well. "And it's great to have you back," the Major said. "Mr Illingworth has done a good job with Corporal Smith as acting Platoon Sergeant, but I'm sure he would welcome an additional pair of hands – integrity of the platoon and all that." Moor and the Major looked at each other and the Major winked. "Yeah," said Moor, "Me and the Platoon Commander have already got an understanding haven't we, Sir?" Moor leaned forward to look across at Paul, who nodded: "I look forward to working together," he said.

"Excellent. And on the subject of which, I forgot to mention one additional logistical piece. The Quartermaster has managed to scrounge additional training ammunition from Brigade: enough for about two thousand rounds of ball per Platoon, and perhaps one thousand blank. Four Platoon have already got their dibs in to do a day on the ranges and have said they don't want the blank. Five Platoon – what do you want to do?"

The Major looked at Paul for the answer but there was a very quick glance to Moor as well. Paul shot in a reply: "We'll use it all. I've planned an ambush exercise for Thursday. It would be great if I can get a range and do it live firing. We rarely practice live ambushes. It'd be a good opportunity…"

The Major was nodding but Moor shook his head: "We won't be ready for that yet Sir. Systems Approach to Training, yeah? You need to work up to that sort of thing. We could use the live ammo for a range day and then the blank to dry train and then do a live ex when we're ready."

"But that's more than one day Sergeant Moor. I don't want to lose this allocation."

"We won't lose it Sir. I'll speak to the Quartermaster. He knows me. If I ask him to keep it back, he will."

Paul was niggled that the discussion should take place in front of the Major. Moor was sitting on the other side of the room. Caught between the two of them, Taggart had to push himself against the wall so they could talk across his chest. The Major looked from Paul to Moor and back again. "Perhaps you might like to do your estimate outside and come back to me with an answer by Fourteen-hundred. Either way I'm sure you can use everything on offer and I will ask the Sergeant-major to make the bids accordingly. Now if there's nothing else, let's get to the day's training."

The men immediately rose, scraping chairs as they did so. Paul and Moor returned to the block together but as soon as they were in the office, Moor told Paul to sit down: "Listen Sir. You've done a good job from what I can see, without a Senior NCO in the Platoon. Delta's done what he can, but he's only a screw. And you ain't been a recruit instructor, so don't understand how training's done. It's got to be realistic but it's also got to be progressive. You can't just go do a live ambush without doing the workup first: we does pairs fire and manoeuvre before we does section. And we does section before we does platoon, get it? It's the way of things. Go tell Casenove we'll use the live ammo but we'll do a range day first. Then we'll do a live ambush when the blokes are good and ready for it. Understand?"

Paul had underestimated Moor. There was more to him than muscle. He would need careful management. When he informed Major Casenove about his revised training plan, the Major was quick to notice Moor had got his way: "Listen Paul, you are on a formal warning. You are in charge of this Platoon, not Moor. Leadership means dominating the environment as well as inspiring others. Moor is part of your environment. I'll be here to support you, if you need advice, but otherwise it's up to you."

Paul felt himself colouring.

"Remember this: Sergeant Moor on your side is unstoppable. Sergeant Moor against you will be unmoveable."

# Montgomery Lines, Aldershot;
# February 1996

It would take time. On the graduate entry programme for Aldi they had been taught about team building; how colleagues had to be allowed to 'storm' before the group would become a team and reach its full potential. Paul had not seen the truth of it at the time, still aglow, as he was, with university socialism. Then at Sandhurst they had been less encumbered by leadership theory, but had been lectured at length about *character*. The relationship between the sergeant and the officer was critical, they said. A happy Sergeant's Mess meant a good battalion. *If you get invited for a drink within six months, you are doing extremely well.* After only a few days Paul was painfully aware of how Moor's return had unbalanced the fragile craft he was trying to helm.

Lance-corporal Quinn lived in Bristol. On the Monday after Moor's return, he appeared in the block at Zero-nine-fifteen, missing the morning parade by over an hour. When he appeared, hurriedly nipping through the NCOs' room and mumbling that he was sorry, the traffic on the M4 had been a nightmare, Paul had stared at him with angry disbelief. He was disappointed. Quinn showed promise and Paul had been giving him more and more responsibility. Now he would have no choice but to discipline him. The Platoon had to know that skipping a parade was unforgiveable. It was week one, day one, lesson one: be on time, in fact be five minutes early. And it was a reasonable certainty that putting a Lance-corporal on a charge would end in him being bust down – *the hardest rank to earn and the easiest to lose*. He was about to shout after him, calling him into his office, when Moor cut him off: "Quinn," he bellowed, and the soldier stopped dead. "Get up earlier next time, or you'll answer to me." The soldier turned, nodded and grinned: "Yes, Sergeant." He disappeared into his room to appear, correctly dressed for the day's training, ten minutes later.

Paul didn't know what to do. There was nothing he could do, not now. Moor had stolen his thunder, undermined him even. Now everyone would think that being late was acceptable.

After finishing the morning brief he asked Moor if he wouldn't mind a quick chat; a quiet one, in the office. Therein, Paul perched on the edge of the desk while Moor stood like a mountain, his arms folded, blocking out the light from the cracked window. Paul grasped for a way to introduce his concerns. His mouth wavered as he sought the words.

Moor pre-empted him: "He won't be late again."

Paul was flustered and embarrassed. It wasn't Quinn who looked clever; it was Paul who looked as if he was not in command: "But..."

"But what Sir?" Moor placed his hands on his hips.

"But next time I expect you to discuss things before you go letting people off a charge..." Paul said.

"Why?"

Paul frowned. This was downright insubordination. "Look, Sergeant Moor. This is wrong. Quinn is a senior soldier, a lance-jack in fact. The junior soldiers look to him. He's a..."

Moor cut him short, his voice a coarse growl: "Sir. His girlfriend's just had a miscarriage. She's had one before and they've been trying for kids for two year. Bennie, her name is. He told me on Friday and I said he'd be all right coming back Monday morning. It's not much. If a bloke's away from his family all week the extra night means nothing. It's just admin this morning. It won't happen again because I said so. And he promised. It's nothing."

Paul's mouth hung open. "I didn't know that. I didn't…"

"Well you fucking should of," said Moor, baring his teeth. "If you want to inspire these men, you better fucking know what's going on in their lives."

# Dartford, East London; February 1996

When it was dark, Liam Gerard left the flat and walked down the road, taking the snicket down onto Crayford Way. He turned right, following the curve of the road past the garage and the little park. With so little traffic, he could hear the indistinct murmurs of the announcer at the dog track.

It was time.

John Major had been told what they wanted but was still prevaricating. It was obvious he was pushing any commitment to past the election in a year or so. That way he'd never be blamed. He was a wily old sod, that one; not quite the fool he looked. Command had said they wanted something special, something that'd tell the Brits the ceasefire was over good and proper. If they were going to fuck around, we'd play the long game too. It had been said before: we only have to be lucky once. They have to be lucky every time.

Liam smiled to himself. It had been his suggestion, the square of big city banks. He'd worked out exactly where a bomb would do the most damage and what time of day would make the biggest impact.

Reaching the main road he walked briskly and found that his sense of purpose made him unafraid of the pack of teenagers balancing on the fence. He was a warrior, a soldier of Ireland. His time had come, once again.

Once inside the phone box, he dialled and the phone was answered immediately.

"Yes."

"It's Liam. It's set, just as I said before. I was there today and there's no police, none at all."

"Undercover?"

"No way. I sat there for hours. There's nobody there. You could easy park a tipper truck and walk away. No one would think anything of it. There's always broken down buses and stuff in London, always."

The line was silent.

"JP?"

"Yes Liam."

"Can I ask you a question?"

"What question's that Liam?"

"Well it's just... I'd like to know what plans you'd have for me afterwards. After this... happens?"

JP was a smoker. Liam listened to his breathing. The teenagers appeared, loping across the walkway to the pub. They looked at him askance. One of them shouted *poof* at no one in particular. Another threw a cigarette aside making a shower of little red sparks.

"How do you mean Liam?"

"I mean," Liam said, "Will you need me again? Or would I be best staying here, under cover, going back to sleep? There's new ideas I could be..."

"You'll do what the organisation wants and what the organisation says, Liam."

The line went silent. He was glad JP could not see him shaking. Sooner or later he would have to tell Mo the truth.

# Canning Town, London; February 1996

"You can tell me if you want, Pauly," Clare said as they lay in her narrow bed on Saturday morning.

"Sorry, love," Paul responded after a while. "Just something at work, that's all." Clare nestled against his rigid body, resting her head against his shoulder. For a moment she nuzzled him but quietly ceased when it garnered no response. His mind was elsewhere so she stroked his chest until he made a move to undress her. Then she let him take her, let him unburden himself inside her, felt his weight upon her. Afterwards, lying interwoven with each other like ivy round a church gate, he whispered: "Thank you Clare; thank you love," making tears come to her eyes.

That afternoon they took the train into town so that he could plunder the army surplus shops for the latest bits of kit he needed: a lightweight sleeping bag and a set of permanent pens. Still buoyed by their morning exchange, Clare happily followed him from shop to shop, holding his hand when the crowd allowed it. Once, when he was busy looking at a rack of camping gadgets, she nipped quickly to the chemist next door so as not to repeat the risks she had taken that morning.

Later that evening she offered to cook but Paul insisted on getting a takeaway, which they ate in the living room watching *Saturday Night Live*. Afterwards, Clare took the plates to the kitchen, leaving Paul chuckling to himself. She stacked them next to the sink and squirted washing up liquid into the bowl. She tested the water for temperature and added more hot from the boiler on the wall. Paul's laughter echoed through from the living room.

She felt the tension in him, even though he denied it was there. Providing for him, calming his soul, made her feel richer than anything money could buy. She was drying the glasses and restacking them in the cupboard when he came through to get a fresh beer from the fridge.

"Let me help," he said, pulling a towel from the rail on the oven door. It was the one for pans, but she did not complain. Being together with him in the tight confines of the kitchen was a sensation she enjoyed. As Paul reached round her to push a mug onto the top shelf of the cupboard, he placed a hand on her shoulder and his body felt proximate and warm.

"It's been a really nice day," she ventured, her eyes fixed on the plate she was drying. "It's been lovely having you..."

"Yes, you too," he replied, quickly. "It's been really... it's been refreshing."

Clare placed the plate on the side and took a wet one from the drainer. Not the most ringing of endorsements, that comment. Her hands slowed their circular motion as a thought sank home. It was not being in the flat that made him happy, but being away from Aldershot. It was not her, but the absence of another. She bit her lip and put both plates away. He had picked up a glass and was trying to rub the grease marks from the base.

She could be angry, perhaps. She could be disappointed, but in her heart she wanted to reach out and envelop him in love. She wanted to make him feel strong, just as he made her feel safe. This was a chance for her to prove she could be trusted. "It must be really hard at work," she said. "You have been so... so worn down since Christmas. Do you want to talk about it? We don't have to. Not if it's too... well, you know."

He would never make a poker player, especially after a drink. He glanced at her, the eyebrows knitted. She took a spoon from the dryer and wiped the bowl carefully. "It's probably best anyway. I'm not sure I would understand."

"It's not that," Paul answered quickly, placing the glass down and pulling himself up onto the worktop, out of the way. "It's not that you wouldn't understand. It's that you don't know the blokes and what they're like. I've told you about Bryan Moor. He was in the Falklands. He was very badly injured."

"This is the same man who was released from prison for that shooting... ?"

"That's him, sort of. He didn't shoot anyone though..."

Clare continued drying the cutlery and placing them one by one in the tray in the drawer. Paul often used the Falklands as justification for someone's behaviour. *He was down south,* he would say as if the concept had a magical, almost religious implication. His face would light up when he mentioned it and she could never understand why. It had been so long ago. She had been at school. There was something on the news and perhaps, now she thought about it, there was a boy at school who had an uncle or a cousin or something... but she couldn't be sure. Then the boats came home. Her father had been delighted because Mrs Thatcher won a second term and set about the unions. Yet the war meant so much to Paul that Clare felt she must try to understand why: "Is he, well; is he a bit strange as a result? Was he affected in some way? Aren't there charities for people who need help?"

Paul laughed. His eyes were bright underneath the bare bulb: "No, he's not a charity case. It made him very focused. And right now his focus is me."

His face was fragile, she thought. He seemed determined to do things his way and yet uncertain as to what that way was. As he sat on the worktop slapping his suede boots together, she wanted to pull him into her breast, to wrap him in her arms and tell him everything would be all right. "I bet that's frightening," she said, gently touching his knee as she closed the cutlery drawer. The towel was wet but the spares were in the cupboard underneath where Paul was sitting and she did not want to disturb him. "I greatly admire how you cope with it all."

"I'm not sure I do cope, Clare," he said after a while. It was the most honest he had been for months. He was asking her for help.

The last time this happened was after Sandhurst. He had been sent to Yorkshire and made to run round the mountains for weeks on end. His feet had been terribly blistered and his back rubbed raw by the rucksack. She had wanted to take him to hospital but all he had done was cover the torn skin with sticking plaster. On the last Sunday he had been so afraid that he had clung to her, unable to say anything at all. He had been too exhausted even to make love. She had held him firmly in her arms until the duty took shape inside him. Wordlessly, he had picked up his bag, kissed her, then limped down the road to the train station. And then on the Wednesday night he had rung to say he had passed and had got into the regiment and would be posted to Oxford for the next month. He had been ecstatic. He had said he loved her, thanked her effusively for everything she had done, then rung off to tell his parents the news.

He had told her first. There was no doubt about it. It had been her dedication that got him through, and she would do so again if it was asked of her. She folded the wet towels and draped them over the oven rail, filled the kettle and pressed the switch before standing in front of Paul, placing her hands on his knees and looking into his sorrowful eyes.

"I am only just in control of the Platoon," he said at last, biting his lip. "And before Christmas I made a very bad error of judgment. It resulted in someone getting hurt. I have to carry the blame for it and I am deeply, deeply ashamed."

She wondered if he was going to cry but then he blinked and looked away before shaking his head and rubbing his face with the heel of his palm. She pulled away, took down a newly cleaned mug and made herself a peppermint tea. Paul drained the dregs from his can and rattled it. She pulled another from the fridge and bent the ring for him. He slurped the bubbles of the top and took a swig. "Do you want to watch a film?" she asked, her voice feeling strange in her throat. "I got *Rob Roy* and *Toy Story*."

He seemed grateful for the change of subject: "*Toy Story*? Excellent!" He slipped down from the counter and went through, but after she had been to the loo she found him nearly asleep on the sofa, the video unmoved from its box.

"Is it too late, Paul? Do you want to just go to bed?"

"No, no, I'm fine," he mumbled, lifting his head so she could sit where he could rest his cheek on her thigh. She sat quietly like that for a while, feeling his breathing deepen.

"You know, Paul; I don't command people the same way you do," she said, brushing her fingers along the cropped hairline on his temple. "I don't have that much responsibility. I mean, I'm just a teacher, and a trainee at that. But I was thinking about what you said.

"You see I have a problem child in my class. He's statemented. Terell he's called. He comes from a broken home. His father is absent and he's the only black child in the school. The rest are white or Asian and are, on the whole, such hard workers. Well one day this child threw the duster at me, in front of the whole class. It really hurt as well. It caught me just here, behind the ear."

The story woke him: "The little fuck! What did you do? I'd be straight on to his mother..."

"It's not like that, Paul, not in teaching. He was just testing himself, testing me. It was an appeal, you see. He wanted attention, wanted to be noticed for something other than being unable to tell right from left. He's dyslexic."

"Couldn't march then? Wouldn't make a soldier?"

"No. Well maybe, in time. The thing is – Sister Maresa taught me this – you have to find the point where you get through to them. Find the point where you reach the real person. Touch it lightly and the child will be yours."

Her voice fell away. She wound her finger round and round the spot where his hair grew in all directions. Paul sniggered. She frowned, realised what he was thinking, then slapped the top of his head: "No, not like that!"

Paul giggled, covering his head with his hands: "Touch me there again and I'll certainly be yours."

But she was right of course, he realised. And even though he was making light of her advice, there was wisdom in her words.

# Aldershot Training Area; February 1996

We are Five Platoon.

It's Zero-four-thirty. We are on exercise. The enemy are due down this track at first light. The Platoon Commander has set the cut-offs and the trip-wires and passes the message down the line: *Ambush Set.*

Nobody moves. For the first hour, you're still warm from the insertion. Your heart pumps. The stars are clear and beautiful against the black-blue sky. But then it clouds over and starts to rain. The sweat freezes against your skin. You start to shake. Your eyes get heavy and you rest the lip of the helmet against the rear sight of the rifle. There's a snuffle from nearby and TP stretches out a boot to tap Dicko on the leg. Sleep's for civvies. We are Five Platoon.

By the third hour you're so cold your fingers don't work. You slowly, silently, pull a boiled sweet from your top pocket and slip it into your mouth. You unwrapped them before leaving the harbour so the inside of the pocket's all sticky. You enjoy the saccharine taste and when it's been in a few minutes, crack it open with your teeth, ducking to muffle the noise.

At about Zero-five you get your second wind. You get warmer as the light improves and you can make out the tree trunks and ferns on the other side of the killing area. You check your weapon. There's ants on the ground but it don't matter. It's nice being close to nature, dark and low in the forest. The darkness is our friend.

At the sound of steps we tighten inside. The enemy enters the killing area and we empty our magazines into them, become blinded by the flash and burned by the hot, discarded rounds. The enemy are in tatters.

We are Five Platoon. We destroy the enemy, collapse the ambush and tab back to the harbour in under an hour. We are pleased with the kill. The Boss is doing OK. Major Casenove watched it all and said we were good.

But here's the thing, right? If you have the skill and discipline to do this, why the fuck do you have to shout a warning? In Ireland you get given rules of engagement, the Yellow Card it's called. It says you have to shout a warning – *Stop army or I fire* – before opening fire. What's the fucking point of that?

## Montgomery Lines, Aldershot; February 1996

The following Friday, after the ten-mile march that marked the end of the working week, Sergeant Moor asked Paul to approve his nominations for those who would remain behind on guard duty for the weekend. Paul looked at the list and nodded; it seemed fair and unbiased and he briefly met Moor's eyes, thanking him for asking. As he did so, his attention was captured by cheering from outside the block. On the gravel below the office window, Rolly and Sergeant Taggart had their Platoon in a circle, deciding their share of the guard rota by tossing coins. Taggart was making laconic quips to the platoon and Rolly, sharp as a pin, riposted with equal speed. The Platoon cheered as each man was either selected or relieved of duty.

Paul watched Taggart with envy. Rolly always seemed to be having much more fun than him. He looked across at Moor, wondering if his expression briefly softened but then the Sergeant shook his head, growling, "You earns it Sir," before striding out of the room. Paul sank into the office chair as if he had been punched in the belly.

An hour later, having done nothing more than stare at the wall, he said farewell to the orphans staying in the block over the weekend, and walked slowly back to the Mess. He felt sombre and tired. In the car park by the front of the Mess, Rolly was on his bike, pulling the visor down. The pair made plans to meet up that Saturday in South Ken, half way between the flats of their respective girlfriends. Rolly sped off, raising one gloved hand.

Paul took a shower. It rejuvenated him. Jumping into his car, he drove angrily up to London, keeping the nose of his Escort up to the tail of the car in front until it pulled out of his way. He got round the M25 before it clogged and was driving through the East End before Fifteen-hundred. He was pleased with his journey time. Anger was good. Parking outside Clare's flat, he sang along when an old U2 song came on the radio: *How long, how long must we sing this song?*

On the kitchen table a note said Clare had gone to the doctor's. She'd be back by eight and he should get dinner for them both and keep it warm. Paul relaxed on the sofa to read the newspaper until it got dark then, just before *The Simpsons* started, nipped out to get some beer and the evening's curry from the parade of shops on Freemasons Road. He watched the news at Eighteen-thirty and wondered what he could usefully do until Clare got home. The Channel Four news had just started when the whole house shook. The sash windows rattled in their frames. Car alarms went off in the street. An explosion like that had to be a plane crash.

Paul ran to Clare's room where he could look out onto the street. The planes were still stacked up, their lights forming a descending line towards the runway. Under the streetlights people were coming out of their houses to ask each other what the noise had been. Sirens streamed past, unseen, on the main road. People looked around, aimless and bovine. He was an army officer; he should be doing something. Taking care not to lock himself out, he went out onto the street but once there found himself as uncertain as everyone else.

"They say it's a bomb darling, a train station in the Isle of Dogs. It's the Irish, no doubt, bloody heathens. It's already on the wireless." The old lady from next door had a radio pressed to her ear. Paul thanked her. It was the first time they had exchanged words. "You're the boyfriend aren't you? The one in the army?" Paul nodded, a little surprised. "Clare's such a lovely girl," she continued. "So thoughtful. Do you know..."

Clare. She could be on that train.

"Look I'm sorry," Paul cut her off, "Has the radio said exactly where the bomb was?"

The woman realised what she had said: "Oh I'm sorry dearie. Is Clare not home? And there's me chatting away. No they ain't said yet. They ain't said where it was exactly. Just it was a train station." Her other neighbour came out of his house; a black man with his hair plaited neatly along his head. "Here, Warren! Do you know where it was, the bomb? This young man is Clare's boyfriend. You know Clare don't you? Lovely girl from this door here; a teacher. She might be coming that way..." Warren shrugged and said he didn't know. The old woman turned back: "Do you know, you might try calling the police..." Paul thanked her but said he would wait inside, pulling the door closed before she could say anything else. There was very little he could do.

The Channel Four news showed the first film clips towards the end of the programme and there was a single-sentence statement on Radio Four at Twenty-hundred. A second and third wave of sirens sped past in the distance. Then at last someone said it was near South Quay and Canary Wharf. It had not been on the main east-west line running from Bank station. There was a chance she would have missed it.

The trains would be disrupted now. Taxis would be non-existent. If he hadn't had so many beers he could drive, but didn't know where she was. Leaning out of Clare's bedroom window he watched people in the street returning home.

The phone rang. Paul only heard it after three rings and was slow to pull himself back through the window and run through the flat to the kitchen. The answering machine kicked in as he got to the handset. "Fuck!" He waited to see if anyone left a message but the line went dead. There was no recall number.

What else could he do? What else would be useful? He should keep calm. The front door opened and heavy feet plodded up the stairs. It was Yvonne.

"Oh Paul. Hello. Where is Clare? There's been an explosion on the railway. Is she here? There is no taxi anywhere."

"No. She was in town. She left a message."

"Oh no. Where has she gone?"

"Town; that's all I know."

"What is she doing there? Why has she gone into town on a Friday night?" Yvonne was still in her raincoat, a scarf wrapped round her neck and bags of shopping in each hand.

"I honestly don't know. Doctor's I think. Look... why don't you settle in and I'll make you a cup of tea?"

Yvonne smiled. "Oh yes, thank you Paul. Very nice. You must be worried. I'm sorry. Is there anything you want to do?" Placing the shopping on the table she removed and folded her coat onto the chair next to the bin then reached out to place a hand on his arm. "Don't worry, Paul. Clare is fine."

But was she? Making some tea, a terrible thought crossed his mind. Would he be upset if she had been killed? Would he really? Would having his girlfriend killed by the IRA give him some special kudos?

The front door banged shut; a sigh.

"Clare!" Yvonne cried, clapping her hands. "You see, Paul! God is great, no?" Breathless, Clare entered the kitchen, her face flushed.

"We were worried about you!" said Yvonne. "We thought you had been caught up in the bomb! Are you OK?"

Paul stepped forward to take her coat and kiss her. Clare pulled a set of earphones from her head. "What bomb?" she said.

# Montgomery Lines, Aldershot;
# February 1996

"We were right in it, right there. My lass, Clare, she was held up for hours. The bomb hit the train in front of hers." Paul leaned back on the rear legs of the plastic chair, his feet on the table in the NCOs' room. Chink was ironing a shirt and the other two were bulling their boots ready for the morning parade.

Sergeant Moor, arms folded and leaning against a locker, shook his head: "She was lucky." He paused then growled, "Wish to fuck my wife was there," making Delta and Weston chuckle. "That's the end of the ceasefire, sure as a pound to a pinch of shit. The boyos are back on the field now. Maybe you'll get a medal after all, Mr Illingworth Sir."

Paul pulled a face of mock thanks and the men laughed again.

"An emergency tour: Armagh for Crimbo, bet you a tenner," said Weston.

"Marching Season," said Delta.

"Sitting on your bergen in a shed in Palace Barracks waiting for Brigade get their act in order," scoffed Chink.

The men quietened into their morning chores and Paul looked happily from one to another. Moor started chuckling to himself; a sure-fire indication of a story: "Wait till you hear this one – you'll like this. My first tour of the province, right? This was back in Eighty-one when those dumb fuckers were refusing their scoff and painting walls with shit. We was doing a foot patrol out by Newtownards or the like, just to show the proddies we love them too. I was a buckshee tom back then and the section commander was this bloke called Jerry Hayfield; Haymaker he's known as.

"And so we're going down this road and in them days all the wives are out with their daughters. They'd do anything for a squaddie in the family, and the women, they was something else."

"Bonny?" asked Paul.

"Honeys, every one. I marries one after coming back from down south. That was before the dragon, but that's another story. So Haymaker's decided he's gonna do a little house search of his own and he's got the whole section in the living room, apart from me. Muggins here is left out on the street, back to the door, sweating like a fat lass at a disco. And then after thirty minutes the crowd has stopped staring at me and I'm just standing there like a dickhead, weapon at the low port and the door opens behind me and I'm pulled inside by Haymaker and told to get into the kitchen – the lady of the house is asking for me.

"So in I go and there she is, sitting on the kitchen table, legs apart and before I knows it she has me by the hair and I've me nose in her axe-wound licking her out. But what d'you know, fucking Haymaker'd already been there. I've me tongue getting a mouthful of his sloppy seconds and the blokes are in the corridor laughing their heads off when I start choking..." The Corporals all pulled faces, mewling at the thought. "And then the dirty old bint slaps me back down. *Don't play with your food, sonny Jim,* she says."

"Aargh, that's rank!" laughed Westy.

Paul, shoulders shaking, checked his watch and the happy smile froze on his face: "I'm late. I've got to see the Adjutant in five. See you later lads." In a second he was gone and a silence settled around the room.

Weston placed a shirt in his locker, taking care not to crease the freshly ironed sleeves. Delta offered his boot cleaning kit around but with no takers, put it away. He did up his shirt buttons and straightened his belt. Chink Hudson locked the padlock on his door and slipped the keys into his pocket. He then thumbed through a training pamphlet to remind him of some of the finer points of the lesson he was to take that morning.

"So what d'you think?" said Moor. The Corporals looked up. "What do you think of the Platoon Commander?"

The Corporals did not respond immediately. Their loyalties had been tested since Moor had returned. They had got used to Paul in his first year and had grown to like him. Moor had turned the clock back.

"I think he's a good egg, Beefy," said Delta. "He worked hard when you weren't here. And his assessment of the blokes in their reports is spot on."

"Couldn't navigate to save his fucking life," said Weston, but he was smiling as he said this. An officer with a map was always a liability. "But he's learning."

It had come close, up on the high ground during the competition. They all knew that. If Mr Illingworth had given in they would have written him off for a weakling. But he'd stuck it out. He'd gripped Delta when he needed gripping.

"So what's new?" asked Moor.

"Nothing Bryan," says Weston. "I think he's all right, just as Delta said. And he's not a gobshite like that cock Rawlins downstairs."

Bryan Moor looked round the room. "So am I being too hard on him or what?"

Delta and Weston glance at each other. They both thought so but had not dare say. They nodded and Moor shrugged: "OK. So I'll lay off him a bit. He's all right really. He needed to be put in his place, that's all."

Throughout this exchange Chink Hudson had been tapping a pencil against his teeth. Being clever, his peers treated him with a cautious distance. He now looked like he had something to say but was wondering how to, the pros and cons of action or inaction bouncing around his mind: "I think you are being too hard on him, Bryan. But there's something else you'll want to know." The others stopped as he reported how the young officer had unpacked the box of Mercy's kit to swap his fleece for the soldier's. The incident had itched inside his memory. He had been unable to work out why it bothered him, but now he knew: "If you ask me lads, Mr Illingworth's diffy the full issue of integrity. He's not to be trusted; not always."

# Clapham Common, London; March 1996

Liam Gerard slowed down when he got to the duck pond. Mo had stopped to retie the thin leather laces on his new shoes. When he had finished, he ran to catch up, hands in pockets, elbows angled outwards and body twisting.

He had become clingy of late, sugary. It made Liam squirm to be so blatant in public. Mo's hand appeared on his arm, pulling him across the railing: "Come on, Fergie; let's feed the ducks..." Liam jerked his arm free and shook his head. He was not in a mood for frivolity and his insides were as taught as a drum skin. He walked on a few hundred yards past the college and sat on a bench, pulling his chin into the upturned collar of his jacket. Out on the grass, a man played football with his children.

When he caught up, Mo sat down too, but not very close.

"What's wrong, Fergie?" he said. "You're cold to me, lover. You're being really uncool at the moment. I don't know what I've done."

His thin face looked childlike with the bottom lip sticking out. Liam didn't know how to say what he felt; the weight of it was just too much. "It's not you, Mo," he said at last. "It's me, I've a lot on my mind. Stuff going on at work, that sort of thing."

A pigeon flapped down under the bench and jerked round their feet, tilting its head. Another joined it, and both walked round each other in fast circles. "Have you... have you found someone else?" Mo couldn't look at him. He was staring at the ground. His new shoes were scuffed already. "I so wanted to come here with you, to show you off," he said, indicating a poster on a notice board. "Pride's here, not at Brockwell, this year. I want us to go together. I've already booked tickets and I think you'd love it. It's really liberating, really exciting, you know?"

Liam said nothing, but kept his chin hidden inside the collar of his coat. The idea of a gay festival seemed too far-fetched, surreal even, for where his mind was.

Mo looked across at him: "Look, Fergie, you're not the only one from a conservative community, you know. My Dad's Egyptian. They'd stone me back home. They'd bury me, or at least flog me." He looked down.

Liam could still not put his thoughts into words. It was just too complex, too large. So that Mo would not notice, he slipped the mobile from his pocket and checked the screen. No one had rung. Something must be wrong: JP never failed to call back and he'd rung him seven times now. He slipped the phone away.

"Mo, it's not about you and it's not about being... about being the way we are. It's something else. It's something back home, something about what's happening that I can't reconcile..."

Mo pulled a face then slid over, placing his hands on Liam's sleeve. "So tell me, Fergal! Tell me! Is it about that bombing? Is it about the war? I see it on the news and I watch how it makes you cringe..."

This was surprising.

"It makes me cringe?"

Mo removed his hands, his voice singing: "Yes! When-ever it comes on, Ireland that is, you tighten up. You turn in on yourself like a... like a hamster when it settles down to sleep."

"I do not."

"You do, Fergie, every time."

"Do I fuck."

"You do. You do so. And you're doing it now. Whenever Ireland comes up, you close down inside yourself. I just think you'd be better letting it out, telling me what's on your mind."

His skin was pure and brown and glowing and his lips creased into a pout. Liam reached out and touched his knee.

"I'm trying, Mo," he said. "But it's hard."

Mo nodded, quietly, brushing something off his cheek. "Well I'll see to that later," he said.

# Canning Town, London; March 1996

It was Wednesday. Paul had been away for twelve days and Clare hoped he would ring if he could. The Wednesday call was a quiet haven in the ocean of her work, a respite from the storms, however brief. It was important to her. Just the sound of his voice was enough to see her through.

She had something important to say, something special.

In the bedroom mirror, her face was unchanged. She had expected it to be different, to show the rosiness, the beauty that only women can show. Her tummy felt tight with excitement. Her heart raced the more she thought about it. How wonderful to have been blessed like this, how precious the gift of life.

Sitting on the bed and looking out the window, she counted again in her mind. She had to be. She was never more than a day or two late and now the yeasties had gone she was much more comfortable. They ought to talk about that as well, she thought, but it was a minor thing in comparison. It could happen on its own, after all.

Clare felt life blossoming. There was so much love and so much beauty all around her. How she hoped Paul was with her to share her joy.

# Montgomery Lines, Aldershot; March 1996

"Have you seen the news, Samuel?" the Commanding Officer asked. "Another gun-nut went crazy this morning, this time in Scotland; a primary school of all things."

"Despicable, isn't it Colonel? Quite incredible," Major Casenove replied. "One wonders how such people are allowed access to weapons."

The Colonel stood by the window overlooking the guardroom. Having just returned from prayers with the Brigade Commander he was wearing full service dress and medals, an MBE and Military Cross adjacent to each other at one end of the row. He sipped at his coffee, holding the saucer carefully by the rim. "Indeed. Indeed," he said. "But no doubt the government will over-react, just as they did with the dogs act."

"For sure." The Major nodded, removed his beret and sat where the Colonel indicated. "But you'll be pleased to know there's already a joke going round the lines."

"The blokes at their best?" The Colonel raised an eyebrow.

The Major nodded: "What do you call the three R's in Dunblane Primary?" The Colonel shrugged. "Reading, writing – and reaction to effective enemy fire." Both men shook their heads, chuckling. Civvies would never understand.

With the Major sat, the Colonel took his chair behind the leather-topped desk. "The reason I asked you here Samuel is to give you a warning order about what is coming your way. I don't intend to issue a formal set of orders, unless directed to do so, but I thought you might like to know what your primary tasks will be for the next six months.

"You will of course be aware of the overall G2 picture but there are some specifics you should be cognisant of. Firstly, Scott Ritter's inspection team are convinced Sadam Hussein is developing sarin for weaponisation. The Americans are applying pressure on Russia and China in the Security Council to up the ante against him, but they've trading interests which they are loathe to lose. The SC is in something of a stalemate.

"Secondly the aftershocks from the Bosnian war are expected to ripple across the rest of the former Yugoslavia, probably to Montenegro first. Bosnia was a bloody mess and the UN are keen to ensure we don't get caught with our trousers down again. The Americans think this is a European problem and it's therefore up to us to sort out. HMG are prone to agree. There is talk of a significant increase in budget and, God forbid, a Euro-corps, whatever that may be. Trouble is, of course, that any deployment will likely be from the armoured rather than light role brigades.

"Thirdly there is, though the government has not made a big deal about it, a small advisory team in Rwanda. They have been looking at ways to shore up the state infrastructure in the wake of the genocide. The civil war has not quite gone away and a rebound wave of killings is still a possibility – although I should stress that there is scant political will for intervention on any particular scale in Africa – no one wants to put the noses of the French out of joint.

"And of course our Irish friends are warming up again after that awful blast in London. There's another attack expected on the mainland although we don't know exactly where. Int suggests the north, perhaps Liverpool, but that would be a little odd given the number of expatriate Irish in the city. They're bombing their way into a stronger negotiating position and need to do so before a general election next year. They're certainly no fools, the IRA.

They've got us by the short and curlies. The poor old PM stuck his neck out to get them to the table and they've knifed him. They're betting on a change of government, I expect. There's a small cell in London run by someone you might recall, a young bomber called Gerard – the Engineer."

The Major raised his eyebrows, nodding.

"But what this means for us is that we have three possible deployment options on the table. Peace support operations in eastern Turkey to protect the Kurds; a stabilisation force in Kigali; and an emergency tour to Ulster. We're not down for another tour until end Ninety-seven, but *if* there's an election next year, or *if* there's a significant increase in violence... well I'm sure you can draw the picture for yourself.

"In short, it seems as though the operational tempo is beginning to ratchet up. We could well be quite busy before long. And as always we need to be ready for anything. The reason I'm telling you is so that you can start to prepare your men for a broad spectrum of operational possibilities. Although the compass tends to point that way, we need to think wider than just Northern Ireland. We need to expect the unexpected.

"I'm going to want you to be the lead Company in any operation we have to undertake. There is precedent for this, and the men will expect as much. You will start to see an increase in training ammunition and access to training estates, that sort of thing. We should even expect to get a few jumps in. The RAF have been told to allocate resources away from the Balkans to meet our needs. We should also, thank god, expect to get another batch of recruits coming through very soon. RHQ has promised me priority despite the fact that the other Battalions are on operations in Ulster."

The Colonel paused, looking carefully at Major Casenove to ensure he had picked up the nuances of his brief. The smile spreading round the Major's face told him that he had.

"But like I say," the Colonel continued, "there's no need to be explicit about this just yet. I'm just giving you a feel for the direction of advance."

The Major tried hard to suppress his glee. "Certainly, Colonel," he said. "It would be good to get some more men; my platoons are down to seventy-five per cent manning."

"Yes I know, Samuel, I know. It's the same across all the companies and of course it's something I've been batting around for some time with the Regimental Council."

"I know you have Sir, I didn't mean..."

The Colonel raised a finger and the Major fell silent. "We are where we are," he said.

After a moment's pause, the Major asked: "Should I tell my young officers do you think, Colonel?"

The elder man reflected before shaking his head slowly. "I don't think so; not until we have something more definite. Are they capable do you think? You have Rawlins and Illingworth don't you? No officer yet for Six Platoon, I fear."

"No, but I have Colour-sergeant Edwards covering and he's doing very well; a good grounding for a Warrant, certainly."

"And the officers?"

The Major pressed the tips of his fingers together: "They're close friends, having come through together. But they're quite different. You'll get my notes for their annual reports very soon. Each has his strengths and weaknesses. Both are regular night time visitors in the Hospital Mess, I gather. Rawlins is the better long-term bet I should think. He has a natural air of command and demonstrates this without being a super-soldier. He knows how to draw a line between himself and his men. Illingworth is the caring sort; very dedicated but somewhat over-faced by his NCOs. It didn't help him not to have had a sergeant for the first year – my fault – but he's got one now."

The Major smiled to himself.

"Was that a good choice, do you think? Giving him Moor?"

"Moor's manner is rather aggressive Colonel – but that's the nature of our soldiers; they're not shrinking violets. It's doing young Paul good to learn to master him. He needs to develop a bit of steel and bite."

The Colonel nodded slowly. "Well it is your decision and no one knows Moor better than you, Samuel. But I'm not sure about your assessment of the two officers. Rawlins is certainly a shiny child; he would look good in overalls I'm sure. But I was watching young Illingworth the other day, the way he spoke to his soldiers and the way they responded. There's something about him. Now that he is a substantive First-lieutenant, and has come off that formal warning, we should up the ante on him perhaps; push him a little harder and see if he still swims."

# Canning Town, London; April 1996

Clare could always rely on Kirsty when it really mattered. All it took was one call and she was round after work: "Oh my god! Oh my god! Get out of the way. Doctor coming through! Let me look at you! Briggsy, you old tart! What would the nuns say, eh?"

Clare cried when they hugged and Kirsty cried in sympathy. Then they both cried and hugged again until eventually, swollen-eyed, they sat on the sofa holding hands, looking at each other.

"So you haven't told him?"

Clare shook her head. Her lip quivered but she took a sharp intake of breath and forced herself out of the fear. "No. I don't know how to. He's never here and at the weekends, when he can come, it's impossible to get through to him. He's..."

"Clare, that's shocking. He's the father of the baby! You have to let him know. You have to make it clear to him what his job is now..."

Clare nodded but then pulled a ragged hanky out of the sleeve of her cardy and started worrying it. Kirsty counted on her fingers: "We've missed Mother's Day... and Father's Day, so you can't give him a card. Have you got the tester? Could you leave it lying around?"

Clare shook her head: "Doctor told me. I had to have a blood test..."

Kirsty thought, then: "OK, what about this. You wait till he's coming home. You get a little bun from Greggs and put it in the oven..." Her smile was so broad and so genuine that Clare could not stop herself snorting, bursting at last into a chortle and then a peel of laughter. Having friends like her was such a blessing.

Her father would be happy, she thought, provided she got married before it was due. And of course her Mum would be delighted; after all, she had had Clare at about the same age. But if only she could be sure about Pauly.

Kirsty produced a bottle of champagne from her bag: "I got this on the way. You won't want a drink will you? But you won't mind if I..."

"One won't hurt," Clare said quickly and the pair snatched some glasses from the kitchen.

"Cheers Clare. Here's to a lovely, lovely baby. Ooh I'm so jealous. I always dreamed of having kids of my own; I so want to be a mummy."

This was probably the first time Clare had done something before her. She was fascinated by everything, desperate to know the details: what it was like, how did she know, what was different?

"You know what?" said Clare, "The funny thing is that after I went to the doctor's, I felt normal. It was like nothing had changed at all. In fact I keep wondering if I'm really pregnant. There's no sensation or anything, not anymore."

"Oooh Clare," said Kirsty, her face suddenly serious. "You don't think there's something wrong do you?"

# Montgomery Lines, Aldershot; April 1996

There was never a moment's rest, being an officer. It wasn't something that could be turned on and off. The responsibility was never ending.

Paul was in the block early because the Corporals' annual confidential reports needed finishing and his training notes were in the file in the office. The doors squeaked when he opened it but he stopped it banging the radiator. On the floor of the NCOs' room he found a soldier asleep in a dossbag, his head resting on his bergen as if he was on exercise. It was Scouse Horne. With Paul leaning over him, the soldier woke, sat up and pulled his face free of the hood. "Sleep well?" asked Paul.

"Oh hello Sir," mumbled Scouse before pulling his wrist free to read his watch. Seeing it was still before Zero-seven he slumped back down.

Paul left him. He probably got back late after a night out and didn't want to wake the others. Or they might have kicked him out for his feet. Had he swamped the bed? The first stirrings were coming from the rooms and still amused by the discovery, he walked quietly round to see the men rising. Scouse shared a room with Banks, Paddy Connelly and Dickinson. Banks was up, dressing, his towel on the floor by his feet. Paddy was still asleep and Dicko was staring at the ceiling, arms crossed behind his head, his Newcastle United duvet cover lying perfectly even over his body. There was someone in Scouse's bed with his face towards the wall: the large head was scarred and bald. Banks and Dicko stared at Paul and the smile faded from his face. He backed out of the room, thinking he would wait for Moor to rise. Dicko tutted as he left.

Why had he not got a room in the Sergeant's Mess? Why pick on Scouse – he was not the crow in the Platoon; that was Twat Carroll. In the corridor, soldiers nodded to him but said nothing. They all knew something. What had happened? TP was taking a piss when Paul collared him: "What's going on?"

"Don't know, LT. I was in bed. Ask them in that room."

"But you know something happened. Tell me."

The big soldier shook his head: "I saw nothing, LT. What did Sergeant say, eh?"

Paul went back to his office. Through the wall he heard Delta arrive and rustle Scouse awake in the NCOs' room: "Up you get, mate. It's Zero-seven-ten. What you doing here anyway? You shit the bed?" There was the shuffling and tugging of a doss bag being stuffed back into a bergen, the opening of a locker and the banging of doors. The voices were indistinct but the tone recognisable. "Who? Beefy? Why?" Scouse responded: "Dunno, Delta; I dunno, honest. If I knew what I'd done, like..." A distant door opened and both voices fell quiet as a deeper voice joined them. Moor was up. A door banged as someone, presumably Scouse, went back to his room. Paul heard his name mentioned and after that the voices shrank to whispers. Paul continued writing the reports.

Five minutes later the office door swung open to bang on the back of his chair. Moor apologised, snatched a towel from his locker and went to grab a shower. Paul focused on his work, expecting Moor to explain in due course. Ten minutes later Moor was in the corridor telling Private Cunningham to bring him a bacon butty from the cookhouse and to get some sugar and ten Marly Lights from the NAAFI. He then reappeared in the office and changed, still saying nothing.

Paul wondered if he was being deliberately obtuse and so forced the discussion: "Good morning, Sergeant Moor."

Moor continued tying his bootlaces, pulling them through the pairs of eyelets in turn, tightening them over the bridge of his foot. "Did you sleep well?"

It could have been going on for weeks and Paul would never have known. There had been no inkling in the Platoon morale, not that he had noticed, anyway. Nobody had whispered anything to him, the way soldiers did. Boots done, trousers straightened, Moor buckled his regimental stable belt before pushing the door closed. Paul turned round in his chair to face him, crossing his legs. "Sergeant Moor, is there something I should know?"

"My wife kicked me out last night Sir. We had a row. It's nothing I can't handle, just a domestic, a one off. I'd have got a room in the Mess but it was too late so I just dossed here. Scouse offered me his pit. There's nothing wrong with that is there?"

Paul frowned. Had Scouse offered him his bed? If he asked, the soldier would certainly now confirm it.

There was a knock on the door and Moor opened it. A hand appeared bearing a paper napkin wrapped round a roll, the smell of bacon permeating the office. A voice said, "I didn't put ketchup on it, that right?" Since Moor lived in a married quarter, he was not entitled to eat in the cookhouse. He seemed embarrassed to be caught in an act of dissembling: "Thanks, Foxy mate. That's superb that is. That's tremendous. In fact I love you like a brother. Well done." The soldier stole a glance into the office and was surprised to see Paul: "Oh hello Sir. Sorry, I didn't get you one as well. I can nip back if you want? They'll never recognise me."

Paul shook his head. "It's fine Foxy. I've eaten, thank you."

The soldier nodded, smiled and bent sideways to pull some cigarettes out of his pocket. Moor placed the bacon roll on the windowsill and reached into his locker for his wallet, scraping coins out of a glass ashtray: "That's smashing, Foxy, smashing. You're a star, you are. How much do I owe you? Pound fifty isn't it? Fucking rip off that NAAFI eh?" Moor counted the shrapnel in his hand, shook his head then pulled a note from his wallet. "Here's a fiver. It's all I've got. Keep the change. It's my turn to get the sugar anyway. Thanks for this, it's great." Cunningham looked uncertain as he backed out of the office. "Now go on, fuck off and get ready for first parade," Moor said, chivvying him away and kicking the door closed.

Paul continued to watch his face as he stripped the plastic wrapping off the fags, turned one cigarette upside down and slipped the box into his pocket. He snatched up his breakfast, gobbled it down, then screwed up the napkin before throwing it in the bin.

Above all, Paul was disappointed. He had held Moor in such high regard that he was almost unable to comprehend a decline into barrack room extortion. He did not know what to say.

Moor looked at him: "What?" The face had resumed its customary scowl. Paul felt his blood draining but could not draw his eyes away from Moor's.

"I hope that was not what I thought it was?" He wondered if Moor would now fly at him, denying everything. But he didn't; in fact he shook his head.

"It's nothing, Sir. Honest. It's nothing," and in an instant he had lit a cigarette and stormed out into the corridor to get the Platoon ready for morning parade: "Right guys. Kit on, let's get out there." There followed a scraping of chairs, the shuffling of feet and the banging of fire doors.

At lunchtime Paul managed to collar Scouse without anyone seeing them together. "Is there something I should know, Scouse?" The soldier shook his head without meeting his eyes. "Nothing Sir, honest. Nothing at all, like." Paul left it at that. There was nothing else he could do.

# Canning Town, London; April 1996

Paul stretched his feet out on the leather trunk and settled back on the sofa as the TV programme started. Clare didn't understand what was funny about the quiz show and she didn't like the arrogant, angular man who hosted, but it didn't really matter. With her head resting on Paul's thigh, she could feel his occasional laughter and sense the warm blood flowing through him. She was tense, but prepared to wait for the time to be right. After the programme ended she thought the moment had come and lifted her head, steeled for the conversation, but Paul flicked immediately to another channel to watch a movie premier: "Do you want to watch this? It's good, I heard; Sean Penn and Susan Sarandon." Clare mumbled assent although the movie looked too depressing for words. It was OK; she could wait a little longer.

Cuddled up against him she put aside a series of whimsical daydreams to consider practical things. The curtains were faded and dirty. There was a damp patch on the ceiling by the window. The carpet was truly horrible. Her wine smelled tart. If she was to have a child, where could they live? What could they afford? Would the army give them a house if they weren't married? She only realised she had dozed off when Paul shifted his hips during an advert break, saying he was desperate for the loo. In the morning they made love. Paul made no attempt to reach into the side table and she made no attempt to make him. There was no need, after all, and he felt broader and more stimulating without the smothering latex. Afterwards, she cradled his head against her chest until his breathing slowed and his body cooled, but even lying with the slug of his cock against her thigh, she felt unable to ask. There was a ribbon drawn across her lips, a doubt she had never voiced. Paul was not ready to have children.

On the previous day's shopping expedition they had driven to Richmond. His frustration with the stop-start traffic on the South Circular had reached a peak somewhere near Catford, where he had been forced to let a woman with a young boy walk across the zebra crossing. They plodded slowly. The child had radiant, coffee-coloured skin and a kicking, stubby-legged gait. The woman held his hand and briefly stooped to wipe his nose. They looked, to Clare, as beautiful as any image of the Madonna and Child. Paul had drummed his fingers on the wheel mumbling, *Come on to fuck, you fat lump* under his breath and stared scornfully at her when he sped off. Clare had been mortified; they had been stationary for less than thirty seconds.

But she had to hear it from Paul himself. Did he ever see himself having children? How would he feel if he was to find out that he would shortly become a father? If she could not ask him in a state of post-coitial somnolence, she would have to get him to come out with it in other ways.

An opportunity arose when they met Rolly and Evelyn for Sunday lunch at a chain bar near Green Park. Having ordered food, the boys started talking about their manoeuvres and laughing at the escapades of their soldiers. Evelyn and Clare exchanged the same pleasantries they did every week until Evelyn noticed she wasn't drinking and started probing as to why. Clare deflected the questions with a sigh. She was trying to lose weight, she said. But how was Evelyn's work?

Although Evelyn pretended to be carefree and blasé about her relationship with Rolly, Clare sensed this was something of an act. They had been going out for around a year, having met in Oxford when Rolly was doing parachute training. She was studying art history at a local college.

Clare asked about their plans. It had been an innocent enough question but Evelyn became cagey, twisting her hair round her fingers. When Paul got up for the toilet Clare asked Rolly directly if he would ever want children. Evelyn studied his face, as keen to know as anyone.

"Sure, of course." Rolly's smile was warm and genuine. His cheeks dimpled. Anyone could see he would make a wonderful father. Paul arrived back at the table at just the right moment and Evelyn blurted out the same question to him, her face a mixture of teasing and revenge: "How about you Paul? Do you want to have children?"

"Sure!" Paul laughed. "As long as Clare doesn't mind..."

There was laughter all round. It had been a witty response and the conversation quickly moved on before she could say anything. Did they want more drinks? Did anyone want a pudding?

She thought there would be other opportunities before Paul got the train down to Aldershot, but by the time he had slept off the lunch his mind was elsewhere. He left at six, pecking her hurriedly on the cheek and promising to ring on Wednesday.

On her own after evening Mass, Clare decided that her instinct was right.

# Montgomery Lines, Aldershot; April 1996

Five Platoon took over responsibility for the guard at Zero-eight-hundred on Thursday. At the bottom of Part One Orders, the weekly directives from the Adjutant pinned to the board in the guardroom, a note reminded the battalion that it was the anniversary of the recapture of South Georgia by the SAS during the Falklands War. In working hours, Paul's duties were to undertake the routine management checks that ensured no one was pilfering from the assets for which they were responsible. He counted the stocks of ammunition in the magazine and the weapons in the armoury. He checked the fuel levels in the tanks in the MT yard. He emptied the phone boxes and games machines in the NAAFI and took the proceeds to the pay office where the tallies were logged. He checked the mattresses and clothing in their respective stores, the meat stocks in the kitchen and the quality of the lunchtime meal, eating in the cookhouse with the soldiers.

At every juncture Paul met a jokey but polite Colour-sergeant with whom he could pass the time of day and at the same time have an interesting discussion about the news or sport or whatever was important to them. Each meeting served to remind Paul that his combative relationship with Moor was unusual. It should not be as it was. And since the other senior NCOs around the battalion were easy to talk to and did not have an issue with his professionalism or manner – they saluted him without question – Paul began to realise that the problem was with Moor, or rather his inability to rein him in.

Should he sack him? It was unheard of, a young lieutenant sacking his sergeant, especially one who had served down south. And if he was honest, Paul was not sure he had the moral authority to take such a course. He would make enemies; and if there was one aspect to his life that he depended on, it was staying in other people's good books. Major Casenove had been quite right, though it pained him to admit it.

Mulling the problem over, Paul returned to the Mess to bull up his shoes and leathers and change into his service dress for the Guard Mount and Defaulters' Parade. In his room, he spread out the financial pages of the newspaper on his desk to protect the surface, placed a tin of black Parade Gloss to the side and filled the lid with water. Holding a shoe upside down in his left hand he applied the polish in small circles with his finger then waited for it to dry. With a polishing cloth only dipped in water, he went round the shoe three, four or five times, circling to push the grease out of the leather, exhaling on it to lubricate the movement. Each time he went round the shine deepened and the reflection of the striplight behind his head became clearer. Pressing play on his tape recorder, he relaxed into his work, doing first one shoe and then the other. To finish, he did the Sam Browne belt. By the end of his labours, some two hours after starting, he had got a little bored and the fiddly straps and buckles of the sword frog did not get quite the attention of the first shoe, but they mattered less. If he stood to attention they were hidden by the wrist and nobody would see them anyway. He finished his preparations by ironing his shirt and tie (remembering to wash his hands first), shining the buttons of his jacket, and then drawing sticky tape over his beret to pull off the dust.

It was Thursday. Having not done so the day before, he knew he ought to ring Clare later in the evening, sometime between Guard Mount and the Defaulters' Parade. He made a mental note to do so and started to dress, thinking once again what he would do about Sergeant Moor.

At Eighteen-hundred, he and Moor mounted the guard, Paul striding round the inspection with confidence and élan. He made the soldiers laugh by reminding them of the South Georgia anniversary and telling them to be polite to any veterans of that operation they saw about the barracks – all of them knowing the Commanding Officer was the only one. After the inspection, Sergeant Moor fell the men out and accompanied Paul round the camp in silence. The two men separated until the final duties of the evening. Back in the Mess, Paul ate a cold sandwich left out for him by the kitchen staff. Rolly was in the bar with the other platoon commanders but Paul did not feel like joining them. It was a rarity to be sober and in a way, he enjoyed it.

There was a single defaulter at the Twenty-two-hundred parade: Private Zhukov, the younger brother of the RSM. Unlike Big Zhukov, Little Zhuk lacked any semblance of work ethic, professionalism or political savvy. Whereas the elder Zhukov would undoubtedly be commissioned, the younger one was constantly being posted from one company to the next as he fell afoul of one Sergeant-major after another. He was now in the Antitank Platoon, always a haven for the soldiers others found uncommandable. There, his sheer size could be put to use carrying the heavy missiles. He was on Defaulters' Parade for being late for a guard mount earlier in the week. If he failed the inspection, he would be summoned by the Adjutant and then placed on Commanding Officer's Orders. The CO, hating personal indiscipline, would undoubtedly jail the man, a punishment that would see him losing all his pay for the time he was incarcerated. Such a feudal outcome seemed wrong. Paul was in far too good a mood to let that happen and anything he could do to irritate the pompous Adjutant – the note on Part One Orders being an obvious bit of toadying to the Colonel – was an opportunity not to be missed.

Sergeant Moor called the soldier to attention and he snapped into position. The first thing noticeable about him was the faintest whiff of alcohol on his breath. The soldier was even taller than Paul, and so his exhalations wafted straight down into Paul's face. His eyes were clear and focused straight ahead but his chin poorly shaven, as if not done since the night before. His buttons were in good order but the buckle of the belt was off centre. One hand had tomato ketchup evident on the fingers. The boots were dull, the toecaps cloudy. Paul looked him up and down again, wondering if the man had done anything well enough to pass him. He had to help himself. The medal on his chest was dirty and the ribbon had threads peeling off at the side. Paul walked round to inspect his rear. The heel welt of his left boot was actually muddy – not dirty – but carrying a smear of mud as though he had walked across a grass verge and skidded. The jacket was misshapen at the shoulders, too small for him. His hairline was ragged and his neck needed a shave. There were sufficient faults in his dress and bearing to send the man to jail for the next millennium.

But at Sandhurst, as a cadet officer, Paul remembered being on Defaulters' Parade himself. An officer from one of the highland regiments had inspected him with such a trivial, petty eye for detail that he had thought the whole process meaningless. Inspections of this nature were relics of a bygone era.

"I'm going to pass you, Zhukov. But next time if I get dressed for you, you do so for me, OK? Fallout."

Paul stepped back to the central position expecting Sergeant Moor to give the order to fall the man out, but he didn't. Standing next to the soldier, he had an expression of unmitigated hatred on his face. Ignoring Paul, he stepped in between them to stand facing Zhukov, where he whispered in low tones. The soldier shook his head or nodded to Moor's questions. Moor froze. The soldier looked straight ahead, as still as ice.

"Have you been drinking?" hissed Moor.

"No Sergeant."

Moor leaned closer, sniffing carefully. A soldier of Zhukov's calibre would undoubtedly know all his rights when it came to accusations of being drunk. Moor continued to hiss at Zhukov who, despite a considerable advantage in height, started to shake.

The grilling went on and on. The idea that Paul had misjudged the situation penetrated his jocular mood. He should have failed the man on first count. He heard the tenor of Moor's voice change as the soldier lifted his chin and pressed his shoulders back. Paul wiped his nose. The guard commander, Chink Hudson, slid the hatch up to see what was going on with the parade but a sideways glance from Moor made him shut it again. Returning his attention to Zhukov, Moor's hiss became a growl and then finally, after nearly five minutes, he abandoned any attempt to hide what he was saying, telling Zhukov he was a disgrace and that his bearing and manner were so bad they were even worse than a pissing civilian's. Then with stiff, curt movements, he strode to the side and swept his pace stick under his arm as if it was a scythe: "Defaulter. Officer on Parade; Dismiss." Zhukov saluted as smartly as a new recruit then disappeared out of sight. Paul knew he was next.

"Sir. A little word in your shell-like if you don't mind." Moor led the way round the side of the guardroom, beyond the flag pole, to stand behind a captured Argentinian machine gun. Out of sight of anyone, he could say what he wanted: "Sir, that's the most fucking unprofessional inspection I've ever seen in this man's army. You pranced round that pillock like a fucking ballet dancer. That man's a nob. He's not fit to soldier. He should be drummed out of the army and sent back to where he belongs: in fucking prison. You, Sir, lets him off. His dress is in rag order, his breath smells of drink, his boots have been polished with a Brillo pad and he stood there like a sack of shit. He was taking the piss."

"I couldn't smell anything, I've a cold..."

"Sir, I couldn't give a flying fuck. If you comes down here again dressed like you slept in that uniform I will tell the RSM your turnout is rank and he will tell the Adjutant and you already knows what he will do."

"Sergeant Moor, I..."

"No, Sir. You fucking listen. I thought you were getting better but that display is the biggest example of cowardice I've ever seen. You've no balls. How the fuck are you gonna lead men down a two-way range if you can't pick up someone for dirty fucking boots!"

Moor's voice had risen to the point of shouting. His nose flared with each inhale. Paul glanced aside, afraid to stare directly at him any longer. Men scuttled past the guardroom and out of sight.

"Sergeant Moor, I..."

"You what Sir?" Moor was so angry that spit flew out of his mouth to land on Paul's chest.

Under the withering onslaught there was nothing left but to go for it: "Get yourself under control, please, Sergeant Moor." Surprised by the vehemence of Paul's response, Moor fell immediately silent. "Now let's discuss this. I will not be spoken to in that manner again; do I make myself clear?"

Moor's eyes widened.

"You may throw your weight around in your own Mess if you wish. You can hang as many chefs as you like for all I care. You can even impose yourself upon... unfortunate specimens like Zhukov... but I will not stand for you talking to me in that way and I will certainly not stand for you bullying the men under my command."

Moor blinked, rocking back on his heels. For a second Paul wondered if he was going to be head butted but the Sergeant frowned: "Meaning?"

"Meaning when I came into the block the other week I found you had kicked Private Horne out of his bed so you could use it yourself. Then you made Cunningham go and get you food to which you were not entitled and also told him to spend his money on your fags. This is way out of line. It is not the behaviour I expect from a sergeant, especially one as widely known and deeply respected as you."

He had pulled the punch but knew immediately it had been a mistake.

"You fucking what Sir?"

"Are you denying it, Sergeant Moor? Are you saying you did not kick Horne out of bed? If so, why was he on the floor when I arrived and you were in his bed?" Paul raised his voice. His left hand was on the basket of his sword and he felt a little ridiculous having this argument in a uniform more suited to a duel.

Moor blinked again. His face became pinched. "Ok, OK. You're right. You are right, Sir. I did kick Scouse off his scratcher and I'm sorry. It won't happen again. In fact it can't happen again cos my wife's gone back to her mother's so I've lost the quarter." He shook his head, a snarl returning to his face: "But that's not the point. The blokes respect me. And they do cos I'm straight with them. They fuck up, I tells 'em. They do well, I tells 'em. And what I see here is you ain't got the balls to grip a soldier who's so far out of line he's in fucking China!" Moor suddenly raised a hand to poke Paul in the chest: "And not only that, but Chink tells me you likes to get your sticky little fucking fingers in another man's kit!"

Paul frowned. "What on earth do you mean?"

"Mercy's fucking fleece, gyppo."

"What fleece..." Paul's stomach ran cold with realisation.

"What would the blokes think if they thought you was gonna rifle through their kit if they got slotted eh? Would they trust you, Sir? What would Major Casenove think if he got to hear of this? Would he think you had

184

an officer's integrity would he, Sir? And you're not even a fucking second-lieutenant any more, are you? You're a full fucking lieutenant and that means you should know fucking better!"

Paul's mouth fell open. His hands started to shake. Moor's eyes were cold and tight, close to his face, frightening, shocking. "It was not like that."

"Oh yes it fucking was. Chink told me. Boxing Mercy's fucking kit you swaps your manky old one for his shiny new one. You stole, Sir, from the kit belonging to a soldier absent, presumed captured. And all you had to fucking do was..." His voice became choked with rage, his eyes hypnotic, his face poisonous. "All you had to do was tape up the fucking box."

Paul could see his career ending in shame. The ash-grey eyes fixed him in his place. "Look," he stammered. "I'm sorry, right? I did swap that fleece and I recognise now that it was the wrong thing to do. I thought it harmless at the time because, well..." Paul blinked, trying to get the words into some sort of order... "Well it doesn't matter why. If you want me to return the fleece to his wife, I will do so. I will post it myself. I did not consciously..."

In the darkness, Paul's voice trails off. The two men stare at each other. Paul is on the brink of tears and a hot flush pumps fear between his kidneys. Moor's expression unwinds, slowly. Both men breathe through clenched jaws, sweat running down their cheeks. A massive fist extends and jabs Paul below his ribs, just hard enough to reinforce the point: "That's all right, Sir. We understands each other now," he says.

* * *

Walking up to the Mess, Paul found his hands would not stop shaking. It felt as if someone had swung a six foot picket and caught him in the gut. His face was long. He was tired, so tired of everything. No matter what he did, it was always wrong. He was on duty but the chances of anything happening so late on a weekday night seemed remote. He needed a drink.

The bar was empty and the barman, Private Bashford, was wiping down the tops and emptying the ice bucket into the sink: "You all right Sir? Want a drink? The usual?"

"No thanks Bash, I'll leave it. I'm on duty. You get yourself away and I'll lock up."

"Cheers Sir," the soldier said and in an instant Paul was alone, melting ice tinkling away in the sink.

Paul signed a chit, poured himself a double, sank it and poured another, altering the two to a four on his chit. The whisky warmed him with a familiar and welcome taste. The door swung open to judder against its hinges: "Oh yes! Drinking on duty eh matey?" Paul shook his head, twisting the glass in his palms as Rolly pulled up a stool and sat next to him, slapping him between the shoulder blades: "You all right, matey? Been in the wars? Ten rounds with Mike Tyson? What's up rainy face? Anything Uncle Rolly can do?"

Paul shook his head again, too tired for joviality. Rolly patted him on the shoulder and silently got himself a beer from the fridge. "Ten rounds with Sergeant Bryan Moor, was it?"

Paul looked up, surprised, then nodded.

"I'm sorry matey, I know. I saw. Clare rang earlier and I told her you were on duty and would ring later. But then she rang again, twice, so I walked down to see where you were. I knew only Little Zhuk was on Defaulters' because I was on duty last night. I wondered what was taking all that time. I saw you and Sergeant Moor having a little chat by the guardroom."

Paul blushed.

"I didn't hear anything matey, honest. It just looked like you and he were calling off your engagement, that's all."

Despite himself, Paul smirked.

"And you seemed to be doing so well of late."

Paul shook his head. Rolly's voice changed as he sat back down: "I know you've got the bad one, matey. There's not a Platoon Commander in this Mess that doesn't know that. And the trouble with Moor is that he's so well known, people keep protecting him, even Major Cas."

"Oh yeah? Why's that."

"Because he sacked him once, a long time ago."

"What?"

"It's true. The QM told me. When Cas was a Platoon Commander way back when, Moor was one of his screws."

"No way."

"Yes way. Ask the QM. Moor was one of Cas's corporals when the battalion were in Germany in the mid-eighties. One night Moor got smashed, stole a tank from under the noses of a cavalry unit, and drove it through Osnabruck smashing into cars and knocking over lamp posts. It was a wonder no one was killed."

"You're fucking joking?"

"Absolutely not."

"And so Cas sacked him?"

"Well, to be fair there was a certain weight of evidence: two hundred metres of track-damaged autobahn, an arrest warrant from the German police, four very small BMWs and a Challenger tank parked on a roundabout."

Paul laughed and when he had finished, laughed again. Rolly slapped him on the back again. "You're all right, matey. You'll be fine. *Nil illegitemi carborundum*, as my granny used to say."

Paul frowned, assimilating the news. "So he was sacked. You mean demoted? Reduced to the ranks? From full corporal?"

"No choice after what he did, matey. Casenove referred him to the Commanding Officer, and the Brig reverted him to the ranks. No pension build up, no job security, nothing. Damn lucky not to get thrown out and sent to prison if you ask me."

"That's why he's so much older than Taggart."

Rolly nodded. "Yes. And don't think I don't know how lucky I am to have someone like Tag. He's young, he's keen. He's officer friendly. He teaches me a lot but does it little by little. He's a great man."

"Yes he is."

"Nice guy, too. I've been round his house, met Kim and the kids: Kylie and Jason."

"No?"

"Straight up. And they're wee terrors the pair of them."

Paul shrugged. "Whatever. Each to his own."

"Aye aye," said Rolly, pushing himself round the barstool. "And talking of wife and kids, Clare was after you, like I said."

Paul tutted, looked at his watch, then shook his head. "Did she say what it was about?"

"No. I talked to her for ten minutes or so, just general shite cos I thought you'd be back any time and I'd hand her over. She just wanted to talk to you. Seemed urgent but she wouldn't tell me what it was." Rolly shrugged, pulling a face.

"I'll ring her tomorrow," said Paul. Her neediness was irritating.

"Fine matey. I'm off to bed. My work here is done."

Paul chuckled, shaking his head: "Yep, fuck off. See you in the morning."

But as he was leaving, Rolly paused in the doorway, looking back: "You know, matey. If you wanted, I could give you some advice?"

If it had been anyone else, Paul would have immediately told them to ram it, but since it was Rolly, he was prepared to listen: "Go on."

"It's the executive order, Paul. You've got to give the executive order. Every time a decision's needed, like the other day on the ranges when you said Weston would be target operator and Moor said Smith should do it, it's Moor always gets his way. It's not you giving the executive order."

Paul felt he had to defend himself: "That was different. I use Weston all the time because he's a sniper. To be fair it was Delta's turn. It didn't really matter that much."

"But when does it matter, Paul? When does it matter that you have the say and Moor does what he's told?"

Paul could not answer. He turned his eyes back to the empty glass.

"Listen. I'm not going to pretend I know all the answers... but you might try what I do. I tell the screws and Taggart that I want to get promoted next year. To do this they gotta make me look good. If I look good, they get good confidential reports. It's that simple." Rolly was leaning on the doorframe, one arm swinging and a chunky silver watch clinking round his wrist. Paul frowned. It was not an approach he liked. "But I'm sure you know how to inspire your men," Rolly added. "Good night, matey; I'm off to bed."

Backing out of the bar, Rolly closed the door behind him. He had not wanted to be pompous but he had certainly sounded it, Paul thought, and the more he thought about it, the angrier he became. Who the fuck did he think he was? Seething, he poured another double but didn't sign for it. He would do so tomorrow, he told himself. It was time for bed.

Taking his glass, he turned out the lights and locked the bar behind him. In the anteroom he straightened the chairs and was about to go upstairs when his eyes were drawn to the painting of Sergeant McKay. Swilling whisky round his mouth, Paul wandered over to examine it once again.

The sky in the painting was blackened with mortar smoke, the rocks and figures unevenly lit by flares and muzzle flash. The sergeant's body position was textbook: the weight low and evenly distributed, the rifle held firm and level. His face was not hate filled but quietly determined, almost serene. The dead Argentinian in the foreground lay across the parapet of the bunker, the rifle having fallen from his hands. On the butt, he had taped a picture. The subject was vague. It could have been a family photo or perhaps a Madonna. Either way it was a detail that struck Paul as incredibly sad. *Command in peace, lacking the unifying purpose of facing an enemy, is often harder than command in war.*

What do these men need from me, Paul wandered? What can I do?

But then a thought struck him. The weight of it seemed incredible. He did not know if he would have the courage to see it through as there would undoubtedly be pain along the way. But if he did it, if he saw it off, his life would be lighter. There were no officers in the painting. There were no women neither.

\*\*\*

The following day Paul said nothing to Sergeant Moor about their argument and the Sergeant said nothing in return. The pair seemed to dance round each other as if wanting to apologise but not knowing how to. It was as if they were married, Paul thought.

But there was one decision made the night before that he would not renege on. The more he thought about it the more his instinct told him it was the right way to go. He and Clare had been going out together for nearly five years. It had been good at times, often wonderful. But surely she would also know it was over. They were different people now, not carefree back-packers any longer. Now his values were formed and he had the responsibility to uphold them for others as well as himself. Recently his very presence had made her moody and erratic.

They had simply moved apart. Her job was nurturing. His was destruction.

In the Mess, the letter rack by the payphone was overflowing with unpaid Mess bills. Paul dithered there for a full minute before going to the phone and picking up the receiver.

His father wanted him to end it. Every week, when he rang home, he asked about how she was in a pointed sort of manner.

Paul dialled: zero one seven one...

He didn't love her. He didn't love her. He didn't love her and in fact he found her rather repugnant. She was fat. She was too shy for even basic social situations and not even particularly clever.

The dial tone rang out so he dialled again, faster this time: zero one seven one four nine...

A new officer, Ewan Kendell, barged in through the front door of the Mess, checked the letter rack with a swipe of his fingers then twisted on his heel to mount the stairs two at a time. He saw Paul by the phone when he was part way up, gave a cheery greeting and then apologised when he saw Paul's face: "Sorry Paul, I'll leave you to it."

Paul waited for the doors to close upstairs then dialled again: zero one seven one four nine five... No, that was wrong. How silly after all this time to make such a mistake: zero one seven one four nine *seven*...

His duty was heavy. It would hurt her. She would be angry and scream down the phone. He could not face the argument and knew he was being a coward. But it should be done right. It should be done face to face. He dialled every number except for the last. The phone clicked patiently in his ear until a rising tonal scale indicated he had timed out. A stern, teacherly voice asked him, very politely, to please replace the handset and try again. Paul partly obliged. He would do it soon.

# Dartford, East London; April 1996

It was still early. Birds were just starting their morning chorus and the faint hum of an electric milk van on the road outside disappeared into the distance. Mo was asleep, turned away from him, and Liam curled up a little so that his knees touched the silky, lean buttocks.

Milk bottles tinkled on the concrete outside. It had to be Mrs Wilson taking hers in. Or was it? She was never normally awake at this time.

When the door went in, Mo leaped out of bed screaming, his body smooth, boyish and naked in the corridor: "Oh my god! Oh my god! Fergie! Fergal wake up! There's men... there's policemen..."

Liam slipped out of bed and grabbed his dressing gown, managing to tie the belt just as the first of them slammed the door back on itself and grabbed him by the throat: "Liam Gerard I am arresting you under the Prevention of Terrorism Act 1974 in connection with the Canary Wharf bombing of February this year..."

A gloved hand squeezed his balls until he yelped. He couldn't breathe. A truncheon swept books and lamps and photos off the dresser. Mo kicked like a frog as a policeman grabbed him by the throat, pushed him up against the wall and punched him violently in the stomach. He dropped to the floor, choking.

Briefly, ever so briefly, their eyes met.

# Canning Town, London; April 1996

Clare knew it was over as soon as the first twinges of pain appeared below her kidneys. The stabbing grew worse by the hour until she had to leave work early, the first time in eight years she had done so. The final hundred metres from the bus stop to her front door were absolute agony. All she could do was hobble with tiny, uncertain steps, keeping one hand on the railings for balance. Short breaths kept the vomit down.

At last inside the flat, she curled up with a hot water bottle clutched against her belly until the ambulance came. After the doctor had discharged her, all she could do for the next forty-eight hours was groan. It took until the following Monday before she could face going back to work, but above all she was determined to put on a brave face. Paul had never rung. He must never know.

# Montgomery Lines, Aldershot; May 1996

Everyone could tell by the buzz of activity in Battalion Headquarters that something was up. The blocks were alive with rumour and counter rumour and the bombing of a Manchester shopping centre pointed clearly towards an emergency tour of Ulster. Young men pushed themselves just that bit harder in the gym. Old hands spent just that bit longer with their children.

In the briefing room, the Operations and Intelligence Officers had spent three hours preparing for the Commanding Officer's orders and rehearsing their parts. The chairs in the front row were labelled for the Company Commanders, the Quartermaster, and the Second in Command. Behind these, chairs were positioned for the captains commanding the support weapons platoons, the signals, the reconnaissance unit, and the medical section, all in descending precedence order. A slide projector was set up with the battalion laptop plugged into it. Maps were tacked to the walls and marked up with labels and string. Printed copies of the orders, peppered with acronyms, were placed on each chair. With five minutes to go, the Ops Officer nodded to the RSM who invited an assembly of officers into the room. There followed a flurry of opening notebooks, folding maps, crossing knees and clicking pens. The RSM remained by the door, as upright as a telegraph pole, keeping an eye out down the corridor: "Gentlemen, when the CO arrives I will invite you to sit up..."

Major Casenove sat in the front row, comfortably placed between the majors commanding A and C Companies. The three of them knew they were the most important men in the room, the ones who would inflict the greatest effect on the enemy. The operation that was about to unfold would be their opportunity for an MBE, perhaps even a gallantry medal. If they dared to dream a little harder, one of them would come out of this with a path cleared for a colonelcy and, possibly, the future command the battalion itself.

The captains skittered about, cracking jokes to make themselves appear cool. This made the majors relax into their chairs a little deeper. It was their moment, the opportunity for them to shine.

"Gentlemen..." At the RSM's bark, the officers sat upright to be told immediately to relax by the Colonel as he strode to the front of the room to stand with his hands on his hips and feet wide apart.

"Gentlemen sit easy, please. You will have heard the rumours but now please listen to the truth. In a matter of weeks we expect to be deploying to Northern Iraq as part of a peace support intervention, Operation Haven. The intent is to protect the Kurdish minority from further gas or conventional attacks by Sadam Hussein or his subordinates.

"That being said, it is not yet completely certain who will be the spearhead battalion for this mission. As at Zero-eight-hundred hours this morning it's something of a toss-up between ourselves and Four-Five Commando Royal Marines.

"In either eventuality we will now actively prepare for warfighting operations. This will involve specific and tailored training at Battle Group level, not least of which will be some refresher training on parachute deployment..."

A cheer, simultaneously sardonic and ecstatic, rose from the assembly to be then replaced by deep, guttural laughter. The Commanding Officer paused, riding the mood like a practiced comedian, then: "Gentlemen, I see you're all as confident as myself and obviously don't need reminding what the slipstream feels like at a hundred and twenty miles an hour." A deliberate pause, then: "But for others in the battalion…"

Laughter rose again from the floor as the Colonel turned and nodded to the Intelligence Officer, before taking a chair set apart at the side of the stage. The Intelligence Officer shuffled his notes on the lectern, looked round the room and waited for the chatter to quieten: "Sirs, gentlemen: the intelligence picture for northern Iraq dated Five, Twelve-hundred hours May 1996…"

\* \* \*

We are Five Platoon.

It's electric. You'll never know if you've not been there, preparing for war.

Gecko is on a chair, leaning forward, while Paddy squeezes the zits on his back, blotting the pus with comfy-bum. Scouse paints them with iodine and covers them with zinc oxide.

Carroll returns from the NAAFI with bars of chocolate and fags. He's started doing weights. He speaks deeper now, and slower. Last weekend he told his step-dad not to slap his mother again or he'd fuck him over. On the stairs, a bloke from 6 Platoon barges into him and in a second he has the cunt by the throat: "Fuck off you…" and pushes him away. That night, the senior blokes tell Carroll he's been in the Platoon long enough. He's not to be called Twat anymore, he's to be Bobby, his name. He can go down town and get a regimental tattoo on his shoulder, same as the rest of us.

Banks is in one of the bunks taking a cadre on the radio for One Section. We know how to use the three-fifty but the three-five-one has more twiddly bits and we have to get it right.

Genghis Khan is packing his kit again, rolling up the excess straps on his webbing and taping them up so they won't get in his way. Rosy asks for the tape when he has finished with it. He cuts off little squares which he uses to cover the threads on his smock buttons.

The Boss is giving orders to the section commanders and afterwards walks round to talk to us all. We trust him now. He's passed the test.

Sergeant Moor is in the office, on the phone. The clothing store has told Cheese Wensley they'll not exchange a pair of trousers that are torn. Beefy tells the guy at the far end that if he doesn't replace them he's gonna come over there hisself. He slams the phone down and tells Cheese to get back over there. The soldier thanks him and leaves. Half an hour later he's got new kegs packed in his follow-on bag.

It's electric.

In the evening the men sit in a huddle in the NCOs' room telling stories. Matt Steele tells us about his best mate Ginge Philby, how he was drowned in Ireland crossing a river. His rifle sling got caught on a submerged branch and he flailed in the water just inches from Matt's straining fingers. Matt hangs his head and the room falls silent. If he ever got married he says, if he ever had a son, he would name the boy after him.

The ghosts of those that went before us stand at our shoulders. They watch over us, silent and tall in the shadows. They wore the same beret and lived the same creed. They carried the torch and set the standards. We are with you, they call across the years. We will steady your aim when you are afraid. We will breathe fresh air into your lungs when your limbs are heavy. We will shelter you when the rain runs down your neck and freezes against your skin. All we ask is to be remembered, to live on in your stories as equals; immortal brethren, soldiers of The Regiment.

# Speakers' Corner, London; May 1996

Paul was sullen and uncommunicative. He was crouched against the railings, eating his ice cream tub. Clare had to stand since her ankles were swollen and her feet hurt. She nudged him with her knee and he looked up, nodding towards the man in the dinner jacket who looked like he was going to mount the dais. There was a look of concern on Paul's face and Clare nudged him again, gently but insistent, and he briefly smiled up at her before scraping the last ice cream out of the bottom of the pot. Clare took his empty, slotted it inside her own and threw them both in a bin.

She liked Speakers' Corner. Sunlight filtered through the trees and the traffic noise around Marble Arch was somehow checked by the human spectacle before her. There was such theatre to it all and today it was necessary to provide a distraction from what was becoming a miserable weekend.

The man in the dinner jacket climbed up and started preaching the way all black missionaries did on the TV. He was vigorous and unselfconscious. A man in bicycle clips raised his finger to ask a question just like the children did at school, but the preacher did not waver. A ring of men, dressed identically in red bow ties and wrap-around sunglasses, surrounded the dais nodding at everything he said. Clare thought it was great they had gone to such lengths, dressing up. In the opposite corner, a woman in a dirty fleece was handing out leaflets and speaking to passers-by in an earnest manner. She could never compete. The crowd migrated towards the preacher as he thundered on, a black book held high.

Paul suddenly turned and wove his way out onto Hyde Park between gaps in the railings, nipping quickly across the cycle path. Clare hobbled breathlessly to catch up: "Pauly, wait for me. What's wrong? Why the rush?" He ignored her and the sight of his shoulders turned away roused a hot flush of anger deep inside her. That morning she had refused his initiations of sex and he had been resentful ever since. "Pauly stop. Don't just walk off like that. Tell me what you're doing."

Paul sat on a bench by the stall where she had got the ice cream. He had his head between his knees, looking for a while like he was going to be sick, but then shook himself and mumbled something about the speaker being scary.

"Oh don't be so stupid," Clare snapped. "How can you say that? You've seen preachers before. We saw them in Kano, during that festival. He's not a Nazi..."

"He's not a preacher either, Clare," Paul replied, looking at her as if she was stupid.

"It doesn't matter what he is Paul. He's got just as much right to be here as the lady banging on about dog mess..."

Paul shook his head, the muscles on his jaw line flexing as he ground his teeth. "Clare. You won't understand, but that's the sort of gang behaviour that threatens our democracy. Did you see them all nodding like that? Did you see how he wouldn't justify his position... ?"

"I won't understand? A threat to democracy? How dare you!"

A woman on the next bench turned round to look at them. Paul stood up and strode off towards Oxford Street, snapping at a cyclist who had to swerve to avoid him. Free of the crowd, he marched on, impatient and driven. His ears were closed. His presence scalded, like curry sauce on chocolate mousse.

Clare let him go, watching the stiff shoulders recede out of view. He would have to wait for her anyway, at the entrance to Bond Street.

She turned to watch a mother pushing a pram down towards Piccadilly. Placing a hand on her belly, she pressed gently into the tender folds. If she wanted a child, she would need a man she could talk to.

# Montgomery Lines, Aldershot; June 1996

The prospect of deployment grew every day. The movement of stores from building to vehicle and racking to bergen became frenetic. The days lengthened. Characters stood out around the battalion and men started to identify who could be trusted when the shit hit the fan.

Paul was as happy as he had ever been in his life. He had found the perfect balance between purpose, ability and aspiration. Because of the training regime he had only snatched one quick and unproductive visit to London and though he had not yet told Clare, this was, in his mind at least, a trial run for being single. Sitting in his office smoking a cigarette he listened to Sergeant Moor chivvying the men to get their wills updated. The laughter and general excitement made him smile. He was doing OK.

Looking out of the window he mulled over Rolly's advice of some weeks before. In many ways, he wanted to follow it, tell his NCOs that their reports depended on the Major's view of him, but being so overtly manipulative rankled. That was not how he wanted to lead. It was not the sort of thing he could say with a straight face: Westy would snort with derision and Chink would shake his head. Delta would laugh then later come and ask for a quite word *in his shell-like,* telling him not to try that trick again. He was not in a position to start losing the respect he had earned.

Paul dare not think what Moor would do if he tried it on with him.

No. He would not say something so crass, so overtly political. Inspiring men was about finding the one thing within them that made them tick, that inspired them. You had to touch them in a way that others didn't and he knew pretty well how to do that for all of them. It always came down to knowing them, caring about them, and understanding their outlook on life. A brief recollection of Clare came to mind and he wondered why. What did she know?

Yes. That would be his way. His leadership style would not be coercive or, indeed, hiding behind his rank. It would be in knowing and respecting the trigger that all men had.

But what about Moor, he thought? That was a nut he was still to crack. And if he got Moor, all the others would surely follow.

\* \* \*

For the first few weeks, the possibility of going to war was thrilling. But having not deployed after a month and a half, excitement waned. Life became one edgy, protracted wait. Senior officers harboured doubts about their political masters. Sergeants felt obliged to enforce battlefield discipline despite the absence of a discernible battle. Soldiers quickly detected changes in the mood music and only reluctantly bent to the tedious routine that was imposed on them. The Operations Officer published a map with a thirty minute circle drawn round the barracks and the Adjutant announced that all ranks were to remain within it at all times. No one was allowed more than two cans on any one day.

On the first weekend, Paul rang home to say they were deploying, adding that he could be away for some time. Captain Oates came from Leeds; his parents would understand the implication. On the phone he had been chatty and buzzing with possibilities. *God bless you, Paul,* his mother had said. He had been silent for a while, wanting to fill the aching moment but had never quite got the words out: how much he loved them; how much he owed them. Instead he mumbled that someone else was waiting for the phone and he ought to ring off.

Since that first weekend he had rung home every Sunday to explain that they had not deployed yet and were still uncertain if they were ever going to. His parents sounded both relieved and disappointed at the same time. Paul felt rather embarrassed about it all, as if he had somehow let them down. After a month of taut anticipation, the Commanding Officer ordered the companies to rotate through a high readiness routine, each for one week at a time, until the Chain of Command decided if the battalion were deploying or not. By mid-July, B Company were on the sixth day of their first rotation as spearhead Company. The men had relaxed into the wait – one of a soldier's essential skills – and they spent the time running or playing volleyball, oiling weapons and repacking their kit; anything to keep minds busy while minimising the risk of injuries or excess laundry.

Paul became fidgety. Ninety-nine per cent of army life seemed to be getting on and off buses or standing round in a clot, sharing fags and stories. For the remaining one per cent he readily expected sheer terror, but to face this with a calm mind he needed the loose threads of his life tidied away. His kit was packed, his rifle zeroed, a new film was loaded into his camera, his will was written, his men were briefed and his family farewelled. There was only one job left and it could wait no longer.

That Saturday, Paul drove Rolly down to the station to meet the lunchtime train from Waterloo. Evelyn and Clare had obviously found each other and waved out of the same window as their carriage slowed along the platform. Having stowed them both in the back seat of his car, Paul drove out via the back roads over the Hog's Back to a small village situated by a bend in the river; a place that felt quintessentially English. Yew trees yawned above a Norman church gate, a cricket green was fenced off between the riverbank and a low-roofed pub, and there had been a wedding that morning, judging by the confetti on the cobbles.

Paul felt out of place. He had hardly been out of the barracks in the past four weeks and the civilian world seemed strangely threatening and innocent at the same time. In the pub he was quick to identify a table in the corner and sat with his back to the wall. Rolly went to the bar as Evelyn popped to the loo. Clare was in a mood: "Hello, Paul," she said, heavily emphasizing the words and he leaned forward over the table to kiss her.

"Sorry, love. How are you?"

"Good, thank you. Nice of you to recognise me."

"Yes, I'm sorry. I was just helping Evey with her bags and we were parked on a double yellow. What did you want me to do?"

"It would just be nice to be welcomed, that's all."

Paul nodded, his lips clamped shut, and leaned back against the wall. After lunch he would take them all home and tomorrow he would tell her it was all over.

Rolly returned with drinks, placing a white wine in front of Clare: "What's up? You two having a domestic? Already?" Paul looked at her, smiled, and reached out to take her hand. She withdrew it, checked her purse, and rose to go to the toilet just as Evelyn returned. She sat next to Paul, which left Rolly to manage Clare during the meal and afterwards, on the way home, it seemed as though both women had preferred it that way. Rolly was charming and sweet to Clare and Paul always found Evelyn both physically attractive and startling in conversation. The tension must be infecting them all.

Back in the Mess, Rolly and Evelyn disappeared up to his room while Paul and Clare remained in the anteroom surrounded by the papers and used coffee cups. There were other officers at the far end, under the big painting, and Paul felt suddenly self-conscious. He wanted to get a fuck before telling her. "Would you like to come up?" he whispered.

Clare shook her head. She pulled a face and shrugged. "I can't," she said. "C'est pas possible."

Paul's heart sank. She was on.

Clare shook her hair free of her shoulders: "Paul, there's something I want you to know. We talked about it at Christmas but you have done nothing to fulfil your promises. As I have said before, I am not going to keep using the pill. You cannot just leave it all to me. You have to start taking ownership of your own actions."

Papers shuffled at the far end of the room and Paul gave a sharp jerk to his head, grabbed Clare by the elbow, and escorted her up to the privacy of his room. She sat on the middle of the bed, placing her bag beside her as he pressed the door closed. She seemed to fill the space, making him unwelcome. He sat on the office chair by the desk, opening the lower drawer to rest his feet.

"Paul, I'm having my period. My cycle has only just got back to normal. In May, I was eight weeks late – and do you know why? I was, for a while, going to have..." The icy façade crumbled as her face creased, tears running rich and thick down her cheeks. "I was going to have your..."

Paul felt a cold iron inside him, solid and unyielding. His face was stone. He studied Clare with a level, uncaring gaze. Curled up as she was, sobbing, she looked pitiful.

"You never even let me tell you. You never answered the phone. You were never there," she sobbed.

Her hair was lank and as dull as Land Rover paint. He could not even face putting an arm around her.

She looked up at him: "Aren't you going to say anything? Aren't you going to speak?"

Paul looked out of the window. In the distance, a plane sliced a white scar across the sky. He wanted her gone now.

"Is this what it's come to? Is this all you can do after five years?"

His conscience pricked, he held her eyes but could not bring himself to smile: "Those five years were very special to me Clare," he said. Leaning forward on his knees, he studied the pattern in her tights, then looked up again at her face. "But I think we both know it has come to an end."

The air crystallised around them. He thought she would scream or slap him but she nodded, looked inside her handbag, took out a hanky, and wiped her nose. Paul leaned back in his chair. The relief was instant but deep inside there was a coil of shame for what he had done. In silence, he drove her to the station where they waited on a two-bar bench painted a thick lime green. They sat apart, Paul leaning forward and Clare primly upright, staring across the tracks to the platform on the other side.

"We are sorry to announce," said a mechanical voice over the tannoy, "that the Fifteen-thirty-eight London train has been delayed for approximately twenty minutes."

Paul clapped his hands and dropped his head.

"You should go," she said. "It's all right. I'll be fine."

"Are you sure?" He knew she expected him to stay but there was no point prolonging the death. He stood and she rose with him. They looked at each other. She reached an arm round his shoulders and kissed his cheek: "I would have followed you anywhere," she said.

"I know," he replied. "But I didn't want a follower. I wanted an equal."

# B Company Block; June 1996

We are Five Platoon.

We stand in a hollow square, the whole battalion formed up and ready for anything. Our bergens lie at our feet, rifles on top. Our time is now. We will prove ourselves equal of those that went before us. We are ready.

We stand in three ranks, each man an arm's length from those around him. We stand easy, waiting for the cautionary word of command, waiting for the RSM to call us all to 'shun. Then every back braces, every neck reaches for the inside of the collar and every man grows an inch.

We stand erect as we wait for the Commanding Officer; as steadfast as we would before the enemy. Each of us knows our place. We have conquered fear and deserve our place in the van of battle.

But when the Commanding Officer tells us they are sending the fucking Royal Marines, we are angry. We are spitting, cursing, kicking, fucking angry.

They tell us to hold our nerve. They tell us we've got leave instead. But we are not satisfied. We wanted war. We go down town and drink our fill and god help any fucking civvy that tries it on.

# Canning Town, London; July 1996

Stopping by one of the pollarded sycamore trees that lined the pavement, Paul changed his mind about going to see Clare. He was afraid of being seen by Yvonne or the batty old neighbour, so he turned round and ambled back towards the main road.

It had been a stupid idea, really. He would go to Rolly and Evelyn's place earlier than agreed, find a coffee shop or something, and wait there. He would read the paper. It had seemed a nice thing to do, seeing how Clare was, but he had lost his nerve. She might resent him for it. She might become angry. It never did any good to turn the clock backwards.

The walk down to the station was familiar but unfamiliar at the same time. A thick tumble of ivy fell over a wall. The newsagent's doorway was surrounded by children. The school was empty and the gates locked. He had gone home for the first week of leave, making himself useful in the garden and taking Bodger, old Mrs Sutcliffe's flatulent staffy, for walks around Baildon Moor. Then he'd met Rolly and Rich and a few of the others up in Scotland. They'd done the West Highland Way and spent a night on the piss in Fort Bill on the way down. Paul hadn't even scored in that tacky nightclub. How shit was that? After a break up he was owed a purple patch; they should be dripping off him, but he couldn't trap his finger in a door.

Rolly had invited him to stay at Evelyn's for a few days and then he was Duty Officer for the last week of leave so would be living on camp. At least he'd have something useful to do, something that would stop him thinking about Clare and how badly he had treated her.

Paul clambered up the steps and over the gantry bridge to the station concourse for the return train into London. A black man in the railway uniform looked at him carefully, knowing he had only just arrived. Paul ignored him and found a place to sit. It had been a mistake to come.

# Lisburn Police Station, Northern Ireland; August 1996

Liam Gerard expected no pity. Their anger didn't surprise him. This time, Inspector Brown was the playing the nice one. He was smart and ironed and spoke quietly from across the table. The man standing behind him, out of sight, said nothing at all. He was playing the nasty one.

The interview had lasted for eight hours so far. Liam had no idea of the time. They had woken him every five minutes for the past three days. His eyes felt like they were made of sausages; his tongue was as dry as stale bread. He just wanted it all to stop; stop for a moment, so he could sleep.

"Oh come on, Liam," Inspector Brown said quietly. "You know fine well they'll kill you. You're not like them. You're a poet, not a thug. I know you believe in a United Ireland and let me tell you, so do I! I'd love to see it, the four kingdoms united – and I'm as Presbyterian as Paisley. So how about it? What are you thinking? Will you help us?"

Liam's head hung to the side. He thought Inspector Brown had a County Down accent but he wasn't sure. He could be just putting it on. His face was round, like a football. Liam shook his head, his eyelids hanging. He was nearly there, so nearly asleep when then man behind him shook his shoulder. The man shook him again. "OK, OK!" Liam said, hoping it would satisfy him, then let his head fall sideways and his eyes close once again.

The blow was clean and precise across the front of his shins. Liam screamed, and then as the pain echoed louder inside his mind, he screamed again. He was jerked back into a man's arms. A gloved hand pinched his face between the nose and the top lip. The pain was incredible as the fingers drew ever tighter. He kicked backwards but the man held his head firm, in the vice of his arms. The pain in his jaw was unbelievable. He squealed and kicked and flailed and screamed again, begging for it to stop. Then he felt the blackness coming.

When the fingers had gone, the pain remained, throbbing across his teeth and into his skull. The man let him fall to the floor.

Brown got up from behind the table and came to stand over him, whispering: "They'll kill you, Liam, you little sodomite. They'll know you talked and they'll string you up by the balls and ram a broken bottle up your fat arse. That's what you want isn't it? You'd like that, you limp-wristed bender. I bet that's what you dream of, you godless little wretch."

Liam shook his head, mumbling. The foot on his ankle pressed slowly down. Liam arched his back, screaming silently, but couldn't free it. "No!"

Inspector Brown's face was close; calm and unyielding. "*Mo* did you say? Did you say *Mo*? Well I'm sorry to have to tell you, Liam Gerard, that Mr Mohammed Samra is being very helpful with our enquiries. In fact to avoid deportation back to fucking Iraq or wherever he's from, he's willing to do anything to help us. Anything at all. Names, dates, times. Who he saw you with, who you called..."

Inspector Brown stood up and reached into his trouser pocket. Liam flinched, thinking he'd be hit, but it was only a box of mint sweets. Brown shook some onto his palm and threw them into his mouth before kneeling again: "Did you honestly think we don't know about that phone box on the corner of the park? Every Sunday, on your way home from Mass? You told your little bumboy that it was to ring your Aunty, didn't you? That's what you said, wasn't it? When every week you were having a little check in with your boss, weren't you? A little check in with Mr John-Paul Murphy? Wasn't that right Liam? It was Murphy wasn't it? Every week you spoke to your handler, John-Paul Murphy?"

Liam's breath was short and sharp in his chest. He was afraid. His head ached and his teeth felt like they were falling out. There was blood in his mouth, blood running down his chin. Inspector Brown slapped him.

"Answer me!"

On the floor by Brown's foot, his father's gold chain and St Christopher medal lay broken.

# Montgomery Lines, Aldershot;
# August 1996

"Gentlemen I hope you all managed to make something of your leave and that you got a rest after the debacle of Operation Haven." The Commanding Officer looked from one Major to the next and each smiled and nodded their assent. "For my sake, I welcome you all back. The purpose of this meeting is to give you a heads up about the programme from now until Christmas."

The Colonel put down his pencil and composed his thoughts, a gesture that alerted the Company Commanders to the fact that something was wrong. The Colonel spoke slowly: "But first of all let me say this. Despite what I said in my last conference, over leave we had something of a slippage in discipline. There are six soldiers who have failed to report back after leave and have been posted absent. I am informed that they intended to be back on time but for reasons unknown, they missed their flight. No fewer than sixteen men from across all companies were caught drink driving in the past four weeks and all have summonses from the magistrates' courts in their respective home towns. One man from Support Company was knifed during a nightclub brawl and is currently in hospital. And I also have a letter of complaint from the secretary of a golf club in Galloway. Apparently a ladies' club match was interrupted by four men from A Company who insisted on playing naked."

The Major commanding A Company sniggered, but a glance from the Colonel made him quickly regain his composure. A silence fell.

"Gentlemen it is difficult to maintain match fitness for long periods of time. The self-discipline required is immense, as we all know. But we seem to have lost something of the edge we honed over the summer. We seem to have let our standards slip. So it is timely that Brigade have given us the opportunity for a major parachuting insertion alongside other NATO nations. We will deploy as the spearhead unit on Exercise Purple Thunder in less than two weeks' time."

The Colonel's face was icy and expressionless. The majors had ten days to get their houses in order.

# RAF Lyneham, Wiltshire; August 1996

Beyond the cavernous hangar the runway disappeared from view in the dawn mist. Dwarfed by the tail fins of the transport planes, and waddling because of the parachute harnesses, lines of men snaked across the tarmac to their allocated aircraft. At their designated plane, loadmasters bullied them up the rear ramp and into the netting seats of the cargo hold. The bulky parachutes made them sit forward and the harnesses pinched between their legs. They were crammed in tightly, thigh to thigh and shoulder to shoulder. They wriggled to find comfort but the loadmasters then passed down their bergens, strapped up and ready for the jump. These were dropped in between the seats in the space where the men's legs should go. Unable to put them anywhere else, the men placed their feet between those sitting opposite. It would be a long trip.

Paul leaned his head against a stanchion. Banks' feet were resting against his thighs and Delta's elbow poked him in the ribs. He lifted his arm to free himself but it made little difference. It was never going to be comfortable. Even though the rear ramp was open the inside of the plane was as airless and hot as an oven. Sweat ran down his body and there was nothing he could do about it.

Further up, on the other side of the fuselage, Major Casenove and Sergeant Moor were squashed together, side by side. Paul watched them with interest. Their laughing made him jealous. As the engines started, Paul asked Delta whether Moor and Casenove had known each other before. Delta nodded. The story about Moor getting bust was true: "I was in the Platoon at the time, a lance-jack. Mr Casenove said he had to sack Beefy cos of what he done with that tank. But what really gripped his shit was how Beefy let us all down. He'd destroyed the integrity of a good Platoon. That was the bastard of it all." Delta related the story in way intended to make him laugh, but to Paul it was tinged with pathos. The shame of it, everyone knowing you had missed the battle down south and then got demoted for being pissed. The medals must weigh on his chest like a mortar baseplate. Delta frowned then shouted above the engine noise as the plane taxied to the runway: "I never thought of it like that, Boss," he said. "But you're right. We all want to be remembered as good eggs – at least by the people that matter."

"Does anyone not matter?" said Paul.

"Well I don't think Beefy's close to Mrs Moor any longer. She's got the kids."

"Were they his?"

"No, course not. Couldn't, could he? He's a jaffa. They were hers. His first wife left him cos she caught him fucking around. Then he married the dragon. Now she's fucked off and he's on his own. No-one to keep his line going." Paul pondered. There was more in what Delta had said than perhaps he knew.

The plane juddered to a halt and paused for a few minutes. Then, brakes off, it jerked forwards and sped down the runway with the soldiers jostling inside like battery hens.

\*\*\*

After two hours, Paul could sleep no more and his bladder forced him to his feet. The toilet was a yellow cone on the side of the fuselage above the rear ramp. He pushed himself upright and wove carefully down the aisle, stepping carefully between the legs of sleeping men. The space between the seats and the rear ramp was filled by a wedge-shaped pallet wrapped in a cargo net and loaded with stores. The loadmasters had been quick to grab it as a place to sleep. All around, men lay in whatever positions they found comfortable, their heads bobbing with the rise and fall of the plane.

A lone soldier was staring out of the small porthole in the side door. It was Private Pietersen and Paul patted him on the shoulder, shouting over the engine noise: "You OK TP?"

The soldier turned briefly and nodded but said nothing. Paul leaned in close to look out of the window but could see only cloud. TP continued staring out, his eyes on the distant horizon. "Is something on your mind?"

The soldier nodded slowly but did not turn round: "It's my kid, LT. My son. My wife told me he's got meningitis. In South Africa that's not a good thing... you don't want a blood transfusion in Joburg unless you bring the blood yourself, eh?"

"I didn't know..." Paul said, quickly checking through his mental notes on his men. Perhaps he had misheard due to the noise of the engines. No, he was sure. Pietersen had never admitted to being married or that he had kids. "When did you get married?"

TP shrugged: "We've been together since we were tots. We got married when we were fifteen. She's the mother of my kids. I've three of them, one boy and two girls. It's the boy, Koos, who's ill."

"Koos?"

"Jacob. We call him 'Koos'. When he was little he could dung like an elephant."

"You keep the family over there?"

"Sure. I didn't know when I came to the UK if it would work. France didn't, man. So we agreed Minnie would stay there, and she's got a job anyway. She's a lawyer. I never told the recruiting office I was married, in case they refused my visa."

"So you don't want to have your family closer? To have a quarter on the patch?"

"No, LT. I don't want my kids growing up swearing and the like. You get a quarter and the kids pick up the language. I was round at Chink's for dinner and you could hear it out on the playing field; the language of the gutter, man. Minnie's from a wealthy family. They won't want to hear them talking like that."

"How often do you get home? When do you see them?"

"Three or four times a year, during leave."

Paul concentrated his thoughts. "If you told the admin office you were married you would get flights for free, you know that? And if your son's ill you could get yourself home – there are procedures for things like this."

"Ja, ja, I know. But it's better for me this way. I get to be a soldier and then get to be a husband. The lines are clear."

"So you don't want me to tell Major Casenove, to get you taken off the exercise?"

The soldier reflected, but shook his head: "No, LT. Minnie knows what to do. She'll tell me." The soldier tapped his pocket. Paul raised his eyebrows. A mobile seemed such a luxury.

"Well let me know how he is, when you find out. I can always engineer something," Paul said, placing a hand on the big man's shoulder. TP met his eyes and nodded.

"Thanks, LT. Really, I appreciate it."

\* \* \*

Ninety-nine per cent boredom, one per cent abject terror. If Paul had wanted to be anywhere else he had missed the opportunity. He could have been sat at home reading a newspaper. He could have been working in the city earning a packet. But he was here, among men, waiting for the order to jump.

The Loadies woke the men with packed lunches which were eaten and cleared in a flash. With forty minutes to go they ordered the men to stand up and fit equipment and the plane suddenly buzzed with jostling, passing, turning and lifting. Each man became intimately aware of others around him. They tightened the straps of their helmets. They propped their bergens against the stanchions to step into the leg loops, before bending to hook the load onto the harness. Painfully, they straightened, then tried to ease the pressure by leaning against the seats. As the plane ducked and wove the weight grew and shrank. The floor of the cabin swam with piss and vomit. The Loadies darted between the lines of men tucking seat belts out of the way, checking straps and helmets and tugging on the karabiners that attached the parachutes to the fuselage cable.

Delta grinned over his shoulder: "Civvies pay thousands for this!"

Paul nodded. He became conscious that he was grimacing when he should be projecting confidence. He was ninth in the port line. On the opposite side of the plane, the man who would jump out of the starboard door at the same time was Private Beckett. Sweat ran in rivers down Paul's back and sides. The bergen was clunky to hold, his arms and neck almost immobile with straps and clothing. His lower back ached. A soldier behind him, a machine gunner, knelt over to be sick. The smell curled round the cabin, making others gulp.

"Get a fucking grip," Westy shouted from down the line, his face red with anger. "Stop showing off." Paul gave him a thumbs up and he nodded, rolling his eyes.

The Loadies at last turned the handles on the side doors, pulling them in and upwards. Cool air flooded in and every man sucked for it, smelling green fields, smelling trees.

It would all be over soon.

Paul needed to piss. This was his thirteenth jump, but only his first full-scale brigade deployment. The orders were simple. The Brigade were to insert by parachute then march sixteen miles to assault a defended enemy position. The insertion would commence at Twelve-hundred, the assault at dawn. Paul's was the left forward Platoon of the lead Company of the lead Battalion. He was the officer at the very point of the brigade assault. His stomach shrank into a tight ball as he thought about it. He felt light headed. Just get me off this fucking crate.

Ten minutes to go.

The Loadies shouted down the line: "Action stations!" Both lines of men stamped down the plane, nudging their bergens forward with their knees. The lead men in the port and starboard lines took up positions in the doorways, one hand on the frame for support. On the starboard side this was Major Casenove, standing erect and proper. Framed by the doorway, his body was silhouetted against the daylight.

The Loadie pressed his earphones onto the side of his head as he spoke to the pilot. The lines of men studied him: "Ten knots, ten knot wind on the drop zone," he shouted, flashing a hand signal. There was a collective murmur of dismay. It was going to be sporting.

Two minutes to go.

The men tightened inside themselves, praying silently, touching their talismans. *There are no atheists in the slipstream.*

The Loadie held up one finger. It was nearly over. Men slapped the back of those in front as much for their own sake as for the other's. Come on. Let's do this, let's get out there.

The engine noise changes. Pistons whine in the fuselage. Men brace, tightening their muscles. The plane slows to jump speed. The rear door shudders and drops open. Men crane to see the sky, the engine fumes, the distorted, tilted earth. Loadies push the heavy-drop pallet off the rear ramp. It tilts, falls and swings away until the massive heavy-lift parachutes snap and billow open. It floats like a jellyfish then sinks out of sight.

Now it's our turn.

"Red on..." The light on the door frame shines in the dark. The message is shouted down the line. Paul is coiled like a spring, ready for anything. The light changes and now there is only one thought: "Go... two... three... four..."

Men leap into space, throwing themselves into pure, clean air. From darkness they enter light. From heat they feel the sweat chill on their skin. The weight disappears from their shoulders, their bodies twist and tumble in space and then, as if slapping them awake, there is a kick and tug and a swing. They look up. The parachute is open and they are still alive.

"Fucking cunt! Right. Get it together. Check above me. Check below me. I'm in my own clear airspace..."

Paul shouted himself through the drills, his heart racing and breath sharp in his chest. Reaching under his reserve he felt for the latches that had to be released to drop his bergen so it hung on a rope below him. To land with the bergen attached to the harness was to invite both legs to shatter at the knee.

The wind was howling. The ground whizzed away below him at an angle. He could see an ambulance on the drop zone. A line of men were already on the ground to his right, their parachutes deflated.

A scream above him. Something heavy whacked his helmet. In an instant Paul's neck was whipped and lashed with cord. Ropes bit into the sinews. He let go of the bergen hooks to clear his throat. His face was covered in silk and then, right in front of him, was Beckett's pale, frightened face. Their parachutes were entangled: "Help me Sir!" He snatched for Paul's harness but could not get purchase. He tumbled away, screeching, to jolt as the ropes stung around Paul's neck. Paul couldn't breathe. Beckett's parachute was snagged round his reserve. The soldier hung thirty feet below him, kicking and struggling in his rigging. There was no time to sort this out. Paul reached again underneath his reserve to free his bergen.

"No! Sir! Please! Don't drop it!"

Kicking in his harness, tugging at the straps, Paul could just see Beckett hanging below him, almost upside down with his foot caught. If Paul dropped his bergen it would hit Beckett clean in the chest and kill him. If he kept it fastened, Beckett might live, but Paul would break his legs. Whatever decision he made, someone was going to get hurt.

What a shame. The horizon was so beautiful; the sky paling from aquamarine to a sublime orange; the fields alive with yellow rape, the line of parachutes floating down in perfect harmony.

Why did he have to do this?

Because he was here. Because he was an officer.

"Beckett get your fucking foot free and prepare to land. Do it now."

The weight below him swung out of sight. He was nearly at the tree tops.

Paul braced himself. He would land and take the weight. He was strong. He would survive this. He always did.

"Beckett, get ready!"

The tree tops were level. He could see the side of the ambulance, the red cross on a white circle. Men were running towards him, carrying a stretcher.

The ground skimmed beneath his feet but he could not tell which way. "Feet and knees together, feet and knees together..."

There was a grunt and cry as Beckett hit the floor. The ground raced up behind him, a blur of yellow grass. Paul crunched himself together, tucking his elbows in. The planet hit his feet and then his knees and then his hips and then his shoulders. Imprisoned by the weight of his bergen and the rigging lines of Beckett's harness, his right leg moved slower than the rest of him and the shin broke cleanly, the bone tearing through the skin. Screaming in pain, his brain reverberated against the inside of his skull like a ball being kicked against a garage door. His mouth was full of soil. His shoulder hit stone. As the agony climaxed, Paul's consciousness left him and everything vanished.

# PART THREE

# HMP Maze, Northern Ireland;
# September 1996

It was amazing, their luck. After all the arrests and the court hearings, they'd still got a gun and eight rounds of ammunition through security; not quite a full magazine but easily enough for the job. Then they heard that H7, the UVF block, had gotten flooded by a broken water pipe and so the inmates were being moved into the north wing of H6, right next door. How lucky was that? With fortune running their way, Michael decided the target should not be just some old codger but one of the big names. They should go for the main man himself, Billy Samson, the Fox of Portadown. That bastard had single-handedly waged war against the Roman Catholic community even from inside his prison cell.

"You're right," said JP. "We won't get a chance like this again."

"But how do we do it? How do we get into their yard?" Michael wondered, standing up on his tiptoes on the kitchen worktop, looking out the high window. Outside, the proddies were kicking a soccer ball against the wall, laughing like wee kids, knowing the echo resounded inside.

"You won't be laughing when we get the Fox, you wee shites," said Michael under his breath.

Liam Gerard stood at the doorway taking occasional peeks down the corridor. At the first sign of Morrison he coughed and the other men quickly jumped down from the window and made it look like they were making a wee cup of tea. Liam sat down by the fridge and said nothing. He was the youngest of all of them and rarely spoke.

The door opened and in walked Mr Morrison, the new guy. He had recently transferred from Wakefield or Sheffield, somewhere over on the mainland. He was ex-army probably, having the look of a man who thought he knew right from wrong and considered himself immune to reproach. He walked the corridors all on his own. Did his mates not tell him they stopped that years ago, after the Eighty-three break out? The men outside the wire said he had married to a girl from Hillsborough and bought an old place that needed doing up.

"Good morning gents," said Morrison, swinging his torch like a truncheon.

"How's about you Mr Morrison," said Michael, smiling away like a boy in P6 greeting his teacher. Morrison noticed the grins, the sternness behind Michael's eyes and must have known he was up to something.

"How's the new house coming on?" said Michael, still smiling like he's chatting to the priest. "Have you got the place all sorted yet? You decorating?" Morrison said nothing, trying to work out if Michael was taking the piss, being friendly or laying a trap. He folded his arms and Liam could see the cogs turning. If there's one thing to say for British soldiers it's that they all think alike. He could always tell when they're gonna strike out and when they'll bide their time. Morrison was no different. Michael would reel him in, bit by bit. All they needed was a time when the Fox would be in the exercise yard; and Michael would get Morrison to give them the nod.

# The Cambridge Military Hospital, Aldershot; November 1996

Paul was embarrassed when Major Casenove came to visit. Being seen in pyjamas by his first reporting officer was demeaning: "Oh hello, Sir, I..."

"Relax, Paul, relax."

Paul collapsed back on the pillows and winced as pain razored down his thigh.

"How are you coping? I'm sorry I didn't come round at the weekend – I had to go up to Inverness to see my wife's family. Did your folks come down?"

"I sent them away. I didn't like them watching me having my arse wiped." He could not help sounding bitter.

"What have the doctors said?"

"Not a lot. They keep dropping hints about medical discharge. Then the Adjutant came round and gave me a load of papers to sign..."

If there was any chance to save his career, Paul would have snatched for it. Being an officer in the regiment was the only thing he had ever wanted. It put him, in his mind, in the upper echelons of society. It provided meaning to his life. He was only just becoming confident as a commander when his whole future had been pulled away.

"Are you still in pain?"

"Yes. It hurts like fuck." He wanted Casenove to feel sorry for him but equally did not want to sound foolish. "Sorry, Sir. It's just I don't want it to end this way..." He exhaled, blinking.

The Major spoke softly: "Relax, Paul. It takes time, an injury like this. You were not the only one. Four other men piled in. And one Land Rover."

Paul smirked, despite himself: "A Land Rover ?"

"Yes. It came off a heavy-drop platform under canopy. The crabs hadn't secured it. It hit the ground at sixty miles an hour and at that very moment we discovered it contained all the spare mortar ammunition."

The Major spoke in monotone. "Just as well you were out for the count. For a while it was like the opening ceremony of the Barcelona Olympics. Men were diving for cover all over the place. There were some very red faces at Lyneham, I should think."

Paul tilted his head back to laugh but the pain stopped him. He breathed heavily through his teeth: "How's Brains?"

The Major hooked a knee behind interlaced fingers. "Beckett is very well. He was knocked unconscious but came round and walked off the drop zone. He completed the exercise. You undoubtedly saved his life by not dropping your kit. You should know that the Brigade Commander mentioned your name as an example of selfless leadership."

Paul couldn't help the grin that unzipped his face: "So he's not slagging me off for my skills and drills..."

"No Paul. And more importantly, every soldier in the battalion knows what you did. Very few would take the hit the same way you did. You're an example. You should recognise that. Your platoon medic, the young lad from Liverpool, he wouldn't leave your side until you were in the ambulance." The Major leaned back lifting his knee as he did so. Although in uniform he was less formal than usual and it gave him an avuncular aspect which Paul appreciated. But it was all very well being a hero if his career was ending.

"It's not over, Paul. You're not finished. And I'm sorry you got bothered by the Adjutant in that way. It's easy, when you're a busy man, to confuse leadership and efficiency. I will have a word with him. Don't complete any paperwork just yet – there's plenty of time. Just get yourself better. In a few weeks you'll be out of traction and then we will see what your recovery looks like, OK?"

Paul nodded. It was good of Cas to be so candid and he was glad someone was protecting him. It had felt, until that moment, that the army would discharge him as soon as he could sit up. He ground his teeth. "So is the Platoon still mine? Will it be there for me if I come back?"

The Major had been expecting this question: "I have not replaced you, if that's what you mean. Five Platoon is still your command, Paul, until we know your prognosis. At the moment Sergeant Moor is acting as the Platoon Commander and it's a good experience for him. Your men are well. I had to jail someone from Four Platoon the other day for missing guard duty, but your men are fine. Corporal Weston has applied to do SAS selection again... his third attempt."

"That's his fourth, actually, Sir. He did it at depot also, when he was a recruit instructor."

The Major nodded, raising an eyebrow.

"You are missed, Paul. That's all that matters. So concentrate on getting yourself back to fitness." He patted the bed gently and despite his embarrassment, Paul was grateful for the fleeting contact.

"There is one other thing you ought to know, though," he added. "Rolly has been identified for early promotion. He will command Four Platoon until the end of his tour, probably mid next year, but will then get one of the captain's appointments."

Paul said nothing. He was glad, he supposed. Rolly was a good officer and a good soldier and had always said he wanted to get promoted quickly.

"Don't think too much Paul. Just focus on getting well. Your men need you back." The Major stood to replace his beret, sculpting it round the corners of his skull. Paul thanked him for coming. After he had left, he studied the patterns of light and shadow on the ceiling until the nurse came round with tea.

# HMP Maze, Northern Ireland; December 1996

It would be a long game, but Michael was playing it like a professional.

Morrison came into the wing on the Tuesday and walked round the common room standing tall, showing them he was not going to be humiliated, not going to be told what to do. There was a bit of Christmas decoration taped to one of the pictures and he pulled it down, just to show he could.

The boys were playing cards with Michael against the wall where he could see Morrison's face. On the cupboard door above the kettle was a photo of Morrison's wife taking his daughter to school. Pretty wee thing she was as well, the daughter. Lovely little curls. She reminded Michael of his own Finula when she had been that age, still blonde. He had a photo on his cell wall to prove it and the two wee bairns were indeed the very spit of each other.

Nobody liked using the bairns. They were not cruel men. But this was war and Morrison was here of his own free will. The moment he spied the photo there was maybe four men left in the deal: Michael, Liam, Shamey and JP. You could see the blood draining when he got the hint. At first he was frozen to the spot, not believing what he saw. Then he went red, angry as anything, gritting his teeth and shaking, pulling the photo down; but the boys just kept playing.

So then Morrison turns to leave, his eyes all watery, and that's the point Michael spoke. If he had gone to the Governor, the plan would have fallen through. Just as he was reaching for the door handle, Michael laid down a pair of eights and whispered all gentle like: "Don't take offense now Mr Morrison. It's nothing personal or anything. It's not about you at all. It could have been anybody, any one of yous."

It was beautiful, just beautiful. Michael had a real knack, so he had, for knowing what it was about someone that made him tick. With Morrison it was pride. He had pride in his uniform, pride in his flag, and pride in what it stood for. If he was convinced we could have done the same to any of the guards there'd be no shame. If there was no shame, he'd crack.

He had his fingers on the handle and his face hidden. He didn't want us seeing him, but you could tell by his voice he was in the dark corners of hell.

"What do you want?" he said. So Michael told him.

# Canning Town, London; December 1996

"Rolly! I wasn't expecting you!" Clare was taken aback by the figure in biking leathers at her front door. He smiled, cheeks dimpling, and Clare could not help smiling back. It was like having Brad Pitt at your door and old Mrs Hutchens came to her window at just the right time. "You'd better come in... I was just..."

Rolly stepped forward and kissed her once on each cheek. His lips were soft and seemed to linger in the act. He smelled delicious. "What a surprise! What brings you...?" Clare asked, closing the front door. Something in his manner made her quieten. "Come up," she said. "Tell me what's happened."

Yvonne was in the kitchen cooking, so she led Rolly through to the lounge, turning the telly off when she got there. "Like some tea?"

He shook his head. "Clare, I wasn't sure, but I thought I ought to tell you. There's no easy way to say this, so I'll just come out and say it. Paul has been very seriously injured."

He was looking into her eyes, watching for a reaction. He was tall and powerful.

"It happened some time ago. He's been in hospital since it happened, nearly three months. He's up and walking but they say he'll need a stick for, well perhaps the rest of his life. He may never run again."

Clare studied his face. "If you didn't think I'd want to know, Rolly, why have you come round? Did he ask you to?"

"You haven't spoken to him?"

She shook her head. "He never rang after we split. I never heard from him after that. No wait – there was one guy who rang, that guy Paul hated; the Adjutant. Said he'd been hurt and I told him we weren't together any more. Why? What happened? Is he... ?"

Rolly told her. A flash of anger rose inside her. It explained the icy absence after Paul had dumped her at the train station. He simply vanished; not a letter, not even a card on her birthday. For a month she had been numb, almost drunk with shock. They had always pulled through in the past and perhaps she had expected the same to happen. But no word came. Then it was as if he was being cruel, wanting to hurt her. How could he behave like that? How could he be so wanton? Then one day she had thought sod it, she was not going to mope. She'd rung Kirsty and the pair of them had gone out, just like in the olden days. Plastered they'd been, getting the businessmen in Soho to buy their drinks. Kirsty had saved her in fact. She'd finished with Dave and then met Teddy and then finished with him not a month later. She'd had Micky on the side and not just the once. Hearing all of this, Clare had realised breaking up was normal. It was God telling her Paul was not the soul she thought he was.

Rolly's eyes kept wandering downwards and Clare couldn't help herself: "You lost something?"

Rolly chuckled but recovered quickly. "Not yet."

Clare smiled up at him. What the heck. She had needs as well.

## HMP Maze, Northern Ireland;
## January 1997

Morrison came through as Michael said he would. He got the paint and told his boss it was spare from doing up his house. No point in good paint going to waste, he said, and the Senior Warden agreed.

Michael now had six part-full tins of paint and a couple of brushes and a roller. One of the young lads was quite the genius with the murals and had a real drawing prepared: Bobby and Francis against a backdrop of some boys in Derry strip playing football. JP took one look at the drawing and said it couldn't be Derry, there was no red paint. The young lad just grinned. There was no white either, just those browny colours. Bobby Sands would be up on the wall as tanned as a Pakistani on a sunbed, and this had the boys all creasing themselves, irreverent as it was.

Then Michael said it would do just fine. The young boy would draw the outline. Then on the day, JP and Michael would be in the yard filling in the spaces, painting by numbers. What they needed, what Morrison had to deliver on, was the exact time the Fox would be in the proddy yard on the other side of the wing. That's when they would strike. That's when they would shoot the bastard.

# Headley Court Military Hospital, Surrey; January 1997

The physio room resounded with cries of motivation, the thump of leather medicine balls and clanking of dropped weights. Rees, the pretty Australian, was outside Paul's field of vision as he laboured along a ten-foot rubber mat: "That's good Paul, that's very good. Let's see if you can make it to the chair. Keep going will you?"

Sweat was pouring down his face. His weight was distributed unevenly between his good leg, the crutch on his right arm and the tentative amount he let the right leg carry. It wasn't painful to walk but the leg was weak, buckling under him. If he had two good arms he could have used the parallel bars but since his left shoulder was still in plaster, bent outwards like a teapot spout, the staff had invented an exercise routine specific to his capabilities. He gritted his teeth and swore at himself, as much for his own sake as to impress Rees: "Come on! Come on!" At the end of the mat, able to touch the leg of the chair with his crutch, he shuffled round as if to do the distance again, returning to the start.

"Don't overdo it, Paul. Take a rest for a minute will you?"

Thankful, Paul collapsed into the chair, the crutch remaining upright. Rees smiled at him. She had crooked teeth and an under bite but there was something about her he liked.

"Just rest, Paul. We don't want to use up all your energy, do we?"

The suggestiveness made Paul smile. She probably did this with all of them, one hour after another. "Is there anywhere to go in the evenings, Rees? Am I allowed out?"

"You can leave Headley when you're P7. You're P8 still, at least until the next review board." She smiled at him, shaking her head, but softened when she saw his face: "But you're not missing much. There's only the *Shoulder of Mutton* and that's all you get in there to be honest. Don't worry. There's time."

She had a hand on his shoulder and her narrow wrist sported a silver bracelet. She probably had a boyfriend anyway.

The whistle blew and the Flight-sergeant shouted for the equipment to be put away and the mats to be stacked neatly under the wall bars. The other men in the room, all training casualties like Paul, shuffled round to his instruction. Rees fetched Paul's wheelchair and helped him into it, pushing him to the double doors where two men stood, arms folded, their berets pulled down low. Rees saw them and immediately walked up to the larger, bull-necked one of the pair: "Excuse me. What are you doing in here? This area is out of bounds unless you're a patient or medical staff. And we don't allow parade boots on this floor..."

Paul could not help smiling at the sight of Sergeant Moor backed against the wall.

"Do you three know each other?" Rees was looking from Paul to Moor and back again. "Well put yourself to use, please. You can take Paul to Block Two, room Thirteen; I have work to do. Paul, I'll see you next time. Look after yourself, OK?"

She walked off, her arm swinging outwards at the elbow and Paul bent his head to look behind him and watch her go. Moor glanced at Beckett and then at the receding nurse, both of them whistling in unison. "You shagging that or what, Boss?"

"Looking like a teapot? You must be joking. It's just as well I'm right handed I can tell you."

"What? Over her? You must be desperate. She looks like a boy."

Paul said nothing, clasping a hand to his heart in mock agony. "That's my beloved you're slagging off."

Moor smiled: "Yeah, yeah. Come on then, Boss. Where's room one-oh-one? Brains – you're the tom, you do the pushing. Easy now! You've already done him enough damage."

Beckett blushed, grinned, and took up the strain on the wheelchair: "Hello Sir. Thought we should come and see you."

The boy was nervous. It could not have been easy visiting someone who had saved his life. Paul was conscious of this but would have done the same for any of them. *There's no rank in the air*. It had been a matter of duty.

"I appreciate you coming chaps," he said, reaching up his good arm to shake Beckett's hand.

Moor walked ahead of the chair and opened the fire doors along the corridor, through reception and across the yard to his block. The lift was cramped with all three of them in it.

"There's half an hour before lunch. Do you want a brew? I've a kettle and stuff, but only two cups."

"Just enough for you and Miss Skeletor?"

"Just enough for me and the massage lady. She's Chinese. Comes round every evening for an hour." They were outside his door and he reached up to press the three digit code so Moor could open it.

"You're joking."

"Straight up. And I can't undress myself so she has to lay me out on the massage table naked and cover me in goose fat..." Paul could not keep a straight face and his head rolled back as he laughed, Moor and Beckett shaking their heads: "Good one, Boss."

Inside the room he was pushed into the corner and Moor sat on the bed. Beckett stood even when Paul directed him to the only comfy chair. "It's alright Sir, cheers. I've been driving. It's fine, honest."

A silence fell and Paul looked from Moor to Beckett as they inspected the room. He unplugged the little kettle and passed it to Beckett to fill at the sink. Moor nodded, shrugging. "Go on then Boss. I'll have a coffee, NATO."

"How are the boys?" asked Paul.

"They're good. The Platoon's in good shape. Best in the Company for sure. Westy's come off selection. That's his last attempt. Taff and Brad have gone on Juniors so they can get promoted. Khan's gone to the army boxing team but will be back at the end of the season. Cheese has signed off but Delta's working on him to sign back on again."

Paul nodded. It seemed to him that when he was away the Platoon started to crumble. His presence kept everything smooth and correct. "Anything else?"

"No, not really. CO's on the warpath about drink driving. Major C's got promoted and will be posted in December." Moor shrugged. "That's about it. Oh yeah. Beckett here said he wanted to come and thank you for not killing him on the jump, didn't you Brains?"

Beckett nodded. He had made two mugs of coffee, passed one to Moor and the second to Paul as he drew up to deliver his speech: "Boss... I'm really grateful... I wanted really to say how grateful..." His cheeks flushed and he looked at the floor.

"It's OK Brains. I appreciate you coming, both of you. I don't get many visitors. So I appreciate it, really. And Brains, I would have done the same for any of the blokes and I'm sure you would have done for me. And anyway I hope you now forgive me for doing your leg."

The soldier burst into a smile. "That were nothing, Boss. It's just that..." He dried up, unable to find the words he needed. Moor filled the silence by quietly suggesting he went outside to start the car. Relieved, Beckett saluted and left.

Paul could not help but smile: "It was good of him to come."

"He wanted to. It weren't me made him."

Paul nodded. There wasn't much he had to say and even less he knew how to. Moor's presence only reminded him of what he was missing, of how his days should be. "I'm going home next week. I should be P7 by then, so I'm off up to Shipley."

Moor nodded, reaching to pull something out of the pocket of his smock: "Good. There's some letters for you. I went up to your Mess and spoke to the Colour-man, said I was coming here. He gave me your stuff. Mostly mess bills I expect." The pile did indeed consist mainly of folded and stapled sheets, but Paul thanked him for bothering. It had been very kind of him to consider it.

Moor looked at him: "But what I came to say, Boss, is get yourself better. The blokes want you back. You've got three months to get yourself fit. There's an emergency tour coming up. The IRA bombed HQNI in Lisburn. It was a double. The primary went off and when the medics were getting the casualties to the med centre the secondary goes off at the cordon. Things are hotting up. It's not like that cake and arse party before leave. This is gen. First London, then Manchester, now Thiepval Barracks. People are saying it's getting like the Seventies."

Paul's jaw dropped open. An operational tour. The chance to get a medal. If only he could be ready.

# HMP Maze, Northern Ireland; February 1997

Michael said Liam was not to be involved in the operation. It was too risky. There was another job for him to do afterwards, something that would become clear in time. Getting the Fox would be down to himself and JP. Liam could stay on the roof and keep watch but that was it.

They were all in the yard painting in the mural. They took their time. JP was doing Frances's hair in a dark brown and Michael was on his knees doing the far end of the football field whistling *Back Home in Derry*. JP had the gun in his overalls. The ladder and iron bar lay on the concrete.

Morrison came round that morning and said the Fox would be getting a visitor sometime between half ten and eleven. Michael said that wasn't good enough. He had better be more specific or his young lass would get it. Morrison had tears in his eyes and was pleading that he was sorry, but he just didn't know. Michael grabbed him by the throat, lifted him clean off his feet: "What time, you Brit fucker," he said and for a second it looked like Morrison was going to press his alarm, but JP grabbed his wrist and held it. Michael yelled in his face: "Tell us. Tell us what fucking time!" Liam looked out down the corridor. There was another guard coming on duty any second. Morrison cursed, cursed like a bastard, but then he cracked. He cracked like a schoolboy. Tears rolled down his grey face as he said the Fox would be out at ten-fifty:

ten to eleven on the dot. That's as much as he could say, just please don't hurt his wee girl.

Michael dusted him down. "There there, Mr Morrison. You go off shift now and take your wife out to lunch. Tell her you love her and buy her something nice. You have my word that the men of the Derry Brigade will under no circumstances do anything to hurt your family so long as you keep your mouth shut."

Morrison's face showed he was eating himself up inside. There'd been no mention of what the other Brigades would promise and now he was a broken man. For the rest of his career they had him at their bidding, and he knew it. He left all bent and hunched up but the boys didn't care. He was just lucky not to be the target.

At eleven minutes to eleven Michael glanced up at the tower on the corner of the wall. At that time of day the sun shone through the windows and if there was someone inside, his silhouette stood out against the thick green glass. It was empty. Michael nodded: "Tiocfaidh ár lá!"

Liam lifted the ladder and JP climbed up, kicking his legs over the edge. Then in a second he was away across the roof like a banished viper and Michael was up and following. Liam looked up at the tower and then at Michael's feet and followed on.

The van in the proddy yard had the back doors open. A prisoner was climbing in, escorted by a guard, and JP reached into his pocket. If he could shoot from here, why go down into the proddy yard at all? Michael grabbed his arm: "Wait. It's not the Fox. It's some other bastard." And sure it was. But the three of them were lying on the flat roof of the south wing of H6 in full view of the towers. If they were seen they could be shot in the back. Outside the ring of guard towers there was the wire and then a dog gap and then more wire and then a wall and outside that there was the road and outside that was the big wall, fifty feet high and six foot thick and topped with rotating drums. And on that wall there were yet more towers and inside them there were not the guards, there was the army. They would shoot as soon as fart. The three men lay still for a whole minute while the first prisoner was tucked inside the van and the door closed.

"Oh fuck! Have we missed the chance? Is he already inside?" JP was so on edge his voice had risen like a girl's. Liam said nothing. He watched the guard who banged on the side of the van and shouted to the driver: "OK, I'm going back in for the second..." and from inside the proddy block the men could hear a voice on a loudspeaker telling the Fox to stand by the yellow line.

The guard at the back of the van turned away. The block door opened and out came the Fox. He was in jeans and wore a yellow check shirt; a weasely little shit in real life, a runt. He had a close-cropped beard and his ginger hair was cut tight. He had vicious eyes; little screwy wee eyes. His hands were shackled and the guard led him down the steps, talking to him all pally as he did so: "So you're seeing the lassie, eh Billy? Getting time in the van alone with her, eh?" The Fox said nothing. He just kept chewing gum and looking mean. He climbed into the back of the van and sat down. The guard got in and then the back door of the van slammed shut.

Now.

The gates were starting to open. There was an orange light flashing and the noise of the engine.

JP went first. Leaning over the edge, he swung his legs round and down. He had been chosen for this mission because he was tall. Michael followed, sitting on the edge then pushing himself off, surprisingly agile for one so large. He pulled the iron bar from his sleeve and ran as fast as he could round to the driver's window. With one wild swipe he smashed it clean through: "Give me the fucking keys you fucker. Give me the fucking keys!" He swung the bar again against the door stanchion. The gate was almost open. The driver twisted over the handbrake to shield his face. Shards of glass covered his legs and body. Michael reached in, turned the key, and pulled it out. The van was going nowhere. One hard jab of the bar into the man's ribs kept the bastard quiet.

JP took his time.

He pulled the pistol out of his pocket and cocked it. The guard would see him but it did not matter. Morrison said he would be unarmed.

JP turned the handle and opened the back of the van. Inside, the Fox was nearest him with the guard sitting opposite. The other man was beyond, in the shadows. The guard dived for the floor, but JP wasn't after him. The target was the Fox.

JP stood straight, legs apart, arms extended: "In the name of Ireland, Billy Samson, you are found guilty of crimes against the Roman Catholic people."

The Fox knew immediately his time was done. He had predicted it. His eyes narrowed and his mouth sneered. He saw the guard on the ground and knew that no one was going to save him. In an instant he was up with one foot on the step and kicking out with the other, his boots flying.

JP toyed with him. The first shot struck him in the shoulder and turned him. His foot slipped off the step and he stumbled down onto his knees. The second bullet hit him in the chest but high and his body was thrown back against the van door. His eyes were sharp as pinheads, full of hate. Blood stained his shirt. JP fired again, this time lower, through the stomach. The Fox doubled over, pushed his legs straight and charged with his head down, taking two steps. He cried out, swinging his manacled wrists like a club, but JP just backed away and fired again and again: "That's for Peter Scullion. That's for Johny Ward..."

After five rounds the gun jammed. JP calmly removed the magazine and shook the pistol until the stuck round fell out. There were two rounds left. He didn't care what happened now. The Fox rolled onto his back. He would bleed to death in minutes. He had done his bit. The Fox was spitting blood from a round through the lungs. "God damn you, Taig," he hissed. There was no point expecting him to beg. One more round was enough, straight through the heart. As it exploded through his chest, a plume of blood sprang out like a geyser, spattering JP's legs, the concrete, spurting across the yard even. JP was surprised by the force of it and blinked, giggling with the shock of the hot, sticky goo on his face. Michael pushed him away: "Come on. The job's done." Liam shouted down at them: "Hurry now. They've seen us from the towers."

There was one round left. The guard was cowering in the van and the other prisoner was backed away as far as he could get. JP let them live to tell how Billy the Fox was gunned down in his own back yard by the men of free Ireland. He put the gun in his pocket, ran to the wall and placed his back against it to heave Michael up and onto the roof, with Liam pulling at the elasticated waistband of his overalls. Both men then leaned over to lift JP.

Back inside their own block Liam went to take a shower while Michael and JP went straight to a cell and shut the door and pressed the alert button on the intercom: "We are soldiers of a free Ireland. We want to see Father McCann. We need to confess and we want to do so now."

# Headley Court Military Hospital, Surrey; February 1997

Paul's letters contained three mess bills totalling two hundred and fifty six pounds. Conversely, the monthly bank statements demonstrated that being injured – and not spending any money – was financially useful. When he was back at full fitness he could replace his old Escort for sure.

The last letter was from Clare and he kept it till the evening when he was alone in bed, the side light providing intimacy and focus. Her handwriting was as curvy as her body, each word glued to the lines on the paper. He could hear the shallow wanderings of her mind as he read but they still made him smile. It had been kind of her to bother. The last paragraph contained a phrase he had to read again and again in order to understand the implication. Rolly, you creepy bastard, he thought.

# Shipley, West Yorkshire; February 1997

"You're sure you want to go back Paul? You're sure it's the right thing to do? I mean you could get a discharge. There'll be a pension for you, if you're wounded."

"I don't want a pension, Dad – at least not one for getting on the jack wagon. And I'll not let them kick me out, not without a fight. This isn't a mine. I'm not dossing... they are my men."

"I don't think the men who lost their livelihoods after thirty years down a pit would appreciate any son of mine calling them dossers, Paul."

"But that's what I mean, Dad... I'm not going to be called one either; least of all think of myself as one."

The whisky was urgent and warm. It had loosened his tongue. Now that the cast was off, Paul could sit comfortably enough. The skin was itchy and the arm very weak. The main problem was his tibia. The scar, where the bone had torn through the skin, was purple and edged with dots where the stitches had been. The brace had been removed but the bone itself was still pinned with a piece of Meccano. It ached if he walked more than a few yards.

When Paul had told his parents he was not going to accept discharge, his mother had wiped her mouth with a napkin and remained silent for a while before saying: "I'm sure you know what you're doing, Paul." But his father had pushed him on the decision, pushed him until he doubted himself. "Why do you keep suggesting I leave? Don't you want me to be successful? Don't you want me to be happy?"

"I want you to be healthy, Paul. I want you to live!" His father was exasperated. "Your mother and I love you, Paul. We love you very much. You are our son. The apples of our eyes, you and Becky."

"Dad I know that. But..."

"All my life I've fought against bad management. All my life I've stood up for the weaker man. And now you're injured and they want you to go back out there..."

"It's not them that wants it, Dad, it's me. Being in command is the only thing that gives my life meaning..."

They had both said too much, but done so without malice. Paul's mother pushed open the door, her face creased by pillow folds. "George, you're shouting. You both are. It's time we all went to bed."

Paul and his father looked at one another and then at her. Both had glasses half full and the bottle was so nearly done. "I'm sorry, Tina love. We'll be quiet now and we'll not be long. I promise."

Paul's mother looked at them sternly then retreated behind the door, pulling it closed. Footsteps receded up the stairs. The room was cooler with a waft of air from the hall.

"I've unfinished business Dad," Paul said, staring at the wall above the gas fire. Years before he had spent three days on that chimney breast, scraping off the woodchip with a stripping knife and filling the room with steam from the kettle. Eventually, his father had decided the paper on the other walls could remain where it was. It held the house together.

"I told you last time I came up that I had the Platoon under control. Well it's not really like that. Soldiers aren't automatons who do what they're told. They're people. They're human beings. They argue back, they ignore you. They say no even when you're laying down the law."

His father stared at the trophies in the corner cabinet.

"It's taken me this long to get a proper grip of the job; to get my men to respect me as an officer. People think you just click your fingers and the men will just run around at your bidding. Well it ain't like that. It's hard. It's fucking hard.

"I've a sergeant and three corporals who were all in the Falklands. They've been there; they've done it for real, all of them. And that was one hell of a brutal war. If you could see the mountain they fought over! If you understood what it was like to fight..." Paul stopped himself getting carried away. "Well the sergeant, Moor you call him; he's... he's a complete bastard at times. And at others he's unstoppable. When he's on my side, life is rosy as the Garden of Eden. But when he's not, when he's being obstinate or he's angry cos his wife left him, then he's a git. A git of the first water.

"At first I tried being pally. That was a mistake. Then I tried being a disciplinarian but he laughed at me. Then I tried pulling his levers but it weren't my style; I'm not a politician. I'm a soldier. But then it just happened. They started doing what they were told. They started respecting me and I'm not quite sure why. I so nearly have them Dad. I nearly have them, in the palm of my hand." Paul held out his hand, fingers curled, the crucible of his being. "That's why I have to go back. I have to prove to myself that I can lead; that I can lead men like them." He reached for his glass and leaned back in the chair, watching the flames flicker from blue to yellow.

"I understand, Paul," his father said at last. "I understand completely." He sat up and reached forward to touch Paul's knee. It was an act of generosity; he was never normally tactile. "And I want you to know that I respect you; that me and your mother respect you very much. I could never have done what you have done: the exams; Sandhurst; that thing in Catterick; the jumping.

"But most of all I could not have been a manager. Not in my twenties. Back then I was too busy causing trouble for management to understand they was trying to do the right thing, same as me. It was just we had different ideas, that's all, about what the right thing was. But you're not afraid to stand up and be counted. Stand up and have the men look at you. It's not easy, I know that. I was in Sheffield in ninety-two and saw the power of the moment go to Kinnock's head. He got giddy. He got drunk on the sensation of it all, standing on the podium shouting *We're all right, we're all right* like a bloody American. Shame really. He were a good bloke, Kinnock."

Paul kept still. There was truth coming.

"And don't think you've done badly because it's taken two year to make people fall in line. Two year's about right in my view. The Union wanted *me* to fall in line and they never managed that in fifteen. And they were bloody lucky I didn't stay any longer, I can tell you.

"It takes two year to get any job right, Paul. One year to learn it and another to master it. That's normal. But what I wanted to say is this. You have to find the Clause Four point if you want to win them over."

"The what?"

"The Clause Four point. It's what Blair did for the PLP, the Parliamentary Labour Party, two year ago. Clause Four was part of the constitution. It said we were all about nationalisation and so forth. It were meaningless. No one actually believed it. It was old fashioned, even then. They tried changing it back in the sixties but the time wasn't right; the unions got in the way. Old fashioned stick in the muds. Awkward buggers. People like me in fact. But the clause was stopping the party get to power. It was making the ordinary folk – not the upper classes but the middle classes, ordinary tradesmen and the like – it was making them nervous of Labour. Then Blair came along and he says if we want to be taken seriously we have to change. We have to reflect the wishes of the population; we have to follow where they want to go. Do you understand?"

Paul nodded. His father gathered his thoughts some more.

"Well Blair changed it. He said we were not socialists but social democrats. He said we were good for our word, what we wanted was what the country wanted. And he was right. He was right all along." He turned to face Paul, pointing: "That's why Blair was put in to lead the party, not Brown. It was because only he could get Clause Four changed.

"So my point is," he said, leaning back in his chair, "do you know what the Clause Four point is for your men? What is it they all hang on to that stops them going forwards?"

Paul looked from his father to the tiles below the fire. A sudden pain sparked inside him and a flush spread up his cheeks. Yes. He knew exactly what it was.

# Montgomery Lines, Aldershot; March 1997

"Hello Sir! Working hard I see." Striding into the weights room, Sergeant Moor was wearing a pair of baggy tracksuit pants and the thin straps of his vest clung round the fibres of his neck. Veins stood out on his arms.

Paul was beasting himself. He had done twenty minutes on the bike and three circuits round the machines, focusing on the muscle groups in his back and stomach. The injured limbs would be exercised at the physio session. He now hung upside down on a sit-up bench set against the wall bars at a sixty degree angle. He had done fifty-five and had forty-five to go. Placing his fingers behind his ears he started again, controlling his breath. Today he felt strong, as though he could go on for ever. The fitness test was in two weeks. If he did the distance within the time allowed he would be signed off as P1; fit for combat. He could take back command of his Platoon.

At a hundred, he stopped and pulled himself up to standing, grabbing his barmat to wipe the bench. He was not out of breath but could feel his body burning. It was the sensation of life.

Moor had sat on a bench against the wall to eat a banana. He was assessing Paul's physique. Paul slumped down next to him and took deep drafts from a water bottle.

"You gonna be ready for the fitness test?"

"Yep. You gonna be ready to let me come back?"

"Course. I'd have less work to do."

The hair on Moor's arm tickled Paul's skin. "Thank you, Bryan," he said.

A cruel smile danced across Moor's face and his voice took on an Ulster brogue: "Listen to this. You'll like this. I watched someone do sit-ups like that once. A tinker he was. We'd a VCP in Andytown, on my last urban tour. There's scrubland underneath the roundabout on the Monagh bypass. The tinkers had caravans and horses in there, as they do. I was checkpoint commander and we had this RUC man with us, just keeping an eye out for a couple of players that the int-cell wants us to locate. But it was Sunday and all the boyos are down the pub so we keeps watching this tinker doing sit-ups on the tresses of his caravan. It was one of those covered ones, like you see at fairs. And he must've done two hundred, on an incline, just like you. He was the spitting image of the guy in *Alien* with the thing in his belly; built like a streak of piss, but couldn't half do sit-ups.

"So it's half ten and the pubs are just closing. I wants to get the checkpoint down and away before the boyos come out pissed up and looking for a fight, not wanting to be confrontational or anything. So I gives the order to Mercy, my second, to pull the blokes in. But the RUC man, he just says no, let's sit here a while longer and see what happens with the tinkers.

"Well sure as a pound to a pinch of shit, out of the boozer comes ten of the boyos, fresh full of Jameson and Nigerian Lager and all of 'em carrying hurley sticks. I thinks hello, we're in for it here; this is gonna to get fresh. So I starts on the radio for backup but the RUC man, he says again no, be quiet; they're not here for us. They're after the tinkers. One of the houses off the Glen Road got robbed the day they came.

"Dead on," says me, and sure enough the boyos ignore us like we wasn't there and go set about the tinkers. Ten against four. Never seen such a one sided fight in all my life. Me and the RUC man just stands there laughing as the four tinkers kick seven bales of shite out of them."

Moor was chuckling, his hand resting on his belly. Paul smiled. To be remembered in one of these stories was to live for ever.

"And the blokes are OK?" Moor stopped chuckling and thought. "Yeah, sure. The blokes are well. But you gotta get back soon. That cunt Rawlins is doing my head in."

"Rolly? Why?"

"He's one of the most selfish officers I've ever seen. Right up his own arse he is. Fucking medal hunters; he wants an iron cross for sure."

"What's he done? He's not in command?"

"No, but that don't stop him. He's always arselicking up at Casenove's office making himself look good. But he's got one bloke gone AWOL and another been caught drink driving by the RMPs and another just come back from a course what didn't get a distinction. One of his toms is suspected of taking drugs but nobody can prove anything. His blokes are in rag order. And you know all that shite that happened over the summer – the CO spitting feathers cos blokes had got themselves in the shit? Well none of them were ours – not one."

"What about Taggart."

"Tagg? He's doing what he can but when Mr Rawlins lays down the law he threatens to do in a man's career if he disagrees with him. So he's sitting it out; doing what he can but sitting it out. And there's no way I want that cunt in charge of me."

Paul smiled to himself. It was a hollow victory, but he had been right all along. He couldn't let his blokes down now.

# HMP Maze, Northern Ireland; March 1997

They knew the Brits were beat. Michael had outsmarted them all the way down the line. They'd got Morrison and the Brits thought that was the end of it. They'd got the intel and the Brits thought that was the end of it. They'd got the Fox and still the Brits thought that was the end of it.

But the Brits didn't know fuck all.

They suffered the beatings. They suffered the block searches and the music, the sleepdep and the quarter rations. But when they'd won a battle, a major battle, no amount of petty shite was ever going to break their spirit, not even the proddies playing the lambeg drum in the block next along. They were winning the war: out-thinking, outplaying, outdoing the Brits in every way. The little jibes only went to show how far they were behind.

After the shooting, the south wing of H6 was cleared of republican prisoners. Michael and JP were put in solitary, as was expected. The young lads were put in H4 and a couple in H2 as other cells got cleared. But just as planned, the prison guards moved the engineer, Liam Gerard, to H1, half way down the eastern wall. And all the coercion, all that painting, all the photos, and all the shooting had been planned for just that one move; because the IRA army council wanted Liam Gerard through the tunnel and out of the prison on the day of the British general election.

\* \* \*

On the day the priority secret signal was sent, Driver Gail Madison of the Royal Logistic Corps was the duty clerk at the Garrison Communications Centre. Her job was to read the overnight traffic, log it in the register then place it in the cubby hole for distribution round the garrison on Monday morning. The job was easy. All the signals were routine: trawls for panel members for a court martial in Catterick, for canoe instructors in Canada, or confirmation of postings.

Despite the boredom, Gail did not mind doing Saturday nights. She had recently got engaged to Jason, a Foreman with the Signals Squadron, and was trying to save money. They were planning to get married in the garrison church in July and she used the long, dark hours of her duty to plan the day with precision. Her mother and father would stay in town and Jason's Dad (his mother had died when he was very young) lived in Winchester so he could get home on the train. Jason's brother wouldn't be there. He was away with the Sappers in Bosnia for the next six months and they wouldn't let him back, not even for his brother's wedding.

Bloody officers. But operations had to come first, she supposed.

The wedding magazine on the desk was plump with possibility. Gail admired it all but was pragmatic enough to know that the dresses so elegantly draped around the famous model could be bought in the high street for a fraction of the price. Her wedding, as much as her house, would be run with value in mind.

The signal printer started clacking away, the paper drawn through by a trolley wheel. There was no point trying to read it until it had finished and so she waited, watching the news coverage on the telly; yet more coverage of the election: Tony Blair visiting the site of the Manchester Bomb; Tony Blair visiting the docklands railway; Tony Blair doing headers with Kevin Keegan.

Gail liked Blair. Like all the men and women in her troop she voted Tory out of habit, the army being culturally conservative. But Blair looked like a keen and boyish captain rather than a crusty and boring old colonel. She rather fancied him in fact. As the printer whirred away she got herself another brew, thinking there would have to be less tea in the future. Caffeine was bad.

Finally, when the printer had fed the pages through to the collection tray, she picked up the latest signal, checking the subject code and security classification: "Fuck!"

She checked her watch. She had to be quick. A priority secret signal from PJHQ about emergency deployments to Belfast had to be processed and dispatched quicker than ten tall indians. She immediately reached for the phone to call the guardroom up at the Brigade Headquarters. They would send a driver down to collect it, if she asked nicely. And if Driver Gail Madison asked nicely there were few men in uniform who would not do what she wanted.

# The last week in April, 1997

There were eight cells in the south wing of H1 but despite this fact, the four prisoners on the wing were paired up and housed in only two cells: the McMahon brothers in one and Liam Gerard and Deccy Malone in another. Their cells were adjacent, so when Liam settled on his bunk to read, he could hear though the wall the scratchings of one of the brothers climbing into his.

It was nearly lights out and adjusting his pillows behind him, Liam pushed himself upright, causing his book to slip off the blanket and tumble onto the floor. Deccy was startled but unbothered, sitting on the bottom bunk with his legs over the side, cutting his toenails. He leaned forward, collected the book and the letter Liam was using as a page marker. He looked at the cover of the book: "Is it in Irish is it? Poetry?"

"It is," Liam said, reaching down with a haste that he knew might betray him.

Deccy ignored his hand and looked at the cover more carefully, then fanned through the pages. He pulled a face, nodding. "Didn't know you were from the gaeltacht," he said.

"I'm not. I'm from Ballymena. I just like languages, but," Liam said, relaxing his arm so as not to appear too worried. He'd be fine provided Deccy didn't open the letter.

"Good Irish name that, Cathal," Deccy said, passing the book and envelope up over his shoulder.

"He's from Donegal," Liam said, pulling the book and the precious letter up to safety. "He writes in Irish but also

258

in English. And I like his poems. They're like songs you know, the old songs – like the Dubliners' one, you know the one I mean?'

"Sure I know it," Deccy said, rolling onto his back to lie half naked on his bunk. "But I'd not spell it to save my life. It's the one sounds like *What Shall we do with the Drunken Sailor* "

Liam spluttered a laugh. "Indeed it does," he said, then sat back looking at the ceiling, fingering the pages and hoping Deccy wanted to sleep. He shuffled down and pulled the blanket up round his chest a little higher and found the page he'd got to last night.

"I thought you were an engineer?" Deccy said then. "At least that's what they call you."

"I am," Liam replied, listening to Deccy thinking below him.

"But you've languages as well?"

"Sure, a wee bit," Liam said. "A little bit of this and that. "French and stuff. A bit of Irish."

Deccy said nothing for a while, then: "I've not got languages myself."

Liam could sense his personal time slipping away. Deccy kept talking, a laugh fluttering behind his voice: "And come to think on it, I was never the man for maths either. Nor geography. I couldn't tell you the capital of Poland, or who wrote *Hamlet*."

"Ach languages are hardly complicated things," Liam said at last. "They're just patterns, same as music or numbers. You just have to find the right ending to the base word and you're home." He closed the book, making sure the letter was safely stowed.

"I couldn't tell you who wrote the Mona Lisa or who painted the Bible," Deccy continued, chuckling to himself.

Liam grunted, thinking he might have finished and would let him read, but then Deccy asked: "And you've Arabic as well? Like all that squiggly stuff and all? Is that true?"

Liam slid the book between the mattress and the edge of the bed with the open side facing upwards. He didn't want to be unfriendly. He was new in the wing and he didn't know the three men well, only that he'd been forced upon their plans and the elder of the McMahon brothers was not that happy. Deccy had been alone for some months and was obviously desperate for a companion. In fact it'd do Liam no harm to make friends with him, in case Clip McMahon took against him.

"Yes. I had a friend who was Egyptian. I learned a little from hi... from her," he said. "But I can't write it. That's much harder, learning a new script, but."

Deccy grunted. "I'll say," he said, then: "So go on then, say something."

Liam thought a while, the corners of his mouth curling into a wicked smile. "Mus zibbiye," he said at last. "Insh'allah, mus zibbiye."

"And what's that," Deccy asked.

"Give it to me," Liam replied, smothering the urge to laugh. There was silence again and then Deccy chuckled.

"I tell you," he said, "every time I was stopped by the army, back when I was a wean, I'd be a right cocky cunt to them, pretending I spoke Irish and all. They'd be asking where you from and where you going and the like and I'd be all *bord na mona* and *pogue ma hone* and there's me hardly able to spell in English let alone in Irish." He chuckled again and then both men let the silence fall as they considered the implications of what had just been said.

"And there's the tragedy," said Liam quietly and Deccy grunted in agreement, just as the lights went out.

Liam turned on his side, face to the wall, and ran his fingers along the fluttering pages of the book, feeling for the torn open corner of the letter. He'd read it again in the morning, when it was light, even though he could recall the words off by heart. His body ached at their memory. He'd never see Mo again, not ever.

* * *

Evelyn came down for the weekend because B Company were once again on thirty minutes' notice to move and Rolly could not visit her up in Fulham. As the election got nearer, an emergency tour of Belfast looked inevitable. "Can we go to that nice little pub again?" she said. "The one by the river?"

"Good idea. What was it called? The Crown? The Cricketers? Paul... we went there once, ages ago."

Paul smiled to himself as he fiddled with the settings of his new mobile phone. It had been the weekend he had split with Clare: "It's called the Barleycorn."

The three of them were languishing in the anteroom waiting for something to happen. Rolly had his feet on the coffee table. The Sunday newspapers and empty cups lay scattered around them. Evelyn lay almost horizontally in a chair, her pink stockinged feet resting on Rolly's thighs. Paul glanced occasionally at her neat, pointy ankles when she wasn't looking.

"You coming, matey?" Rolly asked with a lazy turn of his head, "Or are you too busy phoning Linda Lusardi and all your other yuppy mates?"

"Yes, do come!" said Evelyn, flicking hair behind her ear. Paul looked at both in turn: "I'd love to," he said, and offering to drive sealed the deal. With his savings pot from six months of injury, he had recently got his hands on a 1975 Triumph Stag that had once, so it was rumoured, belonged to David Stirling. He was keen to give it a run.

They arrived early. Scattered groups of people were waiting for the doors to open. Inside, the big-bellied owner placed glasses on the shelves and asked them to take a seat; he would be with them in a second. Rolly walked straight to the table where they had sat before, taking the bench against the wall. Evelyn sat next to him, placing a hand on his thigh as she did so. Last time it had been Rolly placing a hand on Clare's shoulder while Paul and Evelyn had talked about the Southbank gallery. Clare had looked frumpy. The memory of the split was like a rugby match:

the bruises had gone but there was still a vague sensation of pain. It had been ages, Paul realised, since he had last got laid.

Other customers had followed them in and the place filled quickly. Paul went to the bar. He felt good: he was no longer bent over like a chimpanzee and his shoulder was relatively pain free. The shin hurt after the fitness test, but he didn't mind. Major Casenove had asked the PTI if Paul had genuinely made it in on time. The PTI had said yes, then pressed the reset button on the stopwatch. It had been Private Zhukov. After being thrown out of the Antitank Platoon, he had been posted to the gym where he could spend his time body building and shouting at others without being encumbered by rank or responsibility. It was a role eminently suited to him. As he departed, Paul had thanked him and the huge soldier winked: "No worries Sir." Paul had finally been passed P1, fit for everything. If the Company deployed on operations, he would go with them.

After paying, Paul turned to take the drinks back to the table but stopped in his tracks. Clare and her parents stood by the door looking round for a place to sit. She saw him, smiled, and waved. He smiled back and scuttled over to the table: "Clare's here. She's just come in... I've got to go and speak to her..."

As he turned, Clare appeared beside him, her parents remaining some way off. Paul acknowledged them but turned to Clare. Her eyes shone. Her face was carefully made up, her lips full, and skin radiant. "You look fantastic," he said. A grey linen coat with a chinese collar curved round her chest and fell away to cling invitingly to her hips. "Wow, you really do..."

"Thank you, Paul," she said, then smiled brightly at Rolly and Evelyn. Rolly, hemmed into the corner by Evelyn, remained sitting. "Hi Clare, it's really good to see you," he said, raising a hand in a wave. Clare fixed him with a calm gaze, the corner of her mouth curling as she lifted her chest: "It's lovely to see you too, Rolly. Lovely to see you both... together."

Rolly winked. "Situation no change, Clare, you know the score. We had to take Paul out or he'd bore himself to death in the Mess."

Clare looked blank for a moment then smiled. It was deft, by both of them, Paul thought. Clare explained that she had been at Kew Gardens with her folks and remembered this place. Paul apologised but said he had to sit down. Leaning back in the chair, he looked from Clare to Rolly and back again. Clare looked down at him and smiled. He winked back. The only innocent here was Evelyn. But in truth it didn't matter, it didn't matter a fuck. Paul reached out to hold her wrist: "You had better be quick if you want to get a table."

"Yes, we had. But we can always sit outside if it's warm enough. Mum smokes anyway."

Paul pulled himself up to standing.

"You're still injured?"

"I'm fine, honest." He held her hazel eyes, thinking happily of all that had passed between them.

"You take care Pauly," she said.

"You too, Clare."

She walked away with the linen coat wafting, spoke to her parents and then pointed at the door. They'd go somewhere else.

Paul sat down. The meeting had put him in a reflective mood. Rolly was looking at the door while Evelyn looked sideways at his profile, her lips thin. "Get some menus will you, Rolly," Paul said, but just as he did so something in his pocket started to vibrate. The guard commander explained that a priority secret signal had just arrived and B Company were to be called in. "We'll be right there," Paul said.

* * *

"Who says you get to go first? Who says so?" Clip demanded.

Liam shrugged, embarrassed. "Command told me," he said. "I've to go to Libya, to buy weapons."

Clip McMahon folded his arms making Liam feel like he was being judged. The younger brother also stared at him, mouth open. Deccy was looking at the floor.

"You'd be putting us all at risk," Clip said, his eyebrows closing together. "You'll not move as quick as us, once we're out. I'll not be waiting for you, not if you can't run."

Liam shook his head. "Not at all," he said. "It's all been sorted. I'll go my own way. There's a van coming for me. It'll be on the road."

Clip sneered. "Oh is there now?"

Liam nodded.

"A van? On the road?"

Liam nodded again.

"And what if I want a van on the road, eh? You tell me that. This was my idea and my work and my fingernails; mine and these here boys here. It's us that done the work and us that took the risk. Why is it you've suddenly been told there's a van to be waiting on you?"

Liam shook his head and shrugged. "You know the reason," he said. "I speak the language. And that's the way it's to be." He spoke quietly, the same way Michael spoke. He was learning how to deal with people. He was learning how to be powerful.

The following day he got a small taste of what the escape would be like. The tunnel entrance was hidden at the back of a sink unit in an underground cell once used for solitary confinement, now a kitchen for the wing. Kneeling at the opening, Liam smelled the orange, clay rich flavours of Irish soil. With his head underneath the piping, looking down the beckoning tunnel into the distant darkness, he swallowed. He had been in custody for just over a year and it was a good six months since he'd last been near any of the machines in the gym. Alone, late at night, thinking of

Mo and aching with loneliness, he'd eaten chocolate bars and sweets a plenty. Now his belly was flabby and his arse rubbery and broad. This was not going to be easy. Having finally navigated round the u-bend and the concrete wall, he measured distance by the wooden riveting planks. The tunnel was dark and cold and terrifying. Before long he was stuck. He could be down here for ever. A dribble of soil ran across his neck and he panicked: "Get me out! Get me out!" Desperately, he reversed his motion, pulling with his toes and pushing with his arms but a nail had got caught in the belt loop of his jeans. He couldn't go forward and couldn't go back. His breathing became rapid. His lungs pressed against the tunnel walls. He was dizzy. Vomit rose in his throat. He kicked. He whimpered.

A hand grabbed him by the ankle. People dragged him backwards. The nail caught his arm, slicing the skin. He didn't care. After all that time he had only just managed to cover his own body length. Back in the kitchen, Liam collapsed on the floor, breathing hard, holding his arm. Sweat poured down his face and chest. Blood trickled over his trousers.

"I'm just..." he wheezed. "I got stuck."

Clip was leaning against the wall with his arms folded. He had a look of extreme distaste on his face. "At the far end there's even less room, you know that?"

Liam didn't look up.

"You see, engineering boy, it wasn't made for you, was it? It was made by me and for me. For me and my brother and Deccy."

Liam could not reply. Vomit burned in his throat. He clawed himself onto all fours to retch, the sick hot and lumpy on his thumbs.

"So this is what we'll do," Clip said. "I'm going first, no matter what Command says. For one thing, it will help. It'll give the Brits more to think about, trying to catch us all. Secondly it'll make the RA look good; another big breakout, like the one in eighty-three, ok?"

Liam nodded but was unable to do much else. His skin itched. There was soil in his pants, down his shirt, in his socks. His mouth tasted foul. He coughed then retched again, his stomach clenched by an iron talon.

"But most of all you're going to need someone ahead of you to lead the way and dig out the upright. You're too fat to move down there." Clip pressed away from the wall and turned to leave. Liam had no choice but to agree. "And no more chockie bars for you, big boy."

\* \* \*

Once he had tightened the bootlaces, Paul's ankle felt supported. He leaned back on the plastic chair, placed his feet on the office desk and folded his arms in thought. In the corridor the men were humping their bergens and rifles to the bus. Sergeant Moor was everywhere, snapping at their heels. With the general election only a week away, B Company were to reinforce the Belfast Brigade as the Urban Reinforcement Company. Intelligence was certain that an IRA spectacular was imminent.

Paul thought of his father. It was funny that they would both be working on the same election, George doing his bit at the party headquarters and Paul preserving the peace.

Sergeant Moor popped his head round the door of the office: "Blokes are out, Boss. Just your kit to go. You want me to get someone up here to get it?"

"No. I'll take it myself."

"Can you make it?" Moor was looking at Paul's bergen. Paul stood, pushed the chair under the desk and leaned down to grab one of the shoulder straps. It was heavy, for sure. His shin ached when he put weight on it but he would strap it tighter and take a few Brufen. *Pain is a sensation and all sensations are fun.*

\* \* \*

"It's to be Wednesday night," Jamesy said over the phone.

"Why? Why not the weekend? When there's reduced staffing?" Liam demanded, frowning in the dark confines of the phone box. Something was wrong. He'd been true, as true as anyone, but something was happening he did not understand.

"You're inside, Liam. You've not got the feel for what's happening out here." Jamesy's voice was unconvincing.

"Like what?"

"There's an election coming, a big one. It's on Thursday. The whole country will be out voting; lots of cars on the roads, lots of reporters."

Liam scowled, anger making his voice hoarse: "And lots of flipping coppers at every roadside, Jamesy! Surely..."

Jamesy coughed loudly down the phone, reminding Liam of the risk of bugs. He listened for the sound of recording devices clicking on the line. Outside the cubicle a guard walked passed. "I love you too," he said quickly and Jamesy laughed.

"Well that's good to hear, Liam. For a second there I thought you didn't." He paused a little then continued. "Listen, Liam boy; I'm just relaying to you what Michael's said to pass on. There's gonna be a new government in England next week. Command wants you to make a break for it timed with the election. We think the Labour man, Blair, will win. We want him to. But that doesn't mean his people will be any better than the Tories. We made good ground with Major, thanks to the operations across the water – the work you done – but we have to keep the pressure on. We have to keep them guessing. We're nearly there; it's so close we can feel it. There's even talk of getting the prisoners released. All of them, Liam: JP, Michael, Shamey, the works! Just think about it boy, just think about it."

It didn't need thinking about. His instructions were clear enough. They'd all go. And Wednesday night it would be.

\* \* \*

267

We are Five Platoon.

It's like being home, coming here, we've done it that many times. The kerb stones are painted to tell you where you are. The terraced houses have scrubby yards bordered with untrimmed hedges. Paint peels off the window frames. The catholic streets are scabbier than the proddy ones but it don't matter to us. There are good men and bad men on both sides and we've no attachment either way.

We pause at street corners, dropping on one knee. The dickers, kids mostly, reach for their phones. We glide past. A gang of teenagers appears from down the alley where the bins are kept. They jostle past Cheese and spit at his feet. At the next street corner they turn back to spit again, this time higher. They are testing us, seeing how we react. One of them darts for Cheese's rifle, grabbing the muzzle. His mates swarm in close, snatching at Cheese's arms. Tiny Haynes appears from nowhere, six feet four inches tall, and with the body armour under his smock he looks like an ape. He grabs one youth by the throat and squeezes his scrawny neck between two fingers then lets him fall. We move on before they film us. The youth lies on the pavement, coughing. The others back away. They won't try that again.

We're showing a presence. We're telling them the law is the law, even here.

In the quiet moments, when no one's watching, an old lady smiles at Bobby Carroll. We can see she's tired of the violence. There are loads like her. Her car was stolen three times in two years and though the young men tell her it's all for the cause, her insurance company won't now provide cover. With her husband gone she has to take the bus to see her sister up in Antrim. Weekly, at Mass, she agonises over what she saw from her window but the priest says nothing. He dare not speak out. Today she is tired, weighed down by bags of shopping. Bobby smiles at her, greeting her in his friendly English voice. His face is flushed and not yet capable of a moustache. He reminds her of her youngest, now living in London and never coming home.

All of this we see, all of this and more besides.

On the main road we fan out. You feel mighty, walking down a city street with a rifle, a finger resting along the trigger guard. People glance at you then look away and every few paces we turn and check on the men behind.

There are four milk bottles out on the doorstep of number thirty-one. A few days ago there were three. A window is open in the room above the main door, but the curtain is drawn. It's midday. We log it for the debrief.

The boss is with a policeman who has his hands tucked into the arm holes of his body armour. There are three court summonses to deliver down these streets. The police would never come here without us, not to this village within the city.

The int-cell have told us something's up. They hear whispers from the touts and the undercover boys. It's going to be big and we expect a hit. Heading back into Girdwood, we sprint to break the pattern.

We've been here six days. Fourteen hours a day we're out. In camp we debrief the patrol, clean the rifles, charge the batteries, clean our boots, dhobi our kit and finally, eat. On the walls of the bunk are photos of the men we're looking for. Three of them have a big red X across their face. It's in our dreams to get another. After four hours' sleep we're up again and out on patrol. We're running on adrenalin. This is what we joined for.

When you come through training you're keen as fuck. Then you reach battalion and you chill out. You don't march everywhere or shit yourself every time a corporal walks past. Then boredom sets in. You get a few jollies overseas to keep you happy: two months in Norway; three in Kenya; a trip to Belize. You get courses to get you promoted but all the slots are filled by the men who went down south. You get bored and sign off. You'll be a civvy in a year; free and easy, smoking drugs and getting fat and pulling chicks. Easylife. But then the year-end gets closer. The feeling of camaraderie gets weaker. The tattoo on your shoulder starts to itch. Who am I anyway? What am I without all this around me: sleeping in cramped bunks, washing in cold water, starting a foot patrol at four in the morning in the rain?

So you sign on again. Another day, another twenty-seven pounds and sixty-four pence. This is it. This is reality. This is why we joined. Being on ops is the only thing that matters.

We're squashed into one of the bunks for the daily brief. The Boss says we're in helmets tomorrow. We're stepping up the security level as the election gets closer. We're going to do a rummage; have a nose around some scrub land in the Poleglass. There will be media all over our every move.

We listen in silence for every scrap of information. We know it's his cock on the block if we fuck up. He's not ashamed to say he's never done a rummage before and needs the screws, in fact the whole Platoon, to show him how it's done. He listens to what we say and then he makes a decision. He's different. It's like he's real, he's himself without any falseness.

We will follow him anywhere.

\* \* \*

Clip's feet appeared, followed by his knees. Wriggling like a lassie, he shuffled out from under the sink unit. His face was serious: "We'd best get another plank in that middle section," he said. But then he looked round the room and could not suppress a grin. He unwound his fingers. In the palm of his hand was a dandelion.

\* \* \*

Clare did not mind that Tony Blair was not a Catholic; she was going to vote for him anyway and would do it before going to school. Sitting in the lounge, watching the news with Yvonne, she felt sorry for poor old Major. He seemed a veil of a man.

The TV crew were interviewing people round the country, asking them how they intended to vote. The woman from Birmingham, caught in a shopping precinct, was wearing the same coat that Clare had just bought. She would vote Labour, she said. So would the couple from Newcastle, the woman in Leeds and the man in Glasgow. Only one old man, stiffly proper, said he would vote Conservative but the interview made him look rather daft.

In Northern Ireland the British parties never did very well, the reporter said, people usually voting along religious lines. A studious young man with a smiling face and a stripy scarf around his neck said he was voting DUP but he hoped that Labour got in across the water because Thatcher had signed the Anglo Irish Agreement. The reporter then said security had been especially tightened in advance of the election. The Chief Constable of the RUC had called for the assistance of the public and there was a long-range shot of soldiers walking along a road. No doubt about it. The one at the front was Rolly, his jaw firmly set for the camera.

Oh, Rolly. Never had so much been given to so few.

Silently, so that Yvonne would not be disturbed, Clare clasped her hands and closed her eyes. *Please God bring your Strength and Grace to Paul, and all who serve with him.*

# Northern Ireland, 1ˢᵗ May 1997

Clip and his brother had managed to widen the tunnel in time and Liam found Deccy had stayed by the entrance to pull him out onto the cold, wet grass. He lay gasping and shivering while Deccy patted his shoulder, wished him well, and scuttled off through the fields.

Liam pulled himself up to standing. The air stank of rotting food. His pyjamas were filthy and sodden. Between him and the motorway was a field bordered by a blackthorn hedge. He climbed over a gate and tried to run but the soil sucked at his slippers. He cut his feet on a stone and fell, cursing. A hundred yards away a white van pulled up on the hard shoulder. It was his lift; his ticket to freedom, to Libya.

Liam picked himself up and ran the final ten yards through a dense tangle of nettles which stung his feet, his thighs, even belly as he lifted his arms. The gravel scraped the skin from his feet. He bit his lip but drove himself forwards. He opened the van door and fell inside. As he pulled the door closed, the alarms went off inside the prison.

\* \* \*

"Sir! Sir! Wake up! It's Operation Todber. Someone's escaped from the fucking Maze prison. Get up quick. The OC wants all Platoon Commanders and Sergeants in the briefing room in five. Ready to move in twenty at the HLS."

The Company Clerk left the door partly open as he

darted down the corridor, shouting everyone up. Electric light burned across Paul's eyes. He blinked. Bootless, Moor was otherwise still fully clothed from the previous patrol, lying on his back on the other bed. He looked round, nodding; this was it.

In less than three minutes Paul had swashed toothpaste round his mouth, shaved, and pulled on his clothes. He grabbed the orders book from inside his smock. The corridor was puddled with water as men ran to and from the washroom with towels around their waists. The bunks were like hives of wasps. Blokes grabbed their rifles, bergens, magazines and clothing. Paul shouted a warning order to the screws then sprinted down the corridor, skidding round the corner.

Major Casenove was in the briefing room on the floor below. His eyes sparkled with caffeine. Holding a snooker cue in one hand, he checked through his notes on the lectern before turning to the illuminated map on the wall behind him. Rolly, Sergeant Taggart, Sergeant Moor and Colour-sergeant Edwards all raced into the room and sat down. The Sergeant-major closed the door saying everyone was present. The air was tense and expectant; this was their chance to hurt them.

"These are orders for a company cordon and search operation as part of a wider Brigade plan. At Zero-one-fifteen this morning a mass break out occurred at HMP Maze on the motorway south of Belfast. At least four members of the IRA are now free and all of them were seen heading north outside the walls, three on foot and one by vehicle.

"Their perceived intent is to disrupt the mainland general election with a publicity coup. In addition it is assessed that particular individuals were selected for the break out to be sent abroad on fund raising tasks, most likely to South America. We should therefore expect them to attempt to leave the country at the first possible opportunity.

"The Brigade mission is to capture the escapees in order to neutralise any republican publicity. B Company's task is to mount a network of long-term VCPs on the southbound routes out of the town of Newry in County Armagh, between the A1 and the Newry River. The concept of operations is to have Four and Six Platoons forward around the villages of Killeen and Fathom Lower and Five Platoon in depth along the border centred around the road junction to the west of Clontygora." The Major used the cue to indicate points on the map as the Sergeant-major handed out bits of card. "Your task, each of you, is to set up section-sized VCPs at the grids on the card you've just been given. The main roads, the A1 and the Dublin Road, will be blocked at the border crossing points by the RUC supported by the resident Royal Irish Battalions. Company headquarters will be located with them and provide command and control from there."

Paul examined the map, plotting the grids from the card. They were going to be only just inside the border and he could feel Sergeant Moor contracting beside him.

The Major spoke over the rumblings: "Administration: you'll deploy by helicopter and we have alpha-whisky, a Chinook, on task in..." he checked his watch and realising that time was slipping away, started to rush through what else he had prepared: "nine minutes for sixty-five minutes. Drop off and Company RV is in scrubland along the river bank, grid as listed. If we don't get on the chopper, we have to walk. Priority on the lift is Six Platoon then Four then Five. Food will be brought out to you. Be prepared for being out for twenty-four hours. Further orders will be relayed by radio at Zero-seven-fifteen. This is our chance, B Company. Let's go."

Paul had questions but rapping on the door indicated that others were coming in to use the room. The Major was swept away by a Captain from Brigade Headquarters and a Lieutenant-colonel stepped into Paul's chair as soon as he had stood. Everyone was grim faced, turning maps in their hands. Paul felt like a small cog as other much larger ones turned around him. He looked at Moor who flicked his eyes towards the corridor.

"Your kit ready?"

"Always."

"Well let's get out to the HLS; we can brief the screws out there and then at least we're ready for the chopper."

"You're on."

The men were struggling down the corridors leaning over to compensate for the weight of their bergens.

"Pass the message: RV at the fuel store by the HLS in two minutes; orders will be given there. Pass the message on." Paul repeated the instruction to three soldiers. The screws and lance-jacks must already be out there. Sergeant Moor checked the rooms but they were already empty, the chairs scattered and beds misaligned. A single green sock lay bent in a dusty corner. Collecting his kit, Paul ran through his mental checklist: dress, equipment, weapons, ammunition, rations... Sweeping the bergen up onto his shoulder he backed out of the room. Shuffling down the corridor, his shin ached as if straining at the bootlaces. By the time he was outside the transit block, he was limping quite badly. Moor overtook him as they paced towards the HLS and at the fuel shed he dumped his bergen gratefully.

In the dawn mist, shadows darted. Under a blaze of floodlights, a sergeant wearing a high visibility vest and ear defenders stood on the HLS directing the helicopters as they came in to land. Sergeant-majors bellowed for squads of men. Major Casenove, erect and aquiline, spoke to another brigade staff officer. Six Platoon were already clambering onto a Chinook, the loadmaster waving the stragglers to hurry. The downdraft blew paper and twigs across the landing site. Outside the floodlights the world was still sleeping. Paul felt more elated than at any time in his life. His heart raced. The thrill of the hunt coursed through him. Delta had already got the sections into three lines by the fuel store and all the corporals were ready for Paul's orders when he arrived. He briefed them what he knew, divvying up the locations for each section as he spoke. Banks was sitting on his bergen and indicated someone was calling for him. Paul turned round to see Major Casenove walking towards him. He straightened and saluted.

"Sir. I'm giving my orders...."

The Major waved him to be quiet. The Chinook's engines were groaning, the pitch and volume rising: "Paul, I'm sorry but I need you to stay here. We need to provide a liaison officer back to Brigade Headquarters; they're short of watchkeepers. In view of your injury this will be you. Follow that officer there. He will take you to the operations room. Sergeant Moor will command the Platoon."

Paul's face fell: "But Sir..." The Major was already turning away and lost in the business of his mind. "Sir, I want to be with my Platoon..."

Major Casenove turned back, his face reddening and the vein on his temple pulsing. He poked Paul in the chest with a finger: "I'm sure you do. But don't fucking argue; just do it. We can worry about your sensibilities later. Right now the Brigade Headquarters needs another watchkeeper to control this operation. I suggested you. You'll learn a lot from seeing it all happen. Moor is perfectly capable of commanding the Platoon and I will put Rolly in charge of all troops on the ground. Now just do as you're told. Follow Captain Melhish and he will escort you."

The Major was gone in a second, pulling his beret from his head as he ran for the chopper. The tailgate lifted closed as soon he was on board and the vast machine lifted nose first and shot up into the sky. Hot fumes blasted Paul as he turned and knelt, shielding his eyes from grit and leaves.

A man in a ridiculous green hat appeared at his shoulder: "Are you Paul? We haven't met. Simon Melhish. Could you come with me?"

"Just a fucking minute will you?" Paul snapped, then turned: "Sergeant Moor, on me." The corporals,

Moor and Banks all crowded round him. Paul made the immediate decision to look professional despite the bitter disappointment. "I've been retasked to Brigade HQ so the command will change with immediate effect: Major C will be at the border crossing point but Mr Rawlins will command on the ground, each platoon itself being commanded by the Sergeant: Taggart for Four Platoon, Beefy for Five and Colour Edwards for Six. Otherwise all instructions remain unchanged. I'm sorry about this but I have no choice. The chopper will be back in fifteen minutes and you will then be out on the ground."

Paul tried to keep his voice inspiring but could not help enjoying the slight frown that played across Corporal Smith's face: "So you're not coming out with us Sir?" He started to grin. "You'll miss all the action."

The blokes were teasing him already. Captain Melhish stepped closer and Paul looked up and nodded to him before saying: "You'd better catch the bastards without me. Good luck."

Grabbing the strap of his bergen, he heaved it onto his shoulder, bending over to take the weight on his legs. Fuming at the injustice, he ground his teeth and muttered to himself, loud enough for Melhish to glance round at him. He could not look back. His men were going off without him.

* * *

Why did it have to be Jamesy driving the van? He drove like a teenager who'd just got the keys to his Da's Golf. "Jamesy!" Liam snapped. "Catch yourself on. The roads will be crawling with coppers, but. Don't go getting us pulled."

Jamesy looked over his steering arm with a mixture of hate and jealousy. "How'd you get to be the one chosen?" he said, shaking his head.

The pair fell silent for a while, and Jamesy slowed the van to take the Rathfriland Road cross country. Liam wanted to be thankful that the driver was someone he knew, but he wasn't. He didn't trust Jamesy, never had.

At a road junction they both looked left and right, wondering which way was best.

"If they've blocked the border we're fucked," Liam said. "We should go west, down through Fermanagh."

Jamesy shook his head and sucked his teeth. "Don't think so," he said. "It's the double bluff. Command said to do this: straight south on the quickest road. If there's a checkpoint, you just crouch on down and I'll get us through. They'll not have that many policemen on the border, sure they won't. They'll be too busy in Belfast, what with the election and all."

Liam shivered and sneezed. "Well go for it then," he said. But don't just sit here. If we're going to go, go."

Jamesy scowled a little, then turned the wheel and pulled out, following signs for Newry and the A1. Once through the main street they turned at the church and saw the lights of distant houses and farms spread out across the hillside to the south. Distant clouds glowed orange on the underside as the rising sun caught them.

"Shepherd's warning," said Jamesy. "There'll be rain later."

Liam said nothing, tilting with the van as it took the corners. The boots Jamesy'd brought were too big for him. They made his toes hurt. He kicked them off, rubbing the cold skin with his fingers. The overalls were tight around his shoulders and wet from the pyjamas underneath. His legs still burned from the nettles. On the outskirts of Newry the distant wail of sirens kept them both sharp. Liam pulled the boots back on to be ready to run, wishing he had some socks. Jamesy slowed right down, driving very carefully through the town. At the garage there were two cars filling up, the puffs of the drivers' breath rising in the cold air. The police station at the roundabout was lit up but very quiet.

"They're all out and about," Jamesy said and Liam nodded. They were close now. They were so close.

At the junction by the river, Jamesy looked over. If they took a left they'd end up in Warrenpoint, cut off from the south by the river. The car behind them beeped twice to hurry them on just as the lights started to change. Liam thought of Libya and all it meant, all it promised. "Let's go," he said, "Go, go, go."

Jamesy drove through the lights just as they turned red and sped away from the junction, checking in his mirrors. Once over the river they passed a sign pointing right towards a polling station and then finally they were committed. They were only a few miles away now and the excitement ate away inside them as caustic as bleach.

"Fuck!" said Jamesy. "Fuck, fuck, fuck!"

Up ahead, under the rail bridge, a police checkpoint blocked access up to the A1. A tall constable watching the traffic seemed to have locked onto them. He tilted his head to speak into his radio.

Out of instinct, Jamesy immediately bore left on the only road coming off the roundabout that was left open to him, a thin country lane going god knew where. "Best you shifty down there, Liam," he said, and Liam quickly obliged. Curling in tight, he managed to tuck his feet out of the way of the gear stick. He watched Jamesy glancing right and left and back, using his mirrors. He swore under his breath.

The van lurched. Liam bumped his head on the dash and then, as they turned a corner, on the window handle. He protected his head with his hands. The warmth of the engine came through the floor. He could feel the rhythm of the crankshaft and the clutch slipping in between the gears. He imagined the grease and the temperature gradient, the torque models and the design meetings. For a strange moment he thought of Helmut, his boss in London. Had he seen his face in the paper? Did he even care?

Libya. It was all about Libya: almond skin; almond eyes.

The van lurched and then, for what felt like an aeon, sat at a junction as Jamesy looked left and then right and then left again. "It must be this way," he said. "Surely it's this way."

Liam elbowed himself up so he could see. Jamesy made a choice and the van lurched again and choked as he changed gears.

"We're close," Jamesy said. "There's the river and there's the mountains. It's this way for sure. Yes! Yes!"

Liam got into the seat just as they took a bend. The roads were bordered by tall blackthorn hedges, the reason Jamesy had got himself confused. Up ahead, two hundred yards away, an army patrol was setting up a checkpoint. They had to be on the border itself.

"You fucking bastards," Jamesy snapped, instinctively braking to swerve into the driveway of a small, yellow cottage. The van skidded to a halt on the gravel. A red Mini was parked outside the garage. They looked at each other and just as they did so, an elderly woman backed out of the front door and pulled it closed with one hand on the handle and the other on the key. She wore a tweed skirt, a waxed jacket and a scarf over her hair. Liam looked at Jamesy. The two men got down from the van and just as the old woman turned round to look at them, Liam placed one hand over her mouth and grabbed the key with the other.

\*\*\*

Captain Melhish escorted Paul across the car park and round the craters left by the bombing the previous October. He skirted the rubble with an air of one walking on another's grave. The headquarters building had a formal, busy air to it. Shrubs had been tended around the cherry trees. A box hedge had been cut in perfect lines along the wall. The brass plaque by the door had been polished daily and bore the horseshoe symbol of the Brigade. From this building, all military operations throughout Belfast, Down and Antrim were controlled.

"You've completed the junior division of staff college I presume?" asked Melhish. The question was more a statement of one-upmanship than a genuine enquiry. Paul said no, he had not. He was a Platoon Commander. Of course he had not done a captain's course. Melhish looked at him askance, "No, of course not. But that might mean we will find it difficult to employ you as a watchkeeper. Drop your kit here would you, where it won't get in the way." The Captain indicated the well underneath the polished concrete stairs, just inside the door. Paul looked doubtfully at it. "No," he replied. "I'm not putting my kit where it's going to get robbed. And if you want a brew boy or a fucking signaller you can look somewhere else. Have you got something for me or not? If you haven't, I'm going back out with my men."

Melhish raised his hands: "All right old chap; just stay calm OK? I've just been sent out to collect you because your OC said he could spare an officer. I presumed you were fully trained. But if not we'll certainly find some way you can help out. We're a little pushed, you see? Look here, the Commander's just coming in now... Good morning, Sir." Melhish turned towards a senior officer who strode through the double doors and up the steps without giving them so much as a glance. He was followed by three bodyguards carrying short-barrelled machine pistols.

The place seemed busy, clinical and impersonal. While his men were out chasing terrorists, Paul would be stuck in some dark ops room making tea for senior officers. The idea appalled him. Throwing the heavy bergen on the floor, he pushed it under the stair with his boot, hiding it as well as possible from the eyes of passers-by.

"Your weapon as well. You'd better go outside and unload it. There's a bay by the guardroom but if you're not going to have a negligent discharge, just go do it into the bushes." Paul did as instructed then, having stowed his magazines away safely, followed Melhish down carpeted, photograph-lined corridors to the operations room.

Inside the double doors there was a blizzard of chatter and an air of professionally disguised mayhem. A bank of signallers manned a variety of radios. A huge map behind a glass window was illuminated with top lights. Unit location markers and boundary lines were being hastily added by a slender female Lance-corporal. A Major was reading a file and relaying information for one of the signallers to broadcast to the troops on the ground. He was dishevelled; his sleeves were lazily rolled, his shirt half buttoned and a thin, bent cigarette dangled from his lip. A stunning female soldier in Royal Irish uniform placed a mug of coffee next to his elbow, almost curtseying as she did so. He spoke without looking up: "Thank you Petra... now Corporal Malcolm please relay on the PIN that we're looking for four, not three pax as previously advertised. The prison service have at last been good enough to explain who they are: The first is Christopher '*Clip*' McMahon, 26, of Fermanagh and the second is his younger brother James McMahon, 24. The third is Declan Moynihan, 24 of Claudy and the fourth is a Mr Liam Gerard, 31, of Anderson's Road in Bally – oh golly gosh, it's the engineer himself! My my. Well that'll keep the boys focused down on the border won't it? That's the man that kicked off all the fuss we had last year. Petra, be so good as to nip next door and ask the G2 and SpecOps teams to get in here... they'll want to know Gerard is back on the Christmas card list."

The officer took a long swig of coffee, swallowed, extinguished his rollup and in one fluid movement, rolled another from an open pouch on the desk, only looking up at Melhish and Paul as he licked the gum. Bloodshot eyes understood all Paul's weaknesses within the period it took for his tongue to move from one end to the other.

"Hello," he said, coming up to standing. "I'm Peter Haldane, G3 Ops." As the Major extended a narrow, brown hand, one of the phones on his desk started to ring and he turned immediately: "Excuse me; that'll be the Boss just come in... Good morning Brigadier... Yes, what an excellent turn of events, isn't it! Yes, right away. Be with you in three."

The officer swept a jacket from the back of his chair, buttoned it up and placed his cap on his head before carefully balancing his newly rolled cigarette on the side of an over-full ashtray. The attractive clerk appeared with two men at a side door, one bearded and dressed in jeans, the other small and wearing glasses. "Come with me," Haldane said to them. "We'd better brief the Boss together." He turned to Melhish: "Mel: make our new friend comfortable. Petra will get him some tea. Then once you've done that try and get hold of the Chief of Staff will you. We need him in, no matter how trousered he was last night."

Paul looked round the place with wide eyes. It was true: Brigade Headquarters were havens of utter insanity.

\* \* \*

We are Five Platoon.

We're lined up waiting for the alpha-whisky to collect Four Platoon and then it's our lift next. Beefy's out the front, arms folded, body bent against the downdraft as the wokka-wokka lands, arse end first.

It's operations. You step over the dead and injured. You keep going, task in your mind. You can deal with the casualties after it's done.

But something's bugging us. Something's pissing us off. Beefy talks to the screws. He's shaking his head and spits.

Thirty metres away is an officer called Rawlins. He's big and fit. He's good looking, like a photo in a magazine. He is directive and self-assured in manner and we've just been told he's in charge of us. We don't like it. He's a cock: a selfish, medal-hungry, arse-licking cock. So there ain't no way we're gonna let him command us, not if Sergeant Moor has his way.

Beefy grabs Luke Banks and pulls him to the side, speaking close in his ear. Banks is at first afraid then starts to laugh. That's the thing about blokes who went to posh schools like officers. They're dead good at acting and very soon Banks is looking at his handset and shouting across to Duggan, the signaller from Four Platoon: "Duggie! Are you not getting the message? Brigade is on the net; they're after Mr Rawlins. It's urgent."

Duggan checks his radio and shakes his head. He's not getting anything cos of the wind. Banks shouts for Mr Rawlins as the chopper takes off and he comes over all cocksure and swaggering. Banks gives him the handset and he speaks into it. There's nothing there and then Banks shakes his head and shrugs; says it's his fault. But he was sure there was a message from Brigade Headquarters that Mr Rawlins was to go and replace Mr Illingworth.

Sergeant Moor nods. He heard it too.

Mr Rawlins looks round, seeking Sergeant Taggart, but he's just gone out with the last heli lift. He has to make the decision himself. He's smiling. He thinks he's the better officer, the one who should be in Brigade Headquarters. He'll get noticed.

Sergeant Moor can read his mind. He nods: "You best be quick Sir. Get over there and get Mr Illingworth back before the chopper returns."

In a second the officer has picked up his bergen and is taking his swaggering arse across the car park. His Platoon look baffled but we're already spluttering. Then we start giggling. Dicko rolls onto his back, kicking his legs in the air, laughing like a pipe bomb till Westy tells him to shut it.

Fucking officers.

But we want ours back.

* * *

It was impossible not to enjoy deploying by helicopter. The blokes were smiling to themselves, their rifles upturned and chins resting on the butts. The aircraft dropped and wove down the coastline to the Mourne Mountains then swung inland to approach the landing site from a new direction. With the tailgate down Paul looked out the back, mesmerised by the heat-coiled air and the juddering of the airframe.

These truly were awesome machines.

Coming into land, the heather blew sideways. The loadmaster spoke urgently to the pilot and then flicked his microphone away from his mouth: "Go!"

The Platoon sprinted out, bergens in one hand, rifles in the other. No sooner had they thrown themselves into all round defence than the hot downdraft blasted their necks, sweeping twigs and soil up around them. They covered their eyes as the chopper lifted off and away into silence.

South Armagh.

They had landed by a coniferous wood that ran along the banks of the river. Dawn had broken. Paul's ears still rang from the engine noise. Looking west, he made out the motorway and the Dublin road by the backed up lines of traffic on the southbound carriageway. Northwest towards Newry, the houses were sparse and modern; each separated from its neighbour by impenetrable hedges. The terrain had a foreign feel to it; the little differences emphasising the novelty of it all.

Banks disturbed his reverie by holding out the radio: "Boss; it's Zero-alpha. He's after you." Paul took the handset: "This is Two-zero, send message over." The line went quiet. The Major sounded angry: "I was expecting you to be tasked to higher formation. I thought you would be at Brigade Headquarters, over."

Paul did not know what to say. Rolly had appeared in the operations room and said there had been a change of plan. He was to go out on the ground and Rolly would stay in Brigade. He had tried not to sound triumphalist but it was clear he thought it the more fitting way round. Paul had equally needed no second offer. Within a second he was limping back to the HLS just in time for the last lift. His Platoon had been holding the chopper for him and Dicko had run back to help him with his bergen.

"Er, negative. One-zero came to replace me, over." Paul frowned, looking at the handset. Banks turned away, biting his lip. Moor nudged him with his knee. There was silence and then the Major said: "Never mind. You're here now. The other two callsigns are established. You know what you have to do. Orders remain unchanged. Your remaining sections are to operate a roving patrol along the border and provide reserves for incidents as they occur. I will be located here unless the situation changes. Acknowledge, over."

"Roger out."

It was all so haphazard. He studied the map and the grids given in the morning orders until they made sense. If the escapees made a dash south towards the republic they could come this way – all the more likely since the major roads were blocked at the border. He formulated a plan in his mind and knelt upright: "Section commanders on me," he said.

\* \* \*

He'd been lucky, Liam thought, luckier than he could possibly imagine.

The old woman lived by herself. At first she had spluttered and kicked like a wildcat, but then Jamesy had slapped her and she'd gone rigid in his arms, one hand on her cheek, mouth hanging open. The look she had given Jamesy would have curdled milk, but she became pliable nonetheless. In the kitchen they'd told her to sit in a prickly tweed armchair, one she obviously used often. They'd turned it round so she had to face the wall. She winced at the scraping on the tiled floors and again at Jamesy kicking the cats into the bedroom, but otherwise she said nothing, not a word.

The kitchen was small but well planned. There was a counter and beyond that a picture window covered with vertical blinds that hung down to a low bookcase. Peeking out through the blinds Liam noticed the sky fast clouding over. A tiny square of patio, bordered with bird feeders, edged up against a trimmed lawn that disappeared under a tall holly hedge. No one could see in and no one could see out and once again Liam counted his blessings. All they had to do was sit it out and wait for nightfall. The patrols would have to move on eventually – in fact they rarely stayed in one place for longer than a few hours.

He turned to find the old woman looking round at him, her face a picture of prim certainty: "I'll have to feed them, you know, Elizabeth and Diana; my cats. They'll be hungry. I feed them this time of day."

Liam was surprised by her confidence towards him, her lack of fear. "Where's the food?" he asked.

The old woman pointed to a cupboard on the wall and he spooned gloopy chunks of meat into two small plastic bowls, one red and one blue, which were on the floor by the radiator. He filled the white bowl with water and put that down too, then went into the hall to open the bedroom door. The cats ran out through his feet and into the kitchen, leaping first on to the old woman and then, after a time, down to the food. The old woman watched them fondly.

"Do you put them out?" asked Liam.

"In the evening," she said. "They're too old to be out for long, a bit like me."

Liam folded his arms then realised how hungry he was. Helping himself to cereal and milk he incurred a withering stare, which he ignored.

"This is not a robbery," he said. "You'll not be harmed in any way provided you don't start causing any bother, but..."

The milk was slightly off but he didn't mind. The cereal was fresh and novel in his mouth. He had a second bowl then put the kettle on. The woman glanced at the old radio on the counter and he put it on – a classical channel – just to keep her calm. After eating, one of the cats deftly leaped up on to her lap while the other settled into a basket in the corner, curled round on itself, and went to sleep.

Jamesy came in from the living room with a phone in his hand.

"I've said we didn't make it, but we're close. I've said we've gone to ground and we'll just sit it out till later. They say nothing's been announced, nothing at all. They're waiting to see the news in an hour. Then maybe they'll make a statement." Jamesy stood with his weight on one leg, the other bent. He kept passing the phone between his hands like a football. The old woman watched him with interest until he noticed her: "Look at the wall, you," he said, then "I'm away back to the lounge to watch the telly. You'll stay here with Mrs Doyle?"

The old woman tutted and dropped her head into one hand. Jamesy looked down at her as she hid her face, shaking her head. He left. Liam looked at the space where he had stood. The old woman looked up at him with pity on her face. "I was a teacher for years and years," she said. "If there's one thing that's certain, that boy is lying."

\* \* \*

Paul never stopped. The triangle of terrain between the A1 and the river was his personal battlefield and no terrorist was going to get through the net he wove. The forward platoons held the major junctions which stopped any traffic getting into the area undetected from the town. Five Platoon's checkpoint blocked a single minor road that cut away from the A1 to service the villages just across the border. Paul rotated the sections across the whole Company position in order to relieve the boredom and keep the men focused. A roving patrol kept a fervent eye out for snipers setting up a shoot from inside the Republic. With Major Casenove locked into a position up on the motorway Paul was, in effect, commanding the entire Company.

The Major came round the positions at midday with the Sergeant-major, delivering packed hot meals. He congratulated Paul on his efforts and seemed genuinely pleased with the dispositions and routines Paul had put in place. He asked how the leg was holding up. Paul replied that he had not noticed it – the thrill had been too great. The Major nodded before his face took on firmness that bordered on anger: "Now Paul, I thought I had told you to support the brigade staff. I thought I told you, quite clearly, that you would remain in Thiepval Barracks."

Paul shrugged, not knowing what to say. "So did I Sir. But Rolly turned up and said he had got a message from you by radio to take my place..."

"How could I have done that Paul? I was in the chopper?"

"I know Sir, but I didn't question it..."

The Major watched his face closely. Then casting an eye round the throng of men scoffing their fish and chips, he spied Moor leaning against the side of the Land Rover. He was smirking to himself.

"This has nothing to do with you, has it Sergeant Moor?" the Major asked.

"Me Sir? Nothing at all." Moor shook his head, a sly smile playing across his lips. "But I'm really glad *you* decided to swap Mr Illingworth with Mr Rawlins, Sir. Me and this cunt Gerard has some unfinished business. So I needs the Platoon here with me, including the Platoon Commander. And someone once told me, a long times ago, that it's always better to maintain the integrity of a good platoon, eh?"

The Major froze. His face lengthened as Moor winked and turned away to dunk his crumpled chip paper into a bin bag. Paul looked from one to the other trying to work out what was happening. The Major nodded imperceptibly and smiled to himself. "Very well," he said, before accepting the way things were and taking Paul aside. "Listen, Paul. There have been a number of developments you need to brief your men on. First of all there's still no sign of Gerard but the other three have been caught. This is to be passed down by word of mouth only – nothing is to be said on the net. The whole issue has been D-Noticed – the press cannot report it. We will say nothing unless the republicans do. Since they have said nothing, we suspect Gerard is not yet in a safe place. We think he's still in the Province and we think he's heading this way, right towards us. He's leaving it as late as possible to make his break.

"The sneaky-beaky boys are getting close. We know he has a driver with him, a man called James Horgan, from Belfast. And we know they're holed up somewhere, we just don't know exactly where.

"If we can capture Gerard before he gets across the border then we can bang them all back up inside the prison and pretend it never happened. The thing about *Norn Iron* is perception. We have to create the *impression* of peace and stability. We have to pretend normality exists. To pull this off we need to get Gerard back inside with the minimum of fuss. That is what you need to brief your blokes on and get them to stick to. Do you understand what I'm saying?"

The Major grasped Paul's arm. "I understand, Sir" he said. He had to keep Moor under control. The Major nodded, patting his shoulder.

It would be dark in an hour. The Corporals were already getting jumpy about the static nature of their positions. Paul told them they would remain in situ until last light and only then would they relocate. They just had to hope Gerard popped up before then.

\* \* \*

It was dark at last. Liam opened the door a crack and listened to the sounds around the house. The helicopters had gone and the traffic was moving easily along the Dublin Road, so the RUC must be just standing about and waving people on. Was it time to make a move? The van was still in the yard, parked close up against the holly hedge, and the widow's Mini was by the garage as it had been all day. He walked round the yard, decided everything looked normal, and headed back inside the house. As he opened the back door, the cats disappeared out between his legs. He looked over at the old woman: "Mrs, the cats are out. That all right?" She nodded and said nothing more.

Jamesy came back from the lounge again and made himself a sandwich. He found a tin of supermarket lager at the back of the fridge and drank it. "Sure when this is all gone you'll have a story to tell your mates at Mass," he said to the woman. She looked at him and tutted, saying nothing, then cast a quick glance at Liam. He kept his face impassive. It wasn't Jamesy's fault he was an idiot. On the table by the armchair was a King James' Bible with a gold cross on the cover.

Liam brushed the rain off his overalls and shook himself. His feet were cold and he asked if the old woman had any old pairs of her husband's socks or a jumper he could wear. She snapped at him to leave her husband's things alone but then Jamesy told her to be quiet and she was. Liam said he had no choice; he was freezing and his feet were bleeding.

The old woman's bedroom smelled of lavender and she slept in a single, rather than a double bed. On the mahogany dresser, behind the silver backed brushes and a small trinket box, was a large school portrait of a dark haired girl wearing a green jumper and the same gap-toothed smile. An old, curling remembrance poppy was jammed between the photo and the mount. Behind this was a hexagonal wooden plaque bearing a golden elephant on a lurid pink and green background. A brass label on the oak plinth was inscribed, *To Mrs Sandra McKee, hoping you find the bright side of life again. From the Captain and All Ranks, HMS Coventry, July 1982.*

Christ! A prod and a war widow. She could yet be useful, Liam thought.

Rummaging through the heavy, deep drawers of the dresser, he found a vast white, polo-necked jumper and thick woollen socks. They smelled of moth balls but he pulled them on anyway and the warmth immediately spread through his body.

Back in the kitchen the old woman shook her head. "My man died in the service of his country," she said.

"And maybe I am prepared to do so in the service of mine," Liam replied.

The old woman looked at him, her mouth slightly open. "Fool," she said, shaking her head. "Nothing but a fool."

Jamesy appeared again from the living room, a second beer in his hand. He held the phone up in the other and shook it. "Still nothing on the news," he said. "They're onto us, though. Command says we should stay put and be prepared. The border's crawling with soldiers. They're everywhere. We're to be ready." As he spoke, he reached into his pocket and pulled out a small pistol and handed it to Liam. "This is for you," he said, then pulled another from the back of his jeans. "I've an automatic."

Liam looked at the guns and then at Jamesy.

"Why'd you not give me this earlier?" he said.

Jamesy shrugged. "There was no need," he said, then turned and went back to the lounge.

Liam shook his head, placing his pistol on the counter. He went to the picture window and pulled the blinds slightly apart so he could see into the dark garden. Lights from the house illuminated the lawn. One of the cats pranced across it to the back door. Liam let it in and it mewled, brushing against his leg. The old woman whispered for it from her chair, twiddling her fingers. Liam stuck his head out into the cold air. It was unmistakeable, the sound of booted feet walking in unison along the road beyond the holly hedge. He closed and locked the door without making a noise.

"He's going to sell you down the river, you know," the old woman said. "I heard him talking, on the phone, when you went out. They just want you to get caught. Or get shot. It's the publicity they're after, not you," she said.

The cat brushed against her legs, its tail upright. It turned and looked at Liam and sniffed the air, then went on to inspect the blue bowl and then the white one.

Liam shook his head and flushed. He'd left the pistol on the counter. He walked over and grabbed it, ramming it into his pocket.

"Oh, I'll not touch that damnable thing," she said. "And even if you can't see the truth, you might as well listen to one that can."

Liam shook his head again but he felt hollow inside, as vacant as a lie.

The old woman snorted and shrugged then took a sip of water. "Well have it your own way," she said. "But if you don't mind, young man, I need to go to the bathroom."

\* \* \*

It was the last hour of the operation. The radio confirmed that all callsigns were to collapse their cordons at Twenty-two-hundred and rendezvous for collection where they had been dropped off. The drizzle was falling harder and the fabric of Paul's smock was sodden. His legs were soaking. Water sloshed around his boots. He was cold. His ankle was swollen and stiff but he had to show example and keep the men focused through to the dying seconds. They had not found Gerard anywhere.

Voting would be over back home. His postal vote had been made more out of loyalty to his father than any personal leaning. He saw himself as an agent of the state and it didn't really matter who was in power; his duty would always remain the same. As they stood in the rain on an empty road, Paul thought of his father staying up all night, waiting for the counts to come in.

Moor suppressed a yawn: "You only gets one chance," he said. "I've had mine." Paul glanced across at him through the rain. His beret had darkened with the water and the cap badge angled sharply over his eyebrow.

"Is that what you think? You've missed it?"

Moor licked his fleshy lips. "I'll only be remembered for fucking up; Mercy shooting the wee kid. Getting bust down to Private. And having my nads shot off."

His grey eyes were almost luminous in the dark. The rain dribbled down his face and across the exposed part of his chest where his smock was open. He did not feel the cold. A cigarette was hidden in his huge hand and he took a drag, hiding the glow with the lapel of his smock.

That was it. That was all it ever was, the secret Paul had sought for so long. Moor wanted a legacy. He had no children and no bloodline. Even his adopted kids would be poisoned against him. He had been down south, yes, but not in his eyes. On the verge of the battle he had been removed from the line. Men had died; men his presence might have saved. It could have been him in the painting.

"There'll be other times, Bryan."

Moor met his eyes but looked away, blowing out a stream of smoke and shaking his head. There were five checkpoints within a two mile radius and every spare policeman and dog unit in the Province had been in place since Zero-six-hundred that morning. There was fuck all point being soppy. The two men looked down the road into the darkness. Moor turned his head: "You know why you came good in the end? Why they're busting a gut for you?"

Paul flushed. He shook his head.

"It's cos you listens. You puts them first. You're straight and they trusts you..."

The conversation was disturbed by Delta beckoning from the checkpoint a little up the road: "Boss. Come here a second, will you?" Platoon Commander and Sergeant strolled over to him to find his men tense and watchful. Paul was both relieved and annoyed to have his moment with Moor taken from him. Delta pointed along the hedgerow to one of the houses. A skylight in one of the roofs was flashing. Then it went dark. Then it started again.

"It's morse," said Delta. "Cheese noticed it. He said it did SOS then stopped. Then it did it again. This is the third time."

"Kids playing?" said Paul.

"It's nine o'clock."

They looked up. The skylight could only really be seen from above. Paul told Delta to take TP and have a scan round the house. It would be the last action of the day. His receding figure faded quickly into the darkness and then appeared again under a streetlight further down the road. TP was a few feet behind and to the side, avoiding the light. Both Moor and Paul nodded at each other. The big South African would be the next nomination for promotion.

"I'm going to talk to him," Paul said. "He's got a wife and kids you know. He could use the extra money."

Moor's mouth fell open: "Since when?"

Paul nodded. "He told me when we were on the plane, before I piled in."

Moor made a face, nodding slowly. "I didn't know that."

As Delta and TP walked along the road they were suddenly bathed in light as a security lamp came on, set off by a cat. They darted into the safety of darkness and then Delta's voice could be heard on the radio as he plate checked a vehicle. Paul wished they were back in camp, away from these cold, unfriendly houses. A female voice on the radio replied to Delta's query almost immediately: "Vehicle is a black Volvo 340 registered to a Mr Hannah of Belaghy, County Londonderry."

Moor frowned. "What would he be doing here I wonder? Belaghy is a shithole of a place on the way north." The two men looked up the road. Beyond the circle of light, below the street lamp TP was waving frantically. Paul and Moor ran forward, Moor calling Delta's section to collapse the VCP and join them. Very quickly, they formed a line along the roadside against a tall holly hedge. Through interwoven branches Paul could see a neat yellow bungalow with two vehicles parked on the front yard: a white Ford van and a small red Mini.

"I've just plate checked that van. One thing I'm sure of is it ain't a black Volvo."

Paul looked along the line of men. "Anyone notice anything about this place today?"

Cheese raised his hand. "I saw that van drive in this morning. Came up at a rate of knots, two men in the front. But it swerved in here so I never thought much of it. Looked natural enough, like. Bloke in a rush to get home."

"Me too, Boss," said Haynes. "But nothing else, that's the thing. All the other houses have had people going in and out all day. But here, nothing."

The men looked to Paul and he could feel the weight of their expectation. In the earpiece of the radio callsigns reported that they were collapsing their positions and withdrawing back to the helicopter landing site. Exfil would be in thirty minutes. They would have to move quickly or might miss their lift.

But it wouldn't hurt to have a look.

Just as Paul was about to say something, the front door opened. Yellow light spilled across the yard. A woman, her hands held behind her back, was pushed out of the door by a youngish man in a white, polo-necked jumper.

"Let me go," the woman snapped. "Let me go I say. I will not drive you and I will not help you escape. You can do what you want but I'll..."

The entire Platoon shrank behind the hedge, their ears sharp in the darkness. Paul, facing towards the hedge, straightened his legs and raised his rifle into a firing position. He mustn't forget the warning.

"Stop! Army! Or I fire!"

As he shouted, Moor twisted on his toes and sprinted to the driveway to get another view.

Standing, Paul found the hedge too thick to see clearly. The last thing he wanted was hit the woman. Along the hedgerow, TP was the quickest to move. He pushed himself away, searching for a gap between the lower branches.

The man in the jumper proved surprisingly quick on his feet. As soon as Paul shouted, he ducked, dragging the woman downwards as a shield. When nobody opened fire, he pushed her back up the steps and into the doorway, simultaneously pulling a pistol from his pocket. He fired twice into the hedge towards them. Paul ducked. A door slammed. Paul's heart doubled in pace. It was the first time someone had fired live ammunition in his direction. He heard the door slam. Then a rifle clattered and something heavy collapsed on the road beside him.

Paul's mouth fell open. Blood was already pooling around the body where Private Terry Pietersen lay on the tarmac.

\* \* \*

Liam knew better than to stay by the door. With the bolts applied, he heaved the terrified old woman down the corridor and threw her into the kitchen. She shrieked, tripped, and banged her head against the armchair to lie motionless on the tiles.

Jamesy looked at him, his face draining of colour: "Liam, I..."

"Say nothing!" Liam snapped "You've set me up, haven't you? There was no Libya, was there? There is no escape plan or anything. You just wanted a martyr?"

Jamesy stammered a denial, his hands raised, but the more he denied it the less convincing it became. He changed tack: "Look, I didn't know she was signalling did I? I couldn't follow her into the toilet! I saw the light under the door and barged it!"

"That's got nothing to with it! Tell me the truth Jamesy! Tell me the fucking truth. Am I being set up or not?"

Jamesy's mouth worked words without making a sound. Liam slapped the side of his head with the pistol: "Get this straight. I'm getting across that border this night, understand? I'm getting across the border then I'm going away and you'll never hear of me again. I'm through with it. I'm done. You can take your drugs and your beatings and you can ram them up your arse."

His voice had risen. Jamesy detected the fear. He sneered at Liam's threat and chuckled to himself.

"And how you gonna do that then, Audie Murphy? There's soldiers out there, loads of 'em. We can't fight them all off. We're not cut out for that..."

"You're not listening, you stupid wee shite. I'm not going back to prison. The border's a few hundred yards that way and I'm getting there tonight. Either with you or without you."

Liam stuck the stubby pistol in Jamesy's stomach. They both looked down at it and then at each other, their mouths open. Jamesy sneered and shook his head slightly. "You wouldn't fucking dare," he said.

\* \* \*

"He's still breathing."

"Keep him alive. Delta, put men there along the hedge, cover the back and the yard."

Banks was already on the radio: "Hello Zero this is Two-zero. Contact as at Twenty-one-fifty-five hours; two males including the main target have taken a hostage and are armed. Am establishing cordon, out." The radio responded with a blizzard of chatter, relayed information and requests for clarification. Paul ripped off his headset to be able to think: "Banks get the other callsigns in here. We need to assault this place quickly or we lose the advantage."

Banks nodded, pressing the earpiece of his radio to make sense of the chatter. "Boss be careful. Zero's flapping about the hostage. He says stand off and cordon; the target's going nowhere."

Moor had run back to join them. "Bollocks," he snapped. "We've got him. I want him. That cunt cost me. Cost Mercy. He's going down."

Haynes grabbed TP's webbing straps and dragged him across the road, out of any line of fire. He pulled off the body armour and clothing to get to the wound: "I need Scouse here now."

The other soldiers took on a hardness that Paul found frightening, their heads tilted in the firm certainty of men about to fight. Fingers pressed the safety catches off. Eyes lowered into sights.

There was a shot from inside the building. A woman screamed. Paul looked at Moor: "If we don't go now, she might be killed." Moor nodded. Paul looked at Banks: "Where are the other sections?"

"Inbound. Chink in five minutes, Westy in ten. The other callsigns are on their way back to the HLS. It'd take them half an hour to get here"

"Police?"

"I don't know Boss, I..." Banks shrugged, shaking his head. Paul nodded, patting him on the shoulder. "You're doing a great job Luke. Just keep me informed of what they say and relay to them what I do." The soldier nodded.

Paul turned to Delta: "We're going in. But we're going to call their bluff first." He stole quickly round the front of the building using a stone gate post for cover. The hallway lights had been extinguished and there was no movement in the windows. He threw a stone at the door. It banged noisily against the wood: "Liam Gerard. Come out with your hands up and no-one will be hurt..."

Silence. Then muffled shouts from deep inside the building. The woman screamed again. They were at the back.

Paul darted across the yard and up to the front door, placed a foot firmly on the top step, and kicked hard with the sole of his right. Pain razored up his shin. The top bolt shattered but the bottom one held. Paul knelt, ready to barge it. Just as he ducked down, two shots splintered through the door, inches above his shoulders. In an instant he was on the ground and slithering away into cover.

That was stupid.

"Boss. What the fuck are you doing? The other sections are here," hissed Moor from the hedge. Paul rolled away from the building and darted out to join him on the road, calling the section commanders in.

"I wanted to test them. Now listen: Two Section, Scouse to cover TP immediately."

"He's there," said Westy.

"Good. The rest of your men replace Delta's as fire support and cover across the front and rear. One Section, Chink, you're in reserve. I want Three section, Delta, to be the assault. They've seen the men and have a feel for what we're dealing with."

Paul rose from crouching to survey the building. "We'll go round the far side and in the back. Brief your men, but be quick. Watch the blue on blue as we come round the far corner. I don't want any more casualties."

The section commanders disappeared. Banks held out the radio: "Boss it's Zero. He wants you." Paul shook his head. Moor was beside him. "Have I forgotten anything?" asked Paul.

Moor shook his head. "No. Let's get in there." Banks was insistent: "Sir. Zero is demanding to speak to you now. He's..."

Paul turned to Moor: "Sort him out will you. Time is critical."

The sections were snarling at the leash, driving him forward. Leading these men was an art of control, not motivation. Delta's section had already lined up by the gateway and Paul nodded: "Let's go."

In a flash they were round the back of the building, against the hedge, trying to see through the rear windows. Keeping low, Cheese quietly tested the back door handle but it was locked. The men felt precariously exposed in full view of the windows. Paul could not see an easy way in. The blinds in the picture window would ensnare an entrant. The centre window was too high off the ground, the one on the right too small.

From the garden behind them, a woman's voice shouted through the hedge: "Who are you? What are you doing in there?" Lights shone from behind her. Even through the thick hedge she was silhouetted.

"Go inside madam. British army," Paul snapped.

"What are you doing? Show me who you are," the woman repeated. Just as Paul was about to reiterate his instruction, a shot punched a neat hole through the central window and tore through the hedge. The woman yelped and threw herself down: "Jesus, Mary and Joseph."

But Paul now knew where at least one gunman was hiding. There was no time to brief. He had to lead from the front.

Sprinting across the small lawn, Paul raises the butt of his rifle, smashes it hard into the centre of the glass. He reaches in, grabs the blinds and yanks them out of the way. Men cover the entry point. Delta yells to Carroll, who sets a face then scrambles in, pushing shards out of the way with gloved hands. Paul follows, second man in. Others too. Carroll covers the doorway. A man appears, a man in a jumper. He has a weapon, points to shoot. Paul takes aim, snatching the trigger. It doesn't fire. He ducks as noise cracks the air. Pain in his leg. Thump on his helmet. Falling. Men straddle him, shielding. Shooting. Screaming. He is pulled upright. Safety catch on. There are four small black holes in the door where the man in the jumper stood. Beckett has pulled him up; he was not hit. Delta points his muzzle into the hallway, yelling. Paul plunges forwards but is barged aside. Moor shoves past him, weapon low, face set. He sinks, feet apart, yelling, yelling, yelling. Paul is behind him, shouting. In the hallway, the man in the jumper has an old woman by the throat. He has a pistol to her head. He is bleeding. A second man is motionless on the floor, blood pooling. A cat darts across the hall for the stairs. Moor lunges forward using his rifle as if the bayonet is fitted. He jabs upwards, stabbing the man in the face. He falls backwards, clutching for his eye. Moor turns the rifle in his hands and holding the thin barrel, smashes the butt over his nose and then again in the groin. The man screams. The pistol falls free. Stepping forward, Moor places his foot in the centre of Gerard's belly and lowers the muzzle to his jawline: "Now I've got you."

There is silence and perfect stillness.

The old woman is bound at the wrists and spitting with anger: "Shoot him! Shoot the evil bastard!"

Paul lets the voice fall away and calmly, quietly, folds his rifle behind his back. This is his moment. "Stop there," he says. "Do not shoot that man."

At the authority in his voice, the men look at him. Light from the kitchen casts his shadow across Moor's spine. Moor freezes. His head turns slightly but he presses the safety catch off.

"The mission," Paul whispers, "is to capture him without anyone knowing. Your legacy's in your hands, Bryan. Think of the future, not the past."

# Montgomery Lines, Aldershot; July 1997

Pietersen died as a result of his injuries, one week after he was flown back to the Military Hospital in Aldershot. While he was drifting in and out of consciousness in the final days, Paul decided he had to betray the man's wishes and reported the fact of his marriage to the Adjutant. An embarrassed battalion administration made several changes to his documentation and after numerous calls between embassies, his wife was flown over just in time for a clutching, final reunion. The following month was a period of bitter anger and denial by the soldiers of Five Platoon. The loss of one of their number hit them hard, Paul more than any. If he had not shouted Gerard might not have opened fire and the soldier might have lived. Though his men never blamed him, he could not but think of what he might have done differently. A month after the death the coroner released the body and Pietersen was buried with full honours at the military cemetery.

Pragmatic and self-controlled, Pietersen's wife was the picture of composure at the wake in the Corporal's Mess. She was a direct and independent woman and spoke without deference. Paul admired her. Throughout the day she sat with regal serenity, sipping only one glass of white wine. Overcoming his many reservations, he gave his condolences.

"You're the one Terrence called 'LT', that right?"
"Yes it is."

"Well you ought to know that he really admired you. He had many officers in his time. I'm sure you know he was in the NDF and then the Legion..."

"I'm aware of his service history, yes."

"Well what he wrote to me was that there were few officers he had known who listened like you did, who learned. He always said that leadership was like love. You cannot favour one child over another, right? But you do have to put them first, before yourself. He said you did that."

Paul coloured.

"Oh, I know what happened, Paul," she said. "It all came out at the enquiry. *Unlawful killing,* whatever that is. But I want you to know that I don't blame you for his death. I know what wars are like. We've had them in South Africa for the past twenty years and Terrence always said that killing or dying; being brave or being weak; getting a medal or getting shot, was all just a matter of luck. You did your best. That's all. At least I have my son to bear his name."

Paul was embarrassed. He felt stiff and pompous in his service dress, the leather belt inflexible and incongruous. But her words meant more to him than anything. Kneeling by her chair, he placed a hand on one of hers and she in turn did the same for him just as the men from the Platoon came round to place their hands on her shoulders.

The memory of Private Terrence Pietersen would live forever.

A week later Paul was summoned back to Thiepval Barracks for an interview with the Brigadier. In the period of intense blame following the shooting, he had been required to explain the events that led to the killing of one of his men. At first, people doubted his version of events but then the soldiers' reports built up a more detailed picture and Paul's commanders began to see his actions in a different light. He was escorted through the Brigade headquarters and into an expansive, oak panelled office by a fawning Captain Melhish.

The Brigadier sat him down and congratulated him on the job his men had done: "But I'm sorry to let you know that we're keeping this one quiet. There'll be no public briefing and no awards. There was little media interest in Private Pietersen since he has no family here and his wife has now gone home.

"The republicans have kept shtum and so we will too. If they make an announcement we'll downplay the whole story – four men escaped from HMP Maze and were captured very soon afterwards, that sort of thing. Mrs McKee was subject to a vicious and prolonged armed robbery by one James Horgan from the Lower Falls area of Belfast, a crime motivated by pure greed that was resolved by police intervention. She will say nothing more, we've seen to that. The Admiralty recently reviewed her pension and found she had been underpaid since the death of her husband. It appears that she is owed quite a considerable amount, fully backdated of course. And if her neighbours blab about the army shooting guns at night in South Armagh? Well, it's hardly news is it?"

The first time Paul had seen the Brigadier, he had looked officious and incisive. Now, serving him coffee with sugar, he was trying to be affable. But it was difficult to overlook the steel behind the manners and the SAS badge on his arm.

The Brigadier continued: "And now Blair's the new sheriff in Downing Street and that means, Paul, that we have a chance to start afresh with the peace process. The new government are more alive to the media than the last lot – in fact they're making something of an art of it all. Reporting tit for tat killing does nothing to build bridges, you see? What impressed me was that you got the real *essence* of the mission. By keeping Gerard alive you helped create an environment where the peace process could continue.

"We put the escapees back inside and everyone, the nationalists included, could pretend nothing happened. The republicans reinstated their temporary ceasefire and therefore the loyalists could justify re-engagement. Talks started again within a few days. It was a strategic victory, what you did; a strategic victory indeed."

The Brigadier paused, watching Paul's face over the rim of his cup. "But I know that will not appease you, since you lost a man." He took a long sip of coffee.

Paul blinked. "No Sir." He did not know how to voice the depth of his sorrow. "We were a close knit Platoon," he said quietly.

The Brigadier re-crossed his legs and sniffed. "Of that I have no doubt, Paul. Of that I have no doubt. It is one of the reasons, I suspect, why one of your men put himself in harm's way to protect you during the assault. There's a lesson there for many an officer I'm sure. It's quite astounding how the little things one does will secure a soldier's loyalty." The Brigadier fixed Paul with a steady gaze in which the younger man read of many battles, won and lost. "Not only have you demonstrated a thorough grasp of mission command, but you have also demonstrated the selflessness, integrity and tenacity necessary to inspire the fighting man. I would also bet you have had to put aside something of your personal life in order to do this. Is that correct?"

Paul nodded, an image of Clare in the back of his mind. There had only been one choice, really. His men always came first.

"Well these are the attributes that others follow, Paul. If you nurture them, there will be a bright future before you in the army."

The words rang in Paul's mind throughout the flight back to Brize Norton. On his return to Aldershot, he found Major Casenove had a posting order for him. This was something he had expected, since his two-year point had come and gone, but it was far from what he craved. He was to report to the training depot in Catterick one week later and that meant he had barely three days left with the Platoon, men he cared for more than anybody else.

"Your first command never really leaves you," said the Major, reading his face. "But we have new officers coming out of Sandhurst and need to make spaces for them. And we need men like you, experienced officers, to train our recruits."

Paul smiled. "And Rolly? He's not in the Mess, in fact his room's empty. I haven't seen him since I had to go see the Brig."

Major Casenove frowned. "You can't have heard. Mr Rawlins is on leave prior to a new posting as well. He so impressed the Brigade Commander in the few hours he was a watchkeeper that he has asked for him to be his ADC. He starts next week, the same day you report to Catterick. The terrible twosome has had to be separated! Rolly may be a Captain now but you're the one commanding soldiers, Paul. Get yourself up north, shag a few Darlo girls and have a rollicking good time while you do so. Now get lost!"

Paul grinned, feeling like an adult at last. He shook the Major's hand, saluted and turned on his heel, but before he was at the stairs a voice called him back. Major Casenove came out from behind his desk to hand Paul a small, ivory coloured box. Inside was a medal with a green and purple ribbon, his rank and name inscribed along the edge. "Nearly forgot. A signal came through this morning. The Brigadier personally signed a waiver to get you a medal after fourteen days rather than twenty-eight. You're now a dangler. Get the ribbon sewn onto your kit before you report to Catterick. And be thankful for this. If the New Labour government are true to form, there'll be no military operations for a good few years yet. They rarely commit men to war."

Paul nodded and tucked the box into his pocket. The most onerous part of the week was to come.

If saying goodbye to Pietersen had been hard, saying goodbye to the rest of the Platoon almost brought Paul to tears. On his last Friday, Sergeant Moor had them all in the NCOs' room prior to final dispersal. As Paul stepped through the door the room erupted into cheers and chants. The men were applauding him, all of them. He was overwhelmed, too embarrassed to say anything at all. "It's been an honour," was all he could muster, blinking hard.

Moor stood to the side and deftly produced a large cardboard box from behind his back. The room fell quiet, the men smiling. With one hand, Moor drew the box apart to reveal a bronze statue of a soldier in full parachute order.

"We were gonna get you a Northern Ireland figurine, Sir, but since you've only done two weeks the blokes decided you didn't deserve it, even if the Brigadier did." Ripples of laughter swept across the room. Paul blushed, not knowing what to say.

Moor's voice changed: "But what we mean is that you've been a great Platoon Commander, Mr Illingworth. One of the best we've had since many years. It's been a pleasure to serve with you. And we hope you'll stay in the army and come back to the battalion as a Captain in a few years' time. I for one would serve under your command again."

The weight of adulation was almost too much for Paul to bear. Moor called the Platoon to attention and drawing himself up, for the first time in his life, he saluted.

# Afterword

In the Garrison Communications Centre on the second-last Friday in the month, Driver Gail Madison looked up from the Lonely Planet guidebook to tear a signal off the printer. She perused it in an absent minded manner. This was her last day at work before the wedding and the hours seemed to drag by.

The signal was classified as restricted and to her, meaningless. *From MOD London for all units*, it read. *For Commanding Officer for immediate vocal dissemination.*

*One. PIRA has announced its intention to reinstate the complete restoration of its ceasefire effective from Twenty-twelve-hundred hours July Nineteen ninety seven.*

*Two. While there is no intelligence to suggest that PIRA are planning to carry out attacks against security forces prior to the ceasefire common sense indicates that some elements within the PIRA organisation may use the preceding twenty-four hour period as a window of opportunity for attacking security force targets.*

*Three. Units are to remain vigilant throughout the period and all members are to be advised of the need to remain alert.*

*Four. Due to this ceasefire the General Service Medal Nineteen-sixty-two with the clasp reading Northern Ireland will no longer be issued for personnel serving in the Province under Operation Banner. A certificate will be issued in its place.*

Gail Madison stamped the signal with a date stamp and shoved it into the cubby hole for the driver to take round the garrison that afternoon.

Frankly, she had other things on her mind.

# Author's Note

I would like to thank the myriad of people who supported the development of this novel. Foremost of all is my wife, Joanne, who provided, enabled, and encouraged throughout. There were also many consulted for their impressions: the Farsley Massive (especially Steve and Jac Weston, Lee Edwards, Chris and Joss Ivory and Chris Forde), Cindy and KJ Bush, Patty Pops, Julia Richards, Andrew Jackson (the little one), Catherine Stalker (whose influence was pivotal), Adrian and Frances Smith, Margaret Newlands-Smith, Heather Richardson, Peter J Earle, Kirsty Baldwin, Tim Lyttle, Jess Sewter, Martin Ouvry, Neal Sherrington, Rebecca Shepherd, and my parents, Bobbie and Geof. Special mention should go to Neil Howlin, who inspired me to start by giving me a copy of *The War of Art* by Stephen Pressfield. I would also like to thank the staff at YPS, and those who employed me while I wrote: Curzon, Molten, EC Harris, and Lisa S (now Lisa B) at the BBC.

I would also like to thank *the blokes*.

I welcome all feedback on my work. I would like to know what readers think of the ideas, the writing, the characters and how they all hang together. I also write a blog on the Headsail Books website which explains some more of my thinking. If you would like to send me an email, please do so through books@headsailbooks.com.